PRAISE FOR *ROTTEN PEACHES*

In *Rotten Peaches*, Lisa de Nikolits has masterfully written two protagonists that are both thoroughly unsympathetic and utterly compelling. It's impossible to look away as these two women do very bad things in the pursuit of love, happiness, and meaning. And I do mean "very bad"—which makes this book a wild, weird ride, but one that's very worth taking.
—STACY LEE KONG, contributing editor, *Flare Magazine*

Welcome to the world of sales cons, messed-up self-help authors, hotel room hookups and murder most vile. *Rotten Peaches* delivers hilarious thrills and villainous chills right to its final twist. A wild, sexy romp of a book!
—CAROL BRUNEAU, author of *A Bird on Every Tree*

Wow. Just wow. Lisa de Nikolits' *Rotten Peaches* blew me away. A dark, compulsive, and addictive story in which the characters' secrets and needs conflict with each other and fold back in on themselves in an ever-tightening noose, *Rotten Peaches* will keep readers gripped until the very last page. Highly recommended!
—KAREN DIONNE, author of *The Marsh King's Daughter*

A noir page-turner that digs into the darkest corners of the human heart, *Rotten Peaches* dissects the lives of Leonie and Bernice, women who live continents apart but are linked by the attentions of a charismatic con man, JayRay. Leonie, a kleptomaniac chemist for an up and coming cosmetics company in Toronto, juggles her trade show junkets with a taste for petty theft and an abusive affair with JayRay. Meanwhile, in South Africa, JayRay's half-sister Bernice, author of a best-selling series of self-help baking books based on recipes she's appropriated from her Black housekeeper, is in love with a man committed to returning South Africa to white control.

Slowly the two stories begin to merge: as one woman struggles for redemption and self-knowledge, the other slips into a whirlpool of deception and violence. Lisa de Nikolits succeeds in creating a disturbing, mesmerizing tale in which the boundaries of good and evil, justice and punishment, are blurred by family secrets, racism, and sexual obsession.

—TERRI FAVRO, author of *Sputnik's Children* and *Once Upon a Time in West Toronto*

In *Rotten Peaches*, Lisa de Nikolits has written a novel that combines the irreverent energy of pulp with the cool amorality of film noir. With multiple plot lines that weave a tight chokehold of suspense—and characters who are at least as twisted as their stories—this tale of obsessive love, rage, and revenge is sure to make you shiver.

—KAREN SMYTHE, author of *This Side of Sad*

In *Rotten Peaches*, two women grapple with Sisyphean circumstances, paralleled in the seeming inescapable strength of the demons they harbour. Lisa de Nikolits is a skilled craftswoman, gripping the reader from the first page, and suspends her there, brow furrowed, as each new disaster unfolds, highlighted always by our two heroes' inability to turn away from the men they love and the dangerous plots they've been seduced into. With cons, political unrest, poison, sex, and murder plots, *Rotten Peaches* is an unflinchingly cinematic read.

—ROBIN RICHARDSON, author of *Knife Throwing through Self-Hypnosis*

An avant garde page-turner, written with honesty and insight that both caresses and shocks. Set around the corner and across the world, *Rotten Peaches* is an intimate study of human nature in all its imperfect glory. Lisa de Nikolits expertly weaves the lives of four unique characters into a story that rolls out as curiously as life itself. This novel romps with humour and stark private moments in a rhythm that builds with suspense to the climax, a sequence of chilling scenes at a South African farm. Here, de Nikolits uses her art to its highest good to show the reader a vivid and unforgettable snapshot of the

country post-apartheid. In supermarkets, fruit is displayed with the shiny side outward, bruises and flaws hidden behind. While there's no pretending in *Rotten Peaches*, all flaws are front and centre, there is braveness and truth at its pit.
—JENNIFER SOOSAR, author of *Parent Teacher Association*

An intense tale of looking for love in all the "wronged" places ... a telling of mighty meltdowns at a reckless helter-skelter pace. Bernice and Leonie relate with keen insightfulness and gripping candour their individual see-sawing and perilously-brewed stories, born of cumulative despair-festering inner wounds. *Rotten Peaches* is an exploration of damage and shame and prejudice, examining the needs and greeds and horrors thereof. The explosive sensuality, the fleeting, shifting pleasures of *Rotten Peaches* are braided together with anguish and doubt and anger. *Rotten Peaches* is a vivid and gut-wrenching story so forceful that it feels as if it always existed!
—SHIRLEY MCDANIEL, artist

Lisa de Nikolits dramatically explores our time as we try to understand incomprehensible human nature. A gripping, couldn't-put-down tale of impulsive, irrational, and extreme interactions that are raw, shocking, historical, political, and horrific while still being relatable. *Rotten Peaches* is a thrilling escape and a thought-provoking novel.
—MARILYN RIESZ, Registered Psychotherapist and co-author of *Bake Your Way to Happiness*

Rotten Peaches

We gratefully acknowledge the support of the Canada Council for the Arts and the Ontario Arts Council for our publishing program. We also acknowledge the financial support of the Government of Canada.

Cover portraiture art: Jennifer Shelswell
Cover design: Lisa de Nikolits

Rotten Peaches is a work of fiction. All the characters and situations portrayed in this book are fictitious and any resemblance to persons living or dead is purely coincidental.

Library and Archives Canada Cataloguing in Publication

De Nikolits, Lisa, 1966-, author
      Rotten peaches / Lisa de Nikolits.

(Inanna poetry & fiction series)
Issued in print and electronic formats.
ISBN 978-1-77133-529-4 (softcover).-- ISBN 978-1-77133-530-0 (epub).--
ISBN 978-1-77133-531-7 (Kindle).-- ISBN 978-1-77133-532-4 (pdf)

      I. Title. II. Series: Inanna poetry and fiction series

PS8607.E63R68 2018   C813'.6   C2018-904345-8
                                                 C2018-904346-6

Printed and bound in Canada

MIX
Paper from
responsible sources
FSC® C004071

Inanna Publications and Education Inc.
210 Founders College, York University
4700 Keele Street, Toronto, Ontario, Canada M3J 1P3
Telephone: (416) 736-5356 Fax: (416) 736-5765
Email: inanna.publications@inanna.ca   Website: www.inanna.ca

Rotten Peaches

A NOVEL BY

LISA DE NIKOLITS

inanna poetry & fiction series

INANNA PUBLICATIONS AND EDUCATION INC.
TORONTO, CANADA

ALSO BY LISA DE NIKOLITS:

No Fury Like That
The Nearly Girl
Between The Cracks She Fell
The Witchdoctor's Bones
A Glittering Chaos
West of Wawa
The Hungry Mirror

To my lovely Bradford Dunlop.

And with much gratitude and love to the unsung Bettys of this world. There were, and are, many.

Daddy, I have had to kill you.
　　　　　　　—Sylvia Plath, "Daddy"

Now

THE WORLD IS ENDING

LEONIE

I AM NOT A KILLER. I just fell in love with the wrong man.
I went too far this time, and there's no going back. There's no going anywhere, period.

I nearly stayed afloat, but my luck ran out. Luck, that mystical mythical glue that holds the shards of despair together and makes life navigable. But fragmented despair, that's what sinks you.

It's the middle of the day and the ghost of a cat walks across my bed. I am hidden in the downy softness of bleach-laundered sheets, sheets ironed with starch and cleansed of their filthy sins by scalding Catholic water.

The bed is high and wide and the pillows are like clouds ripped from a summer's sky. I bury my head in cotton balls, puffy meringues and whipped cream, and try to ignore the ghost of the cat that is walking the length of my back.

The cat settles at my feet but it gets up again and pads along my legs. When it first started its prowl, I sat up and reached for it but, like all ghosts, it immediately vanished and waited for me to turn away before settling in a warm, heavy lump against my side. Its weight is comforting in a way, like being massaged by the hand of God, but it isn't God. It can't be, because God, like luck, has left the building of my life.

I am here on a business trip. Right now I should be standing next to my table at the tradeshow luring in the poor and the desperate. *Sell SuperBeauty and make Super Money!*

But I can't get out of bed. But I've lost that right, along with the rest of my life.

"My luck has gone," I tell the cat. "The glue has desiccated and all that's left is despair, and despair is gunk in the engine; the engine is dying a gunk-filled death."

So, what? You're going to lie here until you die?

Be hard to do, wouldn't it? Realistically, I mean. Who ever died by lying in the world's most comfortable bed? Suicide by soft, cushy whiteness?

You'd have to take some pills, the cat says. He's trying to be helpful.

"I don't have any pills left," I reply. "And besides, I don't want to kill myself, I just want this hell to end. I want to trade in my current life for a new model, this lemon's run out of gas."

The cat settles like a soft sigh on the back of my thighs and I bury my face deeper into the pillow, wishing I had closed the blinds and blocked out that glittering day, but it's too late and I am not getting up now.

I am pulled down into the undertow of the bed and the day turns to night and even the cat leaves me. It joins God and luck and all the missing socks of my life. It joins the childhood assumption that life gets easier when you get older, not harder, and that courage is rewarded and that fortune cookie guru zen crapfests still make a modicum of sense.

There's a knock at the door and I want to answer it but I can't move, my body won't move. I hear the door being opened and I am relieved. He has come to get me.

"Leo, baby," a voice says and I blink.

I want to move but I can't. I can't even tell him that I can't move.

He explains something to a man who must be the hotel manager. He says, "I've got this, you can go now," and the manager makes a few cursory protesting noises, but he sounds happy to be leaving this mess for someone else to clean up.

"Baby, we've got to be somewhere," he says and his voice

makes my groin hot and tight, and I hate myself for my reaction, hate myself like I always do when I am around him.

He helps me sit up and he props a pillow behind my back.

He puts the coffee machine to work and he feeds me some water, a little at a time and the fog starts to clear.

"What the fuck, JayRay?" I manage. "What the fuck?"

He looks at me.

"It's time to get our shit together. It's time, Leo, it's time."

Then

LEONIE AND BERNICE BEGIN
TO FALL APART

1. LEONIE

SHAME. IT HAPPENS EVERY TIME. The same sickening thud of realization that I am failing again. Failing to keep my stupid crazy impulses under control. My greed will get the better of me yet again. And the most shameful thing of all is that the object of my lust is spectacularly ordinary, thoroughly stupid, and wholly unremarkable. It is a handmade pottery mug, pot-bellied and orange brown, with blue and white daisies etched into the uneven glaze. I want it, not only for the reassuringness of its unassuming shape but because of the insignia inscribed in uneven white cursive icing cake script: *Live your dreams.*

Some crazy part of me is convinced that if I take the mug, I will take the magic too, and all my dreams will come true. If I stop and ask myself what my dreams are, the answer will be that I want to be happy, normal and free. I can't tell you what the specifics of that picture looks like.

Maybe it is as simple as a moment on a sunlit sandy beach, or baking cookies with my kids, or going apple picking. But no, none of these fit the Instagram post of me being happy, normal, and free. Instead, I'd like to ask freedom to unlock the chains of my self-destructive, humiliating urges; yes, that would be a dream come true — to not want to steal other people's shit all the time.

Right now, I am not free. I can only see one thing in the room, the mug, that mug. I can't hear what anyone is saying because the trillions of synapses in my brain are sounding the siren of need, the unquenchable, uncontrollable need to own that mug.

Live your dreams. I need the mug much more than my colleague does. She's got a great life, her dreams have already come true, but mine haven't, not by a long shot.

But how can I get my hands on it? It's surrounded by a protective barrier of post-it notes and papers and file folders and pictures of grandkids.

I realize, yet again, that I should get some pics of Maddie and Kenzie framed for my desk, but somehow I always remember this at the wrong time, like now, when all I want to do is inhale that pot-bellied mug and fill the gaping, yearning hole in my own belly.

I can't concentrate. I'm in the open office plan desk area we call the pigpen, riffing off cops having a bullpen. The pigpen is full, each desk occupied by a happy little piglet, each conscientiously attending to their workerly duties. Except for me. I am obsessed with someone else's magic. I try to distract myself with my usual complaint that I rate a personal office, a glassed-in cubicle at the very least, but my boss says I'm not there often enough to warrant the cost and besides, he says it's good for me to "bond with my fellow colleagues at a grassroots level."

My phone rings. It's my husband, Dave. I reach for it and look up to see my boss signaling. I wave at him and point to the phone.

"We figured we'd make you mac and cheese," Dave says. "Since you're home and all, tonight."

"Great." I feel helpless with hatred. "Sure, Dave, sounds great. I'll be a bit late, an hour or so."

"No worries," Dave says and it always annoys me when he says that. Who is he, some faux Aussie cheerleader: *no worries, mate*?

Two little koalas, that's Dave and me.

The mug-owning colleague starts wrapping up for the day. I

watch her tidy her desk in the time it takes an ice age to melt. She finally gets things into some semblance of order and then she takes her mug to the kitchen. When she returns to collect her purse, her hands are empty.

She must have left the mug in the kitchen. My skin is burning and I scratch at my arms while I wait for her to get the fuck out of Dodge. I manage to sit still for five minutes after she leaves and then I stroll into the kitchen. The mug is drying upside down on a stack of paper towels. I am about to reach for it when my boss comes in and I snatch my hand back and flick the kettle on instead.

"I did the math on the last show," Ralph says and he gives me a high-five. I try to smile. "You did good. Listen, are you sure you're still okay with all this travel? You can start training Sandra any time. She can do the shows and you can focus on advertising and product development."

"I'm developing the product all the time and Sandra's a fucking moron," I say and Ralph laughs.

"Why don't you tell me what you really think? But you are right. She does lack your edge. We'll hold off for a while. But I don't want you to burn out, okay? You'll tell me if you start feeling stressed? You sleeping at night?"

"Yeah," I tell him, thinking of the bottles of Nyquil that give me a couple of hours of shut-eye. Lately, I've been adding pain meds for arthritis, which helped for a while but the effects only last for so long and I need an increasingly heavy dose. I scored a pack of muscle relaxants on the last roadshow; got them from Fred, a regular with a booth piled high with handmade silverware from Maine, two stalls down from me, and I added those to my mix. Despite my ministrations, sleep and rest remain elusive, but I don't tell Ralph that.

"I'll leave you to it," Ralph says and he brushes the kitchen counter with the palm of his hand and wipes it clean on his trouser leg. "Remember kid, you ever need me, my door is always open. Feel free to reach out any time."

I nod. Is he referring to anything specific? But he walks out before I can say anything else.

The kettle has long since boiled but I don't care. I pick up the mug, tuck it under my armpit, and walk back to my desk, my arms folded. I sit down quickly. My heart is a shuddering jet plane in my ears and I am deafened by the fear that I will be caught. I lean down and shove the mug into my purse and it falls with a dispirited clank, hitting something metal. Probably some forks I picked up at the Best Western. I wonder if the mug is broken but I don't dare look. My armpits are slick and the heat rises through my blouse like a steamy forest fog, something raw and unbathed. The other pigs in the pen don't notice anything; they're chatting about some new TV show they love or some crap like that.

Sirens are going off in my head: *put it back, put it back, put it back,* and its usual place on my colleague's desk is already spotlit with loss and accusatory stares. I stare at the glaring absence but I cannot return the mug. I need the magic. The mug is mine now.

Still, my thoughts whirl with confusion, self-hatred, and shame. Why can't I just put it back? I want to but I can't. YOU'LL BE CAUGHT! HUMILIATED! FIRED! EXPOSED!

But I can't put the mug back.

I get up. I am late for Dave and Maddie and Kenzie, and I am late for mac and cheese. But I can't take the mug home. For sure one of the kids will find it in my purse, brandish it, and then Dave will get in on the action.

"That's not your style, Lee," he'll say and he'll want to know the whole story.

I leave work and stop by my storage locker, and I text Dave. *On my way, I'll be home soon.*

I pull up to the garage door of the unit and flick on the light. No one knows about my storage locker. I pay for it in cash and it's my secret. It's piled high with junk that I have stolen over the years. I've had this filthy little secret cave since before I even met Dave. I got it a couple of months after I started studying chemistry, when it became apparent that along with stealing knick-knacks and useless, blameless, worthless shit, I liked to steal samples from the lab. How I never got caught is beyond me. My heart was a runaway train in my ears every single time and I couldn't breathe. The thought of getting caught filled me with terror and yet, still, I had to take. And take and take.

The shelves on one wall hold my most toxic stash. If ever discovered, the chemicals would need to be disposed of as hazardous waste. Why did I take them? For the same reason I took the mug. A sick compulsion. What do I do with my random, shabby treasures? Nothing. Sometimes though, I bring a bottle of water and I sit inside my locker, with the door pulled down and a shallow bowl of water in front of me. I shave off tiny pieces of sodium, one sliver at a time, and I watch the fragments explode into flames and rush around, a skating frenzy of dazzling fire. Somehow this never gets old.

I collect chemicals whenever I can. I have an inside source at the company lab in Mexico City and when I go down to check that they're still producing our products according to semi-official Food and Drug Administration laws, the fellow gives me tiny vials of illicit goodies, cash exchange, no questions asked. Lead oxide, nitrocellulose, acetonitrile, formaldehyde, chloroform, methanol, sodium hydroxide, acetylcholine bromide, ethanolamine, mercurous chloride, potassium cyanide, mercury II thiocyanate, and mercury itself—beautiful, beautiful mercury, heavy, silver, breaking off into tiny balls and coming back together as a whole, sliding, pushed by its weight, its movement swift as light.

I force myself back into the moment. I'm already late for supper. I put the mug on a box of Christmas ornaments I have stolen from various shopping malls and I leave, locking the door behind me.

I go home and eat mac and cheese and pretend that everything is fine. I try to listen to what Maddie and Kenzie are telling me about school, a project they have to do about being sisters, but it's all static noise. I drink red wine and try not to see Dave watching me with a look on his face like he's lost something he once loved.

I drink too much NyQuil at three a.m. and fall into a drugged doze, which makes me late for work. When I arrive, there's a riot in the pigpen and the mug woman is hysterical, trying to find her missing treasure. I have already forgotten about the mug and I can't even remember why I took it. I know they won't rest until some explanation comes to light. I have to fix this thing, find a way to smooth things over.

"Oh yeah, right, look sorry, I broke your mug last night," I say and silence falls, like a snowy countryside in winter, and I think, oh shit, look at the trouble I've brought on myself, and I know it's going to be a hard sell to get out of this.

"I was drying it," I tell her, "and it slipped out of my hands and broke. I threw it out. Here, take this one."

I reach for a gaudy mug on my desk. It's a souvenir from Vegas, a naked, d-cup woman kneeling doggy style. Her big butt is fashioned into a handle and it's so wrong but I don't know what else to do. I stand there, holding the mug out in front of me, and this woman, fuck, I don't even know her name, looks at me with horror. Her eyes fill with tears and she runs out of the room.

"It was just a mug," I tell the quiet, accusing faces and I put the big butt mug back on my desk. I sit down and open my laptop.

"Her daughter made it for her the week before she died of cancer," one of the other sales reps says. He's an aggressive little shit and his numbers are down, which isn't my fault. "Why did you touch it at all? Everyone knows not to touch Moira's mug."

Right. The woman's name is Moira.

"I wanted to do something nice by taking care of it," I say. I sigh, and go and go after Moira. She is in the washroom, surrounded by a colony of angry birds, all clucking and fluffing their feathers around her.

"I am sorry," I say inadequately and this other woman, June, turns on me. June's always hated me. She was in on the business with Ralph when they were a happy hippy startup and she's never forgiven me for kicking *SuperBeauty* into the real world and leaving her on the sidelines, a tired, old, saggy cheerleader.

"Where are the pieces?" June asks, her face red with her useless anger. "We'll glue it back together for Moira."

"I chucked them away," I say and I fold my arms across my chest.

"Let's go and find them, shall we? Garbage won't have gone anywhere."

"I put them in a plastic bag and took them with me. I threw them away when I stopped to get a burger. I thought Moira would be more upset seeing it broken, so…"

June falls silent and I think that will be the end of it. She can't challenge me. I'm the bringer of rain and she knows it. But as she turns to leave, her arm around Moira, she stops. "Funny how things go missing or get broken when you're around," she says, her pug eyes bulging with her boldness. "Think I haven't noticed? We've all noticed. But you're Ralphie's blue-eyed girl, so the sun shines out of your ass, doesn't it?"

Then she looks down, scared witless by what she has said, and the women scuttle out of the washroom. I watch them leave and I soap up my hands and rinse them under the hottest water, cleaning the crap away.

By now, I fully believe my own story about the mug and I can even see myself at MacDonald's, twisting the plastic bag tightly and discarding the broken shards through the scratched, soiled black plastic swing door of the garbage disposal.

Ah fuck it. I tell myself it isn't my fault the whole thing happened. It's just something I do when I got stressed. I take other people's crap. It's a release valve; we all have them, and seriously, it was just a mug. It's not like I ripped off Moira's life savings or anything. I try to imagine the mug in the darkness of the storage locker, but it means nothing anymore, it's a dull and dusty relic, devoid of any magic, power, or memorability. I can't, for the life of me, remember why I wanted it so badly. The whole thing is tedious and boring now.

Thank god I have a show soon. I'll be with JayRay and he will put the whole world right. He will understand, he always does. Because JayRay is as broken as me.

2. BERNICE

I AM PACKING TO GO ON A TRIP. I will be a guest on a day-time television show that is filmed in Las Vegas. *Janette's Daytime Reveal!* Las Vegas. A place I have never been to, nor have I ever wanted to go. I've no idea why I agreed to this in the first place. I hate being on television and I hate flying. I am filled with all kinds of anger and, to make matters worse, I cannot decide what to wear.

"Betty?" I call out and she comes running.

"Yes, Madam?"

I gesture at the bed. "Ag man, I don't know what to wear. I turn to the woman who has been like a mother to me, only really, she is my maid.

"Hmm. This is for television? We should ask Rosie."

"No," I say sharply. Rosie is Betty's daughter and I can't stand her. "We need to decide now. I have to leave soon."

"You hate being on television," Betty says and I sigh. I want her advice on my wardrobe, not her insights into my likes and dislikes.

"Ja, well be that as it may, I was pushed into it. A new book and a great chance to promote it, they said. And I'd had Dirk up to here, so I cut off my nose to spite my face. He didn't want me to go, and that's why I said yes, to prove to him I can do whatever I want. Now, what do you think?" I gesture to the clothing on the bed.

"That one creases badly," Betty points at a linen suit. "You won't be there for five minutes and it will look like pajamas. And remember when we watched the show? Everything was white. The walls, the floor, the chairs and the table, they were white. You must wear a good colour, to stand out. And you must show off your legs. You have pretty legs even if you do not think so. But you need a suntan, so you must wear pantyhose."

"I hate them," I complain but I pull a few packets out of a drawer and throw them into my suitcase. "I'm such a dom-kom, why didn't I see what you saw? About the white and everything?"

She shrugs. "And you must wear nice shoes with a small heel, not too high. It is not a sex show."

I titter. "I don't want to know about the sex shows you watch, Betty."

"*Eish!* I am just saying. You must come across like a person who can cook and be a friend, and be pretty too. Here, this skirt is the best, it is a good length and the fabric is good. And these shoes. With this jacket."

"What would I do without you, hey?" I asked.

"You would be on television wearing crumpled beige paja-mas," Betty says and I see a glint of humour in her eyes.

I sigh and sit down on the bed. "Ag Betty. I wonder if he will ever come back."

She stands next to me and pats my back as if I am a baby. "Maybe he will," she says. "Maybe he will."

3. LEONIE

A S I FLY TO MEET HIM, I think back to the first time I met JayRay. It was at the Southwestern Women's Expo in Los Vegas. I'd been on the road for eight years. After we had Kenzie, Dave promised me I could go back to work and Maddie was hardly out of her toddler onesies when I hit the highway. I told Ralph, when I started working with him, that the road shows were part of the deal. There was no better way to get firsthand knowledge of our clientele. I used his own lingo, telling him that it was the best way "to raise the bar" and "help elevate the brand," never mind how we'd grab all that "juicy, low-hanging fruit." It was obvious that Ralph couldn't understand why I'd want to leave my babies, but it was none of his business. And I told Dave that Ralph wouldn't give me the job unless I travelled to the conventions.

Eight years. And everything was going well. I racked up spectacular sales. And, back at home, I succeeded in motherhood, as long as it was in small doses, and I really did love the kids and Dave.

At the end of a particularly long day, I was sitting in a curved booth in a bar, drinking a rum and diet Coke and not feeling like talking to anybody. It felt good to be alone in the dark bar, staring mindlessly at the cheap mahogany fittings, the worn red carpet, and the fake brass lamps. It was all faux English pub, but clearly American born and bred.

A man slid into my booth, uninvited. I recognized him from

the roadshows, how could I not? That JayRay! *Such a hottie,* the middle-aged women whispered, *he can leave his shoes under my bed any time.*

"James Ray Padgett," he said, extending a hand across the table.

I scowled at my drink. "I know who you are. I'm not in the mood."

"For what?"

"Talking. I don't feel like saying one goddamned thing."

He flashed a movie star grin and I found myself thinking about beds and shoes and how maybe I wouldn't mind either.

"You don't have to say a word. You want another drink?"

I nodded.

"Rum and diet Coke," I said and I watched his perfectly-shaped tight ass walk over to the bar. His short-sleeved shirt showcased impressive biceps and, man, did he ever have a good head of hair. Thick, dirty-blond, and tousled, a bad-boy cowboy fuck who'd make you forget the world for a time.

But I didn't play away from home. I had everything I needed right there. Sweet husband Dave, good old Dave. School teacher Dave, who took care of the laundry and made sure the kids ate balanced meals and did their homework. All those responsible and necessary things, while I ran away as often as I could. Trade fair after trade fair saw me recruiting eager little beavers with a yen to work in beauty and fulfill their deep-seated desires to earn scads of money.

I'm still amazed by the hordes of people who approach the booth smelling of naïve hope, filled with optimistic faith that they'll score tenfold on their not insubstantial investment. They silently beg for my help, as if I have the power to fix their debt-filled lives, and I push those desperate buttons of need and desire. *Yes! You too can become an expert in the world of beauty! You too can earn yourself a Mercedes Benz! I drive a Mercedes Benz! Silver Mercedes for everybody — don't you want yours?*

I'm a science whiz. I hold a master's in chemistry and I'm the one who adds the magic to Ralphie's line of beauty products. I'm the one who gives them that extra zing, mixing the exact blend of ingredients that is *SuperBeauty: Look Seven Years Younger in Seven Days!* I've got shares in the company on top of a generous salary.

The cowboy came back with my drink.

I nodded my thanks, not wanting to look too enthused. Didn't want him to think I was easy prey, because I wasn't. In fact, I had no idea why he was even seeking me out. Must have been a slow evening in his world.

"How are things in the world of anti-aging and reverse wrinklefication?" he asked.

I shook my head. "Not talking. Remember? No conversing. If you are so inclined, you can tell me about yourself, but I'm not talking about me or my world or any of my shit. I'm too freaking bored by it. It's all just the same fucking day, man."

He raised an eyebrow, clearly not getting the Janis Joplin reference. "I'm in security," he said.

"I know. All the boys and girls want to be you, hero cop. How many stop-bys do you sign up?"

"Eighty percent success rate," he grinned. Killer dimples, lips twisted just so. I forced my thoughts away from his smile and back to what he had said, and even I was impressed. I scored seventy on a good day and I thought that was pretty amazing.

"Yeah, well, you've got the looks and the charm," I said, and I wasn't being nice.

"So do you," he said. "All the men on the roadshow want to fuck you."

I was taken aback, not by what he said but by his bluntness.

He mistook my silence for modesty and he nodded. "You're pinup gorgeous. Glamour chick."

A big laugh bubbled up from my belly, the first real laugh I'd had in ages. "Glamour chick. Sure, that's me. What's the story here, James Ray Padgett? Why are you laying this flattery on me? I've got nothing you want, believe me."

"JayRay. I'm called JayRay to my friends and loved ones."

"Of which I am neither," I replied quick as a whip, hoping to flick him away from me, but he smiled.

"Does a person always have to want something?

"Yeah. First rule of survival. Everybody wants something from you. Establish that upfront and at least it's honest." I took a sip of my drink and I wished I had asked JayRay to get some maraschino cherries and I signaled the waiter.

"Then what's honest?" he wanted to know.

"Whatever follows from there," I said and then I asked the waiter to bring over some cherries. "Tell me, Jamieboy," I asked, eating a cherry. "Honest and upfront, what do you want? You know the drill, engage, qualify, present, and close. You've done the first three, what's your close?"

"For me to fuck you," he said matter-of-factly.

I took stock of the situation for a moment.

Truly, I'm no bikini beauty queen. I'm short and close to misshapen. A muffin-top belly spills over my tight jeans, I've no waist to speak of, skinny calves, shapely thighs, and an ass as flat as a pancake. Back bacon folds like wings over my bra straps and my boobs have fed two kids. Yeah baby, this body's not exactly hot to trot.

But I acknowledge one thing. I am pretty. Not beautiful, but pretty, the kind of pretty that makes men pause for a moment, like they imagined I just gave them a blow job and, sure, they know it was only in their minds, but a flutter of hope twitches in their balls like maybe it was still possible.

My big brown eyes insinuate kindness, empathy, and compassion. Add flawless skin, high cheekbones, a cheerleader-perfect upturned nose, and an overbite responsible for a pouty upper lip. My naturally-parted mouth hints at all manner of breathless pleasures to come. I have small, white, even teeth, all the better to nibble you with.

I owe a debt of gratitude to my pretty. It has perpetuated the outward lie that disguises the reality inside. I should thank my parents for their good looks — one positive at least, for the unfortunate offspring of their union.

So I understood what JayRay saw in me, but what would I get in return?

"You've got nothing I want," I told him. "A fuck is a fuck, so what?"

"Clearly you haven't been righteously fucked in a while," he said.

I shook my head. "It's not that. A fuck is never worth what people think it is." I sounded sanctimonious.

"Man, you're hard work," he complained.

"Then leave already. Go." I gazed out the window to emphasize my point.

He didn't say anything for while but he didn't leave either. "I've got a way out of this shit hole," he finally said.

"Yeah? What's your fairytale?"

He leaned forward. "I'm going to be on *Janette's Daytime Reveal!*" He grinned and leaned back.

"How come?" I asked. *Janette's Daytime Reveal* was popular prime-time show in the U.S. that showcased familial dirty laundry for all the world to see. I wasn't a fan but millions of others were and I wondered how JayRay had weaseled his way onto a slot.

"My half-sister. She's a big-time author in South Africa."

"Where?" I asked.

"South Africa. Bottom of Africa. You know."

"Just kidding. Of course I know where it is. But it's too small to have big-time authors." I was just trying to get a rise out of him.

He shook his head. "She's huge in the U.S. of A. She wrote a version of *Eat, Pray, Love*, called *Bake Your Way to Happiness* and it sold millions. Hers is more of a cookbook than *Eat, Pray, Love*; she's got self-help strategies with recipes. You record your emotions and shit like that, and then you have to give the pie, or whatever you baked, to someone in need or someone sad, or share it with a friend, or some bonding crap. All that girlie feel-good shit, but a lot of folks loved it. After that she wrote another one, *Bake Your Way to Good Health* and it had exercises and fitness tips and healthy recipes. And then she did *Bake Your Way to Self Esteem, Bake Your Way to a Happy Family*, and *Bake Your Way into a Fulfilling Marriage* and she's got a new one coming out next year, *Bake Your Way to Mr. Right*. It's all on her website."

In spite of my reluctance to let myself enjoy being with JayRay, I laughed. "The world is such a mark," I said.

"Yeah. Thank god. Anyway, she is worth millions and she's my ticket, baby, she's my way out."

"How come?"

"Because we're blood relatives! Family should share the love! I'm entitled. You'd think she'd be happy to find out she's got a half-brother. The only problem is she won't acknowledge me. Won't pick up phone calls, won't reply to emails, not even real fucking handwritten letters, nothing gets a response. But I got Janette to invite her onto daytime TV. Her name's Bernice. She thinks the show is to promote *Bake Your Way to Mr. Right,* but actually, it's to reveal that this big-time author doesn't give a shit about her own flesh and blood and, so, we'll expose her for the hypocrite she really is. The downside is that the show's a whole year from now. I just got confirmation today. That's how long the lineup is, to get onto Janette's show, plus we have to wait for Bernice's new book to come out."

I was mildly curious. "How did you get to Janette?"

"A buddy of mine made a video of me. It's the only way to pitch Janette and get in. She wants to see your live camera charisma and I nailed it."

"You and Janette are lying to Bernice, telling her it's for the book, and then you're going to shame her? Like that's going to make her love you," I snorted, finishing my drink and pointing to the glass.

JayRay waved the waiter over. "I'm going to help her sell even more books. She'll owe me. You can't buy this kind of publicity and I'm giving it to her on a stick."

"Bring another bowl of cherries," I told the waiter who took our order.

"A year's a long time to wait," I said.

"I know. But it is what it is. Anyway, patience and timing are tools of our trade, not so? Patience is a saleman's best friend. A year from now, I will be on TV. I will never come back! I am not telling anyone, only you."

"Why me? How did I get so lucky?"

"You didn't want to fuck," he said and he sounded gloomy. "Fucking you would have defused the need for conversation, but no, you wanted to talk, so here I am, telling you all my shit. Don't tell anybody. Oh fuck, whatever, tell people, who cares? But no wait, you can't. Bernice might get wind of it and not show up."

His eyes were filled with the enormity of his mistake and before I knew what I was doing, I took his hands in mine and oh shit, talk about an electric shot to the crotch.

I snatched my hands away and grabbed my fresh drink. I swallowed half in one gulp. Getting wasted wasn't a good idea, but I couldn't get off this train. "I won't tell anybody. I swear to god I won't." I tried to forget how good it felt to touch him.

"I believe you. I haven't told my boss either. No one. It could all mean jack squat but I have to try, you know? This trade show shit, it's getting old, man."

"How long have you been doing it?"

He shrugged. "I dunno, like five, six years? You?"

"Eight years. I started after I had kids. I couldn't stay home. I nearly lost my mind. And I have a genius mind, in case you hadn't noticed."

"Maybe so but you talk like a trucker."

"To annoy my mother. I practiced talking like a redneck to piss her off. Now it's my way, although I do try to tone it down when I'm home with my kids. But I'm the brains behind Ralphie's *SuperBeauty* line."

He raised an eyebrow and I couldn't help myself, I had to show off, just a bit.

"People want to see immediate results, right? They don't care if the effects are permanent, as long as they look in the mirror and see a younger-looking face staring back. The trick is moisture. That's all. Plain and simple. But you need penetration enhancers to help drive the chemicals deep into the skin. Most moisturizers sit on the surface, and the skin doesn't look refreshed. But add a careful combination of chosen ingredients and *voilá*, you have a product that makes the skin look younger nearly immediately, even if it doesn't last beyond the next application. And that is what keeps them coming back for more."

"Aren't you giving away company secrets?" JayRay asked and I smiled.

"I'm not worried. You wouldn't know butylene glycol from bisabolol, would you now?"

He shook his head. I didn't add that we mixed the creams in Mexico and that Ralphie's brother-in-law brought them into the U.S. by the truckload. No one ever had cause to tally the percentages against the ingredients listed, which was a good thing for Ralph and me because, to put it mildly, they weren't kosher. Which was why Ralph let me get away with the crap I pulled, like causing shit at work and being off the radar at shows. I created the formula and we were in it together. Ralph had been amazed by my results; sales quadrupled in a matter of weeks. I took Ralph's mediocre but admittedly safe face creams, pumped them full of crap, and the results were astounding.

Selling was a walk in the park. All I had to do was apply a small amount of formula to a woman's face and tell her to walk around for ten minutes and check the results in the mirror. As sure as bears fucked in the woods, the women would rush back, panting to buy a stash of the miracle cream and sure, why not get into the business by selling it to friends and family too?

Of course, when Dave asked me why I didn't use the product that I spent so much time selling, I didn't tell him the truth. Dave's the kind of guy who'd call the cops, wife or not.

I polished off my drink and JayRay called for another.

"Are you drinking with me or just watching me get drunk?" I asked with suspicion and he shot me that killer smile.

"I'm staying sober enough to carry you home. We're on again tomorrow for one last day in case you've forgotten. How many kids do you have?"

"Two. Two girls. Madeleine and Mackenzie. Kenzie's ten and Maddie's eight."

"You gotta thing for M's?" JayRay said and I swatted his hand before I remembered the dangers of touching him.

"How'd you get to be so fucking sexy?" I asked, trying to poke a pin in the elephant in the room and thereby deflate it. Actually, elephants weren't helping. I tried to imagine a tiny mouse instead. A grey mouse. A floppy flaccid dead mouse.

"Just born with it," JayRay sighed. "But it hasn't gotten me what I want. I want real money, baby. I want massages and spas in my house. I want an indoor swimming pool. I want my own chef. I want a warehouse of cars and bikes. I want to lie on a beach all day and play poker all night. And my so-called good looks haven't landed me anything but this endless fucking roadshow of signing up kids and old folk to be pretend-cops. There you go, that's what it's worth, my good looks."

"Why don't you model? Calvin Klein, brands like that? I could see you on a billboard in your tighty-whities."

"I don't shoot well," JayRay sounded mournful. "For some reason, the camera hates me. Fucking hates me. No one can make me look good."

I looked doubtful but he shook his head and pulled out his phone. "Look," he said, handing it over and I scrolled through a bunch of images. Professionally shot yes, but as boring as hell. The animal magnetism had left the building. Instead, JayRay was a Halloween dress-up of an eighties hair band.

I handed the phone back to him without comment.

"You see?" he said and I nodded. "I tried a bunch of photographers. But I'll be a supernova on TV, the video showed it. Hollywood will come knocking, I'll have it made!"

"Yeah, you'll knock 'em dead," I said, feeling the quick pinch of jealousy with a question mark to self. What did I care?

"I'm nervous about it," he admitted. He studied his hands. "Look at me, sweaty palms even thinking about it. Disgusting."

Sweaty or not, I wanted to take his hands in mine but I finished my drink instead. "I gotta go." I got to my feet and I swayed like a willow tree in a storm. Getting plastered in six-inch heels wasn't a great idea.

JayRay stood up. "I'll see you to your hotel."

"You may well have to carry me," I joked, but I managed to walk, holding myself stiffly upright. I allowed myself to hang onto JayRay's arm and I desperately tried not to feel those shapely sculpted biceps under my fingertips.

"I'm in the Howard Johnson," I said and JayRay navigated me across the parking lot.

Neither of us said a word.

He got into the elevator with me and I watched the doors close with a sense of inevitability.

The floral carpet shouted harsh accusations on the way to my room but I ignored it, inserted my keycard and opened the door. I turned to look at JayRay. "One night?" I said and he nodded. "What the fuck," I said. "I deserve a little treat now and then."

"Nothing little about it, baby," JayRay said and he somehow managed to put his tongue in my mouth, maneuver us to the bed, and kick the door shut behind us.

*   *   *

And now I'm sitting on the edge of the bed, watching JayRay's big moment on prime-time TV. We're back at the Las Vegas Southwestern Women's Expo and it's our one-year anniversary.

I've done the unthinkable. I closed my booth early and left for the day. If Ralph found out, he'd kill me. But my numbers are fine and this is an emergency.

I wonder if I'll see JayRay again, once he's embraced by fame and fortune. I don't believe for a moment that Bernice will prove to be a pot of gold at the end of his rainbow but I'm confident he'll be nabbed for a reality show or TV series. I have every faith in his ability to come out a winner, I've seen him in action. My heart is heavy and I'm still annoyed by how excited he is at the prospect of making his world debut, particularly after we've been together this long. I should be enough to fill his world.

I have never understood the chemistry of addiction, despite studying the molecules and the math. But I do now. I'm addicted to him. Hillbilly heroin has nothing on my need for him and the whole thing is a clusterfuck of enormous proportions, two freight trains of need and desire heading bullseye towards certain catastrophe.

JayRay and I were inseparable after that first night. At least, in private. He texted me constantly whenever we couldn't be together and if I didn't have that contact, I would have lost my mind.

My world has become one cliché after another. I sounded like a fucking Harlequin romance novel instead of a scientist with a loving husband, a happy marriage, and two good kids. The scientist part was true anyway. As for the rest, maybe it had always been a lie.

But real love, as I had discovered, is nothing more than the worst kind of torture. When I watched him talk to other women, a feral beast gnawed at my gut. Not being able to wrap myself around him the minute I saw him, to have to hold back, to pretend to Dave and the kids that life hadn't changed, the whole charade killed me. Standing behind my display and advising would-be beauty advisors on how best to sell and market their product was sheer hell. All I wanted was JayRay, in my arms and in my bed. From zero to the speed of light in a matter of hours. Hell, I fell into the black hole of unquenchable love and lust that first night we were together.

The first morning we woke up together, we rolled towards one another, noses nearly touching. I didn't try to play it cool; he knew how I felt and I knew it was the same for him.

"It's like I'm fifteen," JayRay said. He took my hand and held it to his chest. "Feel what you do to my heart."

"How old are you anyway?" I asked.

"Twenty eight. Nearly twenty-nine. You?"

"Thirty-two."

"Hey, Leo?"

"What?"

"This is the real deal."

"I know."

We lay like that until the snooze button on my phone rang church bells and I snapped it off. "Up and at 'em," JayRay said.

"We've got time for one more," I said, and I reached for him.

The first time I had to leave him, I could hardly stand it.

"You have to look on the bright side," he'd said. "We've got each other now. We never had that before. I'm the secret happiness in your heart and you're mine." I realized then that I had watched him for some time, even although I had pretended to myself that I hadn't, and it was clear that he had been watching me too. *Yeah baby, your shoes belong under my bed and don't you ever forget it.*

I didn't want to be a secret. I didn't want him to be a secret. I knew it was insane, how fast it happened, but he was the crazy happiness my whole life had been searching for. I just hadn't known it.

"We have to keep it under wraps for now. Trust me baby,"

he told me repeatedly. "Things will be different once we nail Bernice. She's going to have to play happy families. She'll have no choice since that's what she pretends to be all about. Then I'll get her to pay me to exit her life or we'll get her farm. Whatever, I'll make it work, and I'll play it by ear." You have to stay in character for now. We both have to."

I understood, and I managed to somehow make it through the times we were apart. But it wasn't easy. Dave noticed the change in me, of course he did. He said I seemed distant. And after a few months, when I got home from a trip, Kenzie followed me around. "Are you sick, Mommy?" she asked and I said "No baby, I'm just a bit tired, that's all." And I helped her make me lemon tea with honey.

And then I got back with JayRay and the broken shards of my heart slid back into their rightful place.

And now it is the moment we've been waiting for all year. I settle myself on the bed to watch it unfold. I want him to succeed but at the same time, I don't.

Janette makes her entrance with her usual song and dance and the crowd goes nuts. She lets them roar for a while, finally soothes them with a queenly hand. "Today," she announces, "we have a wonderful show lined up for you! Celebrated author, Bernice Van Coller, who has written a series on baking your way to a better life, has recently released her new book, *Bake Your Way to Mr. Right* and she will be joining us!"

Another roar from the crowd as Bernice walks onto the stage and I crane forward to look at her. I had studied pictures of her online to the point where Dave had caught me and he asked me why I was suddenly so interested in baking, when, to that point, I had shown little aptitude and even less interest.

"Someone mentioned her to me at a show," I said, which wasn't exactly an untruth. "I thought it might be nice for me and the girls to do some baking together." That got Dave all excited and he sat down and started searching for Bernice's books, which wasn't what I had in mind.

"She looks like a skinny grasshopper," he said of Bernice. "You think she'd take her own advice and eat something."

Dave caught me off guard when he ordered a copy of *Bake Your Way to a Better Marriage* and I looked at him warily.

"Something you want to tell me?" I asked and a part of me was hopeful. *End it, Dave, set me free. I'll run to JayRay and I won't have to pretend any more.*

"Nope. Except that why not? We could use a bit of fun, you and me. And the girls can help. Look, there's a chapter for families: 'The Family Who Bakes Together Stays Together.'"

"Sure," I said. "Sure."

"The book will be here by the time you get back from your next trip. Give us something to look forward to."

He was happy with his plan and I nodded, trying to look enthusiastic and not wanting to think about life post-Vegas, which could mean life without JayRay. And, upon my return, the calendar had me stationed at home base for a mind-blowing two weeks before I would be able hit the road again. I had no idea how I would manage.

"Because," I say out loud to Janette on the television screen, who is still introducing Bernice, "JayRay might leave me and hook up with Bernice by the time the show is over. Not in any biblical sense, although I wouldn't put anything past JayRay if it means closing the deal."

I focus on the TV. Bernice is talking. "Ja," she says, and her voice is sweet and girly and upmarket South African. She rolls her r's thickly but she articulates with precision. I bet she went to an expensive school. "My books are definitely a mix of self-help and cooking, which go hand-in-hand very nicely."

"Speaking of hand-in-hand," Janette quips, "is there a Mr. Right in your life?"

Bernice blushes and adjusts her bony body, which is more praying mantis than grasshopper, since even grasshoppers have more meat on their bones. "Well," she titters and her face flushes an unflattering red-grey meaty colour, "I cannot say for certain. There is a current romance, ja, but whether or not he will become my forever Mr. Right, has yet to be seen."

"I am sure you will let your baking work its magic," Janette says. "But for now, we will move onto the reveal part of the show and which might involve a different kind of Mr. Right than the one you are thinking of!"

Bernice looks startled and she clutches her rosebud microphone closer to her mouth, which causes a nasty buzzing reverb and Janette quickly swats Bernice's hand away.

"I thought the book was the reveal," Bernice says, and she looks frightened. "No one said anything about a different reveal. Was my agent informed of this?"

"Oh yes," Janette says vaguely. "It's in the fine print. But never mind that, we've got a big surprise for you! Are you ready?"

"Not really," Bernice replies and she starts to say more but Janette interrupts her. "Come on out JayRay! Welcome to *Janette's Daily Reveal!*"

JayRay saunters onto the stage and he was right, television didn't dilute his looks the way that photographs did. I'm dismayed to see how good-looking and sexy he is on screen. Now the whole world will see it too, and I'm going to lose him for sure. I want to throw up and I can hardly watch. JayRay acknowledges the roar of applause as if he were born to it.

Bernice is shocked and immobilized, her thin mouth is pressed into a tight line. She crosses her arms and I can see her fingers dig deep into her flesh.

Janette's having the time of her life. This is perfect. Her ratings have been falling and she'd been worried, but this show's going to be killer, she can sense it. She turns to Bernice. "He's your brother!" Janette exclaims. "Well, your half-brother. How about that?"

Janette is grinning and JayRay is grinning, and Bernice looks like she is praying that the floor will swallow her up, or that aliens will abduct her, or that show will go to a commercial but of course it will not. It would never interrupt the highlight of the hour and her panicked reaction is playing right into the hands of the show's mandate. Even I watch, fascinated, while she tries desperately, and obviously to gather herself, and get control of the situation.

Janette turns to the audience and nods, and they start chanting *brother, brother, brother,* getting louder and louder and clapping in time to their calls.

Janette lets the cheer reach a crescendo then she whips out a salute and slowly lowers her arm, a lion tamer ordering her beasts to sit and obey. When there is complete silence, she turns and looks at Bernice. "Your brother," she repeats and the crowd leans forward, panting and eager, hoping for blood.

Bernice turns that raw meaty colour again and she unfolds her arms and clasps her hands together. "Ja, I can see that for myself, thank you very much," she replies calmly, her voice like ice.

I watch from my bed, and I can see, clear as day, that she regards JayRay as a scumbag, a cheap scam artist on the make.

I scoot closer to the screen and wonder what will happen next.

4. BERNICE

I'M SO ANGRY I CAN'T SPEAK. I am trapped in a ridiculously uncomfortable chair, live on primetime television, with my book on my lap. I watch the audience respond enthusiastically to the handlers, waving and shouting and punching the air with their fists. It's like I am at a rugby match, and I'm the ball that's just been kicked, and I'm lying there, waiting for more punishment.

I know I have to do something to save the situation, to save my reputation, but what? I was assured that I was on the show to talk only about my book. And now, *this?*

I look over at the man they are calling my half-brother. A good-looking *oke* no doubt, but in a cheap and sleazy way. Those terrible highlights in his hair and that big floppy fringe falling into his eyes, and that wide, lazy, self-satisfied grin. His smile reminds me of a young Don Johnson, and so what if I watch *Miami Vice* by myself late at night and dream about Sonny Crockett smiling at me and undoing my blouse? Particularly on nights when Dirk is home with his wife. What harm is there in watching the camera pan up Sonny's white shoes, his white suit, and pale blue collarless shirt, his sunglasses looped into the neckline, a cigarette pinched between his thumb and forefinger, and his gold wrist watch glinting in the sun? For a moment, I really am lying on my bed, watching my TV, and I'm waiting for Betty to bring me my supper on a tray, steak so rare it bleeds, with blood red wine to match.

My defense mechanism, when I am stressed, has always been to slip into another world and get lost, but I can't let that happen now. I need to get this unspeakable situation under control without losing my temper and, with difficulty, I force myself back into the present. Once this is over, I can reward myself with as much *Miami Vice* as I like and as much red wine as I like, in the privacy of my home, away from this nightmare.

I look over at this half-brother of mine. What kind of man highlights his hair? And he wears his shirt open like a cheap café owner, two buttons too many undone. He looks like he works out a lot and I can just imagine him admiring himself in the mirror at the gym while he lifts weights.

His thin gold necklace glints in the light and I notice without surprise that his beige trousers are a cheap synthetic fabric that never creases, but has turned shiny from being washed too often in hot water. He didn't even get a proper suit for the show, and he probably doesn't even know the difference.

He was a real pain in the neck for a while, what with his phone calls, emails, and letters. He tried to persuade me to meet him but I refused, to the point where I thought I had successfully shaken him off. Clearly, I was mistaken. And while I had forgotten about him, he was busy planning this nonsense.

I turn to Janette. "What exactly were you hoping to achieve with this stunt? Please enlighten me."

I'm dismayed to hear my accent. It is guttural and harsh, and much too South African. The careful training of my elocution lessons falls apart whenever I am caught off-guard, which doesn't happen often.

Janette looks stunned. "I thought you'd be happy. In your books, you talk about the importance of family. I did my homework and I found your brother for you. It wasn't easy, believe me. I had to do some serious investigating. I thought you would be happy. You're always saying how family is everything."

She's such a liar! JayRay tracked her down, like he did with me. She wouldn't have had to do a thing! I want to expose her lies, but I keep my cool. I remember to inflect more of a British lilt into my tone and I make my voice go light and happy when I speak.

"Janette," I say, and my voice is even and soft, "Ja, you were right about one thing. I was aware of this man's existence, thank you so much. He chased me with as much subtlety as a vuvuzela at a church choir. And frankly, I have not been in touch with him because I did not want to meet him. I did not want to meet him by choice. You didn't find him, Janette, he found you. And I bet he was most persistent about it too." I force my lips into a small smile, tilt my head to one side to indicate positive body language and I use a "smiley" voice to show there is only goodwill on my part, that I'm not being difficult in any way, I am simply stating the facts.

I refuse to look at my half-brother and I focus my gaze on Janette who is still looking perplexed, as if she truly cannot understand why this good deed is being punished. Meanwhile, the crowd is loving the drama of the whole thing and Janette knows it.

I refuse to say anything more. I study my nails and wait for Janette to make her next move.

"Maybe he did come to me," Janette amends. "We get hundreds of requests and it's hard to keep track. But," she says earnestly, "flesh and blood. Think about it. He's your flesh and blood. Your family. Don't you want to know more about that? Don't you want to know more about him? And about the father you both share?"

"Flesh and blood," I repeat, and I look out at the audience who crane forward in a wave of motion. I sit up straighter in my chair and I clutch my book to my stomach for strength, using it as a shield. "Flesh and blood. Yes, Janette, I couldn't agree with you more."

She looks surprised, she did not expect such an easy victory, and my ridiculous half-brother gets this triumphant look on his face but I continue, and I don't stop talking for a while, and I use that same, even, soft, firm voice. "He is exactly, and only, that. Flesh and blood. The blood and bones of a stranger. I could have met with him any time I wanted to, had I wanted to, but I did not. You say we are family. Why? Simply because we share the same sperm donor? We share a father, you say? No. My father is the man who adopted me when I was two years old. My father is the man who gave me his name, and who supported me in every way, from teaching me how to ride my bicycle, and ride my pony, to buying me my first car, and to seeing me through university. To listening to my problems, my hopes, and my dreams. That is what a father is, that is what being a father means. A man who impregnates a woman he is married to and leaves when the baby is six months old, well, that man is no father. A sperm donor is all that man is. And, on the basis of sperm, you think that I should have an interest in this stranger, in this vehicle of flesh and blood and bones? Half-brother? You've been watching too many soap operas where strangers rush into each other's arms on the basis of a DNA strand, crying and exclaiming love and affection and bonds forever after."

I turn away from Janette and face the audience directly. "Family, she says? What does this man know of my scraped knees from falling off my bicycle? Did we ever fish together as children? Did we learn to shoot BB guns together? Did we learn to ride horses together, or read each other's comics late into the night? Did we cover for each other as naughty teenagers? Did we comfort one another's disappointments as we grew into adults? The answer is no, we did none of that, and we have none of those memories. And that is what family is. No, people, that, sitting over there, that is no more than a stranger's body of flesh and bones and blood and muscle. We have neither shared soul, heart, history nor memory. And *that* is what family is."

I come to a stop and I sit back in my chair. I look over at Janette. She looks stunned, and horrified. I have no idea of the sleazy man's reaction because I refuse to look in his direction.

The wall of silence shatters as a wild cheer rises from the audience. The assembled crowd shoots to their feet, clapping, hooting, and whistling. The applause seems to go on forever and Janette's expression changes from one of hatred to delight; delight mixed with tears of joy. I swear that bitch even makes a show of wiping her eyes. She joins in the applause and my half-brother also stands and claps along.

After what feels like several lifetimes, Janette calms the crowd and they sink slowly back into their seats. "Wow!" she says, pretending to wipe more tears from her eyes, "that was incredible! People, there you have it. You have been told! Family. Shared souls, hearts, history, and memories. Come here, Bernice, come and stand with me."

I stand up awkwardly and I join her and she puts her arm around my waist and hugs me close, which I hate.

She smiles at the audience, grabs my book from my grasp and waves it. "Each lucky member of the audience will be taking a signed copy of *Bake Your Way to Mr. Right* home, along with a cookie cutter sponsored by Royal Baking Flour! Thank you, Royal Baking Flour for being a proud supporter of this show today! Bernice, is there anything else you'd like to say to the audience before we sign off?"

I take a deep breath. The book. I have to remember my precious book. I have to save the moment.

"Ja, for sure there is," I say, and I take my book back from Janette and hold it out to the audience, returning the central focus to it, and not me.

"What I always want most for my books is that they will be a friend to you. That they will help you achieve your dreams, and give you love, advice, and support in tough times. If you are looking for Mr. Right, I hope this book will help you find him. But I also hope it will help you during the times when you have not yet found Mr. Right or perhaps Mr. Right is not behaving as perfectly as he should. This book is about *you*, and it is *for* you, and I hope it enriches your life and brings you joy."

The audience claps and cheers appreciatively and I give them the biggest smile I can, even though smiling is the last thing I feel like doing.

Janette jumps in before I can say anything else. "There you go, what a show! We'll take a few minutes for commercials and come back with our next guest, the stylish and beautiful influencer Elaine Jane Wheeler, who has more than eighty thousand Instagram followers! But, people, we know something about her perfect life that she doesn't! Viewers at home, don't go anywhere!"

The moment the off-air signal is given, we leave the stage. I wave to the crowd on my way out and they wave back and I make sure my smile is plastered in place.

Janette is ecstatic. She high-fives her producer and does a little victory dance. Out of the corner of my eye, I see JayRay standing in a corner, ignored. He looks confused, with his hands shoved deep into the pockets of his cheap trousers.

"That's what I'm talking about!" Janette shouts. "Anger! Passion! Ha!"

"Congrats," the producer says. "Great TV, the best kind. Your ratings will be through the roof. And Bernice will sell even more millions of her books. It's a win-win! Everybody should be happy." He looks pointedly at me.

I want to voice my fury. The interview was supposed to be about the book, not an invasion of privacy. But I can't find my voice. My hands are shaking and the room spins. I want to sit down but more than that, I want to leave.

Janette meets my eyes and I silently agree to concede.

"I've got to get back out there," she says and she gives me a nod, which I take to mean, *let's leave it at that.*

I grab a bottle of water and watch the set from the sidelines as she strides back onto the stage. I'm dying to leave but I need to hear what she will say about our segment.

"Wasn't that amazing?" Janette coos. "Legendary! Don't forget to buy Bernice's book, all of you out there at home. And again, each lucky member of our audience will receive a copy of the book, along with a cookie cutter brought to you by Royal Baking Flour, the proud sponsor of our show! Be sure to spread the word; family is not just flesh and blood but shared souls, hearts, history, and memories. Amazing! And now I'd like to introduce you to Elaine Jane Wheeler!"

She continues her babble and the next victim of her show is ushered onto the stage. I grab my purse and coat and I rush out of the studio without a backward glance. I push my way through gathered staff in the corridor who are too busy gossiping among themselves to care about me.

Once outside, I stand on the street corner, unsure what to do next. The studio is one street off the Strip and I turn in a hurry and find a slipstream with the fast moving crowd of Vegas sightseers. My phone is beeping and buzzing with emails, tweet alerts, and Facebook comments, and I know I should answer them but I can't trust myself to talk, not even via text. Especially not via text. To vent online now, is to regret it later. Better to be silent. What had my publicist been thinking? And if she had no idea this was going to happen, it's even worse. She had put me in a hornet's nest when it was her job to protect me from exactly that.

I stare at my phone again. Why are there no messages from the only person who matters? Where is Dirk? True, he didn't want me to be on the show; a woman's place is in the home, not on the world's stage. Even if that woman is only his mistress, not his wife, and even if she is an enormous success in her own right. In fact, all the more reason for her to stay at home, be demure, self-effacing, and humble.

But I'm no Afrikaner *vrou*, I am no man's wife. Not for lack of trying or wanting. I sigh. Dirk is punishing me with his silence and he's succeeding.

My pantyhose crawl around my legs like *shongololos* and I

stop and scratch at my thighs, not caring who sees me. I grab the waistband of the offending garment through my skirt and try to yank them up but when I catch a few curious stares, I stop.

I double-check my phone again. Maybe the signal was briefly down. But there is nothing from Dirk. I hate him at that moment. He's probably out with his *Volksraad*; he thinks I don't know about that but of course I do. His "Parliament" of righteous Afrikaners who are intent on saving their language and heritage at all costs.

I'm not even sure why a proper Afrikaner like Dirk is seeing me. He is an *opregte* Afrikaner, as he tells me just about every time he sees me. He's given to quoting Hendrik Bibault's cry of *Ik ben een Africaander*, reminding me that the rallying cry was first uttered in 1705 and that he is still waving that same flag. Not to mention that Dirk's ancestors were among the Voortrekkers on the Great Trek in the 1830s. I have never had as many history lessons in my life as I do with Dirk. At least he doesn't make me speak Afrikaans with him.

Actually, in the beginning, he tried but he said I was butchering *die moedertaal*, the mother tongue, and could I please stop. I stopped with pleasure. To my mind, Afrikaans was nothing more than a relic of the past, a second-language I half-heartedly studied at school.

I sigh. I want to smash my phone and break it into tiny pieces, as if it's the phone's fault there are no messages from the man I love. But that would be cutting off my nose to spite my face, as my father used to tell me when I was having a fit of fury and looking for vengeance.

I stop at a corner store and buy a packet of cigarettes and a lighter. Since it is Las Vegas, the lighter is shaped like a naked woman but I don't care. I gave up smoking for Dirk but I needed a smoke now. One? I want to inhale the whole pack in one go. Dirk is one of those sanctimonious ex-smokers and I only stopped because he nagged me endlessly.

I sit on a bench on the Strip and smoke three cigarettes in

a row. I need some wine. Some good South African red wine. I'm going to have an entire bottle to myself and maybe not stop there.

I walk back to my hotel as fast as I can and when I get there, I head straight for the bar. I consider going to my room but I don't trust myself to be alone. I might smash the mirror, destroy the room, break the chairs, and behave badly. I have a temper. A bad one. My rages were the only thing my father admonished me about when I was a child. I would scream like a banshee and I threw things, breaking whatever I could lay my hands on.

Betty would wait for my rage to subside, and then would slip silently into the room, a dustpan and broom in hand. When I was a teenager and filled with the blinding rage, I used a blade on my arms and leges and I scored cuts, nothing neat, a mishmash of angry marks, not deep mind you, but still, a frenzied attack that momentarily eased my demons. I wore long sleeves for a while. As I grew older, I learned to turn my anger inward, and I became depressed instead.

And that old familiar anger surges through my blood now. I won't self-harm, but I'm craving an act of violence and destruction. However, achieving infamy as the self-help author who turned her room upside down in a fit of temper would not be judicious. No, best to stay out of my own way until I calmed down.

I climb onto a tall barstool with relief. I order a bottle of Boekenhoutskloof Cabernet Sauvignon 2012. At least the bar has good South African wines.

I study my reflection in the mirror behind the bar. My skin is a dark putty colour, a colour I hate, and the thick TV makeup exaggerates the uncooked sausage tone. Man, I look old. Betty used to tell me that angry never makes for pretty, and she was right. And the whole world saw me: puce-faced and fuming. But let's not forget that I won.

I grab a napkin and wipe my face roughly, pausing to down

a glass of wine and pour another. "Tough day?" the bartender asks and I ignore him and focus on my drink.

I polish off a second glass and my composure tiptoes back. My phone continues to chirp and buzz and everybody and their brother message me. The whole world chimes in, but there is still nothing from Dirk. And the rest of the world can wait until I'm good and ready to say what needs to be said.

I can't stop thinking about that man, James Ray, that sleazy man, trying to ride on the coattails of my fame with his claim to be my family. How foolish to think I had shaken him off. I had been a little surprised that he had slunk off into the shadows so quickly, but for the life of me, I never expected him to pull a stunt like this.

I sit at the bar and finish the bottle in short order. My anger recedes. I can go to my room, tear off these godforsaken scratchy pantyhose, tie them in a knot, and throw them away. I will close the blinds, order another bottle of wine, and drink until I pass out.

I get up, unsteady on my heels and I concentrate on grabbing my handbag. I sling it over my shoulder, and the world wobbles a bit. I turn to leave and who do I see but that con man, James Ray, sitting alone in an alcove booth. He is watching me. How long he has been there? I lean on the stool that is still warm from my bottom and I stare straight back at him.

I do not move.

5. LEONIE

SITTING ON THE BED IN MY HOTEL ROOM, I watch the TV in horror. My poor JayRay. My poor baby. Once that bitch got going about flesh and blood, she made it sound like he was a mangy, scavenging dog and I could hardly bear to watch. He wasn't so much sidelined as discarded like garbage. He'll be devastated. All his hopes destroyed, with nothing left but the dead ashes of a dream.

I'm not sure if I should rush off and try to find him or leave him be for a while. I know he will have followed Bernice back to her hotel and I scramble through my texts to find where she's staying. I decide that I have to find him. I grab my purse and walk quickly to Bernice's hotel.

I wrench the bar room door open and stop short. A standoff is in play between Bernice and JayRay. Bernice is at the bar. She looks wobbly and half-cut while JayRay is sitting at a booth and he's slicing her with a chainsaw look.

I don't move, neither does Bernice, and JayRay keeps his radar glare locked in place.

"Sorry, excuse me, pardon me," a hefty man wheezes past me and breaks the spell. I march over to JayRay's booth and slide in next to him. Now both of us are staring Bernice down.

Bernice hooks her purse over her arm, picks up her coat, and makes her way across the room. I was right; she's liberally drunk. She walks straight past us and I can't help myself. "Hey," I call out. "You. Bitch. Who died and made you the queen?"

She stops and turns around. She looks at us for a moment and then she comes up to our table and eases into the booth and faces us. "Okay, fine. Here I am. What do you want? Money? Is that it?"

"I wondered about you my whole life," JayRay says quietly and he isn't smiling. He actually looks classy when he isn't smiling, although I've never told him that. When he grins, you can't help but see a guy on the make — that kind of beauty has to be asking for something in return. When his face is still, he's believable as an honest, sincere guy.

Bernice is taken aback by this quiet new charm, this guy without a play in hand. Her shoulders relax slightly and her fingers stop their frantic cuticle digging. "Wondered what? What did you hear anyway?" Her accent is like cheddar and raw onions.

"Dad often talked about you. He felt bad for leaving you. He didn't know what else to do."

"So he divorces my mother when I am six months old, marries some new woman in two shakes of a lamb's tail, gets her pregnant, hightails it to Canada, and then we never hear from him again. He takes his new wife and starts a brand new family, and you and your brothers and sisters are set while he leaves my mother high and dry. And I'm supposed to be happy he talked about me? Tough *takkies* if you ask me."

Brothers and sisters? JayRay told me he was an only child. I want to extrapolate the truth from him, but I acknowledge that the timing isn't great and I'll have to wait.

"Have a drink with us," JayRay says quietly, keeping his believable sincere face in place. "Please don't rush off. Hear what I have to say."

Bernice hesitates and she looks at me. Unlike JayRay, my game face is my smile and I slap it on now, not too much, somewhat shy, even apologetic. "I apologize for shouting at you," I say to her. "Please stay."

My plea works and the waiter comes to take our orders.

"A cappuccino," Bernice says and JayRay follows suit. I order a bottle of red wine.

"So now, what next?" Bernice asks. "What do you want to talk about?"

JayRay shrugs. "You. Do you have any kids? Are you married?"

Bernice shakes her head and I know that JayRay has the answers already.

"She had a dog called Snoopy when she was a kid," he told me after our first night together. "Like how unoriginal is that? A beagle. You would have thought that as a future bestselling author, she would have shown more imagination. And a cat named Fluffy. Her mother died from ovarian cancer when she was thirty-eight, and her adopted father died eight years ago, and he left her everything."

"What's everything?" I asked.

"Millions. A mansion in Johannesburg, where she lives, although she grew up on a farm several hours north west of Johannesburg. They've still got the place. Imagine us, living on a farm in Africa."

"Wasn't there a movie like that? It rings some bells: *I Had a Farm in Africa*, that type of shit?"

JayRay shrugged. "No idea."

"How are we going to get this farm?" I asked. "What kind of farm anyway?"

"Sheep. I think. The last reference I found for it online said it was sheep. Sheep are easy to manage. We'd figure it out."

"And if you piss her off on the show, how do you plan on worming your way into her life?"

"You know me," he had said confidently and yes, I did, and right now, sitting in a sitting in a shiny upscale bar in Vegas, with the sound of slot machines clanging in the background, he's got Bernice exactly where he wants her. But I've got no idea where he'll take it from here.

"I won't discuss my private life," Bernice says and she is firm. "Tell me about you."

I turn to JayRay enquiringly. Dollars to doughnuts this story will be different from anything he's told me.

JayRay sighs and looks at his hands and I lean forward and wait. "I was born in Johannesburg, like you."

Liar! You were born in Halifax!

"My father brought me to Canada for a better life, a safer life. My mother was raped at knifepoint by three thieves and my father never forgave himself. They came into the house one day when she was alone and he blamed himself because he worked with one of the guys, a mechanic. Of course, the police never caught him, they were as dirty as he was."

Bernice nods, her face expressionless. She's sobered up pretty quickly although she's barely touched her coffee.

"My mother never recovered," JayRay continues. "She was scarred for life. She got pregnant and she didn't know if the baby was from the rape or from my father, and she carried that child, me, for nine months not knowing."

Bernice takes a sip of her coffee and doesn't say a word.

"When I was born, they did some tests and I was my father's child. But my mother equated me with the rape and she hated me. She couldn't bear to look at me or touch me. That's why my father took us to Canada, to try to start fresh. My mother had two other children after me and she loved them. It was only me that she couldn't stand."

Liar! You told me that your mother loved you more than anyone in the world! She told you that you could be anything you wanted and she bailed you out of jail for petty thievery, and she forgave you when you stole from her, and she let you break her heart over and over again.

I'm not sure, anymore, if I do want to hear this version of his life but it's too late to leave.

"I was never close to my brothers and sisters. How could I be when they were loved in a way that was denied to me? But I my father believed in me, he taught me everything I know."

Seriously? He must have taught you that from prison, eh?

Your father's a bank robber who shot up a bunch of innocent bystanders. He's still in prison, no chance of parole.

"He taught me to hunt and fish and work with machines and how to fight and stand up for myself. He had a tough life. Life in Canada's no piece of cake, I'll tell you that much. He struggled to put food on the table and he struggled to give us kids the things we needed. He worked two jobs and he encouraged us to go to school and make better lives for ourselves."

"A real upstanding guy," Bernice comments and I pour myself a generous second glass of wine. JayRay's annoying me with this line he's working. I know he'll have a reason for it, he always does, but, still, he should have looped me in. I'm an outsider watching him work and I don't like the feeling at all. He must sense it because he leans back in the booth and slides his hand under the table, and he pretends he is rubbing his thigh meanwhile he's caressing me. His touch loosens me up, regardless of my intentions to be standoffish.

"I understand that he hurt you," JayRay returns his hand to the table. He clasps his fists and looks earnest. "He often told me how much he regretted it. He wanted to get in touch with you and I know he tried but your mother wouldn't let him."

Bernice studies her coffee as if it holds the secrets of her life.

"Where is he now?" she asks.

"He died." JayRay is somber. "He was exhausted from working all day and then, later that night, he was working on a car, he was lying under it and it fell on him and crushed him."

Ah. It makes sense now. The sad story of a boy rejected by his mother, fatherless and alone, estranged from his siblings because of his mama's prejudice towards her perceived rape baby. All elements that Bernice could relate to. Her mother died when she was young, her father loved her but he too was gone, and she has no other family. JayRay and Bernice. Two little peas in a tight little pod.

"I got your emails, you know," Bernice says. "I had no interest in meeting you. I still don't care about you. You or your brother and sister."

"They don't know about you," JayRay adds quickly. "Dad only ever told me about you. I don't even know if Mom knew and if she did, she never said."

"From what I heard, your mother knew, oh ja, for sure she did. Your mother knew that my mother was married to your father and still, she flirted with him, fell pregnant, and ripped him away from us. But from what my mother said, your father was no great loss. And I won the lottery with my stepdad. Just like I told the whole world, with you as my witness." She pushes her coffee cup away from her. "After you kept emailing me, I had you looked into."

Her expression challenges JayRay and his face changes, hardly at all, but I see it. The sincere-guy-look melts around the edges and his eyes glint with anger as his jaw tightens. I sense more than see that he's defensive and wary, as if he knows what's coming. I brace myself.

"You're rubbish," Bernice says. "And your father was rubbish before you. He's in prison. You haven't got any brothers or sisters. I've got no idea why you'd think I would care either way, but you just lie, it's what you do. You open your mouth and lies come out. You were born in Halifax. Your mother's a drunk and she lives off welfare and the pennies you send her. You're a mommy's boy who sells second-rate security courses at trade shows to people who don't know any better. You ride on your good looks and what you think of as your charm. You're scamming me right now, or at least you're trying to, and I'll tell you this much, if you so much as come near me again, I'll put a lawyer onto you. Do not email me, do not call me, do not contact me again." She eases out of the booth and puts on her jacket.

"But," JayRay starts to say, "I've got something big on you, you should know...."

Bernice's eyes widen and a look of fear crosses her face. She stoops down slightly, as if she's going to listen to what JayRay has to say, but she shakes her head emphatically in a childish motion, and I half-expect her to stick her fingers in her ears.

"Whatever it is, I don't care. Got it? I don't care what you know or what you think you know. Besides, you don't know anything, because there isn't anything *to* know." She slings her purse over her shoulder and looks at me. "Such a loyal little puppy dog. I feel sorry for you." She marches out and I notice she's a lot steadier on her feet than when she first walked over to our table.

JayRay rubs his temples in a way that he does when he is furious and I shouldn't poke a stick at him but I can't help myself. I don't like the way Bernice made me feel.

"Engage, qualify, present, and close. No so much, eh?" I say. "Good job, honey bunny."

JayRay looks at me and he clenches his fists. I can see that he wants to hit me, punch my face to a pulp, but he instead, he smashes the bottle of wine onto the table. Glass explodes everywhere, red wine floods the table cloth, and a piece of glass flies into the softness of my cheek and lodges deep, burning me. I touch it with shaking fingertips.

"Look at what you made me do," JayRay says. He peers at my face. "Hold still now." He plucks the glass out and he's not exactly gentle. He drops the shard on the table. "I'm going for a walk. Don't follow me. And pay for this mess."

Wine puddles in my lap and blood trickles down my cheek. The waiter comes over with a mop and some rags. "I'm sorry," I tell him.

I edge out of the booth, mindful of glass in my lap. The manager rushes over with the bill and I pay him. "I can take you to our in-house doctor, if you like," he says and I nod and follow him. I wonder if JayRay has scarred me for life.

But I already know the answer to that.

6. BERNICE

I LEAVE THOSE TERRIBLE PEOPLE and take the elevator up to my room. I gnaw on a knuckle, thinking about JayRay's parting words. There's no way he can know. I only found out by mistake when I had Dirk's marriage and finances looked into. I wanted to know the truth out about his marriage. I hoped it was in a worse state than Dirk had let on and, affirmative, it was on the rocks big time. Haha, Dirk's fine upstanding *vrou* was, herself, having an affair. And Dirk's finances were none too shiny either. He gambled too much on his own racehorses, none of whom were winners.

It was routine for me to investigate new boyfriends and random people who came into my life. Being born into money and making millions more, I was never sure who was befriending me on the basis of my sparkling and engaging personality, as it is *not*, or on the basis of my sparkling and engaging bank account.

I'm a plain woman. All us girls want to be tall and slender and I'm tall, but I'm skinny and bony. Sexless. My hands, feet, and knees are too big. My bottom is flat, my waist is square, and I've got no boobs to speak of. I'm a long, tall box. I'm the antithesis of my beautiful model mother. Her sensuality glowed even when her hair was turbaned in a towel and she was swathed in a shapeless dressing gown. She was so beautiful she took my breath away. And I wasn't alone. All she had to do was look at a person and they felt as if it they had been singled out for the most special kind of praise and love, and they never wanted that feeling to end. I watched it happen, time after time. Except that she never looked at me in that way. She never really looked at me at all.

I studied my face for hours, examining the similarities and differences between us. I went so far as to cut up a picture of her and a picture of me and I put her nose next to mine, her mouth next to mine, her eyes next to mine. I was embarrassed when my father caught me, and he tried to assure me that I was lovely in my own way but we both knew he was lying.

My features are oddly miniaturized in a big oval head. I have a large, high forehead, a tiny, pinched nose, and a small mouth with thin lips. As far as I can see, my only assets are my eyes, they are large and round. But they are too wide-set and too big, and they aren't a definite colour. Are they blue? No, they are not. Are they brown? No, they are not brown either. Sparse eyelashes don't help and neither does thin, ginger-coloured flyaway hair that frizzes like a cheap doll's at every turn. I spend half my life straightening it and trying to make it bend to my will. And don't forget the off-putting tendency of my complexion to flush the colour of raw meat when I'm anxious. If you add all of this to my ugly rages and depression, plus the fact that I have no sense of humour, the package is no great shakes.

During the fourth year of my postgraduate study at the University of the Witwatersrand, I fell into a deeper gloom than any passing funk previously experienced. Life was pointless. Nothing had any value or meaning. It was impossible to get out of bed. I stayed under the covers for days, the thick curtains drawn tight against the light. I had realized, without a doubt, that apart from my money, I had nothing to offer the world. Nor could I expect anything in return. Neither friendship, love, or companionship, or, that most alien of concepts, fun.

I was unlikeable and unloveable. My own mother had been unable to love me. I was irrelevant to the human race.

I was alone in Johannesburg at the time. My father was at the farm, and I couldn't bring myself to call him and tell him I was hurting because it wasn't pain, it was a terrifying numbness. That I got out of bed at all was thanks to Betty. "Madam, you must get out of bed. You have been in bed for two weeks now. You are not sick. If you do not get out of bed, I am going to telephone your father."

"I am sick, Betty. Sick in the mind."

"Lying in bed will not fix it. Come with me. Come on, get up."

Betty. By all rights, Betty could and should have left me after the ANC came into power, but she said she had her doubts that I could fend for myself. Certainly I could not iron, or make a cup of tea or cook a meal and she said why should she leave when I would just get someone else who would do a poor job? No. Betty said that she had looked after me all her life and until the time when I was happily on my own two feet, with a family of my own, she wasn't going anywhere.

I was grateful in a way that I could never tell Betty but I increased her wages, which drew scorn from Rosie. Rosie had wanted Betty to leave and she didn't mince her words. Rosie didn't mince her words. It was beneath her mother to clean up after a white princess, even if that white princess offered her mother more money when she said she'd stay.

"Blood money," I heard Rosie say. "Money from white men is blood money."

"And jobs are jobs," Betty had replied. "And I like mine. I will keep it, thank you, Rosie."

I heard Rosie's disgust at her mother's comment. "One day I will make enough money so that you won't have to wash the panties of a spoilt rich white girl."

So, after lying in bed for two weeks, when Betty knocked on my door, I did not tell her to go away. She came in and sat down on the bed and she stroked my forehead. I listened to her talk and I got up when she told me to.

"We are going to bake," Betty declared. "We are going to make a *melktert* and you are going to help me."

Food had never interested me and I sighed, wanting only to return to the safety of my dark room. The world stung my eyes and seared my skin.

But, as I followed Betty's instructions and mixed the butter and sugar together, I felt the slightest lifting of my spirits. I added the egg yolks and beat the mix until it was light and fluffy. I sifted in the cake flour, the baking powder and the salt, and I folded and stirred while Betty watched approvingly.

"You are a natural," she said and I wanted to smile but I grunted and added vanilla essence and milk.

"This is fun," I finally conceded. "Why haven't you ever taught me before?"

"You never lay in bed for this many days before. I couldn't think of anything else to get you up."

This time I let her see my smile. "Ja well. You helped me, Betty. Thank you. Where did you learn to cook so well?"

"My mother taught me, and she learned from a strict *tannie* who was a cook on a big farm. She learned traditional South African food. And your father, Mr. Ruan, he hired me for my cooking. He told me that he liked to eat well and he said he had a beautiful wife but she did not like to cook."

I laughed in agreement. "I don't think my mother could make a piece of toast."

"You are right, she could not. Now, let me tell you my secret ingredient that nobody knows. I have added something along the way, to all these recipes." She opened up the spice cabinet and I watched her closely.

Yes, I learned each and every one of Betty's secrets.

"What will we do with this pie?" I asked once our *melktert* was ready. "Seems like a waste, only you and me to eat it."

"We must share it," Betty said, sprinkling cinnamon sugar on the top. "Food is a blessing to be shared."

"I'll call Theresa to come and have tea with us," I said.

Theresa was my best friend. My only friend, really, and I had ignored her during my funk.

I took to baking with a passion that startled Betty and she struggled to keep up with my requests for new recipes. I baked cakes and pies and tarts and cookies and I gave them to the homeless people who hung around the strip malls looking for handouts. South Africa has no shortage of hungry people to feed and for a while I provided some of them with a steady supply. I baked my way out of the pit of despair and I studied Betty's methodology, making meticulous notes, annoyed with myself for making the same mistake twice.

I finished my doctorate as quickly as I could. I told Betty that, in my opinion, the fastest way for a person to become completely depressed and unhappy with their lives was to study psychology. The minute after graduation, I threw myself into developing my first book, a combination of baking and self-help and it was an instant success. Betty told me she was proud of me, as did my father, and my books became my life. I got hundreds of letters from people around the world, telling me how I had changed their lives and given them hope. I replied to every letter. I felt good about myself. I felt real and I mattered.

A professional photographer took my portrait for the book and the results were pleasing even to me. I looked less like some kind of alien, bug-eyed sea creature in print than I did in real life. I even looked pretty. My father insisted that I was pretty in real life too. He said I made the mistake of comparing myself to the wrong people. By which, of course, he meant my mother. Would it have made a difference if she had told me I was pretty? Or showed me how to fix my hair or apply makeup? Or shown me any kind of attention at all? Sometimes I wished she had hit me, or shouted at me, anything, just to prove that she knew I was there. But I was never a part of her world and I hated myself for not being able to get past my need for her love.

Apart from Betty and Theresa, I kept the boundaries of my life close, limiting my love affairs to short-lived dalliances with married men who were good in bed. No one breached the barbed wire perimeter of my affections until Dirk. Big, powerful, charismatic Dirk.

Dangerous Dirk, whose affiliation to the secret underground group, the *Volksraad*, poses a torpedo threat to my untarnished reputation.

The *Volksraad* are a group of racist Neo-Nazi Afrikaans South Africans. Their mission is to inflict as much damage as they can to to fragile, post-apartheid South Africa, in a bid to keep their language and culture alive. It is absolutely imperative that no one ever finds out about Dirk's allegiance to this powder keg group.

I am dismayed by the onslaught of uncomfortable memories and fears that my unfortunate encounter with JayRay has stirred up. I don't want to think about my mother or my past. Of course, I can't stop thinking about Dirk, but that's another matter. By this time, I am safely ensconced in my hotel room and I pace up and down.

But how could JayRay have found out about the *Volksraad*? They were news to me, but I must not have been reading the newspapers carefully because after I found out Dirk was a member, I saw mention of them everywhere.

Is that what JayRay was going to tell me? But what else could it be? I couldn't risk hearing what he knew. It was better to walk away, even if it meant not knowing what cards he was clutching in his horrible con man fists. Was there a way to find out what he knew? No, it was better to ignore him; he was a one-way ticket to trouble. What a mess. Dirk, JayRay, everything.

After I found about the *Volksraad*, I wanted to tell Dirk to leave. I wanted to tell him that I knew what he was up to and that it was despicable, but I couldn't say anything. He's the only man I've ever loved. I am so in love with him that I will do nearly anything to keep him by my side, but I also know that associating with a Neo-Nazi is the kind of bad you don't recover from.

I remind myself again of the famously disgraced journalist Jani Allan. So beautiful and so untouchable. At the pinnacle of her power, she trotted off blithely to have tea with Eugene Terre'Blanche, leader of the *Afrikaaner Weerstandsbeweging*, the Afrikaner Resistance Movement. Her meteoric fall from grace was both spectacular and mesmerizing. The country watched in fascinated horror as the blonde beauty and the hefty boer met secretly in parking lots and left embarrassing messages on answering machines. Buttock sighting through keyholes were gleefully reported and the whole affair was career suicide for Jani. And all because she had been "transfixed on the flame of his blowtorch eyes."

I was only a child of ten when she sued Channel 4 for libel, but her story hooked me from the start. Who on earth, I wondered, could be so stupid as to let someone that damaging into their lives? Where was Jani's sense of self-preservation? Where was her discipline? I vowed that lust would never lead me down the garden path of any such stupidity, but now it appeared that I had not only walked that path, I had opened that very door, the door to the secret garden which, unless I was extremely careful, would not remain a secret for much longer. And it would be my undoing.

I can't let myself be damaged by Dirk. But neither can I live without him.

I'm exhausted. I can't think about it right now. I strip off my clothes and throw them in the trash. I want to destroy the evidence of this ghastly day. But I fish them out and pummel them into the corner of my suitcase. There's no point in throwing out an expensive outfit. Betty will clean it and fix it, like always.

I have a long hot shower, wrap myself in a toweling gown, and turn on my laptop. If there isn't a message from him, I will die. There has to be a message.

Hundreds of messages flow into my inbox and I scroll through them quickly. All from fans, congratulating me on what a great job I did. Nothing from him. He is telling me that me and my pain come second to him and his family, and that he doesn't care. He won't let himself care. He is married and he is an honourable man, an *opregte* Afrikaner who will stand by his wife and his children.

I hate him. How could I have let this happen?

I lie down on the bed and curl into a ball. What if we'd met at university? He wouldn't have looked at me once, never mind twice. But he looked at the blonde Afrikaans girl in her bobby socks, didn't he? And he did more than look.

He got her pregnant in their third year at university. He sat in his future parents-in-law's living room and ate homemade rusks while he apologized for the unspeakable predicament by asking for her hand in marriage. He would be an honourable man, he told her parents, a good man. He tried to look responsible and serious as he dunked the rusk into his tea, fearful of looking gauche for doing so, but more terrified of spraying crumbs everywhere.

"Her roommate came to me," he told me. "She said 'Chrizette's late.' One didn't say vulgar things like 'she fell pregnant' or 'she missed her period.' You just said 'she's late.' I knew what she meant. I replied instantly, 'I will marry her.' I meant it. I never thought she'd look at me in the first place. Never. But I noticed her the minute I walked into the lecture hall. She was sitting in the front row. The Sunshine Girl I called her because she was so wholesome and so beautiful, and when I asked her out and she said yes, I couldn't believe my luck. And she fell pregnant and we got married and I promised her I would be true and I will stick to my word."

"Ja, but you're not true to her," I said, wanting to crush him under the boulder of his lies and self-deception. "You love me and you know you do. And I am sick and tired of hearing how you thought she looked all wholesome and pure and I am sick of hearing you congratulate yourself for being an honourable man. You visit me and you come in my hand and you come in my mouth. And you still call yourself an honourable man!"

"I have never been inside you," he said, his eyes pebble cold. "My penis has never been inside you. Therefore I have never slept with you. Therefore we have never had an affair."

"You've been fingering me and making me come for a year," I spat at him. "A full year. We celebrated our anniversary. We shared secrets, fears, hopes, and dreams. And yet we are not having an affair?"

"I have never been inside you," he repeated as he got dressed. "And now I am leaving you for good. Good luck with your trip. You'll be amazing, you always are. You don't need me in your life anyway."

"I hate you," I said and I threw a box of chocolates at him and they flew through the air, a hail of brown stones. "You and your stupid chocolates. You stupid hypocrite."

And that was the last time I saw him before I left. And now there is no message from him. I fold into myself, with my arms hugging my belly, and I cry. I wonder how many times I have let him shatter my heart and I wonder if this really is the end and, if so, how will I carry on with my life? How many times have I let him shatter my heart? Is this really the end? And if it is, how will I carry on with my life?

"Some things aren't forever, *poppie*," my father once told me. "You take what you can while you can and then you try your best to live with it or let it go."

I miss my father. I have no one to talk to. My agent is fed up with hearing about my stupid love life. Theresa is tired of hearing about Dirk and Betty doesn't count.

I pick up the phone and order a bottle of red wine. Then I sit down and attend to the texts and emails. I attend to them with professionalism and dignity, while tears pour down my face and I drink my wine.

7. LEONIE

I LEAVE THE DOCTOR and walk back to my hotel. I am worn out. My face stings under the large bandaid on my cheek and I'm worried the cut will leave a scar. I wonder if JayRay will be waiting for me, drunk, angry, and truculent. I hope not. We always give each other room keys although usually JayRay stays with me.

I slide my key card into the lock and open the door hesitantly.

"JayRay?" There's no reply for which I am grateful. I close the door behind me and lock it. After everything that happened, I need some quiet time. I run a bath of steaming water and climb into it. But I keep my phone close to me and as I'm about to sink down into the water, it rings.

It's JayRay. I was on the mark. He's drunk and truculent. He spews his rage like vomit and I'm unable to get a word in edgewise. I soon tire of listening to him. I put the phone on speaker and lay it on the toilet lid, and his voice echoes out into the bathroom. I crack open a tiny bottle of vodka I grabbed from the mini-bar. JayRay's rant continues and I wonder why I don't hang up. Eventually his vitriol sputters to a halt, replaced by silence. I pick up the phone.

"You still there?" I ask into the void.

"Yeah. What are you up to?"

"I'm in the bath. Listen, I'm sorry it didn't work out, baby, I really am. Bernice is a bitch. I'm sorry I wasn't more supportive. She pissed me off too, made me feel like I was a cheap whore."

"I just wanted to get us a farm," JayRay starts crying. "I was only looking out for our future."

"I know. We'll figure out something else, okay? We'll come up with something."

"But what? This was our golden egg. She was our goose. But I've got something on her, I do, I wasn't lying. I've got a Plan B. I wanted Plan A to work out, but it failed."

"Forget about Plan B, JayRay. You heard her. Leave her alone. She's brutal. You do not want to fuck with her."

"But I've got the goods, babe, I've got them. I can make her pay."

"You can't get near her to give her the goods. Let her go, JayRay. End of the road. Accept it."

He is quiet for a moment, then he says, "But what if I can't let it go?" and he sounds so sad it makes me want to cry.

"Then you won't see me for a while." It's an idle threat but one I have to make. This can't go on, this Bernice obsession.

"You don't mean that," JayRay is confident and I sigh.

"I'd like to mean it. C'mon, babe, let her go. We'll figure out a new angle."

"And we go home tomorrow." JayRay states the obvious.

"If you think that depresses you, think how I feel. Back to being a wife and a mom."

"I want to marry you," JayRay says out of nowhere. "I want you to be my wife."

"A bit complicated unless I divorce Dave." I sit up straighter in the bath and slosh water onto the floor. *Mine! He will be all mine!* But I can't let him know what this means to me. I force my tone to stay neutral and I even manage to sound a tiny bit amused, as if challenging him to make the impossible happen.

"We're in Vegas, let's get married. Have a ceremony. Come on. We'll know it's true, you and me. True love."

"I'd like a proper proposal," I say and I stand up and slosh more water onto the bathroom floor. "You know, you on bended knee, with a ring. Anyway, you hurt my face." I want him to know that what he did is not okay. He can't pretend like it didn't happen.

"I'm really sorry," he says and I can hear he means it. "I was so angry I couldn't see straight. Did you need stitches?"

"No. But I hope it won't leave a scar. And I don't know what I'll tell Dave."

"Tell him you were having a drink after work and some drunk guy smashed a bottle and you got hit by piece of flying glass. It's the truth."

"It is that," I agree. "The real truth is that I don't know how to be Dave's wife anymore. Or a mom."

"You were always a shitty mom. Dave's a much better mom than you."

"Hey mister," I tell him. "I do my best. It's better to have a mom than not."

"I don't know so much. I mean my mom loves me, she dotes on me, and what good did that do? Kids need one good parent and your girls have Dave."

"What's your point, JayRay? Are you asking me to leave my family and be with you?"

There is silence. "I thought not," I say, and I'm like a kid who realizes that Father Christmas is a whore in drag. "Then, why don't you back the fuck away from my parenting skills? Where are you?"

"A bar." I can hear JayRay looking around and he sniffs loudly. "I don't know which one."

"Come to me, baby. Come on, I'll make you forget about this crappy day."

"I am getting fucking older by the fucking minute and all my dreams are gone. I thought that my phone would be ringing like a fucking crazy thing with offers from Hollywood. Stupid, eh?"

"Not stupid. Hopeful."

"I'm running out of time, Leo. I'm my best asset, my only asset, and I'm losing it. I'm like the fucking fruit basket in the room that no one wants. I'm the rotten old fucking peach and pretty soon the fruit flies will be circling, moving in for the kill."

"You'll always be my peachy boy," I say absently, wishing he'd stop being so dramatic and haul his ass over so I can cheer him up in person.

"I'm a rotten peach," he says mournfully. "I never had a good heart. I'm rotten to the core. Even my father said so. He said, 'boy, you may be the apple of your mother's eye but you're a rotten peach, just like me.' He used to sing this song by Elton John, about peaches rotting in the summer sun. 'That's you and me, boy,' he'd say. 'Rotten peaches, rotting in the summer sun.'"

He falls silent.

"Nice. If anyone was a real peach, it was your dad. Come home to me, baby, I'll make you feel better. Home is with me. Come on."

"Okay." JayRay sounds defeated. "I'll have one for the ditch and be right there."

8. BERNICE

I DRINK THE NIGHT AWAY. I drink steadily, red wine, and I chain-smoke cigarettes. I weep, slowly at first and then I howl with rage, my face pressed into a pillow to muffle the sound. I stand close to the open window, looking down at the glittering Vegas Strip and thinking about all the happy people out there. I hope the smell of cigarettes won't carry into the next room. I'd booked a non-smoking room. I always hated those disgusting and smelly smokers' rooms even when I smoked, but how could I have known what a disaster this trip would be and that I'd once again need my friend, nicotine?

I refuse to go downstairs and smoke outside. I'm convinced that those terrible people, JayRay and his girlfriend, will be lurking around, lying in wait and, besides, I can't risk anyone seeing me. I look dreadful. My face is so swollen that my eyes are nearly shut.

I have a vicious headache. Wasps are stinging my eyeballs and I chew a couple of aspirin and smoke more cigarettes and drink more wine. I keep checking my email. I can't stop myself. I curse Dirk, then I switch to telling myself that I'm better off without him. I know I should eat something, but my stomach feels full of bricks and I know I won't be able to keep anything down.

I'm aching to go home. I'll hide in my house and find a way to figure things out. I lie down on the hotel bed, my head pounding, and think back to how I met Dirk. I was the star, the guest of honour. I was the one they invited. The event was part of a book promotion that my agent had set up. Dirk was big into horse racing and one of the rich racehorse owner's wives' had a book club, and her husband had thought it would be a treat for the ladies to come out and meet me. I generally avoided those kinds of events like the plague. I'm great with my fans on email and Facebook, but please don't ask me to actually talk to anybody in person because, really, I don't have anything to say.

But I couldn't find a way to get out of it, so I called on my friend, Theresa, and off we went.

Theresa had studied psychology at university with me but instead of becoming a therapist, she moved into statistical research and development. We got on fine because we exchanged tales of doomed love affairs over tubs of ice cream and bemoaned the lack of good men.

"I don't even like horse racing," I told Theresa, who was pushing up her cleavage while we primped in the ladies' room. "I am only going because it's a paid appearance."

"Not that you need the money. Goddamn, my breasts are small. Heiress, bestselling author, you hardly need pocket money."

I shrugged. "Amelia insisted that 'important' people will be in attendance." Amelia is my agent. "By the way, your breasts are no smaller than mine."

"Like that's any consolation, Miss Flat Chest. I'm hoping that I will meet my rich sugar daddy husband today," she joked and she shoved her breasts up another inch and I laughed.

The rich wives didn't seem interested in me, which was great. It meant I could relax and enjoy myself. The suite was well catered and there was an elegance and gentility to the day that I liked. The crowd was affluent and beautifully dressed by local designers and it was a nice place to be. And it got even nicer when I spotted Dirk.

He was built like a rugby forward, big and strong and wide. He had a laugh that came right from his balls, and I instantly wanted him to fuck me. I'm not promiscuous by definition, but I have appetites and as long as there were no emotional ties, I did whatever I wanted to do. I wasn't sexy by anybody's standards, but that didn't mean I wasn't horny. I was often extremely horny, and while my bedside table was stocked with all manner of toys and personal enchantments, I preferred the real, hot and throbbing, turgid thing.

At one point, Dirk stood behind me while I placed my bet. I couldn't stop myself. I arched my back, stuck my bottom out and gave his balls the tiniest bump. I wanted to turn around and check his reaction but of course I did no such thing. I pushed my money towards the cashier. When I turned around, casually pretending I hadn't even noticed he was there, he grinned at me and I knew he knew what I was thinking. I forced myself to breathe in a controlled manner, a trick I had learned that sometimes helped stop my complexion from turning that dreadful tomato soup colour. Breathe out, a little bit in, more out, don't think about how much you want him.

Later, I couldn't help myself. I pointed him out to Theresa. "Who's he?"

"Hot, hey? Dirk Villiers. The *skinner* is that he's married to money. She's a real bitch. He's good looking, né? I'd like to suck his dick just to get back at her."

"I don't see how sucking his dick would get back at her," I said, wanting to tell Theresa that if there was going to be any dick sucking, that it would be done by me.

"Because she's viciously jealous. Everybody knows it. She totally freaks out on him all the time. But I'm not wasting my time on Dirk, revenge or not. I want marriage material."

"I've got someone in mind for you," I said. "My publicist. He's coming later to join us. You met him at some of my book launches, remember? Ben Sheppard-Smith. He and his wife split up a while ago, they had one of those starter marriages. They were together for a year and then they divorced. It's not like he's on the rebound or anything, the marriage was just a mistake."

"What does he look like again? And why haven't you mentioned him before, in this critically important context?"

"He's tall and skinny and he looks very British, which he is. And I never mentioned him because you'd have nagged me incessantly to set something up. I thought I'd wait until it happened organically."

"Organically? What a load of rubbish!"

"Hello, ladies. I don't believe we've been formally introduced. I'm Dirk," a voice interrupted us and I felt a hot sensation in my belly. My nerve endings tightened with awareness, as if a big-maned lion had strolled into our pride. I willed my face to stay a normal colour.

"My wife is a fan of yours," he said to me. "Unfortunately she couldn't be here today. Will you sign this copy for her?"

"Absolutely," I replied, keeping my voice light and pretty. "And what is your wife's name?"

"Chrizette," he said, and he slowly spelled it and I signed the book, along with some generic message, hoping I wasn't making any Freudian slips about how much I wanted to fuck her hunky husband. I also thought that Chrizette was a particularly horrible Afrikaans name; was it a combination of Suzette and Christal? I would bet money on it. Afrikaaners loved making up names for their kids and I wondered if Dirk and Chrizette had any weirdly monikered, daddy-loving offspring. Not that I would let that get in the way of my pursuit of the big man.

"And where is your lovely wife today?" Theresa asked. "She let you out all by yourself? I'm Theresa, by the way."

Dirk smiled and I felt crazy with lust. I wanted to swat Theresa away, like the annoying insect she was being. I threw her a glance, telling her in no uncertain terms to step down.

"She lets me out every now and then," Dirk replied. "In fact, I come racing most weekends. I have shares in Piet's horse as well as some of the others."

"I need some more wine," Theresa said, holding up her empty glass and Dirk sped off to grab a bottle.

"Ag no man," Theresa said, looking at me.

"Ag no man what?"

"You like him in that way. I can tell. You go all quiet and I can feel these weird vibes coming off you. I wasn't flirting with him, just so you know."

"Ja, well, he's attractive for sure. I didn't expect to be attracted to anyone so soon after Matthias, it caught me off guard."

"You and your Afrikaner-married men. They're like your version of a bad-boy rock star. I don't get it. The Afrikaners are beyond uptight, especially these days, now that they're an endangered species."

I giggled. "I don't think they'd be too happy to hear you say that. And you're right, I do have a weakness for them, so sue me."

When Dirk came back with a bottle of wine, I couldn't help but notice that he let his fingers brush against mine and later, when we were sitting together and he was explaining how best to place a bet, his thigh was warm and reassuring against mine.

And when he asked for my telephone number, because he thought that his wife's book club might be interested in having me over for dinner and a conversation, I didn't put him straight as I usually would. I didn't tell him that only junior authors and losers attended book clubs, and that my books sold themselves thank you very much.

I said I would be delighted and that I hoped to hear from him. I didn't mention anything about his wife.

When he phoned the following day, the book club was not mentioned. He said he had been trying to find a copy of my first book as a gift for his wife but he couldn't find one anywhere. I told him I could give him one, no problem, and if he wanted to stop by the house and collect it, that would be fine too.

He arrived that night and we continued the pretense for a bit while Betty served coffee and cake and he made some snarky comments about my collection of African artwork, asking me why I would I buy rubbish like that when I could pay for real art by proper artists. Of course, I had no idea then about the *Volksraad*. I thought he just was another embittered Afrikaner, mouthing off. I knew I should take umbrage at his comments but I was too horny to think about politics. I put my cup down on the table and that was when he moved towards me, as naturally as either of us taking a breath, and I folded into him, under him.

But he would not have sex with me. At first, I thought this was quaint and charming and even sweet in an old-fashioned schoolboy kind of way, but as soon as I realized he truly meant it, it became annoying and childish. And frustrating. Very, very frustrating. He did astounding things to me with his fingers and his tongue but it was his cock that I wanted, his cock that I craved. He had a stumpy flat cock, shaped a bit like a hammerhead shark. It was lacking in length and it was strangely flattened and I wondered if he was with-holding it from me because he believed it would not satisfy me but I knew it wasn't that. It was his code of honour, his self-directed "fidelity" that was more akin to "Paradise by the Dashboard Light" by Meatloaf, only I was the one who was in hot pursuit.

He said he could not "go all the way" with me. He would not commit that terrible sin against his Calvinistic God, that sin being infidelity. I nearly threw him out that first night. I couldn't believe his gall. But he returned the following day and I let him in and so it went on.

"Oh for god's sake, just fuck me," I told him repeatedly, which I interspersed with: "I don't care. Don't fuck me then." Then, "oh fuck me for god's sake." Then, "fine, don't."

Dirk explained, *ad nauseam*, how the soul of the Afrikaner was made up of two aspects: church and state, and they were intertwined. Being an Afrikaner came part and parcel with the Calvinist God and all His rules. To break a rule was to cease to be an Afrikaner and that was unthinkable.

Instead of fucking me, he practically drowned me in superb wines, Belgian chocolates, glittering jewelry, the best fragrances, massive bouquets of flowers, and bath salts. He took me out for long lunches and we ate and drank from noon until late evening, satiating our lust with the inadequate substitute of fine dining.

Following which, drunk on Chardonnay and gluttony, he took me home and left me alone with my longing and my anger.

I threw him out of my life more times than I could count and he sometimes stayed away for a while but never for very long. Arguments were swept under the rug and we fell into each other's arms, Romeo and Juliet, breathless, fuelled by the *sturm und drang* of it all.

We had a year of this on-again, off-again, violently passionate, love-driven, hate-filled frenzy. We were never calm, we never rested together, it was all cravings, addictions, and madness, and I kept thinking that I would win and that Chrizette would lose.

But before I left for *Janette's Daytime Reveal!* we had another row and it felt different from the others. We were both tired of the situation. He hated the fact that I was leaving him to promote my books. Although he couldn't and wouldn't commit to me, he did not want me to be out in the world, talking to people, flirting, he said. He was a jealous man, which I, at first, took to be a measure of his love for me, but it wasn't. It was a measure of his sense of ownership.

Nevertheless, I hated leaving him too. I was convinced that he would realize that he didn't miss me at all. So both of us, armed with tired but sharpened swords, faced off in that final battle with vicious intent to our blows.

It was on the tip of my tongue to tell him about Chrizette,

tell him that his precious wife was hardly *opregte* herself. Although, at least she was keeping it in-house, sleeping with the Commandant-General of the *Volksraad*, Gerit Venster. The Commandant-General was a short man with a groomed, bushy, little Hitler moustache, a Führer-styled beetle-black pomaded haircut, and the same downturned mouth of self-importance.

I knew saying anything about Chrizette would be the death warrant to our relationship. Instead, we threw stones and rocks and knives at each other, and I kept that nuclear warhead to myself and he finally stormed out, telling me it was over for real.

I told myself he would come back. He always had in the past. But he didn't and I cried on Betty's shoulder, packed my suitcase, and flew to Vegas, staring out the window of the plane at nothing, and biting the skin around my cuticles until I drew blood. Then I sat on my hands, not wanting to arrive at the show looking like a self-mutilating freak with raw fingertips.

And then, the silence after the interview on *Janette's Day-time Reveal!* The bastard. He would have known how much I needed him.

I down valium with red wine on the flight home. I'm relieved to fall out of a taxi and find myself finally safely at my front door, fumbling to get my key into the lock. My first thought, as I stumble inside, is that the alarm hadn't beeped to let me know to disarm it and I freeze. I tiptoe cautiously into the living room and am immediately convinced that I'm about to be murdered in my own home, because there's a man on my sofa, a huge man, and he must be there to kill me. But my scream falls silent in my throat when I see that the man is asleep and as my thoughts settle with clarity, I realize that the man is Dirk.

He's fast asleep and he's snoring loudly. He's wearing old track pants and a wrinkled T-shirt and he's barefoot, and the nakedness of his feet and the awkward paleness of his ankles is slightly revolting to me in a way I can't understand. Surely I must have seen his feet before? I try to focus and I know I am still drugged and numb from the pills and the wine but I can't figure out what's going on.

What is he doing there in the middle of the day? What day is it? Had I given him a key? Oh, yes, I had, and I gave him the alarm code too. Oh, brain, come on, think! What day is it? Friday? No, it's Saturday. So why isn't he at home with his wife and ever-important children? I sit down on a chair in the living room and that's when I see his phone on the coffee table alongside a mess of newspapers, a pile of pizza boxes, and a filthy beer glass that is nearly empty. The floor is littered with beer bottles — ag, for *fok's* sake, he knows where the kitchen is! If there's one thing I hate, it's a mess. Where, for god's sake, is Betty? I know I should be delighted to see Dirk but all I can see is the trash in my living room, piled high like a rubbish dump. How long has he been here? Judging from the remnants of food and drink, he must have moved onto my sofa only hours after I left.

A prickle of hot rage runs across my scalp. I clench my fists. I want to throw the mess at him, bombard him with sour-smelling bottles and garbage, and tell him to get the fuck out. But I will myself to calm down. I had wanted to see him more than anything, but now that he is here, in my space, soiling my haven, intruding unexpectedly and in such an ugly and depraved fashion, the only thing I want is to have a long hot bath, climb into bed and get some sleep.

And those feet, I can't stop staring at those feet. I want to slap them for their insolence. How dare he help himself to my life while I was away? He spurned me and then he made himself welcome, without so much as a by-your-leave. This wasn't part of our deal at all. The anger and hurt from the past few days poisons my heart like a filthy abscess.

But then, just as suddenly, I'm delighted and my heart is as light as a summer-time balloon. He's here, with *me!*

I turn to leave, to go and have my bath, but he wakes at that moment and he lies there, with one arm behind his head, blinking the sleep from his eyes. He hasn't shaved in days and there are food stains on his T-shirt.

"So," he says and he is nonchalant. "Here I am."

"Ja, I see that. And to what do I owe this honour?"

"Chrizette kicked me out."

"What?"

"She knows about our affair. She had me followed and she pulled my phone records. She showed me all kinds of evidence."

"Did you tell her you've never fucked me? That you've never actually been inside of me? Did you explain that all important dividing line between morality and fidelity, between Godliness and sin?"

"Ag, of course I tried to explain. She said she didn't believe me. She said if that was true, why would you keep seeing me? She also said it was the most childish thing she had ever heard, and that I was beyond stupid for thinking that my virgin dick, virgin with regards to you anyway, could make up for the time and money I spent on you. She said that if penetration was my code of honour, I could shove my dick up my arse or, as she less than politely put it, I could shove it up your frigid cunt. She said it's over for good and she's going to take me for every penny I've got. I've never heard her talk like that. I didn't even know she knew words like cunt."

"I see." I sit down. "And so you came here."

"Where else would I go? Aren't you happy to see me?"

"Why didn't you email me? Or text me? Or phone me? I had that shitty bloody interview and if you tell me you didn't watch, then you can fuck off right now."

"Ag, of course, I watched. You were magnificent. You didn't need me to tell you that. I've had a lot on my plate, a lot to process too. I lost my entire family for you."

"For *me*? Ag ja, now that's rich. Before I left, you gave me the boot, don't you remember? You have the most convenient memory in the universe. It's like a black fucking hole, a death star, the things you choose to forget. You make me impossibly angry. What makes you think I even want you here?"

He gets up and walks over to me and pulls me to my feet. The minute I feel his arms around me, I forget my anger and my hurt. A part of me wonders why I had been angry with him at all, while another part of me curses my desire, the desire that overrides every rational thought.

"We belong together," he says. "I couldn't leave Chrizette, that is true, but now she has kicked me out, she failed in the marriage, not me. It's no longer my fault. It's hers. I never left her. I stood by her, and I did no wrong. And, you and me, we are meant to be together. Don't be angry. I wanted to come and get you at the airport, but I wasn't sure what you would say, or if you would be happy. I hoped you would be, of course, but I had no idea. Maybe you like me being married, maybe you like your independence and your freedom."

"No. All I want is you. I wouldn't have it any other way." And, in that moment, I mean it. I also want to say that he can fuck me properly now, but I'm afraid to mention it in case he finds some new excuse to deny me.

"I have to go and have a bath," I say and I pull away. "I'm exhausted. It was a grueling trip. And that man, that horrible man, who says he is my half-brother, what a con man. He thinks he is God's gift to the world and I suppose some women might agree. His girlfriend does, that's for sure. She shouted at me! She called me a bitch. What a pair, the both of them. I wish I could sue *Janette's Daytime Reveal!* but I've got no doubt that all the i's were dotted and t's crossed."

I walk down the hall and stop at the kitchen for a bottle of Perrier water. I fill the bathtub, adding bubble bath as well as bath salts. I peel off my clothes and I climb into the hot scented water. It feels fantastic to wash that off that disastrous trip. I lather up sponge after sponge and wash my face with the strongest exfoliants in my arsenal.

Dirk wanders into the bathroom as I am drying myself.

"That JayRay, he said there was something I should know," I say, turning to Dirk who has shed his sweatpants and his dirty T-shirt and is sporting an enthusiastic erection. I drop my towel and move towards him. "I wonder if I should have asked him what it is. But all I could think about was getting away from him. I told him that if he ever contacted me again, I would put the police onto him."

"Never mind that now. I want to introduce you to someone," Dirk says and his voice is husky and it's clear he hasn't been paying the slightest bit of attention to what I said. "I want to be inside you," he says. "I want to introduce you to my cock, my cock that wants to be so deep inside you that you will come forever."

About bloody time, I think, and then I stop thinking and enjoy this long-awaited fuck.

9. LEONIE

I'M AT HOME IN THE KITCHEN trying not to scream. I take the teabag out of my mug and squeeze it, burning my fingers and splashing drops of tea on the granite countertop. I throw the teabag into a stack of unwashed cereal bowls in the sink. Why are there dishes in the sink when we've got a perfectly good dishwasher?

Maddie and Kenzie are playing video games in the living room and they're dancing around, shouting and singing. Dave is at the old oak table, engrossed in homework or something, and somewhere in the house, a radio is playing. And, breaking news, we have a dog. The family acquired a puppy while I was away, and by the way, Dave, thanks for involving me in the decision-making. The dog is a ratty little mongrel, a teacup terrier of some kind. They named the creature Muffin and right now Muffin is yapping at the top of her tiny but powerful lungs.

Hockey equipment lines the hall and the kitchen table is covered with sporting gear, with Dave having cleared a tiny space for himself. I clean up a puddle of Muffin's pee and when my phone rings, I lunge for it, praying that Ralph will need me at the office.

"Well hello, Leonie," my mother-in-law says. "Nice to hear you're home for once. How long this time?"

"Two weeks," I say, thinking I might have to kill myself before it's over.

"Truth be told, Dave gave me the heads-up that you'd be

home. I need product. Don't forget to add more of your secret ingredient to mine. I need to pick up extras to sell but only add the zing to mine. My friends tell me I look like I am going backwards in time and they're buying stock like crazy but I don't want them to look as good as me."

"Sure," I say, thinking how trusting this woman is, letting me mix up a lethal blend of poison for her to spread liberally on her face. Good thing she doesn't have a heart condition or she'd be long since dead and we'd be down a granny and a nanny. "Come on over any time you like, we'll be here all day."

"I'll be right there," my mother-in-law slams the phone down and I look at my watch. Half an hour and she'll be ringing the Chopin-chimed doorbell.

"Who was that?" Dave asks, looking up from his book, his pen still for a moment. I peer over his shoulder and am immediately pissed off. He's filling in Bernice's ridiculous self-help book.

Bake Your Way to a Happy Marriage arrived while I was away and the minute I got home, Dave tried to get me to do a worksheet with him. He wouldn't stop telling me how great the book was, but I couldn't bear to look at it.

"I was skeptical too," he said, misunderstanding my lack of enthusiasm. "But it's based on solid psychology. This woman has a doctorate and she's incredible with emotions and the human psyche. Just reading it makes me feel more cheerful."

"You weren't cheerful? You seemed cheerful."

He shrugged. "I'm okay. I could be happier, and this book could help us."

"No us, buddy. I am perfectly happy, couldn't be happier."

He looked at me and he knew I was lying and I knew he knew, but I couldn't go there. I couldn't go anywhere with this discussion.

"We're adults," I said. "Happiness is a fairytale. Actually, happiness is the end of a fairytale and since no one gets to step behind the curtains of 'they lived happily ever after,' we'll never know the truth."

"Suit yourself, Lee. I'll do the book by myself. At least one of us wants to be happy. And not only do I want to be happy, I believe I can."

To which I did not reply and he opened his book and started filling in a worksheet and now he is at it again, writing like a possessed man while his accompanying worksheet recipe, toffee crunch cookies, bakes its way to cookie-ness in the oven. They smell heavenly, I will acknowledge that. Bernice might be annoying but the skinny bitch knows a thing or two about cookies.

"Lee? Who was on the phone?"

"Your mother. She's on her way over." I put my mug into the dishwasher with exaggerated slowness, trying to point out that we actually have a dishwasher and why is he using the sink?

"Dishwasher's broken," he says, reading my expression. "I've got to get someone in to fix it. Let me guess. She wants more face gunk, doesn't she?"

"It isn't gunk," I'm affronted. "It's our biggest seller. Ralphie says he can't believe how well we're doing. We keep growing. My formula's a winner, baby."

"With your brains, you could be using your skills to help people. Instead you jet off to sell face creams to desperate middle-aged women in mid-West America. You could be doing something important, like helping save lives."

I am saving lives. I'm saving my own, by getting out of here. I'm saving your and the kids' lives too. If I stayed home, I'd murder all of you.

I glare at him. "I do what I need to do. Plus I pay the property taxes and insurance on this." I wave my hand around the mansion that Dave inherited from his father.

"I pay my way," Dave looks annoyed. "You know I do. And you're lucky, you've got me to play mommy when you're not here."

"We've had this discussion Dave," I say. "Don't try to pull a guilt trip on me. What's going on with you? All of a sudden you're not happy, you're ordering self-help books and attacking me, and sounding self-righteous and wounded."

"I'm just tired." Dave admits and he rubs his face hard. "The kids are full-on. Their homework and after-school activities take up a lot of time. And I struggle to keep them off their computers and I worry that they aren't outside enough, learning to be kids like we did when we were young. And I worry about who they hang out with at school. I worry about bullies. I worry about their safety. There's a lot I worry about." He sighs.

I look at him. He does look tired and I go over to him. "I'm sorry, honey. I don't mean to be a bitch. I feel guilty, you know, like I should do so much more than I do. I feel bad when I come home and see how hard you work. What can I do to help? After your mom leaves, how about we go to Boston Pizza? Have a nice meal out?" I want to do something to make it right even though I know that everything is wrong and it's all my fault. None of this is on Dave. He has no idea that the root of our discontent comes from me, and here he is, shouldering the blame.

He stands up and I hug him and he relaxes into me. "I miss you so much when you're not here," he says and I feel his erection through his jeans. "You bring him to life," he whispers. "He missed you too."

"And I missed him," I lie and I'm about to tell him that I have a bladder infection and we can't have sex until it clears up, when Maddie runs into the kitchen to tell me that Muffin has thrown up on the Persian rug in the living room.

"What the frick are you feeding that dog?" I snap at Dave, my grumpy mood instantly back. "Tell me again, where did you get her and why can't we take her back? She pees, vomits, shits, and barks the whole time. I'm not seeing the appeal."

"It's a he, not a she," Maddie says and she bursts into tears. Dave frowns at me as he gets a rag to clean up the mess and we follow him into the living room. I watch him spray Windex onto one of the many family heirlooms in the house and

I want to ask him if what he's doing is a good idea but I can't be bothered.

"Your mom didn't mean it," he says to Maddie and I apologize.

"Come here Maddie," I say. "Give your mom a hug. Have you brushed your hair this morning? It's grown about two inches since I was away."

"I don't want Muffin to leave," Maddie sniffs and I wonder what Dave's feeding her to make her such a roly poly.

"He's not going anywhere, mommy is sorry," I say and I give her a hug. "You want to go out for pizza tonight?"

Maddie's face brightens. "Yes! I'll tell Kenzie."

She runs upstairs and I sink into the sofa and watch Dave finish cleaning the throw-up. The once-elegant oval living room is full of kid's clothes, scattered toys, DVDs and jewel cases. I wonder, not for the first time, how Dave and the girls manage to cover every available surface of such a vast house.

The fifty-two inch TV screen is frozen on a Minecraft game and I study the farm that Maddie was building. I don't under-stand what she sees in the game. It's ugly, with distorted pixels creating bitmapped images in shades of olive and blue. I reach for the control and switch it off. I want to comment on the surrounding mess but I know that will come back to bite me.

"What are you feeding that kid?" I ask instead. "She's getting fat. She needs to exercise."

"She's not fat," Dave says and he no longer sounds simply tired but exhausted. "She does exercise. She's a hockey kid; she plays and she eats. She's a little kid, Lee. You need to be supportive of her, not critical."

"I didn't say anything to her," I protest, lying down and arranging a cushion behind my head. Like everything in the house, the sofa is worn and threadbare.

"She can sense what you are thinking," Dave mutters. "Kids are like that. You should know that better than anyone."

I stand up, furious at the criticism. "I do the best I can," I yell at him and a recriminating silence falls throughout the house.

The kids' chatter falls silent, Muffin stops barking, and Dave stops scrubbing. Only the radio keeps playing, a song from the eighties, something I recognize as early Billy Joel.

"I'm going to lie down for a bit," I say. "Wake me up when your mother gets here."

But the doorbell chimes and I sigh. "No rest for the wicked," I say, and Dave nods and gives me a look.

"You've got that right," he replies.

Dave's mother, Nancy, is a fancy old dame who lives in a downtown high-rise condo, close to the Elm Street Spa and the Arts and Letters Club. I don't think she ever cared much for me, a solidly mutual feeling.

Dave air kisses his mother and I take Nancy upstairs. The girls rush out of their room to see her and she hugs them.

"Come see our friendship tree, Granny," Maddie says and I follow. Not having been in the girls' room since I've got back, I have no idea what they are talking about.

Maddie and Kenzie still insist on sharing a room, which I think is ridiculous since they could each have two apiece. Then again, their one room is nearly the size of the house I grew up in, plus they have an en suite bathroom with pastel-coloured geese and piglets in the relief pattern of the wall tiles.

Their bedroom is painted a pale robin's egg blue and a large crystal tear-drop chandelier hangs from the high ceiling. During my first tour of the house, I jokingly asked Dave if the place was a chandelier showroom, which made him grin.

The kids are showing Nancy a large cut-out brown paper tree that is stuck to the wall, with branches extending in various directions, and a liberal pasting of green leaves. Pictures of the girls are pasted onto the leaves, showing them at their various activities with their friends, at school, with Dave, and with Nancy.

"There are lots of Muffin too," Kenzie points out as Nancy oohs and ahs at the artistry. I wonder if she notices, as I do, that there are very few pictures of me and the ones that are there, are from years ago. I also wonder when Kenzie took up ballet. I don't want Nancy to know I don't know, so I file the question away for later.

"Come on girls," I interrupt them, wanting to move Nancy along, "I have to talk to Granny in my study. You can come with us if you like."

"Boring!" they both chorus and Nancy hugs them again.

"See you Tuesday," she tells them and I inwardly sigh. Great, she'll be back.

"We take trips to the library every week," she tells me as I lead the way to my study. "Gives Dave some time off to catch up with things." I wonder if her comment is a pointed one. It probably is, but I ignore it.

I want Nancy to take stock of the place, I want her to wince at the not-so-genteel deterioration that is clearly visible at every turn but she doesn't seem to notice. She truly doesn't care. Things have rapidly gone downhill at 66 Ashdale Drive since her reign of unlimited budgets and dedicated housekeepers, but Nancy doesn't give a damn. I notice new stains on the carpets, and wallpaper that is peeling at an alarming rate and I'm sure there's some kind of rot crawling along the ceiling cornices. The truth is, Dave and I have no right to live in a five-million-dollar home that we can't afford to maintain, but neither of us wants to admit it.

I let Nancy pick out her selection from my wares and I think back to how I met Dave. It's ironic that I met him the same way I met JayRay, in a bar. I was sitting alone, drinking, when a guy rushed in clutching his gut and asking if he could use the washroom. He dashed past me, his expression focused and fearful. He was gone for a good half an hour and I know because I timed him. I also knew he'd stop by to chat when he emerged, which he also did, looking pale and drawn. I waved him to sit down when he asked if he could. He was good looking, sturdy, and wide. He reminded me of Matt Damon mixed with Jeremy Renner, a nice guy, earnest.

"Soda water with lime," he asked the server and he grinned at me. "Spicy food," he said. "Never again."

Dave was a good Canadian guy from old money. He still lived at home, home being 66 Ashdale Drive, Rosedale, one of the most fêted and wealthy areas in Toronto.

"Dad's in hospital," he said, immediately launching into his life story. "Been there for months. His heart. And mom's out playing tennis which she does ninety-nine percent of the time." It didn't take long for me to gather that his father was a real piece of work, full of patriarchal bullshit about men being men and claiming their rightful place at the top of the world, ruling universes both seen and unseen. His mother nearly made the pro circuit in her youth, but she wasn't quite good enough. She dealt with her disappointment by marrying a rich guy and she spent the rest of her life slamming balls on local courts, enjoying her status as a small-time celebrity, and obediently working the room at cocktail parties.

When Dave first took me to the house, I tried not to look as impressed as I felt. The place was a palace of regal rose brick, lead-paned windows, high chimneys, and pitched gables. Layers of overlapping roof shingles made me wonder just how far back the house went. I soon found out. The upstairs boasted five bedrooms, four bathrooms, and a central oval yellow living room with a fireplace. Each room was decorated with a signature wallpaper, matching bed linens, drapes and throw rugs. The ground floor housed another oval living room, a replica of its upstairs counterpart, only the downstairs version was painted a virbrant, rich aqua. A dining room followed, with a mirror-slick ornate cherry wood table that seated eighteen, followed by a family room, an enormous marble and stainless steel kitchen, an expansive, well-stocked pantry, two powder rooms, and a masculine study complete with a fixed-gaze deer head, several mounted fish trophies, and teak and glass display cabinets. It was also home to a double-sided partner's desk, a bunch of caramel leather-studded easy chairs, and green and brass reading lamps. The room screamed machismo and the stench of rich cigar smoke was nearly overpowering. Downstairs, Dave led me around a finished basement that could easily house a family. His grandmother had lived there, he explained. "Spent most of my life down here when she was alive. She died when I was ten and Dad sent me to boarding school, which I hated. He called me a namby-pamby, but he eventually gave in and let me come home."

He showed me the four-car garage, his father's black Bentley Continental in one spot, the other empty, save for an ugly oil spill.

"What does your mother drive?" I joked. "A Rolls?"

"A Porsche. It leaks oil like crazy. Drives Dad nuts. Dad told her only the *nouveau riche* favour Porsches, but Mom just laughed at him. It's bright yellow too. Mom's a rebel in her own way."

What a nice life it must be, to wear the badge of rebellion by way of a yellow Porsche.

Neatly trimmed topiary trees and bushes graced the front garden, with an abundance of rose bushes in the back. "Dad said roses are *nouveau riche* too," Dave said. "He's very particular about those kinds of things. And it made no sense about the roses, since they were my grandmother's and she was hardly *nouveau riche*. My dad wants me to live here after he's gone. Continue the legacy. This place has been in my family forever. Dad wants me to fill it with kids and live his life all over again. Except, ironically, he was never really here, it was just Mom and me after Gran died, plus, Dad never even liked me. But I'm his son and he's a conservative traditionalist in that way.

Dave took me back up to his bedroom. It was more austere than the rest of the house, with polished hardwood floors, dark blue walls and spotlights studded in the sloping ceiling. I sat down at his desk, noticing how neat it all was. Three shelves of hockey trophies lined one wall and Dave nodded at them.

"Wore my body out. Not what Dad wanted for me anyway. So now I'm a grade school teacher, not what he wanted either. And yet, he still wants me to have this place."

He picked up a trophy and rubbed it with his sleeve. "Dad's already signed the house over to me. Some complicated legal thing so I won't have to pay inheritance taxes." He sat down on the bed and faced me. "The cottage will go to Mom. It's in Muskoka, near Three Mile Lake, which is right near Echo Beach. Some locals say it inspired Martha and the Muffins to write that song."

He started singing and I joined in, "*Echo Beach, far away in time, Echo Beach, far away in time.*"

"I'll take you there some time if you like," Dave said when we finished the chorus which turned out to be the only part of the song we knew. Then the refrain was stuck, an earworm in my head.

I shuddered and laughed. "That's okay. I've had enough rural Ontario to last me a lifetime."

"I think my mom agrees with you. I bet she'll sell it as soon as dad dies. She's already got her eye on a condo. She says she's had enough of taking care of this place. She wants to play tennis and bridge with her friends, and not have to worry about anything."

Dave lay down on the bed, his hands behind his head and I went to lie next to him. He turned to face me.

"I love this place," he said. "Because of my grandparents. They were the real deal. Good people, with a sense of family and real tradition, not some fake macho imitation. They weren't like my dad. I want a family too. I love kids. I don't want uptight rich kids like the ones I grew up with. I want real kids and a real wife. I want a noisy, energetic love-filled life. With Christmases and school stuff. When I grew up, this place was always so quiet, but I can imagine it full of happiness and laughter. I don't want it to be like it was when I grew up. Mom couldn't have any more kids after me."

He kissed me and I melted into Dave's dream. A family. It had never occurred to me that I could have anything like that either. The complete opposite of my loveless upbringing. I could see it too, yes. And I could be that person, I could. And, to live in an area that I had never even had occasion to visit, well, that blew my mind. In a mansion! Me! I hoped my father could see me now. And Dave was solid guy. I could trust him.

So there it was, me at twenty-two, Dave's wife, pregnant after our honeymoon in the Dominican Republic. We had two kids in a row. There was a symmetry to our lives and I didn't have to control anything or be wary of anything.

Dave and I planned to live in the house and rent out the basement to cover expenses but then Dave inherited more money than he thought he would and he turned out to be a savvy investor. We never had any spare cash, but we didn't need to have tenants in, for which we were both grateful.

I loved the house so much it hurt. It wasn't the reason I married Dave but it was like winning two big prizes in a row when you were already ecstatic to have won one. Dave, the house, and my happy-ever-after were all rolled up into one big bundle that winked at me like a bright shiny future. When I was first pregnant, with Kenzie, I wandered from room to room, exploring everything. I loved the expanse of walls and floors and ceilings and light. I was princess in a foreign land, a land of peace and beauty. It was the only time in my life I ever felt calm and happy. Dave was at work at the school, and I was alone in that beautiful, luxurious place.

Dave's father, Edgar, thought I was the bees knees. Granted I only met him a couple of times in the hospital when he was wired from head to toe with cables. He was shrunken, like a mummy, hardly able to talk, but he approved of me. His eyes lit up whenever he saw me like maybe Dave wasn't such an idiot after all.

Dave even said that I helped him out, that his father died with more respect for him than he'd ever previously had. The moment Edgar shuffled off his mortal coil, Nancy moved out of the house and she sold the cottage too, just like Dave said she would. She packed her couture wardrobe, her sizeable collection of jewels, and her numerous trophies. She also took the portraits of her playing tennis, huge life-size paintings and photographs of her frozen in mid-serve or hammering a ball down the line, her muscles stretched like a cheetah in flight, all power, no mercy. She and Edgar had clearly shared an appreciation for her beauty and I was glad to have the evidence of the blonde über-Wonder Woman removed from the hallways and rooms.

I loved sitting behind Edgar's desk in his study. I pretended to be him, a hot-shot banker, wheeling and dealing, ordering my minions around with scorn and condescension. It was interesting that Nancy had left one portrait behind, of her and Edgar. She was in her tennis whites, her hand on his shoulder. He was seated in one of the leather chairs, his hands behind his head, his legs stretched out in front of him. He was a bland, well-groomed man, made generic by pampered middle-age, and he looked as if he wasn't ecstatic by how things had panned out but he felt it beneath him to complain. I took the oil painting down and hid it behind the sofa, knowing Dave would neither notice nor care.

When it came to having kids, I had no idea what to expect. I guess I thought that two obliging mixes of mini-me and mini-Dave would pop out, the best of both of us, two compliant and malleable little people that we could usher around and play with. Only I was never one to play with dolls.

I was happy when Maddie and Kenzie were babies. But when their own selves started to show, selves that I didn't particularly like or understand — not that I could admit that to anyone, especially not Dave who marveled at their every utterance and movement — things changed for me.

"Who is this kid?" I asked Dave when Kenzie started talking and she never shut the fuck up except to sing and dance. Oh, how she loved to sing and dance. Dave and Nancy and just about everyone else thought it was super adorable, but I found her incredibly annoying. What did the kid want? To be Selena Gomez at two? All I knew was that I had to get out of the house or I'd lose my mind. Maddie was like Dave, solid and silent, but Kenzie got on my nerves.

"I thought we'd create our kids," I blurted out to Dave one time. "Meanwhile they pop out from god knows where, these opinionated little strangers. Instead of a ready-made family, you get a bunch of strangers you have to live with. Like look at Little Miss Rock Star, where on earth did she come from?"

"That's a really weird way to look at it," Dave said and he looked perplexed, and somewhat horrified. "I don't see it that way at all. They're each their own miracle. That's the best bit, getting to know them. And anyway, I see lots of me and you in both of them. Our lovely Little Miss Rock Star is you when you get excited or allow yourself to feel happy, and Maddie is the quiet, reserved side of you."

I nodded, just to make him happy. I shouldn't have said anything and I hoped he'd forget about it.

I started looking for jobs around the time that Kenzie started her tiny tot Selena Gomez impressions and I came across an ad calling for a science grad to help sell beauty products. When I met Dave, I was working at my first post-university job as a lab tech. It was hardly glamourous and I knew I never wanted to go back to that. I did some research on *SuperBeauty* and I stopped by to check out the place. It was no more than a startup in the back end of industrial nowhere-land, in one of those brown brick low-slung offices, the kind that all have "Industrial Service" as part of their names. Even Ralph's setup was called *Super Beauty Industry Service Management* which was ridiculous. But I immediately realized the potential. I got all gussied up and I persuaded the receptionist to let me see Ralph and he never stood a chance against the force of my persuasive vision. Ralph's a nice guy, just overly given to catch phrases like: *knock this one out of the park* and *let's gain some traction here*. He thought I was a kindred spirit when I littered my pitch with the tired, meaningless business speak.

I asked Ralph where he got the idea for *Super Beauty* and he said he saw a niche in the market and, more importantly, there was a market in the niche. Which didn't answer my question. From what I could gather, his sister had started a line of organic products in her kitchen and Ralph had taken over when she lost interest. And then I stepped in and transformed the operation.

"Will you mix more of your magic powder into mine?" Nancy asks and I'm wrenched back from memory lane into the present.

"Sure," I say, loading up a tiny scoop and adding to her night cream. "Wow, you're taking quite the haul."

"Making tons of money," Nancy flashes her expensive veneers. "All us old ducks think we look ten years younger than we did before we started using this. But remember, the extra zing is only for me. There's a new boy on the block, Oscar Dollars we call him, seventy if he's a day, and I want him to wine and dine me, not anyone else!"

I take care of Nancy, usher her out the door, and then I go and lie down.

Homework. Hockey. Laundry. TV. School lunches. Ballet Getting the kids ready for bed. Getting them ready for school. Listening to their chatter, and attending to their endless need for attention. The noise, the never-ending noise. Watching them eat their breakfast and wondering where they learned their manners and then remembering, oh right, Dave. Dave's a good man and I remind myself that I loved him once. But since I hooked up with JayRay, Dave's more like a colleague to me than a husband or a lover, and it's like we're running a business on tired old dreams with the cash flow trickling dry. But we've got two kids, I have to make an effort. Besides, what is my alternative?

The next morning, I push the scrambled eggs around on my plate and wonder what JayRay is up to. When we left the show, he said he needed some time to think, and that he would text me once he figured out what to do next. I asked him, since when had I started interfering with his thought processes, and why did he have to push me away? I said, "I'm the ally in this, remember?" The thought of not hearing from him when I was back with Dave was more than I could bear. I asked him if he was ending things between us. Was it over?

He refused to meet my eyes and he carried on packing up his boxes and there was nothing I could do except walk away, without letting anyone see how upset I was. No one at the roadshow had any idea what was going on and I needed to keep it that way.

Once I was home, I expected to hear from him. At first, when there was no contact, I understood that he was still bummed out about what had happened with Bernice, and I forgave his silence. But I grew increasingly furious with him for hurting me.

After four days of silence, my anger turns to panic. Why hasn't he messaged me? I break down and send him half a dozen texts, begging him to tell me what's going on.

What happened with Bernice wasn't my fault. I had even warned him there was a good chance it wouldn't go the way he hoped it would, and that he should be ready for that. But fault or not, here I am, stuck in an aging Williams Sonoma kitchen, eating sunny yellow scrambled eggs and feeling not so much blue as black, black and blue, heartbroken. I toy with the colours of my feelings, lost in my own thoughts until Dave interrupts my privacy.

"Do you think Ralph will ever get some help? It's not fair that you have to travel so much," he says and I shake my head.

"No one drives sales the way I do," I tell him and I sound proud. "And only I can personalize the creams on site."

"Not exactly a sound practise if you ask me," Dave says.

"You're coming to my practise today?" Maddie interrupts us, anxious.

"Yes, honey, of course I am." Great. Another Saturday gone to hell in a handbasket, holed up in the local hockey rink, drinking crappy coffee, and trying to make small talk to other parents, most of whom are more viciously competitive than career politicians.

"We're all coming," Dave says. "Family outing."

"Tell Mom to leave her phone at home," Kenzie mutters and I look up sharply.

"What did you say?"

"Your phone. Leave it at home."

"I will not," I retort. "Work could need me."

"You're always on your stupid phone," Kenzie says, not for the first time and I hate her for her watchful eye.

She's right. I had always been on call for Ralph before JayRay, but once he and I got together, the phone became my lifeline, my intravenous drug fix. I'm like an obsessed teen, grabbing it when it buzzes and trying not to smile stupidly when tapping a reply to him. And I noticed Kenzie watching me, like she knew it was more than work or maybe that was just my guilty conscience. Even Dave started making snide comments and for the past few months I retreated to the washroom to send messages in private. But I can't help myself now. I keep picking up my phone and scrolling through it, as if telepathy and desire will force a message from JayRay to pop up on the screen.

"Listen, it's just great that Mommy's here," Dave makes an excuse for me, trying to smooth things over. "Let's be happy about that, okay? Finish up princesses and get ready, it's a two-hour drive."

I sigh and Dave waits until the girls have left the room.

"I know I haven't exactly been Mr. Cheerful since you got back," he says. "I have been tired. Like I said, the girls are a lot of work. But I love them and I love my life, and it's not like I'm depressed or anything. And I was really looking forward

to you coming home for longer this time but here's the thing."
He stops and rubs his head. "You've been weird, Lee. For close
to a year now. It's like you came back in another world after
one of the shows and I don't even know who you are or where
you are, in your heart and in your head. And the girls notice
it too. I tried giving you time but it's getting worse."

He's spot on about the timing. JayRay and I did celebrate
our one-year anniversary, despite the debacle with Bernice. I
shrug and try to look apologetic or interested but the truth is,
I don't have the resources to placate him. I'm growing increasingly distraught that I haven't heard from JayRay. Is it over?
Would he even tell me if it was? I can't concentrate on what
Dave is saying. Why does he need to talk about this now? All
I want to do is stare at my phone. I've run out of words to
fake the emotions that have deserted me. I once cared about
this little family but that was before JayRay. Now I can only
view my family through a thick pane of glass and their voices
are muffled and indistinct.

"Where's the dog?" I ask.

"Upstairs with the girls. Don't change the subject. What's
going on? Is there someone else?"

"No!" The words shoot out, a reflex, and I'm astonished
at how horrified I sound. "Of course not! I just need a bit of
me-time and when I come home everybody's so glad to see me
which is great, but I need some space too. That's all, Dave, I
swear. I wish I could sit by myself for a whole day and not say
a word to anybody, not have to listen or talk or think or feel.
I get so tired sometimes of the enthusiasm we are supposed to
have for every fucking thing."

Dave studies me. "Maybe you're the one who's depressed.
You sound pretty damn depressed to me. You used to be a
positive and happy person."

"I'm not depressed! I ask you to give me space and what do
you do? You categorize me further and you ask me to justify my
fucking life. Thanks for the support Dave, thanks for nothing!"

Kenzie comes back into the room and stares at me, her eyes like slits. "If you want to be alone," she says acidly, "then don't come today. Dad and Maddie and me will go. We don't need you. We don't want you. I lied when I said I missed you. I don't miss you and when you're here, you sit on your phone all day. You don't know who my friends are anymore; you don't know anything about me. I don't want you to come, okay?" She runs out of the room and Maddie, who came in halfway through her tirade, glances at me and takes off after her sister.

"Great." Dave says and he follows her, pausing at the doorway. "Actually, I can't say I disagree with Kenz. Maybe you should stay here, Lee. Take that me-time you wanted where you don't have to talk to any of us. See you later."

I think about getting up from the kitchen table and protesting: no, I really do want to come, I do. I want to say that I've been looking forward to it, that I'm proud of Maddie and I love hanging out with Kenzie, but I don't move. They leave and the car starts up and pulls away, and I hate myself for being such a loser mother but I grab my phone and scroll through it, thinking that maybe it has gone to sleep and JayRay did text me but, somehow, the phone hadn't signaled me. But there's nothing from him, nothing at all.

Fuck. I can't take it anymore. I dial his number, thinking that if he doesn't answer, I will die there and then.

"Hey puddytat," he says, picking up on the second ring. "How come you're phoning me?"

"How come you never texted me back?" I can't stand the neediness in my voice. "What's going on?"

"I told you," JayRay sounds surprised. "I need time to think. I thought you got that."

"But you shut me out." I shout. "How could you not text me? I thought you loved me, JayRay."

"Listen, honey, it's been a tough time for me, okay? I do love you. But it's been super rough."

He's upset and I find myself sobbing, at a loss for words.

"Hey, hey. Come on, puddytat. You want to meet up?"

I manage to hiccup yes.

"Then come over baby doll, come on, daddy will be waiting for you, okay? But can you drive? You sound in bad shape. You want me to come and get you?"

"I'll be fine. I'll leave now."

In my haste, I forget about Muffin. I don't see him rush out the back door as I'm scrambling to find my keys. All I can think about is JayRay and I drive as fast as I can, crying all the way.

10. BERNICE

I WATCH DIRK SLEEPING and I marvel at the miracle of him being there. He's mine! I hadn't thought it possible. It's been four months since I arrived home and found him asleep on my sofa and it's been one long honeymoon. The only fly in the ointment is that the sex is lackluster at best and I'm increasingly convinced he takes Viagra to get it up because he definitely needs a lot of lead time before the fucking commences. There's no spur-of-the-moment passion like we used to have, no insatiable appetite to explore one another's bodies. Our carnal relations have gone from being a ride in a Ferrari to an outing in the family sedan.

And then there is his kids' lack of enthusiasm to visit their father at his new home.

I had, in a gesture of goodwill, set up a bedroom for both the boy and the girl, and I had, along with Dirk, taken them to Ikea and let them choose their own furnishings. Neither child showed the slightest bit of interest, playing games on their phones instead and annoying the hell out of me. Dirk had no rapport with them, which surprised me. From what he'd told me, I imagined a strong bond between them, but he was awkward and non-communicative, leaving me to try to fill the conversational gaps and, of course, I didn't have a clue how to begin.

The children visited every second weekend, arriving on a Saturday morning and leaving on Sunday afternoon. They were quiet, unobtrusive, and well-behaved, and I attributed this to their Afrikaans upbringing, with old-fashioned morals and respect for their elders. Respect perhaps but not like. They whispered a lot to each other in Afrikaans, so quietly that I couldn't make out what they were saying, not that I would have been able to understand even if I could distinctly hear them.

Another thing that annoyed me was how upset Dirk was that I had started smoking again. But I needed it, and I wasn't going to give it up again, just for him.

And when Chrizette served him with divorce papers, Dirk dug in his heels and refused to sign, a move I simply could not understand.

"She kicked you out, it's over. Why won't you sign?"

"I need to come to terms with my failure as a husband. I can't sign yet. It's agreeing in writing that I didn't keep my side of the bargain. Divorce is breaking a sacred bond that was never supposed to be broken, never."

"You're worried it will be misconstrued that you didn't keep your side of the bargain?" I was outraged. "You're right, you didn't keep it. You had a mistress. You were unfaithful."

He shrugged. "You don't understand. Church and state. One and the same. I never had sex with you. I never technically sinned in the eyes of God."

"Ja, for sure, I don't understand. I don't understand. But let me ask you this. What will you do and how will you feel if Chrizette wants to remarry?"

"What?" Dirk shot up as if he had been stabbed by a cattle prod. "She would never!"

"Why not? She's a looker and she's still young. Why wouldn't she? For all you know, she could be seeing somebody. Why else would she kick you out so fast and not give you a second chance to make things right?"

I was sick and tired of Chrizette, the patron saint of women, particularly when I knew the truth about her. I was also furious at Dirk's refusal to sign the papers and the relentless drama of the whole thing. And I had other problems. I was due to start writing my next book, but I had nothing left. Perhaps I could write *Bake Your Way to Nothingness*, an existential book for the philosophers out there, but I couldn't imagine there being a vast audience.

"You think Chrizette's having an affair?" Dirk was furious and he got up and grabbed his keys. "Are you out of your mind, woman? I am going over there right now. If the mother of my children is fucking some stranger then I deserve to know about it. What kind of mother would do that? Where are her morals?"

The same place as yours, I wanted to say but he had already left.

I watched the car speed down the driveway and stop impatiently at the electronic gate. I wondered what Chrizette would make of Dirk's accusations and I hoped that she would insist that Dirk sign the goddamned papers, tell him that she was moving on, and that it was over for good.

I busied myself with the rituals of setting up my office for the start of a new book. I tidied up the paperwork, I brought in a stack of new reference cookbooks and magazines, and I put my pencils, highlighters and pens just so. I lined up scented candles and arranged my notebooks and my stack of post-it notes.

I took a shower, slathered myself in expensive body lotion, and got into my favourite silk pajamas. I made a cup of green tea, filled a bowl with chocolate-covered peanuts, and I sat down at my desk.

My computer was ready, the new files and folders were waiting. But I couldn't think of a single thing to say.

I got up and went to find Betty into the kitchen. "Any new recipes, Betty?" I asked hopefully, but Betty shook her head.

"You've got them all, Madam."

"Ag come now, can't you think of any new ones?"

Betty shook her head. She was being uncommonly stubborn. We had been in this boat before and back then she worked with me to come up with new ideas and we'd had a fine old time of it, concocting dishes and ideas. I sighed and told her she could go to her room for all the good she was doing, and I went back to my desk.

I wondered if it was time for me to change tack and write a novel. I was convinced I had a novel in me. I had a thousand ideas that had never amounted to more than a roughly penned paragraph that stuttered and ground to a halt, but maybe as one door was closing, another was opening.

I sighed. If I was clutching at old clichés as a lifeline, then I was definitely "not waving but drowning." All my life, I have been much "too far out, not waving but drowning," just like a poem I'd read a while back said. Oh dear god.

I could to write about JayRay and his assumption that we had any kind of connection. I could write about Dirk's misplaced sense of honour and his allegiance to a way of life that was all but gone. I could pay homage to my stepfather. I could explore the concept of family and what it meant.

I watched my impassioned speech on *Janette's Daytime Reveal!* and there were some good ideas there, surely enough for a book? But where would it go and what would it say? Secrets, lies, and self-deception were players, yes, but they were everyday pieces of the chess game of daily life, nothing new.

Hours pass since Dirk left. I sit at my desk, feeling lost and angry. Where is he and why he hasn't he come back yet? I'm afraid that I pushed him too far. Have I pushed him back into the arms of Chrizette?

Night falls and I'm hungry. Betty has vanished and I make a ham and cheese *sarmie*. I need to talk to Betty about her moodiness, but not now. I can't face another confrontation. I close the thick curtains and pour a large glass of wine. There is no book, my man is back with his wife, and I am alone and afraid.

I sit down on the sofa with my untouched sandwich and I wait. My ears are keenly pricked for the sound of his car and the slow whine as the gates swing open, followed by the engine's roar up the driveway. But there is no sound at all.

11. LEONIE

IPULL UP AT JAYRAY'S PLACE and yank the keys out of the ignition. I look up at his apartment with a sense of foreboding. Something bad is going on with JayRay. He's never been like this towards me, not in all the time we've been together. He usually texts me six, seven times a day, charming little messages that pave the passage of time until we can be together again. This time he left me at the mercy of my family with no support.

I sit in the car for a moment. JayRay's apartment is on the second floor of a two-storey block. The yellow brick is tired and filthy and the flimsy steel balconies are shedding white flakes of paint like dandruff. Each apartment is stacked over a garage, with a cracked, grey asphalt forecourt in the front. The apartment block sits on the edge of a busy industrial area on the outskirts of Toronto, much like Ralph's setup, only Ralph's is on the other side of town. It's a place filled with warehouses and peculiar little churches that set up dingy shop in empty office buildings, all of which are flanked by shabby fast food strip malls. I had asked JayRay why he chose to live in such depressing surroundings and he shrugged, and he said it was irrelevant. He was waiting for his ship to come in and once it did, he'd move.

I only visited him once. It was a rule that we stayed away from each other when we were back home. JayRay wasn't interested in hearing about Dave and the girls, they bored him. In fact, I wonder, while I look up at his apartment, which has one broken curtain pulled half-shut, what we do talk about? It seems like I can't remember at all.

I'd had to visit him, that one time. It was after our first Vegas hookup and we were back for the same interminable two week stretch as now.

"I need to see where you live," I told him and he gave me his address. I couldn't get there quickly enough. "I need to be able to picture you," I told him as I fell into his arms. "I need to know everything about you."

"Stay for a while," he said after we had sex like crazy teenagers.

"I can't. I have to get back. But I had to see you. I love you so much it hurts." And then I ran away. I ran back to my shiny silver Mercedes-Benz SUV courtesy of *SuperBeauty*, back home to Dave and the girls, and I left JayRay to the cheap shambles of his messy apartment and the paltry ornamentations of his life.

I look at my face in the rearview mirror. I'm puffy-eyed and my hair is flat and dirty. I fix myself up as best I can and get out of the car. I climb the steps with a sense of doom. The last time I'd been here, I felt entitled. This time I feel out of place, not so much unwanted as invisible, which is infinitely worse.

I knock on the door and he answers, pulling me to him but his gestures feel false and overly-hearty. "Puddytat! What's up, baby? Hey, why the face? Come to Papa, come on, baby, Daddy'll fix everything."

He holds my hand and takes me into the bedroom and undresses me, and my body breathes again and the tightness lets go, just like that. I close my eyes and then he's inside me and the world is perfect.

Afterwards, we lie in silence. "So," he says. "What's going on? You never come to my humble abode."

I pull the sheet over myself. "Humble is right," I sound sharp. "Why don't you get some quality sheets? A nice thick duvet? This one's thin as anything. And your pillows ... I've seen thicker pancakes at a Best Western."

"Leo," he says quietly, "what's up? Spill the beans."

"I can't do it," I say and my eyes fill with tears. "I can't bear to be without you."

He doesn't reply, which isn't a good sign. "I need a wife," he finally says and I sit up and let the crappy sheets fall to the side.

"I'll divorce Dave. I said I wouldn't, for the sake of the girls, but I will."

"Hon," JayRay says patiently, "you don't understand. I apologize. I wasn't clear. You're already my wife, you know that. You're my love-wife, but what I need is a rich life-wife. I need a money-mommy-wife. You're right. Look at this dump I live in. I can't take it anymore. I need to find a rich woman and marry her. You heard my bitch of a half-sister — my looks are fading. Let's face it, I need to find a rich woman while I still can."

My heart is pounding and I feel hungover, and there's acid in my gut and poison in my veins. "What? Are you serious?"

"Deadly." He moves around and kneels on the bed in front of me. "This doesn't change anything between you and me. You're my real wife, my true love. But we need to find me a big old moneybags wife."

"We?"

"Yes, we. We have to think long-term here baby. If you leave Dave, and move in with me, then what? We live like this forever?"

I shudder. The thought is repulsive and he nods. "Yeah, see what I mean? We need a wife I can make some money off of. Bernice was supposed to be our big meal ticket. That bitch. We were supposed to get *something* from her! I worked on that plan forever and now the whole thing's gone belly-up. Talk about no return on investment. I spend over a year working and waiting for that gig! What a waste. I'm still super bummed out by what happened. Do you think I want to marry an old bag? I don't. I love you too. And hey, you couldn't really leave the girls, could you?"

"I love them. I do. I want to be a real mom to them, but you left me alone and I'm crazy without you, JayRay."

"I'm sorry I left you alone, hon, I am. I had to think. I needed time to figure out what to do. And now I know. When we get back on the circuit, we'll put our plan into play. I've been thinking and Iris is the best candidate."

"Iris? The old duck who runs the Canadian shows?"

"That's the one."

"Are you fucking kidding me?"

"Why? She's rich. She's a widow. She's got it all."

"She's *old*, that's what. And what makes you think she'll be interested?"

"She'll be interested," JayRay is confident.

"What happens once you marry her?"

"I get the lay of the land and see what I can do."

I'm silent for a moment and I get out of bed. "I need to have a quick shower and go home. I put my trust in you JayRay, and you fucked me over. I should have known you would."

He jumps off the bed and grabs me. "I have *not* fucked you over. I am thinking about us, our long-term. You always agreed we had to think long-term. You told me you wanted to be a mom to your kids. That you never wanted to be a parent like your own parents were. And what long-term plan have you ever come up with? How were you thinking we'd fund our days together? That we'd live off the petty cash you take from the shows or from the money you skim off the company credit card? Or the product you sell off the books? I *am* thinking about *us*. You're the one who's being short-sighted."

"I'm a terrible mother," I say and I slump with the admission of my failure. "I wasn't exactly winning gold stars before I met you and now I'm worse. You said so yourself. Dave is a better mother than I'll ever be. But at least now I know how I figure into your future."

"Why can't you see that I am only thinking of us?"

"If that's true, then why didn't you tell me?"

"I couldn't exactly text you, *hey, hon, I'm thinking of marrying Iris. Isn't that a great idea?* I needed to see you. I was going to tell you as soon as we saw each other."

I give a half smile. "Yeah, that wouldn't have gone down well. But you didn't have to disappear. I've been a crabby bitch to Dave and the girls. I'm going to have to make it right. They won't be happy." I look over at the alarm clock on JayRay's scarred pine bedside table. "They'll be back soon. I'll stop by Walmart and buy them presents and say I was there the whole time."

I have a quick shower, come back into the bedroom and start pulling on my clothes.

"Let me ask you something." I've been afraid to broach the subject but I have to ask. "Did these mean anything to you or were you just fuck drunk and out of your skull?" I point to the tattoo on my pubic bone. It isn't a pretty sight, the tattoo is scabbing and the hair is growing back and the whole thing looks diseased. He flips the sheet aside and shows me his, which isn't in much better shape.

"It means the world to me. I take it Dave hasn't seen it?"

I shake my head. "I managed to evade him. My fucking bush better grow back quickly and cover it. Not like he examines me down there or anything."

"So, Iris?" I can't help but comment as I gather my purse and keys. "For real? Good thing no one knows about you and me at the shows."

"There is one other way," JayRay says quietly and I stop, deadstill.

"What?" I ask.

"Dave…" JayRay says vaguely, waving his hand around. "All his money. His family's moola. Moneybucks Grandma Nancy … I don't know. That pile of cash you live in."

"You've seen where I live?" I had told JayRay about the place but as far as I knew, he'd never been there.

"Of course I do, sweetcheeks. I've driven past a few times. I even stopped outside for a while. You never saw me. But I saw you, not looking too happy might I say. Can't you get Dave to sell that big old castle and split the money with you?"

"No," I say, through clenched teeth. "I cannot. Nor would I, ever. You might be happy to skin your half-sister alive JayRay, but I would never do that. How can you even think that? Not an option. Anyway, he'd never sell. He'll rent out the basement, do shit like that to keep it. It's all fucking falling apart anyway. Place looks like a giant shithole inside. And Dave said investments are down right now, so we're living off his salary and mine. And Nancy? There's no way we'd get a penny out of her tight-fisted, tennis-toned ass. She hates me. Plus she's selling my product for extra cash, so you've got your answer right there."

JayRay shrugs. "Had to ask," he says, nonchalantly. "No Picasso's on the wall, shit like that you could offload?"

"No Picassos. No nothing. Forget about it JayRay. Shit, I can't believe you even thought about it."

I glare at him and he jumps off the bed. "Listen, Leo honey, I was only thinking of you and me. Bernice is history. You think you don't want me humping Iris for our lottery win? Well, neither do I. I was just exploring all the avenues out there."

I relent. I guess it was an obvious question for him to ask, particularly if he's seen the house. Anyone would think we had money coming out of our ears.

"Well it's not an avenue, cross it off your list. I'd better get going. I'm in more shit than I can tell you. See you in a few days."

"You are my everything," JayRay says and he holds me close and kisses me goodbye. "You know that, right?"

I nod and close the door behind me. My focus is back on my family. I have to put things right. My fix taken care of, I'm horrified by how I missed the hockey game and I'm shocked by my own actions. If JayRay's going to make other plans, then I'd better make my own too, and that means making things right at home. My family are my own personalized Hallmark card come to life, a safe haven from the pain. I need that comforting cocoon of familial chaos within which to lose myself.

I turn on the car and swing towards home, trying to figure out what gifts I can buy to make amends for what I have done.

12. BERNICE

I FINISH THE BOTTLE OF WINE. Dirk still isn't home.

"Madam?" It is Betty, faithful Betty still wearing her neat pink-and-white servant's uniform, her turban neatly in place, her apron tied in a perfect bow, and not a crease in sight despite her long day.

I sigh. "Ja, Betty, what do you want?" I am still annoyed with her for being less than co-operative about new ideas for another book, and for disappearing and not making me supper.

"Madam, would like something to eat?"

"No. I didn't know where you were so I made a *sarmie*." I gesture to the dry uneaten sandwich and Betty makes a disapproving sound.

"That looks very bad," she says and I nod in agreement.

"Ja well, I'm a bit drunk to be honest, Betty. I don't know where Dirk is and I'm worried."

"He will be back, Madam, do not worry."

"Do you think so? How can you know, hey?"

"Men," Betty says. "Come, Madam, let me put you to bed."

"No, I am fine here, I am going to wait."

"Then I will go to my room. You will be all right?"

"Ja, I'll be fine, Betty, thank you. Have a good night."

Betty nods and leaves. I try to think back to the men that Betty has seen come and go in my life and I wonder what Betty thinks of me. I know so little about her life. I know that Rosie is twenty-six and that she's gone from being an angry, lazy, lout of a girl to an angry, couture-wearing, go-getter with a big career at the South African Broadcasting Corporation. My father paid for Rosie's school fees and sent her to the same private girl's school that I attended, but she was ten years behind me and I never saw her.

These days she comes into the kitchen and scowls at me, as if I am holding her mother hostage, and she mutters in Zulu, things that I know are not complimentary.

Betty has been a part of my life forever. She came to help my mother shortly after my first birthday. Betty is more of a parent to me than my own mother ever was. Betty isn't even that old; she's nearly fifty-five. My mother would have been fifty-four had she lived. My mother had me when she was nineteen, and when Betty arrived a year later, she was only a year older than my mother.

I wasn't happy when Rosie was born, but Betty made sure that I hardly noticed her. Betty kept her strapped to her back, wrapped tight in a blanket, in the traditional way of carrying children, and all I ever saw of Rosie when she was a baby was her tiny head. When Rosie grew up she was a vortex of spinning fury who hated the world and everything in it. I stayed as far away from her as I could.

We lived on the farm back then, and it was to Betty that I turned when I needed affection or solace. My mother spent most of her life in a darkened room, resting, and emerging briefly to host parties and socials and teas for the other bored farm wives.

My mother died suddenly of ovarian cancer that had spread. She was only thirty-eight when, out of nowhere, she fell ill and very shortly after that, she was dead.

I was nineteen at the time. The same age that my mother was when she had me. I had just started my studies at the University of the Witwatersrand and I was finding it hard to get into the rhythm of adult life after the safe and cloistered confines of the convent boarding school and the equally cloistered summers at the farm. No sooner had things settled for me, in Johannesburg, when I had to return home to bury my mother.

"She hated the farm, you know," my father told me as we prepared her funeral arrangements. "She married me because she thought I could save her. She hated modeling for a living and she had you to support and she thought I offered her a way out. But instead of being her salvation, I brought her to live in a dusty hell. When I asked her to marry me, I told her that we would live on a farm, and I explained our way of life in detail. I told her she was more of a city girl but she said that wasn't true. She said the city had hurt her and she couldn't wait to leave. So she accepted my marriage proposal but I don't think she understood what life here would really mean."

"I don't care what she thought or felt," I said, linking my arm through his. "You saved me. What would have become of us if you hadn't married her? Modeling doesn't pay the rent for long and god knows she could never have gotten a real job. The only thing she was good at was being a coat hanger for pretty dresses, and giving tea parties."

"Ah now, don't talk about her like that," my father was reproving. "She was a creature made to decorate this world. She had her beauty and that was her gift to me and to the world. But I would like to think I made her happy in some kind of way."

"You did," I insisted. "You gave her everything she ever wanted and she did love it here or she would have left."

"And gone where? With what money?"

"She would have made a plan," I was certain. "Ma would never have stayed anywhere she didn't want to be. You must know that?"

My father looked doubtful. "Well there's nothing I can do for her now except miss her. And miss her I shall, every moment of every day. Come on, *poppie*, let's plan a tea party that would have made her proud."

After my mother's white, lily-strewn coffin was lowered into the family burial ground on the farm, I walked away with my father. I glanced briefly over my shoulder at the large feather-winged marble angel standing guard over my mother's grave. Who was the woman who birthed me? She was the shadow of a butterfly, pretty, distant, and vague, paging endlessly through fashion magazines and making her dresses from bolts of cloth that she had delivered to the farm.

We held a fine afternoon tea and the neighbours came. Betty baked *kooksisters* and *melktert* and other traditional treats, and the table was weighed down by the array. We drank Rooibos and Earl Gray tea and there were tiny cups of espresso coffee for my father, only he was crying too hard to drink anything. He sat, immobile, trying to swallow his tears, and I watched his face, so still, awash with tears that he dabbed with his already-soaked pale blue handkerchief. My mother had made those handkerchiefs for him; he had a drawer full of them.

I was hardly aware of the neighbours, although one woman in particular seemed inappropriately upset. Certainly, my mother had been known to throw a good party but it wasn't as if any of them had been her real friends. After they left, I sat on the sofa in the quiet darkening of the late afternoon and I looked at my father who hadn't moved.

I was thinking about my mother's room. I had not crossed the threshold of that room since she died. I was a stranger to her room, having visited only twice when I was a child. The feeling of trespassing was thick in the air and I knew to leave as quickly as possible.

When I came home for the holidays from the boarding school in Johannesburg, I lived in my bedroom, reading, or I hung out in the kitchen, talking to Betty, or I took my horse out for long rides. After a formal but simple dinner with my father, I spent the evenings with him in his study, reading or playing games or watching movies. My mother's absence was an accepted fact. She joined us for dinner now and then, dressed in one of her sparkly creations, but I preferred the evenings without her. It had never occurred to me that my mother might be depressed or have problems of her own; to my mind she was simply inordinately vain and selfish. But she never sought me out either.

"What will you do with her room and all her stuff?" I asked.

"Keep it exactly like it is. I can't bear to lose her in that way too. When do you go back to university?"

"In two days. Pa, I don't think I want to be a lawyer. I want to study psychology."

My father rubbed his chin. "Hmm. Too much introspection is not a good thing. It's better, if you ask me, to learn a trade. Law is a trade. It's objective, it is this or it is that. But psychology deals with the grey area of life and grey can be dangerous."

"But it's what I want to do. I signed up for Psych 101 and it's fascinating. Law is dry and boring."

"I will always support you, *poppie,* in everything you do. And if that is what you want to do, so be it."

"You always have supported me." I went to him and put my hand on his shoulder. "I love you, Pa, you know how much?"

"How much?"

"A gazillion pieces." I smiled at him.

"And I, you, *poppie*, and I, you."

And he was good to his word. He loved me in spite of everything. In spite my anger, my sadness, and my loneliness.

My anger, my sadness, and my loneliness. The worst of these was my anger. It was the main reason I wanted to study psychology. My father knew I had a temper but he didn't know the depth of hatred that lay beneath my skin like a virulent second dermis. A dermis that crawled with impotent rage, hating life, hating my mother. I hated her beauty and her, for giving none of it to me. I hated her fragility that I knew was really her armour.

I knew I needed to untangle my feelings about her or I'd never be happy. Besides, being that angry was exhausting.

I graduated when I was twenty-six, in 2008, and I published the first *Bake Your Way* book a year later. My father died in

2010 and I was grateful that he had witnessed my success. I buried him next to my mother, under the watchful eye of the six-foot angel. I did not have a party or invite any of the neighbours over because I couldn't bear to share my grief. And I understood then why my father kept my mother's room untouched. I too, could not bear to change a single thing on the farm. My father's world had to remain intact, as if he might come back at any moment.

But I sold the sheep and I locked the farm up tight, leaving Isaac, the groundsman, to mow the lawns, keep the gardens alive, and see that no harm came to the place. I had no idea if or when I would ever return but I needed it to be there, because it was my childhood home.

I was already living in the Westcliff house that my father had bought for me, and Betty lived with me. And, according to my father's wishes, I continued to pay for Rosie's university tuition, as he had done mine.

Still hoping to hear the sound of Dirk's car, I open a new bottle of wine and wonder what my father would think of Dirk and the current mess I am in. I'm sure he wouldn't approve but I am in too deep and I don't know how to fix things.

I think about faithful Betty, asleep in her room, with her bed set high on bricks to keep her safe from the *tokoloshes*, while Rosie toils late into the night at her fancy job and dreams about being an even bigger shot. She is fueled by her own brand of anger, and here I sit, drinking to drown my sorrows, not that this is anything new. Sometimes I find my life ironic. I am, after all, a world expert on happiness and the state of the human psyche. It's a good thing no one knows the truth.

I try to call Dirk again but his phone stubbornly goes to voicemail.

I drink until I fall asleep on the sofa. Betty wakes me the next morning, a cup of coffee in her hand. Dirk is still nowhere to be seen.

13. LEONIE

"IT'S GOING TO TAKE MORE than cheap crap from Walmart," Dave says and he's angrier than I have ever seen him. "Do you have any idea how upset the girls were?"

It turns out I let Muffin out and were it not for the observant eye of a neighbour, Muffin would be history.

"The old guy across the street saw Muffin running out and he managed to grab him," Dave tells me while I unload my parcels onto the kitchen table.

"Yeah, that guy watches us all the time," I say, trying to lessen the magnitude of what he said, but I am sick to my stomach.

"Thank god he does," Dave retorts. "The girls were hysterical when we got home and found him gone. We searched the house for hours. You can't imagine. First, they were extremely upset that you didn't come with us. Maddie played badly and Kenzie was so stressed. And then we got home to find Muffin gone. They were out of their minds. It took an hour of them wailing and me looking in the garden before the old guy thought to come over with Muffin. The kids were so noisy he must have heard the commotion but, still, he waited. Anyway, thank god he had him. I don't know what I would have done. I can't carry on like this, Lee. The girls can't carry on like this. We love you but what's up?"

The question was an echo of the one JayRay had asked me. JayRay, who texted me five times after I left, declaring his love and undying commitment such as it was. At least that was back to normal.

I had stopped at Walmart and bought Kenzie's favourite bubble bath, a new Maple Leafs T-shirt for Maddie, and chocolate-covered pretzels for Dave, and I drove back home wondering how bad the wrath would be, hoping it would be negligible and that I would be able to breeze through it. And, were it not for Muffin, things would have been manageable. Stupid fucking dog. I'm annoyed that no one paid any attention to my gifts. No one was giving me credit for trying.

"I don't know," I say to Dave, and I pour myself a rum and diet Coke. "I really don't."

I don't want to talk to Dave at all. I want to think about how fantastic it felt to be in JayRay's arms again and I need to untangle his insane idea about Iris. My brain cells are occupied. I don't have time for Dave's domestic issues.

Yes, I had been filled with fear at the thought of losing my family, but as soon as I found them at home, it was like they didn't matter anymore. JayRay was the only thing that mattered and I had to come up with an alternative plan to his.

"If you're going to stay with us, you need to get some therapy," Dave announces loudly and I turn around quickly.

"What? What do you mean *if* I stay with you?"

"You're not being a mother or a wife, and you haven't been for a while. I kept giving you leeway, making excuses for you. I told myself that you were busy building a career and said that things would be different if I gave you some time, but it wasn't that. It's you. And if you want us to be a family, then you need to see a therapist about your issues and we both need to see a marriage counselor."

"What issues?" I'm genuinely stunned and I sit down and drink half my rum and diet Coke in one go. "What are you talking about?" The girls are playing Minecraft and Muffin is yapping and I'm going to lose my mind. I try to think of a way to stop Dave from talking but he's like an oncoming train.

"Your intimacy issues. You've never let me get close to you. I don't even know who you are. You prefer being on the road to being home. You prefer working to hanging out with us. You don't seem interested in the kids, and you aren't the slightest bit interested in me."

"Dave…" I don't know what to say. It isn't like I can tell him it isn't true, because it is true, all of it.

"You see, you can't even reply. You never talk about anything meaningful. Do you even think about life and what we're doing here or things like that? Or how much you love the kids, if you even do? Do you think about our marriage? We never talk about anything."

Maybe Dave's right. Maybe I don't have anything to offer anyone. Look at JayRay and me. What did we talk about? We bitched about the roadshow vendors and we had sex and got drunk. Maybe that was all I'm good for, have sex, get drunk, and work. Maybe I'm more like a man that way, while Dave is like a woman, needing to talk about his inner feelings and what's going on with the kids. Either way, I can see I'm going to have to make more of an effort with him and with the girls.

"Dave," I try again, "I realize I have been in my own world a lot recently. I feel guilty about being on the road as much as I am, but I love it. I need it. I love you and the girls, too, and I need you, more than you can know. I think about you all the time when I am away."

I look at him. I put my glass down and I really look at him. I look at his earnest, kind face, and I know that I do love him. I love him for giving me everything I ever wanted, an extraordinary home, a family, a stable, supportive environment.

After those long lonely years, struggling to survive my mother's rejection on the one hand, and my father's icy cruelty on the other, all I wanted, growing up, was the noise and excitement and easy affection that I saw in other people's normal lives. I wanted the cotton batting of family love to protect me from the emptiness that hollowed me out. My dreams came true and

I got my family, but it didn't protect me in the way that I had hoped. Most of the time, I still felt like I was empty inside: no bones, no blood, no organs. Hollow. Dave tried to save me from that. In the beginning, he made me laugh but I stopped letting him. I became more and more like my father.

And I realize, sitting there, that I'm just like my father. I go over to Dave and put my arm around him. His shoulders feel odd and unfamiliar, and I want to ask him, *who are you?* But I rub his back and try to find my way back to some kind of familiarity.

I'm shocked by his ultimatum and I can't help but think that if my family had any idea how rotten to the core I am, they'd boot me out, brush the dust off their hands, and get on with their lives. They don't need me, but I need them. *For fuck's sake, Leonie. You're like a psychotic fucking pendulum, caring, then not, then desperate again.* I am my own worst mistake.

"I didn't realize how bad I was getting," I admit and at least that's partway honest. "When I come back from my trips, I am tired out and you guys seem to have everything in a groove. It's like you don't need me and I don't try to make myself fit in. I admit, I've been lazy and I've let things slide. It isn't up to you or the kids to make me feel needed. It's up to me to be a part of this family and I haven't done that. I realize that now. And I will go and talk to someone, I will. I am tired of being me. I am tired of keeping you and the girls at arm's length. I never wanted to treat the girls the way my father had treated me. I want to love them and make them feel loved and wanted and needed. I'll fix it, Dave, I will, okay? Will you let me?"

He nods. "You can start by apologizing to the girls. Be a mom to them, not some kind of aunt who tries to win their love with gifts from Crapmart."

I try to hug him but he moves away. "No. You don't know how much you've hurt me, Lee."

I put my hand on his arm. "I will make it right, you'll see. I'll go and see the girls now. I am very sorry about Muffin. That was fucking careless of me. I'm sorry about that and I am sorry I missed the day with you and the girls. I am sorry about everything. I'll make it up to you, you'll see."

He doesn't reply and I go into the living room to face my daughters.

14. BERNICE

DIRK COMES HOME THREE DAYS LATER. By this time, I have called the hospitals, the police stations, and anyone I can think of. I would have called Chrizette, but I don't have her number. It is odd, when it comes down to it, how little I really know about this man I love.

I had Theresa call his horse-racing friends, but they hadn't heard anything.

Theresa came over for a while and she visited with me and we sat there, knowing there was nothing we could do, nothing but wait. I couldn't even watch *Miami Vice*.

When Theresa left, she patted my hand but she didn't say anything. What could she say?

And at last, Dirk comes home. He stinks of alcohol and cigarettes and he's covered in bruises. I guess he's started smoking again; at least he won't be bugging me about that.

One arm is broken, one eye is swollen shut, and he has stitches in his lip. He hasn't shaved in days and when I look at him, I hear James Sonny Crockett saying: *Things go wrong. The odds catch up.*

Betty and I exchange a glance. We heard him at the gate and we stood together on the verandah and watched his car crawl up the driveway with none of his usual, exuberant style. He staggered out, slamming the door behind him. His clothes looked as if he had slept in them or perhaps he slept under a tree.

He looks up at us. "Betty," he calls out. "Run me a bath,

make a big pot of coffee and some sandwiches."

Betty turns to do as he says but I stop her.

"Who are you to tell Betty what to do, hey? You disappear for three days. I thought you were dead. But never mind that, Betty doesn't do what you say, you are a guest here, have you forgotten that?"

"Ja, of course. I am sorry." Dirk climbs the stairs with the weariness of an old man and lowers himself onto the small verandah couch.

"I will make coffee," Betty says quietly to me and she disappears into the coolness of the house.

I look at this broken man. I try not to breathe in his foulness.

"And so?" I ask. I'm still leaning against the railing, watching him.

"Ja, you were right. She is seeing someone." Dirk starts crying. Clearly not for the first time. "How could she do that? The mother of my children. And never mind that, it is *who* she is seeing."

"And who is she seeing?" I ask, knowing full well.

"Gerit Venster."

"And who is he, when he's at home?" Of course, I know but I can't tell Dirk that.

"He is ... ag man, it's a long story."

"If you want to stay," I say and I sit down next to him, "I suggest you tell me everything."

"I belong to a group, we call it the *Volksraad*. It is our parliament, our government, the real one, the one that should be in power, instead of the blacks who are ruining this country."

I stay silent and I keep my hands folded in my lap. I don't look at him, I look out, straight ahead. I watch the evening lights start to flicker in the city below and I wait for him to continue.

"We just wanted to keep our language alive, our culture alive, our history and traditions. We started it after Mandela came into power, and it was big. Huge. Ten of thousands of us. But over the years, a lot of people have emigrated and others, it seems, decided that black South Africa wasn't as bad as they thought it would be, and they left the group. There are only about three thousand of us left now across the whole country and the organization is mostly online. The leader is a guy named Gerit Venster. He thinks Hitler is the bee's knees. You should see him, he even looks like Hitler. His hair is stuck down with Brylcreem and he shapes his moustache the same as Hitler did."

"And Chrizette is having an affair with him?"

"Ja." Dirk is crying again. "I went to see her and I confronted her and she admitted she is sleeping with him, and that they have been seeing each other for nearly three years."

Longer than we have been together, I want to say but I don't.

"That's longer than you and me," he says and I nod.

"I had no idea." He looks utterly bewildered. "How could she? How could he?"

"What happened next?"

"She told me that the kids love him. They've loved him from the start. They knew all along. The bloody kids knew. What a fool I've been. Anyway, after three years with Gerit, she says she suspected me of having an affair and she gets me followed and then kicks me out."

"I will have you know," he says, "I only ever had one night stands before you and I never had sex with any of them either. I was faithful to her, but she cannot say the same. They both betrayed me."

"But if she and Gerit were having an affair all this time, and the kids love him so much, why didn't she ask you for a divorce long ago?"

"You just don't get it, do you? For the sake of morality, that's why. Gerit didn't want to betray our church and our way of life, neither did Chrizette. None of us did. But Chrizette said that once she had the evidence of my affair, that she and Gerit figured the whole thing was broken anyway."

"Ja, you are so right. I don't get it. And I never will. So what happened next?"

"As it turned out, there was a meeting of the *Volksraad* the night I left you to confront her. It was the perfect opportunity for me to set the record straight. We have a strict agenda and one of the issues tabled is that you can report a fellow member if you have evidence that they have betrayed the code. There weren't a lot of people at this meeting and it seemed to take forever for us to get to that part. And when we did, I stood in front of Gerit who sits behind a huge desk, like a judge. He has a gavel and he wears a black gown and a hat in the *Voortrekker* style and all of a sudden, he looked ridiculous, so self-important. Anyway, I stood there, and I didn't say anything.

"Eventually he asks me what is it that I want to say, and can we please move on. Because he knows. Of course he does. I turn and face the room, there are maybe eighty people there, and I shout that he is an adulterator and a fornicator and a man who breaks up families and he should be kicked out. 'He is a disgrace,' I shout and I wait for the people to tell him to get out but no one says anything and I turn back to Gerit and I grab him by his stupid gown and I pull him across the table. I throw him on the floor and I start to *donder* the shit out of him. And then, everyone runs up and starts punching me! *Me!* Gerit was the one who made them stop; they listened to him.

"He calls the meeting to a close and he tells them he needs to talk to me. By now, my arm is killing me, my face is covered in blood, some of my ribs are broken, and I can hardly breathe.

"They leave and Gerit sits on the floor with me. He is in much better shape than I am. I hardly started on him when they climbed on me. And he tells me, 'Look, admittedly it's not ideal what happened, but then again, nothing is.' He says that maybe we were married to the wrong people to start off with and that 'this is God's way of putting things right.'

Something occurs to me and I tell him that since him and Chrizette were screwing each other before you and I even met, that I will sue her for desertion and take her for all her money. The bastard laughs and says Chrizette is ready for that. Her lawyers are all lined up. She'll give me a million bucks and that's it. A million rand. Worth shit these days. And I will only get it once I sign the divorce papers. And Gerit's going to adopt my kids once the divorce comes through. And here's the kicker, literally. He chucked me out of the *Volksraad* because I instigated a fight. Apparently, according to his rules, we are now allowed to fornicate, but hitting each other is out of the question. Ag, *fok,* they can have it, they're a bunch of self-righteous bastard hypocrites. I was the only one who tried. I was the only one who said we should make a real statement, blow up the fucking ANC, do something. But no, they said that was too extreme."

He looks at me. "You don't seem very surprised by any of this," he comments.

"I'm processing what you're saying. I thought you were dead, or that you had gone back to Chrizette."

"Never," he cries and he wraps himself around me as best he can, but he stinks like a filthy wet dog and I untangle him.

"Maybe after you have brushed your teeth," I suggest.

"Ja, of course. I am sorry about the state I am in. I admit I was not exactly sober when I went to the *Volksraad,* which was stupid. I started drinking after I spoke with Chrizette and I was shit-faced when I confronted Gerit. But the nerve of that guy! He said he doesn't want me to see my kids. He said they don't want to see me either and if I try to see them, he'll make sure that I'm *taken care of.* Him! Take care of me! I tell you. And my kids! What did I ever do to deserve this from them? I was a good father. I was a good husband."

He gazes off into the distance. "Everything has changed. I thought the *Volksraad* would bring back the past and make things right. But they are useless wankers, good for nothing except to talk big time out their arses. It's all gone. Everything I stood for. Nothing has any meaning any more."

"You may still have one thing," I point out and he looks up at me.

"I know I still have you, and I am grateful for that. And I am sorry I disappeared."

"I said you *may* still have one thing." I study my hands. "What makes you think I am willing to put up with this rubbish? Look at you, crying like a baby. Do you think I care about Gerit or Chrizette or any of them? Do you think I care about your kids? I only tried with the kids because of you. I never wanted kids. I don't care about them and frankly, from what I saw, you don't either. You hardly spoke to them when they were here, and you say you were a good husband and father. I won't comment on that any more.

"But I will say this. I loved you. I took you into my home. I made the children welcome. And you treated me like crap. You ran out on me. You ran after Chrizette like a love-struck schoolboy. I was worried out of my skull. I thought you had died in an accident. I couldn't think of a reason you didn't contact me. You left and you got drunk and now you have come back to me crying. Here's what I have to say. Leave now, go and think about your life, and if you can think of a reason why I should take you back, I might do it. But for now, I want you gone."

He looks at me, his mouth agape. "You can't be serious," he says.

"I have never been more serious in my life."

He puts his head in his hands for a moment and then he looks up at me. "I am sorry. Of course, you are angry. I know I must look weak to you. I must look like a loser and a hypocrite. Please, don't hate me. Please let me come home."

"This is not your home. You left me. And now you must go."

"No," he says and he pulls me to him. It's awkward, what with that broken arm and he smells disgusting. And yet, with the return of his arrogance, so returns the flicker of my lust for him. Despite myself, I lean into him, ever so slightly, but it's enough so he knows he has won.

"I am sorry," he says. "This will never happen again. Me losing it, I mean. You are my world and I will make it up to you. It will be like this never happened. You'll see. I am going to make you happy."

He reaches under my dress and tugs my panties down and he pushes me back on the sofa and although it only lasts a minute or so, it seems that for once he doesn't need Viagra. I lie underneath him and hold him close.

Happy? What does that even mean?

15. LEONIE

"IRIS?" I ASK AGAIN. "Seriously, just to double check we're talking about the same person. You do mean *that* Iris?"

"Give it up Leo, yes, that Iris."

We're in Vancouver, at The Marketplace for Gifts, Garden and Home, and I look over at Iris who's helping set up a stand. Iris has her standards and she is showing a newbie the ropes, the exact ropes. Iris is the Executive Director of the Canadian Trade Show Association, the CTSA, and she has a manual on booth presentations and regulations. The newbie's eyes are glazed as she watches Iris read from the booklet and point out items of supreme importance.

"That should be an exciting roll in the hay," I comment. "Oh, James, put your penis here, no James, a little more to the left, wait, straighten up a bit, now a bit deeper, yes, thank you, James, now you've got it, well done."

JayRay laughs. "Yeah, I'm sure you're right."

"Why Iris?" I'm aware that I sound whiny.

"Because she's the perfect candidate. She lives in a mansion in Mississauga, she knows the trade show gigs, she won't object to me being on the road a lot, she'll only hang out with me at the Canadian shows, she's rich, she's the right age—"

"She's old!"

"She's the right age. She's our meal ticket, Leo, she's the one."

"I hate this," I mutter.

"Suck it up. You have to go to therapy and I have to get

married. The alternative is you and me stuck in my shithole apartment for the rest of our lives, gigging shows. You want that?"

I shake my head. My recent brush with losing my nice life had made me nervous. "Go do your thing. Hey, she's a client of mine; tell her I say hi. Bring her over later, I'll mix her a special batch and say nice things about you."

"Don't tell her too much," JayRay warns. "You don't know me that well, remember. But from what you do know, I'm a standup guy. Don't elaborate."

"I know how this works. I'm on our side. I know what to do."

I try not to throw up when I watch JayRay walk up to Iris. I know he's making sense, and that a plan of some kind is needed to action the necessary change in our lives but I hate this particular idea.

I choke on my bile and set up my display. Everything is ready for the opening that evening and, knowing that I can't bear to watch JayRay for one more minute, I leave and I walk back to my hotel room where I close the curtains and lie down on the bed.

My life is falling apart. Therapy. Fucking therapy. I shudder. Dave suggested I go and chat to our family doctor and see if she had any recommendations for therapists and I reluctantly went. She gave me a list of websites and told me to do some research, to find someone that made sense to me.

"I have to find my own person," I told Dave.

"But how?"

"She gave me a bunch of websites. I'll do it. I promise I will, after I get back from Vancouver. I'm not procrastinating. I leave tomorrow and there's a lot of prep to do."

Dave was quiet. I could tell he thought I should be online right away, scrolling through therapists, making decisions, and setting up appointments. Instead, I was sitting on the sofa, reading a copy of *The New Scientist* while the girls were doing their homework at the kitchen table.

The next day the girls were at school and I was getting ready to leave. The house was sunny and Muffin was sleeping in his basket in the corner. Dave was folding laundry and I made a move to help him but he stopped me. "You fold things badly. You leave creases."

Anger bubbled inside my chest. "Hey, mister, do I do anything right? Are you even interested in having me around anymore?" My eyes filled up with tears and I folded my arms. "Stop punishing me, okay? And if you can't forgive me, I'll leave." My heart was pounding with fear as I said this, fearful he would say yes, go, leave.

He turned to face me. "You keep telling me you need time. I need time too. This erosion has been going on for a while, it's not going to fix itself. And I'm going to find a marriage counselor, that's my call."

"If things have been this bad, why haven't you said so? Why tell me now that it's a catastrophe, with no warning?"

"Because, like I've said a bunch of times, I kept hoping things would improve. I hoped it was just a mood or a phase and that the next time you came home, the real Leonie would come home with you too. But this time, you were even worse. You didn't come to the game, then you nearly lost Muffin, and it all came to a head. If I had tried to talk to you before, you would have dismissed me outright and said I was imagining things."

I didn't know what to say but I had to ask. "Dave, is it over? If it is, I'd rather know."

He rubbed his forehead. "I don't want it to be. I don't."

"I need you to show some compassion at least. It's like I'm on parole."

"You haven't earned compassion, Lee. Go to your show, come back, get some therapy, I'll sort out some counseling and we'll take it from there. I can't give you more than that right now and you don't deserve any more."

I felt shamed and humiliated and I left the kitchen without a word. I went upstairs, and packed my suitcase. I wasn't ready to leave. I needed to think. I sat down in the reading nook that I loved so much when I first moved into the house and I looked out the window. The garden was a tangled and overgrown mess, it was a wonder that the neighbours hadn't complained. It seemed like the house and its surrounds were falling apart just like my life. Whereas I once felt like a princess in a foreign land, now I was in exile, in a place I could no longer call my home. I looked around our bedroom, at the white rose chandelier, the high cherry wood sleigh bed, and at my dressing table. Even my dressing table looked unlived in. It was spotless and tidy, barren, in a house that exploded with life at every other opportunity.

My body turned to concrete. It took all my will to swing my legs off the nook and get moving. I wasn't welcome here anymore. It was time to leave.

Dave was waiting at the bottom of the staircase and he looked up at me as I lugged my bag down. "It wasn't fair of me to treat you like that. I'm not your father. I would never want to be like that."

"You just were." My chin quivered. "Bad girl. You're right, Dave, this isn't working for either of us right now. Let's hope we can fix it."

I tried to brush past him but he put his hand on my waist and pulled me towards him. "But do you really want to fix things, Lee? Have you even asked yourself that? How much do you want to?"

Two big fat tears rolled down my cheeks and I bowed my head. "Well, I certainly don't want our life to be like this. I want us to be like we were before, when I could trust you, trust you with me."

He nodded. "But you broke my trust, Lee."

"So you keep saying."

We were at an impasse and I realized I'd have to do something. Dave. I'd always loved his sensual mouth and I focused on that now, his almost girly, full upper lip. I leaned in slowly and kissed him, knowing he wouldn't be able to resist me, in the same way I can't resist JayRay.

I kissed Dave slowly and deeply and even I felt our connection. I let go of the handle of my suitcase and I put my arms around him. I felt his arousal and I undid his belt buckle and I slid down to my knees and took him in my mouth. He groaned and cupped my head with his hands and he slowly lowered himself to the floor. I pulled off my jeans and I straddled him and rode him and we came together and I lay crumpled on top of him.

"Well now," Dave finally said, "I don't know about you but that sure felt like a step in the right direction to me."

I looked at him and grinned. "I second that." I rolled off him and pulled up my panties and we lay there, looking at the ceiling. I felt for his hand and held on tightly.

"Whoa," Dave shook himself awake. "I was dozing off. I'd better get up. Imagine if the girls came home now, we'd scar them for life."

I laughed and sat up. "I must be going anyway. I'll text you later."

I kissed him goodbye, a kiss I hoped would wipe my record clean but when I arrived at the show, Dave had texted me; *Don't think this means you're off the hook for therapy... xo* and I ground my teeth.

And to top it off, now I've got to watch my beloved JayRay sniffing around old Iris.

I lie in my hotel room with a cool wet face cloth on my forehead. I am bereft and hopeless, as if the life has been sucked right out of me.

16. BERNICE

TIME PASSES AND I CAN'T QUITE FORGET how Dirk had behaved. I try to push his weeping and hysteria to the back of my mind and I succeed to a degree, but the memory calls to me, waving a red flag and disturbing the purity of my former love. He was weak, he betrayed me, and he took me for granted. Nor can I forget how he chose to run back to Chrizette until she kicked him out for good.

Am I am happy or just coasting? I miss the thrill of my affair with Dirk. There's no adrenalin now. And, since things got finalized with Chrizette and Gerit and the kids, there's been no excitement at all. I chastise myself for thinking that, and for needing more.

We settle into a routine. I write during the day, or I try to. He goes to his job, selling life insurance. We have dinner at seven, with too much wine, followed by sex every other night. Blue pill sex. I know my suspicions are correct because I searched his closet and I found the Viagra hidden in a pair of shoes.

It kind of kills the joy of it for me, imagining him having to pop a pill to get it up with me. The whole act is so premeditated and lacking in real passion. But once he takes me in his arms, it doesn't seem to matter as much. Hard is hard and what he lacks in imagination, he make ups for by pushing the buttons he knows I like.

But he's stopped being magical with his tongue and fingers and I mourn that loss.

"You used to fingerfuck me so exquisitely I thought I'd die," I tell him. "And your tongue. Oh my god! Why don't we do that anymore?

"Because we're the real thing now," he says without even looking at me. I want to tell him I'd exchange the real thing, in a hearbeat, for the passion of our early days, but I don't.

We are very different people and we don't have much to talk about. At first, we drank while we binge-watched television but we didn't have the same viewing taste and we switched to drinking and reading instead — me, a book and him, a newspaper that supported his right-wing way of thinking.

I decide to write a memoir. I can't think of a single cooking thing left to do and without Betty's help, I'm sunk. I had thought of *Bake Your Way Through Grief*, following the loss of a spouse, a thought that occurred to me when Dirk had vanished for those three days and it was easy to envisage my future life as a widow. But he returned and I lost the emotional thread and Betty continued to be unhelpful and it seemed like the time to admit that the *Baking* series had run their course.

I like the idea of writing about my family, and JayRay and my father, and I figured that *Janette's Daytime Reveal!* would have piqued interest in my personal life thereby creating a market for the book, not that I had been grateful for that at the time.

The first few chapters of the book fly onto the page as if they've been waiting to be written. I chronicle my mother's short stint as a model and her love affair and marriage to a biker. The only thing my mother had told me about my biological father was that he had been "beautiful like a young Robert Redford, only he was drunk and on a Harley." The way she told the story, I imagined the song "Leader of the Pack" as the soundtrack to their relationship, only he hadn't died, instead he ran out on her and their newborn child.

I imagine my mother's passion for a certain kind of man, a man doomed from the time he was a boy, a drunk long before his first beer, his eyes glittering and wild, his body sweet smelling, smooth, and unscarred. A boy-man whose beauty carried the promise of forever. And my mother, a catalogue model from a small town north of Durban, alone for the first time in the big city of Johannesburg, drifting into a crowd of bikers and marrying her first boyfriend.

And then, he leaves. Just like that, he abandons her and their six-month-old baby girl. Divorces her quickly and marries another girl from the biker gang and then he leaves for the east coast of Canada because an uncle there said life was good and who doesn't love the promise of something fresh and new?

My mother, by pure happenstance, meets a man on a shoot. The art director of the shoot decided that they needed a prop: a Ford Model T from 1920, and a guy knew a guy who had one. The guy's farm was a few hours north west of Johannesburg and the fellow would bring the car down. And thus, my father met my mother.

At the end of the shoot, which only lasted a few days, my mother returned to the farm along with the Ford Model T Phaeton, my father, and me.

"I told her I would keep her safe, and that I would keep you safe. That neither of you would never want for anything again," my father told me.

And to my mother, already tired out by what had happened to her in the short span of her life, and saddled with a child towards whom she showed no affinity or affection, the solution must have felt akin to winning the lottery.

A farm. A gentleman husband. Never having to work again or worry about money. A nanny for the baby.

I reach that point of narration and the writing grinds to a halt. I have no idea where to go from there. Who was my mother when she was at the farm? What happened to her story then? How had she felt about my biological father? Had she loved him? Was she heartbroken when he left? I don't have a clue. And I have no idea how to answer these questions. My mother is a mystery to me.

I reread JayRay's emails, hoping to find a prompt that will jog the story forward but his messages are nothing more than poorly written entreaties for us to meet, with promises that he can tell me stories, oh yes, he can tell me stories.

One evening, I leave my computer on, with JayRay's emails on the screen, and when I return to my study, Dirk is behind my desk, reading everything.

"Excuse me!" I'm instantly furious and I snap the off-button of the screen. "I would never help myself to your computer. How dare you?"

His jaw clenches and I see the anger flash in his eyes. I remember that in his world women are second-class citizens and, to his mind, he has every right to read the contents of my diary, or search through my computer or closet drawers. The thought makes me shiver and I recall him telling me how he opened and read Chrizette's letters, and scrolled through her computer and poked through her drawers. How on earth had I been okay with that?

"Let me set you straight," I say now. "This is my house. I am not your wife, I never will be. Keep out of my things. If you don't, that is the end of us."

Dirk stands up, his hands raised in supplication. "Fine. So that was the guy on the talk show? Piece of work, né? Are you going to get in touch with him?"

"I don't want to talk about him," I say through gritted teeth. "It's none of your business, Dirk."

His face turns an angry purple, a lot like mine does, only his eyes bulge and they water slightly.

"You women don't know your place," he says in a tight voice and he says it quietly, and just as quickly he realizes what he has said and he apologizes.

"I am sorry. You are right. That was very old-school of me. I wasn't thinking and it will never happen again. You have my word. I'm sorry." His tone is contrite and I want to believe him. I tell myself that a lot has changed in his world. I can't expect him to be an entirely different man than the one he has been all his life.

I know that a large part of him is still trying to please his father, *die Predikant*, the preacher, who had threatened fire and brimstone from his pulpit, instilling in Dirk the good *boere* values of a righteous Afrikaaner whose wife had few rights and whose children were his possessions.

I also know that Dirk misses the *Volksraad*. He misses the camaraderie of it, the brotherhood. He was a member for over twenty-two years. He's still a believer in the cause but he has no outlet of expression, a thought which concerns me because I know that that energy cannot simply have dissipated.

Of his day job, he never offers nothing except to say "Life insurance. It is what it is."

And I wonder if he misses Chrizette and their life, and his kids.

There's so much I don't know, and so much that he doesn't tell me. I resolve to be more understanding about what it is that he's going through and I go over to him.

"Ag now, don't worry about it," I say. "Let's go and open a good bottle of red and relax. We've both been working hard. Let's just be happy we have each other."

Platitudes and clichés. Banal feel-good slogans to save the day, when really, the day cannot be saved at all.

Then

LEONIE ON A
COLLLISION COURSE

17.

IT'S MIDNIGHT AND I'M WIDE AWAKE, wondering where JayRay is and if he's scoring with Iris. There's a knock at my door. JayRay grins at me when I open it and I let him in. I wordlessly hand him a keycard to my room. This time he doesn't give me his, which makes me feel ill. I'm already locked out of his life. I don't want him to see how hurt I am, so I go and lie back down on the bed.

"It's going to be harder than I thought," JayRay admits. "Iris is a savvy old bitch, I'll give her that."

He lies down next to me and nuzzles my neck and I spoon into him despite my hurt. No matter what, I can't resist him. "What happened?" I ask.

"I offered to help her with some boxes and she brushed me off! She acted like I was the hired help who had come in through the front door instead of using the kitchen entrance. It was humiliating."

"Yeah, I know the feeling," I say, still stung by how Dave had talked to me. "What's your next move?"

"I don't know. Send her flowers?"

"No, too smarmy. We need her car to break down or something and you happen to stop by and help her."

JayRay turns to me. "You're really going to help me now? You haven't exactly been onboard to this point."

"You're my guy and if you're going to do this, we'll do it right."

"And it's for you and me, babe, you do get that, don't you?"

I shrug then kiss his lower lip and nibble on his chin. "I don't trust anyone, but I hope you won't let me down. If you do, I might have to kill you."

"You won't have to kill me," JayRay assures me, and he cups my buttocks with his hands. "Tell me, how do I reel Iris in, hook, line and sinker?"

"Later. Right now your mission is to make me forget about everything."

He laughs and holds me tight. "Come here, you."

Afterwards, we lie back and JayRay turns to me. "So?" he asks. "What do I do?"

"I'm not sure yet. Don't worry. I'll think of something."

"We don't have much time," JayRay is worried. "We're only here for four days."

"We'll start first thing tomorrow. For now, get your beauty sleep. You're going to need it."

The next morning, I nudge JayRay awake. Usually I ride him hard and wear his cum on me all day but there's work to be done. I've decided that if it takes my buy-in on the Iris gig to keep him with me, then so be it.

"Come on babe, get up and get pretty. Let's head down and see what the old gal is up to."

I pause. "You need to be her friend. Don't hit on her. Talk to her, but mostly listen to her. Ask her about her life. Find out if she is happy or lonely. If she's lonely, you're in. If she's happy, look for her vulnerabilities, make her feel weak and lonely and afraid, and then make her feel better. Make sure she knows that she feels better because of you. Make her feel attractive but be respectful. Don't touch her too much or too soon. Take your cues from her."

"Good thinking. But I'm not sure how to do it in practical terms."

"You'll figure it out as you go." I'm confident. "Rule of thumb: less is more."

"I've never understood what that means."

"It means less is best. Shut the fuck up unless you are sure what you are saying is the right thing. Watch her body language. If her shoulders stiffen even slightly, you're on the wrong path. If she tightens her lips, purses her mouth, it's a bad sign. If she frowns, if she crosses her arms, if she touches her purse, fiddles with her jewelry, if she doesn't make eye contact—"

"Fuck me," JayRay says and he stretches out. "This is too intense."

"You cannot use your usual methods," I insist. "You will drive her away. Let's review what we know about her. She's about sixty—"

JayRay gives a muffled shriek. "She's not sixty! She's fifty-two. I found that out. I don't want to marry my granny, thank you very much."

"And you are twenty-nine. Twenty-three years difference. Hmm, it might be too much for her to buy into."

"I can't make myself older," JayRay says. "Everything's on the net! You can't lie about that shit these days." He pulls out his laptop. "There must be some celebs with that age difference, we have to find them. Look, Cher, Madonna, Mariah Carey, Geena Davis, JLo, and Cameron Diaz. We're golden. What else do you know about her?"

"She's been the Executive Director of the Canadian Trade Show Association for the past ten years."

"She's been around us the whole time. She can't know about you and me, can she?"

"I doubt it. We've been super careful. Don't worry about it. And if she asks, tell her we are friends, and that we look out for each other, that's all. She's a widow, I know that for sure."

"Yeah I know that too. I would be stupid to be going after her if she was married."

"She still wears her wedding rings, she's old-fashioned, tra-ditional. She lives in Mississauga—"

"Yeah, I know that, Comanche Drive, in one of those mega

houses where hopefully I will be installed one day, pulling up in my new Mustang, and strolling into my man castle."

"Getting a bit ahead of yourself here. I can't think of anything else. She may have kids, who knows? These shows mean the world to her, we know that too, and she's extremely particular about how everything is set up, so she's a perfectionist. And JayRay, don't pretend to know anything you don't, like if she asks you to order a bottle of good red wine, tell her you don't know about wines, and ask for her advice. Let her teach you, be guided by her. Let her talk, and let her show you her life. Don't compete. Don't be afraid to be inferior and admiring, but not too admiring. Never admire her possessions. Material possessions aren't important to you. Relationships are. You've watched her work, you admire her work ethic, you worry that she works too hard, but you don't want to express that worry too much or too soon."

"You are stressing me like crazy," JayRay said and he jumped out of bed. "I'm going to take a shower, then let's get this show on the road. I am fucking freaked by all this talking. Usually my smile is all it takes to get me what I want."

"I know but this is a different animal we are after, and we have to adjust our game plan accordingly."

We get dressed, him in his security uniform and me in my white lab coat, white blouse and white trousers, and we walk down to the conference centre, discussing what to do.

"Oh my god," I say and I point. "Look, there she is and she's carrying boxes, go and help her. Don't ask her if you can help, just do it! Go, go, go!"

JayRay rushes through the crowded lobby and intercepts Iris. I watch him say something to her and before she can reply, he takes the boxes from her. Iris looks annoyed and I wonder if she'll grab the boxes back, but she nods sourly at JayRay and marches off with him following at a trot.

I swing behind them as they round a corner and go into an empty conference room. I pretend to be looking through the stash on the freebie table, all the while keeping an eye on what's going on. Iris has thawed slightly and she's letting JayRay help her unpack the boxes. She even manages a reserved smile at something he says. JayRay gives Iris a mock salute and a mile-wide grin and he turns to leave, but he grabs a piece of hotel stationary pad and scribbles something. He grins at Iris and holds out the piece of paper.

Iris doesn't take it and eventually JayRay puts it down on the table. Iris says something and JayRay looks boyish and earnest and he nods. He leaves and I watch Iris pick up the piece of paper and put it in her pocket. I rush to catch up with JayRay.

"What happened? What did you write on the paper?"

JayRay jumps. "Shit, what are you doing, Leo? Fucking gave me a fright. I gave her my number and said I would be happy to lug any boxes or shit that she wants, she just needs to phone me. I also wrote down my stall number and said if she wants any home security equipment, she should stop by, it'll be my pleasure to help her out."

"And?"

"And she thanked me. That's all. She wouldn't even take the note."

"She picked it up after you left," I tell him and he beams.

"We'll have to see what happens," I say. "We can't rush this. Things like this take time. Speaking of time, we must assume our positions at our stalls. Let the games begin. See you later, 'gater."

I open up my stand and see JayRay across the way, getting his table ready. I look around. The quiet before the storm. The opening the previous night was a huge success and we are ready for a bumper day.

The exhibition hall is the same as all the others, an expansive hangar, sectioned into narrow, partitioned-off rows. Standard wire-bristle blue carpeting covers the floor, and the perimeter of the hall is circled by stand-alone partitions divided by black curtains. Warehouse spotlights hang from high steel beams and the world has an unnatural pallor to it. Sometimes I imagine we're on a different planet, or we could be on a space ship, speeding away from our complicated lives on Earth.

I marvel at the expense and detail that some of the vendors go to, to create a stage set. *SuperBeauty* is designed to resemble a high-class dermatologist's office, pristine to the point of sterile but with a good dose of pretty thrown in for good measure. I got Ralph to shell out a few hundred dollars to an artist to do a stunning watercolour illustration of a beautiful woman walking down a Parisian-styled street carrying a bag of *RealBeauty* cosmetics. The poster is enormous and after grumbling for weeks about the unnecessary expense, Ralph soon changed his mind when, in his terms, "it elevated the brand and knocked one out of the park." The booth's fixtures are silver and white; I ditched Ralphie's motifs of daisies and organic herbal health, that sad, tired, old, hippie oatmeal made-in-your-kitchen look. "We want them to know we're serious about skin care and aging," I told Ralphie. "None of that fuzzy save-the-planet shit. We're here to help you reverse the signs of aging. If you don't see a change in an hour, you get your money back. Hard-hitting, tough-love, serious scientific approach. People love shit like that. It tells them they can trust us. We need to take a deep dive with this, no more swimming in the shallow end."

I know Ralphie had his doubts in the beginning but now he loves it. I'm also lucky because Ralphie has booth staffers in all the cities. They bring the exhibit up from the shipping dock to the warehouse and get it all set up for me. They rig the lights, hang the signs, and create my stage. When the show's done, they dismantle the set and ship it to the next location. Sure, I have to unlock the booth and get my daily display organized, but I don't have to do any heavy lifting.

The doors to the hall open and the crowd swarms inside, filling the aisles like a human tsunami and in seconds the noise level rises from quiet to deafening.

I have no shortage of visitors and I'm kept busy, explaining ingredients and skin care routines, and the day flies by. As the evening crowd dwindles, I look up and there's Iris, looking tired and earnest.

"Hey, Iris! How are you?" I'm careful to sound like I always do, cordial but not overly happy to see her.

"I'm fine, Leonie, fine. I do need some more of your creams though. I have to say, they really do make a visible difference. I used Lancôme for years but your line is so much more effective. Any chance of adding more of your secret magic?"

"Sure," I say, thinking I should cut down on the amount of people I tell about the secret ingredient. "But you don't need it, you look great, Iris. How do you manage it all? You run all these shows, you work so hard."

A slight frown crosses Iris's face and I wonder why. "I must be more in need of your cream than I thought," she says with a wry smile. "That young man over there in security told me the same thing today, that I work so hard. I must look tired."

I look up. "You mean JayRay?"

"Yes, James. I prefer to call him James. JayRay sounds like a hip-hop artist and I hate hip-hop." She sits down on a stool next to the table. "My feet are tired today," she admits. "I shouldn't have worn new shoes."

"Can I offer you a mini-facial?" I ask and Iris looks around. "It won't help your feet," I say, "but it will relax you."

"But I don't want to take any business away from you."

"The day is done, people are leaving," I wave around the emptying hall to make my point. "Don't worry. Anyway, it looks good if I'm busy, it will attract more people."

I put a clean towel around her shoulders and apply a facial cleanser, gently massaging her face and Iris relaxes. Her shoulders, usually coat hangers up near her ears, ease, and I know best to remain silent.

I apply toner and moisturizer and Iris inhales deeply. "It smells divine," she sighs, "Like lilacs in the springtime. I love it because it does a great job but it also smells heavenly."

I smile. I'd had a hard time convincing Ralph that he needed to add a subtle fragrance. He naysayed the idea until I got him to test a couple of focus groups and the results were overwhelming. We kept a fragrance-free range as an option but the scented creams were the winners by far. Between that, the new look, and the upward trajectory of the sales, he never questioned me again.

"We have a new line of makeup too," I say. "Can I try some on you?"

"You're spoiling me rotten!" Iris gives a high-pitched nasal girly giggle and I grin, thinking how much JayRay will love that.

"Hot date tonight?" I ask as I brush mascara onto Iris' lashes.

"No, nothing like that. Early to bed, I am worn out."

"You want to get something to eat? I'm going to close up after you, we could have a snack in the hotel bar if you like. I hate eating alone."

A lie but Iris seems to believe me.

"Sure, why not? That would be lovely, thank you, Leonie. Most people give me a wide berth. They worry I'll find fault with their displays."

"I don't know why we haven't had a meal together before," I reply. "I guess we get into a zone and do what we do. We don't think of each other as real people, we're in business mode."

"Very true." Iris admires her reflection in a mirror that I hand her. "Very nice. I'll take a mascara, eyeliner, blush, and foundation. And the day cream, night cream, toner, and cleanser. I'll take one of everything, and all of them with more of the special ingredient, if you don't mind."

"Thank you Iris!" I infuse my voice with delight and I mix up the night cream, adding more octinoxate and mercurous chloride with a tiny plastic spatula. My secret ingredients. I pause for a moment, uncap a tiny vial, and add a micro amount of potassium cyanide. A secret ingredient just for Iris.

I've had the potassium cyanide for years. It has been lying

dormant and quiet on a shelf, but I found myself veering off on my way to the airport and stopping at the locker. I rushed in, grabbed the tiny container, and shoved it into a side pocket in my check-in bag. Yes, I'm ready for Iris. I just hope the cyanide hasn't lost its efficacy.

I put the products into a glossy white *SuperBeauty* bag and tie the top with a silver and white ribbon. I can see JayRay eyeing me, waiting, but I avoid looking in his direction.

I'm worried that my invitation to dinner is too much. All of a sudden me and JayRay are paying particular attention to Iris? Will it seem weirdly coincidental?

I hand the bag over to Iris and close up my stand while Iris waits patiently.

I bend down to straighten a few boxes under the table and when I stand up, JayRay is standing there.

"I was wondering if you ladies would care to join me for a bite to eat?" he asks and I want to laugh. We need to synchronize our plans.

I look at Iris. "Iris and I were going to the pub for a quick bite. Iris, what do you think? Shall we add some security to our party?"

Iris finds this hilarious. "Yes, let's! Hello James, thank you for helping me earlier. Look at this lovely bag of goodies Leonie gave me, I'm going to look ten years younger by tomorrow!"

"You don't need to look a day younger," JayRay insists and Iris gives her high-pitched girly giggle. I'm dismayed to hear her flirting with JayRay already, but I remind myself that it's part of the plan and that I should be happy that things are going well.

I tag along behind them, feeling like an unwanted kid in the playground. We walk through the lobby and Iris suddenly lunges towards me and grabs hold of my arm. "Quickly! That man over there, Mr. Reid, Dips and Delights from Nova Scotia, he loves to talk! He'll have us here for hours! Whatever you do, don't make eye contact with him. Look at me, that's right, we're cannot be disturbed!" She giggles again and I sigh. It's going to be a long night.

The hotel bar is packed but JayRay finds us a booth.

"If I'm honest," Iris confides in us both, "a lot of vendors try to wine and dine me, but I prefer to keep to myself. One doesn't want to become overly familiar. I'm not sure what they hope to achieve, it's not as if I can sway sales or give them better locations in the main hall. That's up to them. And most of them hate my interfering in their displays and what-have-you, but we do have standards to uphold. And it's vitally important that we—"

"A drink, Iris?" JayRay interrupts.

"Yes, thank you, James, I would love a glass of champagne. Did you know that Winston Churchill loved champagne? It was one of his favourite beverages, along with sherry and scotch."

"Champagne for the lady," JayRay tells the waiter and he pauses. "Make it a bottle," he says grandly and Iris giggles.

"Now, now, James, we have a long day tomorrow." But JayRay and I notice that her objections are mild at best.

I give an inward grin, thinking how much both JayRay and I hate champagne.

"I love champagne too," JayRay says earnestly. "It makes me happy. The bubbles, you know."

"Exactly!" Iris was delighted. "The bubbles! So, tell me about both of you. Leonie, tell me about you."

"Not much to tell. I have a degree in chemistry and I help mix the cosmetics—"

"And she does such a stellar job of it. I tell you, James, I used Lancôme for years and it never had any effect on my skin. But after just a week of using *SuperBeauty*, I saw a real difference! All my friends noticed too but I didn't want to tell them what it was, because I didn't want them looking better than me." She giggles again.

The champagne arrives and we raise a glass in a toast.

"To the best show ever," JayRay says and Iris nods.

"B.C. is one of my favourites. I love coming here. The mood is different to Toronto. I love the people here. I mean I love the crowds back home too, but this is lovely for a change. I also love the Halifax crowd. You both work the American circuit too?"

"We do," JayRay nods and looks serious. "We're at a show pretty much twice a month, except for December when there's only one and there are none in April. For some reason, April is awfully quiet."

"What's your favourite American one?" Iris asks as she lays her hand on JayRay's arm and I chug half my champagne.

"Vegas," JayRay replies instantly. "The neon. Bright lights, big city. I love it there. It's wild and free and fun. Do you want something to eat, Iris?" He pours another round of champagne although I notice that he has hardly touched his. I'm unpleasantly reminded of how I got toasted the first night we got together while he hardly touched a drop. Was he playing me then? But to what end?

"Yes, thank you. A nibbly would be lovely."

JayRay raises his hand and the waiter appears. "A round of appetizers," JayRay said and Iris smiles sweetly.

"Tell me about you, James. Funny how often the three of us have worked together and we've never talked. Amazing!"

"I would like to say I have had a happy and easy life," JayRay says and he looks sad. "But I lost my longtime partner to a brain aneurism about a year ago and I still haven't recovered."

I'm sipping my drink when he says that and I snort before I can control myself. Champagne shoots up my nose and I have a small coughing fit but neither Iris nor JayRay notice.

"Oh my word," Iris says, her eyes wide. "How old was she?"

"She was forty-nine. Nearly twenty-five years older than me. I don't mean to sound like a weirdo, but I've always been attracted to older women."

"My word, that is quite a bit older," Iris says and I can see her trying to calculate JayRay's age in her mind.

"I'm twenty-nine," JayRay offers helpfully and Iris sits up straighter and plays with the top button on her blouse.

"I'm sorry about your wife," Iris sounds wistful. "She died so young."

"We weren't married. But we had been together for eight years. A long time."

"A very long time," Iris agrees and the waiter arrives with the food.

"Oh, yummy," Iris says. "I love to eat. People often ask me how I can eat as much as I do, but I've got the metabolism of a racehorse."

She eats a piece of bruschetta with precision and JayRay looks on admiringly. "I always drop half of those on my shirt," he admits sheepishly and Iris smiles.

"And so what if you do? Eat up, both of you. James, I am, in fact, thinking of installing some more security in my house. I might give you a call when we are back home."

"With pleasure," JayRay says, "I am sure I'll have everything you'll need. Do you have family in Toronto, Iris?"

Iris wrinkles her nose as if something unpleasant wafted by. "I do," she replies shortly. "But I don't like them. They're from my husband's side and they want the money. They think they can fool me but they can't."

"Oh, you're married, of course," JayRay indicates her rings.

"Widowed," Iris says and JayRay nods sympathetically.

"I was his second wife and I was young when we got married. He too was much older than me. I was his secretary, back in the day when secretaries were powerful and important. I attended to his needs and when his first wife died, we became close. It was quite the scandal in those days. I was only twenty-seven and he was fifty-five. People thought I was after his money but I wasn't, I was in love with him."

"I know what you mean," JayRay said sagely. "Elinor was also rich and her family hated me. But I didn't care what they thought."

"Exactly!" Iris finishes the bruschetta and moves on to the olives and crackers. She chugs champagne and while I know that this is going better than either of us could have hoped, I'm bored out of my skull and I can't wait for the night to end. I try to meet JayRay's eye but he's in the zone, leaning into Iris and nodding.

"They wanted to have the will contested," Iris is indignant. "After he died. We had been married for over twenty years! How ridiculous is that?"

"Ridiculous," JayRay agrees.

"But it was thrown out of court. Is there more champagne?"

"As much as you like." JayRay tops up her glass. "How long ago did he die?"

"Two years ago now. He liked me doing these shows. 'Iris,' he always said, 'you have to have a passion in life.' I miss him. We had such fun together. He came to the shows because he had retired by then and we'd stay on and I'd drive him around to see the sights. We loved going sailing too. He was a sports lover. Golf, sailing, fishing, cycling. It was a terrible shock when he died. He seemed so strong, I thought he would live forever."

She seems to be sinking into a dark mood and JayRay takes her hand. "It's harder than people know," he says, and his voice is low and meaningful. "The loneliness is brutal. We have to be brave, Iris. But we can find comfort in friends and work."

Iris perks up. "You are very right, James. I apologize. I nearly ruined our lovely little party. Thank you!"

The appetizers are gone and she drains her glass. The bottle is empty. "That's it for me. Time to hit the hay and get ready for tomorrow."

JayRay signals for the bill and he signs it to his room with a flourish. "My treat."

"Maybe we can do this again tomorrow night," Iris says and JayRay beams.

"I'd love that," he replies and I mumble something and nod my head.

"Terrific!"

We walk across the empty lobby.

"I love it when it's like this," Iris says dreamily. "Everything is quiet, everybody has gone to bed. The world is waiting in the wings for the play to begin and when it does begin, there is nonstop action and it's all hustle and bustle!"

"Iris, you should be a writer," JayRay says admiringly as he holds the elevator door open for her. "That was beautiful."

"Why thank you James! I am going to write my memoirs one day. I've had rather an interesting life. Here is my floor, nighty-night to both of you. See you tomorrow!"

"Night, night!" JayRay calls after her and when the doors close, he turns and beams at me.

"Talk about a hole in one!" he says, and he gives several fist-pumps. "What do you think? We're in!"

"We're in all right," I say and my eyes fill with tears. "We're in."

"Oh baby, don't be like that. It's business. Come on, let daddy make you feel better."

But I shrug him off. "You should stay in your room tonight. You never know. Iris might get frightened by a spider and call you."

"She doesn't know what room I am in," JayRay says but I shake my head.

"Sure she does. She knows everything about the vendors."

"Are you sure you aren't upset with me?"

"I hate this, JayRay but I need to come to terms with it. And anyway, I need to answer my kids' emails properly and act like a good mom to them. See you tomorrow."

"Hey, Leo, I love you baby, you know that, right?"

"Yeah, I do. I do." I let myself into my room and close the door, leaving him standing in the hallway.

I lock my door and sink down onto the carpet and draw my knees up to my chest. I want to cry, sob my heart out, but I'm too drained to do even that.

18.

IRIS DOES NOT FIND A REASON to call JayRay to her room. Not that night anyway.

The next morning she's beaming positivity from every pore. I notice that she finds reasons to saunter past JayRay's stand more than a few times, and she stops to chat with him. There's a bounce to her step and she looks wired and perky.

I want to throw up. It's bad enough that this is happening but to have to watch it is nearly intolerable. By mid-afternoon, I'm ready to run.

"Dinner and drinkie-poo's later?" I look up and see Iris standing at my table, her hands clutched in a prayer pose, a schoolgirl grin on her face.

"I don't feel that great," I say and it's true. I'm sweating and shaking and I know it's a reaction to what's happening but that doesn't help. "Why don't you and JayRay go? I know he'd love that."

"Oh! Do you think he would? Poor dear, you don't look good."

"I'm sure he'd love it. I must have a bit of a tummy bug, don't worry."

"Okey dokey! Toodle-loo! Oh, p.s., how are your sales going?"

"Great, everything's great!"

"Fantabulous! See you later, Leonie."

Iris trots off and I notice that her skirt is several inches shorter than the previous day's version and her heels are two inches higher. I also notice, with no small dismay, that Iris has some great gams on her. And her ass isn't bad either. I wonder if the bitch works out. She must. And look at her now, taking off her faux-Chanel jacket and showing off those toned arms. She's chatting to JayRay and her hip is cocked to one side and JayRay is liking what he sees and who knows, maybe the jacket isn't faux anything but the real deal.

"Hello? Excuse me?" A woman waves a brochure at me, wanting to know about *SuperBeauty* and I force myself to concentrate. If my numbers drop, Ralph won't think twice about taking me off the shows and giving my slot to that twat Sandra who's dying to prove herself. Ralph would put me on desk duty or send me down to check on the lab, shit like that. I have to deliver so I can be around to see how this plays out. No way am I letting JayRay out of my sight.

I sell my little ass off and the woman summons her friends who are texting and instagramming at Starbucks and I sell them each a sales kit and enough product to last a lifetime. It's one of my best days ever.

When closing time rolls around, I'm exhausted. I pack up and I'm about to leave when JayRay appears in front of me. "Leo, you okay?"

"No, I'm not. This is killing me."

"Oh, puddytat. How can I tell you how much you mean to me?"

"You can't. There isn't anything you can say. I'm sick from this, literally sick. I'm sweating like a pig. I've got a fever but I'm ice cold. I'm sick as a dog. I can't do this."

"You have to. For us. Come on, baby, come on." He pauses. "I'll come by later if I can."

"No, you need to be available for her. I'll be okay. I'll cope."

JayRay looks worried but I wave him off. "Go, leave, go. Iris will be waiting. Go on. Do us proud."

He leaves and I double over. My stomach is laced with violent, sharp, shooting pains and sweat pours down my temples. My shirt is drenched. I try to straighten up but it hurts too much and I lie down on the floor. Worried that someone will see me, I crawl under the table and curl up in a little ball, hidden by the long tablecloth, with my head resting on my purse.

I fall asleep and when I wake up, I have no idea where I am. I lie still, trying to remember what had happened. Oh right, I am under the table. I crawl out and lean against the wall of my booth, taking shallow breaths and testing my stomach with tentative fingertips. I feel better. I can breathe and the river of sweat has stopped. I reach for my phone and check the time; it's after midnight.

I wonder how JayRay is doing with Iris. It's all champagne and giggles no doubt. I stand up and clutch the table for support. The hall is eerily quiet, with drapes covering the stands. It's eerie being the only person in the cavernous place. I hope the main doors aren't locked but they open easily when I try them. I give a sigh of relief. But then I stop. Wait. Think. Not a security guard in sight.

I stop because I am overwhelmed by my shameful need. I can't leave without taking something. I need to scratch this vicious itch until it bleeds. My need is as strong as a fist in my throat and there's only one way to achieve release. But what can I take? We operate on trust, all the vendors do. We lock up our valuables, but we leave the rest out. I can't betray that code. But my need is stronger than honour. I'm standing next to Mr. Reid's stall, the guy from Nova Scotia. I lift the cloth covering the table and there's his array of tester jams and dips. I glance around. There aren't any cameras that I can see. I open my purse and throw the jars into it. I take every last one of them, and then I ease my way out the main door.

Still no security guard in sight. I creep into the lobby and approach the desk clerk, startling her. "Any messages? I've been out all night. Room 494."

The desk clerk checks and shakes her head. "Nope, nothing. But they could have left a message on your phone. Let me know if you can't retrieve them, I'll walk you through it."

"Thank you! Penelope? Penelope. I'll call you if there's anything. I'm Leonie by the way. Great pubs in this town! Hey, what's the time?"

"Nearly half past midnight."

"Thanks a bunch!" I sound like Iris and I grin and stroll off to the elevators.

I fumble with the keycard; my hands are shaking. When I get in to the room, I grab a teaspoon from the complimentary coffee set and I sit on the floor. I empty the jams out of my purse. Four jars of jam and three kinds of dip. I open them and I can't eat fast enough and I curse JayRay as I shovel the shit into my mouth: *look what you made me do, look. Look.*

I lean against the wall when I am finished. My hands and face are sticky. My stomach is distended and painful and there are food stains on my uniform blouse.

The food rises in a lump and I scramble to my feet and run to the washroom. The jams and dips shoot out of my mouth in a single projectile of rainbow vomit.

I push myself away from the toilet and sit on the bathtub. I want to cry. This is so bad. I lost control. What if there were cameras? What if someone saw me? And what will I do with the empty jars? What if they search our rooms and find them? There would be no limit to the humiliation.

I don't know what to do. But I pull myself together. I can't lose everything over this. I won't. I take my clothes off and put them into a laundry bag and shove it into my suitcase. I take the jam and dip jars and put them into a trashbag and I put that in my luggage too and I lock it for good measure. Fortunately I travel with two uniforms or I'd be in real trouble.

I have a shower and take a sleeping pill. I need to rest. I have to sleep. There's too much at stake.

19.

THE NEXT MORNING, I am resolute. I dress and go down to breakfast. Along with grabbing the potassium cyanide from my storage locker, I pocketed a vial of tranquillizers and I dissolve one under my tongue as the elevator descends. I find a table and in no time at all, I'm feeling quite pleasantly numb.

I look up to see JayRay and Iris coming into the dining room together and I am so calm. I even give them a little wave. Which is a mistake because Iris comes trotting over, with JayRay in tow.

"Hello, hello!" Iris is ebullient. "And how are you feeling today, my dear?"

"Fine, why?" I'm immediately on edge, thinking that Iris knows about my jam thievery.

"You had a stomach bug yesterday," Iris reminds me. "You looked terrible. You do look better today. I'll go and get us coffee, James. Do you want anything to eat?"

"Yeah, but I'll get it."

"No, let me. What do you want?"

"Everything!" JayRay winks at her. "Eggs, bacon, waffles, a muffin, toast, everything."

Iris trots off and I look at JayRay. "Worked up an appetite, did you?"

"Yeah." He has the grace to blush.

"How was it?"

"Ah, Leo, hon, don't do this. She's kinda sweet, really."

"Sweet. Good. Fine." I push my plate away. I assume the

crushing hurt will come later when I'm not as medicated. But in a way, now that the worst is over, I feel relief. He slept with Iris and it didn't kill me. I'm still alive. Which is remarkable.

I'm still contemplating my fortitude when Iris returns with plates of food for JayRay and he falls on them, devouring the spread with greed and happiness.

"Today is our last day here," Iris says, as if I don't already know. "How I wish this conference was longer. Oh dear, there's Mr. Reid and he's heading straight for us. I may not be able to duck out of this one. Hello Mr. Reid and how are you today?"

"Someone stole my samples!" Mr. Reid is close to hysterical. "The only thing I didn't lock up and they were taken. Who would take my jams? They were nearly full. And the dips? It's the principle of the thing. What kind of gig are you running here anyway? What are you going to do about this?"

"We're going to see security immediately," Iris says. "Don't you worry, Mr. Reid, we'll get to the bottom of this." She looks perplexed. "This is the first time in ten years that anything like this has happened. I must say, this conference certainly is throwing some surprises."

"It's unacceptable," we hear Mr. Reid say loudly as they walk away. "I won't have this. I'll have you removed from your post for this, Iris Papadopoulos."

They move out of earshot and we don't hear her reply.

"Was that you, Leo?" JayRay asks quietly, shoveling eggs and waffles into his mouth.

I nod. My head feels like it's moving in slow motion and I carry on nodding because something about it feels reassuring. JayRay doesn't say anything; he carries on eating. When he finishes, he pushes his plate away, wipes his mouth, and throws his napkin on the table. He downs the remains of his coffee and gives a loud burp.

"You stupid fucking cow," he says. "Stay the fuck away from me. Don't poison me with your crap, do you hear me?

I've got a real chance with this. If you fuck this up for me, I will fucking kill you."

"I'll tell her you're playing her," I burst out and JayRay looks at me.

"Yeah? You will? And she'll believe you? I'll say you're so crazy in love with me, you'll say anything. You're mad with jealousy. She'll believe it. I'll get you banned from the Canadian shows and Ralph will boot your ass out the door. Now, what were you going to say again?"

"Nothing," I whisper. "I'm sorry. What if they find out it was me who took the jams?"

"What the fuck where you thinking?"

"I wasn't, you know that." And he does know. I've told him everything about my past and he never judged me. Not until today when it affected him directly.

I tell him how I tried to alibi myself with the desk clerk and he shakes his head. "It would have been better to not say anything. Instead, you drew attention to yourself. I'll let you know if Iris tells me anything. But I'll text you. I don't want to be seen talking to you."

I nod and he leaves.

I dig into my purse and find the bottle of pills. I dissolve another tranquilizer under my tongue. I'm going to need more of these. I'll find a therapist and get a prescription from my doctor. No more fucking about. There is only one solution to this. I have to get over JayRay. I'm an addict and he is my drug and I need to get him out of my system, cold turkey, detox. I can do it. I had been leery of him from the start, but I fell for his charms and it nearly cost my family and my job. I can't let him ruin anything else. Iris is welcome to him. I'll deal with the jam situation. If they find out it was me, I'll say I was delirious with a fever and Iris will attest that I wasn't feeling well. I wait until the pill calms me down and I walk slowly to the conference hall, ready to face the rest of my day.

20.

"I STEAL THINGS," I TELL MY FAMILY DOCTOR. "I can't help it." I describe the jam episode. "I couldn't stop myself. I was lucky they never found out it was me. Their cameras weren't working. I would have been fired. I need you to help me. I'm losing control of my life. I had to take Xanax to get through the whole thing and now, here I am. And I need more Xanax."

My doctor doesn't look at me while I speak. She scribbles on her notepad, scribbles until I want to scream: *Look at me, me, I am here, I'm the one with issues not the fucking notepad.* But I hold my anger in check and pick at my nails instead.

"My relationships with my children and husband are strained, maybe broken. I'm full of pain and fury all the time."

The doctor finally stops writing and she looks at me. "I gave you a list of therapists the last time you were here. Did you get in touch with any of them? I'll give a prescription to alleviate the anxiety, but you need to see someone and the sooner the better."

"I didn't have the time to find a therapist yet. But I will, as soon as I get home. I need more Xanax. No anti-depressants. That shit fries your brain and I'm a scientist, I know the facts behind the advertising crap. And I'd love something to help me sleep too, some zopiclone, that's the least harmful. I can't sleep at all. I get like maybe like two hours a night."

"Difficulty falling asleep or staying asleep?"

"Both."

"You're wrong about anti-depressants but I'll leave it up to you. And I believe you can handle a lot more than you think, you're just struggling right now."

The doctor's vote of confidence cheers me. As do the prescriptions for Xanax and the sleeping meds. And then there's the happy fact that the next conference is in Los Angeles and I won't have to see JayRay with Iris.

I haven't spoken to him or texted him or heard from him since he left the breakfast table. He and Iris were everywhere and their happiness radiated like a fucking lighthouse on a stormy night.

When I got home, I was momentarily comforted by the noise and chaos of family life and the girls appeared to have forgiven me for the Muffin episode. Despite our great-sex sendoff, Dave was cautiously welcoming but he was definitely holding back until I took some action.

I get home from the doctor and I look up the therapists online. I like the look of Dr. Gerstein and, bonus, she works from home, not even ten minutes from our house. I phone and make an appointment and I tell Dave as soon as he comes home. That news wipes the Miss Priss pinch off his face and I feel rewarded by the warmth of his approval. Then I think back to my father and I hate myself for needing approval at all, and for responding to it, like a good little doggie.

"I need to talk about my childhood," I tell Dave, wanting to get his opinion, if not his approval. "I need to talk about my father. I'm stuck in the past."

"I agree. You've got a lot of anger about how he treated you. But your mother hurt you too, by not standing up for you. You're angry about her too and yet you never acknowledge that."

Of course I can't tell Dave the truth about why my mother hates me. I wonder if she's still alive, up there in Coldwater. I assume someone would tell me if she died. Or maybe not. Whatever, I can't think about that right now. I fall into gloom.

"I'm not angry," I object. "I'm sad. And maybe there's too much to fix. Maybe I can't be fixed."

"Honey, you're not that broken. Trust me, you can be fixed. I want you to be happy, that's all. I want us to be happy and we can be."

I'm exhausted. "I'm going to take a nap. I need a rest from all of this."

I lie down on the big sleigh bed and fall asleep. I wake feeling better, stronger. I go downstairs and sit down at the kitchen table with the girls.

"Mommy's going to help you with your homework. How about science? Mommy's a science whiz, you can ask me anything."

"Anything?" Maddie looks at Kenzie and grins.

"Anything," I reply and for a moment my heart is happy and I catch Dave's eye and we both smile.

21.

WE'RE IN LOS ANGELES, at the Craft, Hobby, and Security Show. JayRay's there with his usual mile-wide grin. And he's there with Iris. Iris, who is giggling with happiness and hanging onto JayRay's arm.

"You were the matchmaker," Iris bubbles and giggles her thanks to me at the same time. "I never thought I would be this happy again. If you hadn't invited James to dinner that night, I would never have ended up with him. He is very grateful to you too."

I am sure he is. I dissolve another tranquilizer under my tongue and try to smile. I'm feeling all kinds of discombobulated, and it isn't just JayRay; it's the feelings that Gerstein the therapist has unearthed. The muddy bedrock of my life has been unpleasantly stirred up and the murky waters are clouded and threatening.

"I couldn't be happier for you," I say distantly to Iris and she beams.

"It was his idea I come along to this show. I've never been to any of the U.S. shows. I know, I should have but I stuck to my job of overseeing the Canadian ones. This is such fun! To be a visitor at a show! And afterwards, James and I are going to Long Beach and then he has another show. How you people do it, I have no idea! Busy, busy, busy! I might stay home for that one. You know," she lowers her voice to a whisper, "James has moved in with me. I know it's rather sudden but when love hits, it hits, and the heart knows what the heart wants. I am having a gym built for him, as a surprise. He is so athletic and he hasn't had much gym time since we got together and he's moved all the way out to Mississauga for me. I know his apartment was much more central, being downtown, but he says he can't bear to be away from me."

I try to imagine JayRay in a gym, hopelessly unsure how to use any of the equipment except perhaps the stationary bike. My tranqs protect me like a hazmat suit and although I can hear Iris, what she's saying doesn't penetrate.

"He's a kind and generous man," I articulate carefully. "He cares about people. He's a real people person."

"He is that. Listen, Leonie, I need two more jars of the nighttime cream. I have been using more than usual, wanting to look my best for him. Can you mix me up a new batch?"

"Of course," I assure her. "I'll do that right away."

"I'll come back later and pick it up. I'll skedaddle now. You've got people waiting for you."

I look up. It's true. Good thing I have my spiel on autopilot. I move over to the lineup and begin my pitch. I sell a bunch of starter home kits and look at my watch. Only two hours have passed and my numbers are good enough that I can leave and go back to the hotel and sleep off the rest of the meds but then I remember Iris's cream.

I look up at JayRay across the way, he's talking and grinning and selling like a madman and I hate him with all my might. I notice that he is deliberately not looking in my direction. I reach under the table for my bag of secret ingredients and I mix up Iris's cream, trying to steady my shaking hands.

The shakes must be a side effect of the meds and I'll happily take them over feeling the pain of JayRay's betrayal. I'm not sure if it's my unreliable hands or my hatred for Iris that makes me add a little too much mercurous chloride to her jar but I don't care one way or the other. Iris is going to get what's coming to her. I try to remember the side effects from too much mercurous chloride penetrating the skin and I recall something about nausea, vomiting, diarrhea, and dehydration.

I pause and then I add a micro amount of potassium cyanide. A tiny bit more than the last time. *If you want to look good for your man, you have to do what it takes. At least then, when you're throwing up your intestines, your skin will look as pure and smooth as a baby's bottom.* I smile at the thought and package up Iris's products, tying the bag with a large bow.

True to his word, JayRay hasn't been in contact with me once. Not a text. Nothing. And I, in retaliation, have not sent him one message either. If he wanted our relationship cut off, then cut off it is.

I think about what Gerstein the therapist said. Her theory, after listening to my version of my childhood, is that I'm still trying to fill the void that my father's cruelty left in my life. Which sounded like a crock of shit to me, a real textbook cliché. What I hadn't told the therapist was how my father had ultimately shamed me. I never told anyone what happened, not even Dave or JayRay.

My father. A beautiful man. Tall, like a Grecian god, with dark curly hair and a distant look in his eye. An inventor with fine hands and long fingers. None of his inventions ever came to anything, but he was from old money, so it didn't matter. He spent his days secreted up in a cabin in the woods, endlessly working on a prototype for something or other that would change the world. We lived just outside of Coldwater, Ontario, a village that was hardly more than a hamlet, and my father financed his endeavours by selling off parcels of the once-extensive family farm to greedy subdivision developers.

My mother was an aspiring figure-skater but she blew out her knee with one catastrophic landing that shattered all her dreams. I have memories of my mother lulling me to sleep with tales of how my father loved watching her glide and swirl. And, when she fell, he was the first to rush onto the ice and hold her hand while she waited for the stretcher to carry her off, never to return.

My father was rich, good-looking, aristocratic, clever, and aloof. All of which made you think he was worth so much more than he was. He was also unloving, disinterested, and cruel.

I craved my father's attention to the point of obsession. I sat outside his cabin, a couple of feet away from the front door. I'd read or do my homework, or wait for him to come out and show me the slightest bit of attention. Of course, I was never allowed to knock on the door, or go inside.

And one day, while I was waiting for him, I needed to go to the toilet. Not a number one. A number two. I needed to go badly and I knew I wouldn't make it back to the house. The spasms came out of nowhere and my stomach needed instant relief. I didn't even have time to rush back into the woods; I simply had to go right where I was. I ripped down my panties and squatted and my stomach relieved itself in a hot fluid rush.

And then I was stuck there, squatting, unsure what to do. I was eleven, such a vulnerable age. It strikes me in a flash, that's the same age Kenzie is now. Had Kenzie's eleventh birthday triggered my current emotionally wrecked state? No, it has nothing to do with her and everything to do with JayRay.

I force myself to continue thinking about that event. There I was, squatting, terrified my father would come out and find me before I got myself cleaned up. I had no idea what to clean up with. I gathered a leaf and tried to wipe the mess with it but I only succeeded in smearing the shit further. I grabbed my panties and tried to clean myself with those and that was how my father found me, covered in excrement and rubbing at my legs with my soiled panties, stinking and shamed.

He opened the door to his cabin and looked out at me. It was the first time he had looked at me in years. He stretched and cracked his back. He straightened up slowly and walked towards me. I was frozen and I watched him walk towards me and neither of us said a word. I couldn't move from my crouched position and he stood over me for what seemed like forever.

Then he turned and walked back to his cabin and he shut the door.

I rose to my feet, my legs aching with squatting and I ran back to the house, still holding my panties in my hand.

My mother was ironing and she rushed over when she saw the state I was in. "What happened? Are you all right?"

"My stomach," I said and I started to cry. "I had an accident."

My mother soothed me and ran a bath for me and helped me clean up, but later that night, I could not sit at the dinner table with my father. I blamed my stomach again, saying I had to lie down. I had no idea how I would ever face my father again.

I heard my mother urging him to check on me and he mumbled an impatient reply. I lay as still as I could, listening for his footsteps reluctantly climbing the stairs. When he finally stood over me, I pretended to be asleep and I hoped he would leave but he didn't. "Such a dirty little girl," he finally said and he left.

I cried after he left, and I hated him. I never went near the cabin after that and I was polite to him but that was all. I told myself I would have my revenge, I didn't care how long it would take, but I would have the final word. And, I did.

When I am with JayRay, that dirty little girl doesn't exist. I feel clean with him, understood. I had been waiting for Dave to discover I was unworthy and now he has. But until the jam episode, I never had to worry that dirty little Leonie would humiliate me in front of JayRay.

Now I am that shamed and unloved girl again. I look over at JayRay and I hate him through the soggy numbness of my medicated self. I know that I will have my revenge with him too. It's simply a matter of time.

I have to stop taking so many tranqs. They're interfering with my brain and I can't trust myself. Not that I can trust myself at the best of times, but I feel even less in control than usual. I make a vow. I will not steal and I will not break down about JayRay in front of the whole roadshow, but I do need to get myself back. This anaesthetized state is worse than anything.

"I'm back!" Iris pops up and I hand her the big shiny bag.

"Thank you, my dear. Would you like to join James and I for dinner tonight?"

"Sorry, I've made other plans," I say and I smile. "But maybe another time."

"Perhaps the next show? I plan on accompanying James to all the shows! He says he can't bear to be away from me for such a long time. Isn't that the sweetest thing?"

"Very sweet." I make a note to change stalls. There's no way I can stand watching JayRay for days on end, aching to touch him, missing him with every molecule of my being. I remind myself that he's just an addiction, and that all addictions can be conquered and managed. I will be kind to myself, protect myself, and see myself to the finish line of managing to live happily without him.

"Well then, toodle-loo," Iris waves her fingers. "See you soon, sweetie."

I wave back and start closing up my display. We're moving to Long Beach the next day and as soon as I finish packing, I exchange stall numbers with a woman an aisle down who sells handmade animal-shaped fluffy slippers.

"But yours is a prime spot," the woman is confused, "on the main aisle. Are you sure?"

"Absolutely," I say, hoping that my numbers won't drop and Ralph won't fire me. "I like this spot of yours. I'm desperate for a change of scenery, you know how that goes." The woman agrees that she does. We exchange paperwork and it is done.

When we get to Long Beach, I know I made the right decision. It's a relief not seeing JayRay and my new neighbours are friendly. I don't even have to take any meds.

I am startled, at the end of the day, to look up and see JayRay standing at my table. He looks forlorn and beautiful and I want to welcome him and tell him how much I missed him and that I still love him but I don't.

"Look what the cat dragged in," I say instead and his shoulders droop even further.

"I miss you. Why did you move? I liked you where I could see you."

"That's exactly why I moved." I had resolved not to say anything about Iris but I can't help myself. "Your love life is moving along swimmingly. Congratulations."

He brightens. "Oh Leo, she's really nice. She's kind and funny and considerate and energetic and all the things I need her to be."

"And rich and generous and giving," I add and JayRay grins.

"Yeah, that too. How are you doing?"

As if you care, I want to say. "Fine," I am short with him. "Good."

I start to fill in my sales sheet and JayRay clears his throat. "I'll let you go. See you later. Take care, Leo." He walks away.

Two fat tears fall down onto my paperwork and I blot them up. I force myself to concentrate. My numbers are fine. I have two more days left to go. I can fucking do this.

22

I LIVED THROUGH LONG BEACH. I lived through Seattle and Philadelphia. The months passed and the seasons began to change and it never got easier, seeing JayRay and Iris bounding around like teenagers in love, holding hands, *holding fucking hands!* and frolicking like they just finished making out in the back of a Cadillac with the top down.

Iris seemed in good health whenever I saw her. She must have had the constitution of an elephant or my doses weren't high enough. She had mentioned her high metabolism and I wondered if that had anything to do with it.

Back home, I dutifully attend therapy sessions. I have sex with Dave. I am enthusiastic at the kids' after-school activities and I do their homework with them. I walk Muffin, I buy the kids an aquarium, and we have fun. We go to the movies and on shopping trips to the mall and I even take up gardening and get the unruly mess in our backyard under control. And all the while I feel as if my heart has been cut out with a pair of shears and there's a big black hole where it used to be. But Dave and the kids seem happier and JayRay is lost to me, and there is nothing else I can do.

One day we go for a bike ride on the trail along the edge of the muddy Don River. It's early spring, with a clear, high blue sky. The sun is shining and it is unseasonably warm.

"Just a short ride," I say to the girls as Dave loads the bikes into the car. "Parts of the ground will still be frozen, we must be careful of patches of ice."

"I'll ride ahead and check," Dave says. "We'll take it easy."

The girls are overjoyed at the prospect of a ride to the Bloor Viaduct where we can watch the subway trains clacking back and forth behind the enormous steel girders, with the city skyline behind.

The river still has chunks of ice from a recent storm and there are patches of snow in the shady parts of the adjoining marshy fields. We can hear the traffic from the highway as we pedal along, with leafless brown trees lining the way. We are gloved and hatted up and, with the sunshine on my face, I feel the glimmer of something that might be close to happiness.

But a tiny field mouse springs out in front of me, directly in the path of my wheel and there is nothing I can do to avoid it. I hear an awful pop as its little skull blasts open. I am riding at the back and I don't want to tell the girls or Dave about the horrible thing that has just happened, but I slow down and look behind me. Yes, there is the tiny corpse.

Yet again, life reaches out and slaps me in the face. You think you can be happy, Leonie? Think again. But was I the one crushing my potential happiness, just like I killed that hapless mouse? Or was I the mouse, with an inevitable fate and a bad sense of timing? I tell myself that the mouse isn't my fault. I didn't have time to swerve. It ran directly under my wheel. I feel sick as I pedal to catch up to the girls and Dave and I try to focus on their happy chatter.

* * *

"Do you think we can learn to be happy with ourselves? I mean be content with our own selves and not need anybody else?" I ask Gerstein the therapist. "By the way, I'm getting tired of these sessions. I don't think they're helping at all." I get up and walk the length of the room. Gerstein's office is a converted granny cottage behind the house, a cosy, low-beamed place, vaguely reminiscent of a hunting lodge. Both the main house and the cottage look polished and well-maintained, Restoration Hardware all the way, whereas ours continues to sag like a defeated circus tent left out in the rain. I sit down again and rub my sleeve on the edge of Gerstein's immaculate sofa and wonder how long it would take Muffin to destroy it.

"We aren't supposed to not need anybody. We are humans. We need other people. But not at the expense of ourselves. It's not unusual that you want and crave affection and acknowledgement. We all want that. From our parents, our peers, our family. We want to feel needed and included. But we also need to realize that other people are their own islands too. They have their own scripts running through their heads, things we can't even imagine. Therefore, most of the assumptions we make about what they are thinking and feeling about us are inaccurate. But we base our happiness and self-esteem and moods on those very things."

I looked out the window. "My parents didn't care about me either. You'd think I would be used to it."

"You judge yourself harshly," Gerstein observes. "You are who you are, you have the needs you have. Why question them? Ask yourself if what you need is positive, and is it something you can control? These are pertinent questions, but don't judge yourself for needing what you need."

I don't agree with Gerstein. "I want to change my needs. I want to be able to control my them. That's why I'm here."

"And you can change them, to a degree. But maybe we over-estimate the happiness levels we feel we are 'owed' in this life."

"I need to lower my expectations?"

"Perhaps first ask yourself what they are. What do you want from life?"

To live with JayRay forever, amen. "Um, I don't know. To make my family happy, to be a good wife to Dave, to work hard and make a lot of money."

"Making your family happy, that would make you happy?"

"It would make me feel like a good person and feeling like a good person would make me feel happy."

"I'm not sure happiness is a consequence of something like that. Like you can say, *I'll feel happy when I pass this exam* and you are, for a bit, but then that happiness goes away. We're looking for something deeper here. Something where, if you fail your family and you fail your husband and you fail your job, you can still feel happy."

I give a sharp bark of laughter. "You're living in la-la land, doc. And I would rather make other people happy and be miserable myself than be happy myself and make others miserable."

"One does not necessarily come at the cost of the other."

"Not necessarily, but usually it does. That's life." I reach for my purse and stand up. "Thanks doc. I'm not being sarcastic. I'll try to think about what would make me happy. Maybe I don't feel things the way other people do."

"You might be surprised by how many people think and say exactly that. See you when you get back. Where is it this time?"

"Orlando. I like being by myself. There's something that makes me happy. I like being in the airport alone. I like being on the plane alone. I like being in my hotel room alone."

"Then enjoy that and don't hate yourself for being happy in those moments," Gerstein says and she holds the door open for me. "It's all much more complicated and much more simple than we think."

I nod and walk out into her neat and tidy garden, feeling more miserable than I had when I arrived. I always feel worse when I leave. I told Dave that and he said it meant that progress was being made. He says things are being shaken up and that's good.

Easy for him to say.

23.

"**O**OOOH!" IT HAS TO BE IRIS, that squeal. I look up. Yes, it's Iris. "Look!" She flashes an enormous diamond ring under my nose.

"Whoa, JayRay went all out," I manage to sputter.

Iris blushes. "Yes, he did."

How does it feel to have to buy your own ring? I think, still holding Iris's bony little hand. *Tiny bird hand, like a sparrow. Iris the sparrow.*

"When's the big day?" I ask.

"We're already married," Iris says breezily and I might die right then.

"Oh?" I manage.

"Yes. It was a civil ceremony and James looked very handsome. Like a movie star. Look." She scrolls through the pictures on her phone. Yes, indeedy, James looked like a dream. My dream guy, beaming at his blushing bride while she gazes up at him adoringly.

"Were your family there?" I ask, sitting down on my high stool and leaning on the table, glad that it's a solid support. I scrabble to find a tranq in my purse under the table, and I swallow it dry. "Bad headache," I say as Iris looks concerned.

"Sorry to hear that, my dear." Iris shakes her head. "I don't have any family to speak of. But now I have James. He's all the family I need."

"Did you have a honeymoon?"

"Not yet. But we're going on a cruise when this show ends, to the Caribbean. James has been working so hard, he deserves a rest."

A rest. You certainly got what you wanted here, JayRay. Motherfucker.

"Congratulations," I force a smile. I wish I could lie down on the floor and never get up.

"Thank you, my dear! I must dash, I want to get some shopping done before James and I meet up for dinner. Toodle-loo! Have a great show!"

I watch Iris flutter off, waving hellos this way and that, flashing her enormous ring and beaming.

Gerstein the therapist had suggested I write a journal, to check in with my moods every so often in the day. Gerstein said I might surprise myself by being happier than I thought I was. So much for that.

How do I feel? Crappy. Let me count the ways. Shitty, fucked, gutted. Sad, angry, want to punch something, hit something, hate something, hate people, hate the world, hate the universe, fuck everybody, hate everybody, hate, hate, hate. I've always hated the show in Orlando and now I hate it more than ever.

I'm worried I will lose my shit in front of everyone so I take another pill.

I have to kill Iris. She should be dead by now but the bitch clearly needs a higher dose. I'll make up a gift basket, a wedding gift, with enough poison to kill a town. The thought cheers me up. I want that the skinny old bitch six feet under.

But wait. Has Iris written JayRay into her will? Has she bequeathed everything to him? Is he going to end up with millions? Because if that's the case, that fucker JayRay needs to die too. There's no way he's going to come out of this all roses and sunshine with money to burn. I will kill both of them. But what if there's a chance JayRay will come back to me? But he's shown no sign of even acknowledging my presence. It's over. So they both have to die. It's the only way I'll be able to live.

"Leonie, are you all right?" It's my neighbour, Sandi, purveyor of chakra remedies and cosmic laxatives, guaranteed to flush the bejesus out of your colon for goddamned good.

"Wha...?" I realize I can hardly form the words. I'm slurring badly. "Uh..." I can't seem to form the words, "bad ... migraine, took too many meds."

"Yeah, Leonie, I think you did. Look, it's nearly closing time. I'll take care of your stall. We've been neighbours for two shows now, so don't think I've been stalking you but I know the ropes. You go to your room, okay? Don't worry about anything, just make it to your room, okay?"

"Yeah. Shanks, Shandi. I owe you."

"Not a problem. Here's your purse. Here, I'm going to loop the strap around your neck. Where's your hotel key?"

I dig into my bag until I find it. "Here."

"Good, okay off you go. If you wake up later and want to catch up with me, I'm in Room 508. Wait, I'll write it on your hand."

She scribbles the room number on my hand and waves the security guard over. "My friend here isn't feeling too good. Will you see her up to her room?"

The security guard nods and he grips me by the elbow. "Sure thing. C'mon, ma'am."

I lean against him and he guides me through the conference hall, across the lobby, into the elevator and up to my room. He takes the key card from me when I can't manage and he swings the door open. "Come on, in you go."

I stumble across the room and fall on the bed face-first, with my purse crushed under my belly.

I hear the door shut and I bury my head in the coverlet. JayRay had married Iris. Things cannot get any worse.

"You're a pretty thing," a voice says and I struggle to raise myself up onto my elbows.

"JayRay? You came!"

"Whatever, baby, yeah, I'm that guy."

But something is wrong, JayRay is pushing my blouse up out of my trousers and he's being rough, coarse. It doesn't feel like him.

"Are you drunk?" I ask him and my phone rings in my purse and we both look at it and something about the ringing brings me back into the moment and the reality of what's happening.

"You're not JayRay," I say and the guard pushes me back on the bed. My phone continues to ring and I'm flat on my back, ridiculously clutching my purse, while the security guard tugs at my belt.

I reach for the bottle of water on the nightstand and I hit the man with it. Water pours over him and he growls and rears off me for a moment.

"Wild cat? Yeah, baby, bring it."

I take advantage of the moment to roll out from under him and I fall off the bed. I grab a can of hairspray off the table, thanking god and my guardian angels for something so mundane. Kneeling, I spray the guard full on, and more goes in his mouth than his eyes and he spits and chokes and I manage to get to my feet.

"Get the fuck out," I yell, but my voice is no more than a weak croak. "Jerry, yes, that's you, and don't think I won't report you, get the fuck out of here now!"

Jerry is still gagging on the hairspray and he staggers out, spitting as he goes.

I fall on the door after he leaves and lock it. My purse is still tied around me but it's upside down and a trail of debris snakes across the floor.

I pull the bag off and drop it onto the floor. I flop down on the bed, face-up this time, leery of the ghost of Jerry but before I know it, I'm out cold.

I wake several hours later and the room is dark but light is shining in from the building outside. I have no idea what happened. Why am I still in my work clothes? I can't remember what happened. The last thing I recall was that I was at my stall, and now I'm here. I run my hand through my hair, which is matted and sweaty, and as I do, I notice something written on my hand. *Room 508, Sandi.* What does that mean?

I slide off the bed, horribly sober, and frightened by the lack of knowledge of the past few hours. I grab my wallet and key card. I find Room 508 and I knock on the door.

A woman opens it. Right, my stall neighbour. "Hey, Leonie, good to see you. How's your head, girl?"

"I'm okay. What happened? I woke up in my room now and I can't remember anything."

"Here, sit down, have some water. You took one too many migraine pills, and I got Jerry, the security fella, to walk you up to your room."

"Jerry." Something about that rings a less than popular bell but I'll figure it out later.

"Yeah. Listen, a few people stopped by, I sold some of your stuff for you. I'm going to get myself a starter kit for when I'm at home. I read your brochures. Your product is awesome! But don't worry about that now, don't worry about anything, we'll sort it out tomorrow. You go back to your room, get something to eat and have a bath. Water is purifying and cleansing, and I don't mean just for washing but for healing."

"Good thinking. Thanks Sandi."

"No problem, see you tomorrow."

I return to my room and sit down on the bed. My life is in the toilet. No, my life is in the sewer. Now I'm having blackouts too. Something happened with some turd named Jerry. I don't know what it was, but I know it wasn't good. And a horrible memory flashes its way to the surface of my pain, a big shiny ring that glitters and sparkles and cuts my heart to bleeding ribbons. JayRay married that skinny bitch Iris.

Never mind finding the happiness within. I have no reason to live.

I have the sudden thought that my phone is awfully quiet. What if Ralph had tried to get in touch with me? He did that randomly, when I least expected it. And what if he had a spy in the conference hall, someone who alerted him that I had left my stall? You were never allowed to leave your booth, not even if you were dying. I'd packed up early a couple of times now and I had left my stand and product in the hands of a stranger. I wouldn't put it past Ralph to have eyes on me.

I dig around in my empty purse and try to find my phone, hoping it is buried in a side pocket but it isn't there. I feel sick, where could I have lost it? I kneel down on the floor and look under the bed but there's nothing. I search among the debris on the floor, throwing things aside, but still, nothing. I look in my suitcase, and I look in the washroom, among the towels that I had thrown on the floor that were still there because I had requested no housekeeping. No housekeeping meant the housekeeper couldn't have stolen my phone but someone has, someone has taken my phone, with my contacts and my loving messages from JayRay, not to mention my lying texts to my family.

I don't know what to do. As a last resort, I pick up the landline and dial my cell. To my amazement, I hear it ringing, a muffled and distant sound, and I realize it has to be in the bed. The phone is buried under the comforter.

Thank god. I slam the landline down and fish around in the bedding, rooting through the sheets and blankets. I finally find it. I sink down onto the bed and scroll through my missed calls.

Much to my relief, there's nothing from Ralph. There's nothing from JayRay either. But there are over twenty calls from Dave. Twenty calls? And a bunch of voice messages that range from worried to angry, to spitting mad. Something happened to Kenzie. Oh no, not Kenzie! I can't dial the numbers fast enough and Dave picks up on the second ring.

"Nice of you to call," he says, and his sarcasm is thick and heavy, like a forced accent in a bad movie.

"I had a migraine, I passed out. What the fuck Dave? What happened to Kenzie?"

"You don't get migraines."

"I did today. I'm telling you the truth, I passed out. Are you going to tell me what happened or not?"

"She got hit by a car. Some old lady jumped a red light and she hit Kenzie."

"Oh god. Is she okay, Dave?"

"She'll be fine. They're keeping her at the hospital overnight."

"Shouldn't you be there?" I'm crying, thinking of my baby alone in the hospital, all alone.

"It's midnight, Leonie. She's asleep. Maddie needed to come home too. Anyway, Denise said she'll stop by and check on Kenzie. Sam's in to have his tonsils out and Denise was going to go back anyway."

"Denise? Sam? Who are you talking about?"

"Sam goes to school with Kenzie, they're in the same class. Denise is Sam's mother. We've gone to their house for parties and Sam often comes here for playdates with Kenzie."

Dave's talking slowly and carefully like to a person with an exceptionally low IQ and I lash out in anger. "Oh, cut it out, Dave. So I didn't remember Denise or Sam, like that makes me a bad mom. I had a killer headache, why don't you care about me? Maybe I've got a tumour or something, maybe I'm dying. I'm telling you, I've never had pain like this. I nearly died."

"And yet look, you lived. When are you coming home?"

"We're due to pack up tomorrow afternoon. I'll get the first flight I can, get there by early evening. I can't cut the conference short, you know that."

"We don't need you here anyway," Dave is cruel. "I know there's something you're still not telling me, but frankly I don't care. Hot and cold, that's what you are, Lee. You blow hot and cold and right now, I can't be bothered to deal with you. Maddie is in shock too. She saw the whole thing happen, and she was hysterical. She's more traumatized then Kenzie."

"Did she, Kenzie I mean, did she ask about me?"

"She did not. Neither did Maddie. Seems they don't have very high expectations of you, Lee."

"Dave, what's going on with you? I thought we were getting better? I'm trying, I'm really trying."

"Having sex doesn't mean our relationship is better. And yes, you're seeing a therapist. But I guess it takes a while for it to kick in. We still have to find a marriage counselor. I keep meaning to look for one, but in between the laundry, the dishes, and the homework, I guess you could say I'm a little tired out come the end of the day."

"Hey, this isn't my fault, Dave. I wasn't happy to sit on my ass and be a stuck-at-home mommy. And when I told you it was driving me nuts, in the real sense of loco, you told me I could do anything I wanted and that you'd support me. And now you're throwing it in my face. Nice."

"Yeah, well maybe I didn't figure on a job that would take you away from home so much of the time." Dave is exhausted. "I miss you, Lee. At least, I miss who you used to be."

"I miss me too," I say and I mean it. "I miss us. I don't know what's going on with me either Dave, but I swear, I'm fixing it. You'll see. Here's what I want you to do. I want you to call someone to sit with Maddie and I want you to get Kenzie's bear and take it back to the hospital, so when she wakes up, her bear is with her. And I want you to tell my girls that mommy loves them and that I'll be home soon. Will you do that?"

"Sure." Dave is resigned. "I'll call the service and I'll take Kenzie her bear. I should have thought of that. Okay, Lee. Listen," his voice breaks, "I'm sorry I attacked you. It was a tough day that's all, and I couldn't understand why you weren't picking up. I'm sorry your head was bad. Are you okay?"

"Better than I was," I say, and it's the truth. "I'll be fine. Call me tomorrow with an update on Kenzie. Did they do an x-ray?"

"Yeah, they did everything. Her whole back is one big bruise, it breaks my heart. Those little bones, she's so little, Lee."

"I know." We're both crying now, and I know we aren't just

crying about Kenzie, we're crying about our marriage, crying about how hard it is to be an adult, and we're crying about life in general. And there's relief. Kenzie will be okay. But it's all so damned hard.

"We'll be okay, Dave," I say and I try to sound sure of myself. "Okay? We had a wobble, for sure, but we'll be okay."

"Yeah," Dave says and he sounds calmer. "Yeah, we'll be okay. You get some rest now Lee, we'll talk tomorrow."

I click my phone off. I strip my clothes off carefully, as if they're a life I'm leaving behind. I take a shower and scrub hard. I scrub my scalp, my armpits, and my buttocks. I brush my teeth until my gums bleed and I wash my face until it's shiny and red.

I clean up the mess in my room. It's nearly two a.m. when I climb into bed. I set my alarm and take a half a sleeping pill. But despite the pill I can't sleep. I just lie there, thinking.

24

I CAN'T GET HOME FAST ENOUGH. The plane is stuck in the sky, an unmoving puppet. When I finally land, I rush to my car and fumble to get the key in the ignition. I text Dave and he's waiting for me at the entrance to Sick Kids.

"They're releasing her in an hour or so," he says by way of hello. His face is drawn and older, there are bags under his eyes. I nod and follow him mutely. "They did x-rays, nothing broken, just bruises. They were worried about a concussion, so they kept her here. We've got to keep her quiet for the next couple of days. That's the easy part, the tough part will be calming Maddie down, she's still freaked out."

I nod again. We're in the elevator and I'm terrified of seeing my own kids. They have every reason to hate me and that makes me want to cry even harder. Maddie rushes towards me as soon as I enter the door and I crouch down and hug her. As big as she is, I pick her up and she doesn't mind and I go to Kenzie who's in her pink fairy ballerina pjs, looking tiny.

"I'm so sorry I wasn't here, honey," I say, kissing her forehead and Kenzie reaches up and hugs me. "It's okay, mommy. I'm fine. I didn't even break a bone!" She's so proud of herself.

"That's amazing, honey. Does it hurt?" I blow my nose and wipe my eyes.

She nods. "It hurts when I breathe. And when I sneeze."

I turn to Dave questioningly. "Bruised ribs," he said. "But you'll heal soon, sweetheart," he tells Kenzie. "Healing is like a super power, you'll see. A couple of days and you'll be good as new."

A whirlwind commotion spins into the room. A woman the size of a linebacker sweeps in and halves a big bunch of helium balloons she's holding. Yellow and silver balloons with brightly-coloured emojis. "Here you go, Kay-Kay," she says and Kenzie grins. Kay-Kay? Ah, right, Denise. Former hockey great, now I remember. She and Dave must have so much in common. "Sam's getting out today, you too?"

Kenzie nods and Denise has the wherewithal to finally notice me. "Hi Lee," she says breezily and I want to tell her that only Dave calls me Lee. JayRay calls me Leo and I'm Leonie to the rest of the world. But I don't say anything, and I manage a semblance of a smile. Not that this woman would let me get a word in edgewise.

"They'll deliver it the day after tomorrow, around three," she says to Dave, "and the tuner will be there around five. I told him to text you first."

"My piano!" Kenzie sits up, clutching her balloons, delighted.

"Denise's piano," Dave corrects her, "we're just borrowing it."

"For as long as you like," Denise says and she swings in my direction without warning. "It was my mother's. We tried Sam on it. To say he was not musical would be an understatement. But your sweet girl here has talent coming out of her ears, so we thought why not?"

We? I look at Dave who looks at his shoes. "Great," I say flatly. "Thanks Denise." At least she understands that's her cue to leave.

"A piano?" I say into the silence, feeling like the bad guy.

"My teacher at school says I'm very good," Kenzie says, still grinning. "She's going to give me extra lessons after school, three days a week. And then I can practice at home."

"That sounds amazing!" I try to inflect my voice with an enthusiasm I'm not feeling and we all fall into an uneasy silence. We're all relieved when the nurse comes in, trailed by the doctor who says Kenzie can go home. "Rest up young lady, no trapeze acts for at least a week," he says and the girls both find this hilarious.

"My car is here, who's coming with me?" I ask, convinced the girls will say they're going with Dave.

"We will," the girls both chorus and Dave nods.

"We're low on groceries. I'll meet you back at the house," he says. We get Kenzie into her shorter than short shorts that I really wish she wouldn't insist on wearing and I watch her struggle to bend forward to pull on her little white cowboy boots. Ever the rock star. I curb my critical thoughts and wait in silence. I follow Kenzie out the door. She's clutching her balloons and I want to grab them and let them float away, the unwanted evidence of my bad mothering.

I load the girls into the car and listen to their chatter and I thank all the gods I can think of that they are okay, that my family is still intact,and that that I haven't lost everything. Screw Denise. I'm their mom. I'm Dave's wife. I will not be usurped. The woman has no idea who she's dealing with. I take the long way home, just to be with the kids for longer.

"How's Muffin?" I ask.

"Good. We had to take him to the vet, he ate some rubbish and the vet had to cut his stomach open, but he's fine now." Maddie is happy to chat, Kenzie just stares out the window.

"You young ladies have had a few adventures. Let's try not to have too many more. Mads, do you have a game tomorrow?"

"Nope, only next week."

We pull up into the driveway and Maddie lugs my suitcase inside for me and I help Kenzie up the stairs.

"I'm going to make you guys the best dinner ever tonight," I say and they both looked uneasy. "Or we could get any kind of takeout you like." This is met with more enthusiasm and I grab them both to me and hug them hard until they squirm away.

"Fine. I'll stop now, Mommy's got some paperwork from the trip, you guys have homework?"

"We don't have any, because of the accident. Can we watch TV?"

"Sure, I'll come and sit at the dining room table so I can be near you."

"Mom, we're fine," Kenzie says. "Dad said it was an accident, and that accidents happen but not every day. Stop worrying, okay?"

"Okay." But I sit where I can see them and I study them, pretending to be working. They're so grown up. When did they get to be so grown up? They are both tall and Maddie looks like she's dropped some weight but Dave's right, I can't make that an issue. They're so pretty and I can see some of me and Dave in both of them. Maddie's more square-jawed while Kenzie's face is heart-shaped. They both have my nose. I want to tell them how sorry I am for everything and how I really do want to make things better, but I can't think of what to say.

I log onto my work spreadsheet server and check my sales. Thanks to Sandi, my numbers are better than ever. I realize, with a shock that this is the first trip where I came straight home and didn't go to my storage locker to stash a pile of shit.

My email pings and it's Ralph congratulating me on a stellar performance.

Good one, scout! You took it to the next level again! Take some time; you've earned it. Take the kids to Wonderland, do some fun stuff. I can get you free day passes for Sunday if you like.

"You kids want to go to Wonderland tomorrow?" I ask the girls over the noise of the TV.

Shrieks of happiness tells me that yes, they do and I message Ralph who sends me the tickets.

"We're going to Wonderland tomorrow," I tell Dave at dinner and he grins.

Later that night, I straddle Dave with the hunger of one who has had a narrow escape. And afterwards I fall into a beautiful dreamless sleep.

25

MY BEAUTIFUL DREAMLESS SLEEP is broken by a nightmare. Dave, the girls and I are on holiday at a seaside cottage. We take a trip into town and hear news of an approaching tsunami. I turn to gather the kids to me but they have disappeared. I turn to Dave but he too is gone. They must have gone back to the cottage. I climb into an abandoned SUV while around me people are screaming and running in all directions. I put my foot on the gas but the tarmac heaves up in front of me and splits apart like a special effect in a Hollywood movie. Ten-story waves crash down on either side of the car and slam down on the pier. The road has become a wooden dock, a thin strip heading out into the treacherous ocean. The waves miss me but only just. I somehow make it back to the cottage and Dave and the girls are not there, but my father is, with his distant gaze and his Grecian beauty and his fine aristocratic hands that twist and turn as he examines something he has made. I want to scream at him but my voice catches in my throat and I jerk upright, gasping.

Awake, I reach for Dave only to find that he really is gone. I am in bed, alone.

I sit up. What happened? Where is he? But then I hear the sound of crying and I jump out of bed and rush down the hallway to the girls' room. The bedside lights are on, throwing shadows across the room.

Maddie is sitting up in her bed, her eyes wide and worried.

The bright and cheerful room is at odds with the sound of sorrow. Dave is rubbing Kenzie's back. Kenzie has her face to the wall and she is sobbing, huge gulping cries.

Dave sees me arrive and he looks up at me and shakes his head.

"What happened?" I ask Maddie and she too shakes her head. "She just started crying. I didn't hear her in the beginning but then she got really loud. I don't know why she's crying. She wouldn't say. So I got Daddy to come."

"Let me try," I say to Dave and he gets up. I sit down and stroke Kenzie's hair. "Sweetie, is it your ribs? Are you in pain?" She cries harder and Dave gives me a look. I lie down alongside Kenzie, something I haven't done in years and I carry on stroking her hair. I spoon my body into hers and I'm struck by how tiny she is, how thin. "Baby, tell Mommy what's the matter, please."

"Wonderland," she finally manages, "too sore. I can't..." She stops.

"Oh sweetie." I feel terrible. "I should have thought of that. Of course you can't go. What was I thinking? I'm so sorry. You don't have to feel bad, okay? I never should have suggested it. My bad, okay? Please, honey, stop crying."

She stops sobbing but she's still hiccupping and it's hard for her to breathe. "Kenz, honey, I'm really sorry." I murmur this again and again to her, and I rub her little shoulder and I start crying too. I cry quietly so she can't hear me but hot tears roll down my face. The soapy innocence of her freshly-shampooed hair makes me hate myself even more. This little person. I brought this little person into the world and I made her cry like this. What a shitty mother. I'm critical of everything she does and how she does it. This kid doesn't deserve me. Not the me that I am. I have to change. "I'm going to stay here with you, baby, okay? We'll go to sleep and then tomorrow maybe we can go to Eggspectations or Cora's or anywhere you like and you can have pancakes or waffles or anything." She gives a small nod and her breathing starts to ease.

I hear Maddie settle down, with Dave murmuring behind me. I carry on rubbing Kenzie's back and she soon drifts off into sleep. But I don't sleep. Thoughts of my failure swirl around in my mind followed by resolve followed by doubt, all wrapped up in a big ugly blanket of shame.

I have an appointment to see Gerstein the following day and not only am I going to go, I'm darn well going to succeed at this, whatever it takes. So, when I'm sitting there, across from Gerstein, I tell her the truth.

"Whatever I tell you is confidential?" I ask and Gerstein nods.

"Fine. I had an affair. A year-long affair. I loved him and he broke my heart. That's why I went crazy recently and Dave made me come here. I wasn't crazy; I was heartbroken. Dave's got no idea."

"Tell me what happened. From the beginning. We can have a double session today, I had a cancellation."

I'm not sure I'm up for a two-hour interrogation, but a part of me badly needs to talk about JayRay. I can't talk to anybody about what happened, so in a way, I welcome this opportunity.

I start at the beginning and I tell her pretty much the whole truth. I tell her about Bernice, and I tell her that JayRay is a con man, but I leave out how we got married in Vegas, and how I'm a polygamist, even though the marriage isn't a legal one.

The wedding happened after JayRay came to my hotel room, following the Bernice debacle and after he cut my face with the green glass from the broken bottle, even though he hadn't meant to. He was drunk when he arrived and he asked me to marry him. He even got down on one knee. I said yes, of course I did, and we took a taxi to the Little White Wedding Chapel Drive-Thru Window and we got married.

I kept the certificate and because we couldn't get wedding rings, we had matching tattoos done instead. The tattoos are small, about the size of a quarter , but I still made sure to keep covered up around Dave until my bush grew back. Thank god he never commented on my sudden tendency to wear a robe instead of wandering around our bedroom in my usual naked state.

JayRay got his tattoo above his balls, near the base of his penis. The tattoos are an utter cliché, a blood-red heart pierced by an arrow. I was surprised that JayRay would agree to something so girly but, then again, he was drunker than I had ever seen him. I loved mine so much at the time but now it's a constant reminder of JayRay's betrayal. It's a good example to my girls of why they should never get tattoos, but I know this is one story I'll never get to share with them, or with anyone. Not even Gerstein.

"And how do you feel now?" she asks and I force myself to concentrate. I had just finished telling Gerstein about my most recent, supremely disastrous trip. I told her I about my blackout and I told her about Sandi helping me and saving the day.

"He married somebody else. It's over. And I feel like it's my fault Kenzie was hit by a car. It's because I'm a bad mother. I passed out because I took too many pills and I wasn't there for her. And now I've been given another chance and I'm not going to fuck it up this time. For some reason, I have been given this free get-out-of-jail card and I'm not going to squander it."

"Leonie, why is it that you never talk about your mother?"

I know exactly why. Because that would mean telling Gerstein another nasty truth and if I do that, she'll give up on me and rightfully so. So I deflect her.

"My father was a cruel man," I say and she takes the bait.

"To her too?"

"No. He loved her."

I remember something. I came home early one day, when I was about fifteen. I had bad period pains and I wanted to lie on my bed in the fetal position and hold a hot water bottle close to my stomach, while I waited for the painkillers kick in.

I opened the front door and I heard music playing, some schmaltzy song from the fifties and I expected to see my mother sitting next to the record player daydreaming when she should have been vacuuming. But instead I saw my parents slow dancing and my father had his eyes shut and my mother was holding him gently and they were swaying in time to the song.

I met my mother's eye and her expression was clear. I closed the front door quietly and crept up the stairs, foregoing my hot water bottle.

"You and Dad do that often?" I asked later and I could see my mother weighing up the decision whether or not to answer me.

"It makes him happy. Your father gets the blues you know. He always has."

I jerk forward in my chair. "My mother said that my father got the blues, he always had. I never knew that. I just thought he was mean. I never forgave him for making me feel humiliated and I wanted to punish him for what he said."

"What did he say?"

"That I was a dirty little girl." I take a deep breath and I tell Gerstein about the episode in the woods and therapist nods.

"That would have been extremely damaging," she says when I come to the end. "That was unspeakably cruel of him."

My eyes flood with tears. "Thank you. I guess, all these years, I wanted somebody to say that. I was so afraid that instead, I'd be told that I was a filthy, disgusting little thing, just like my father said. So, thank you."

I blow my nose, wanting to move the conversation away from my father, just in case she wants to explore my emotions about his death, which isn't a good idea. I don't want to talk about my mother either.

"I'm going to be okay," I say. "I need to learn to communicate better with Dave, I know that. And I need to learn to be more demonstrative. It's JayRay. He derailed me."

"Obsessive love can do that. But, a word of warning. He may not be done with you yet. What you two had was too intense to fade away without some kind of comeback. How does it make you feel, me telling you there still may be hope?"

"Afraid. I worry I won't be able to resist him, and I can't afford to let him back. He's as toxic as a deadly poison, as lethal. And I know my chemistry."

"We'll equip you with some coping tools," Gerstein says, and her confidence cheers me up. "Then when he tries his tricks again, you'll be armed and ready. You'll have weapons to protect you."

"Sounds great!" I'm optimistic. I lean forward. "Let's visit the armoury, shall we?"

26.

IT DOESN'T TAKE LONG TO ARM ME, according to Gerstein anyway. "The first step is awareness. Have you ever had a food addiction? Something you craved, every day?"

"Not me but a friend of mine had a thing for Cool Whip. She'd buy a can every day on the way home and eat the whole thing. Just Cool Whip, nothing else, piled up like a fluffy cloud in a bowl. And she couldn't stop. She wanted to but she couldn't."

"Excellent. Not for your friend obviously, but helpful as an example for you. I want to you to imagine that JayRay is a can of Cool Whip and you are your friend. And yet, you are also you, and you can see how craving a can of Cool Whip a day isn't good for you."

"Got it."

"The first thing you do is notice the craving. Awareness; I am craving JayRay. And then you imagine JayRay with a can of Cool Whip in his hand. JayRay is like the Cool Whip. Now imagine eating a bowl full of Cool Whip. Awful, right? That way, he'll become negatively associated with Cool Whip, a thing you don't like, a thing which you know isn't good for you, a thing which, in excess, will make you sick. And, once you're at that stage, you pick up your next weapon, which is distraction."

"Distract myself how? I'm telling you now, my thoughts will swing back to him."

"The mind is like that. We each have as many as fifty to

seventy thousand thoughts a day. That's thirty five to forty eight thoughts a minute. We don't have an exact count for repeat thoughts, but a high percentage of our thoughts are repeats. Very few of them are new. You don't have to have new thoughts instead of JayRay thoughts, you can think of anything. Think about work. Or maybe make a grocery list. Or plan something fun you want to do with the kids. Find a new hobby or have a selection of books or magazines that you are reading and think about something you have read in one of them. You need to divert your thoughts and I'm not saying it will be easy. You have to keep at it. It's like anything in life, nothing comes fully formed the first time you do it, you have to work at it. And your brain and your heart and your mind are in the habit of thinking about him. We all know how hard it is to break even the most simple of habits. So, awareness is the first step. Distraction is the second."

"And then?"

"Breathe. I know it sounds simple, but think about your actions and before you do anything, stop and breathe. Before you do anything, before you turn on a kettle, or pick up the phone, or take any action at all, breathe. Because, be aware and be warned, the smallest action can lead to the biggest disaster. Let's use an example. Let's say JayRay texts you. And let's say he asks, *You free for a quick coffee?* It's just coffee and it's just a text, but the consequence of engaging will most certainly result in the loss of your marriage and the loss of your family. Therefore, breathe and don't do anything before you list the consequences to yourself. Tell yourself, *I will lose everything that matters to me.* And it does matter to you, or you wouldn't be here now."

"The smallest thing can lead to the biggest disaster." I echo. "You're right. Yes. Okay. JayRay holds the Cool Whip. Cool Whip in a bowl. I will lose everything. Distract my thoughts by focusing on other things. Breathe, don't do anything, don't reply, don't respond. Anything else?"

"Yes, there's more but you've got a lot to deal with so this will do for now. Do your best and be on your guard. Men like JayRay are more like heroin than Cool Whip. Be careful."

"I will, but I'll be okay. Besides he's still a newlywed, in love with Iris's money and not interested in me. I don't think he will come back, and yes, there's a part of me that does want him back. A part of me thinks fuck the consequences. I want him to the exclusion of everything else, but I know rationally that I will lose any real chance of happiness if I give into that."

"Don't be hard on yourself for still wanting him. Try not to judge yourself. Don't accuse and condemn yourself because you want him. We're not responsible for that which we desire. Don't see yourself as a failure for it."

I exhale and slump into my chair with relief. "I thought that after I told you how nasty he is, that you'd ask me why I'd even want him. I thought you were going to be impatient with me like we've resolved this, why haven't I learned my lesson properly?"

"No, that would be the voice you learned from your father, the nasty judgmental voice telling you that you are a dirty little girl. That's not your voice and it doesn't have to be any voice at all. You can learn methods that will help you to shrug off that internal narrative. You're not dirty or bad or wrong for loving JayRay. But he will destroy the good in your life, and that's why we need to focus on extricating him from your life."

A double-session and we are out of time. "I'll see you when I get back," I say.

"Text me if you need to," Gerstein says. "I mean that. You're not alone in this. You'll be okay, you can do it."

I feel happy after that appointment, confident. There's hope for me. I say that to myself but I know I'm lying. Gerstein doesn't know the full truth but of course, I do.

She doesn't know how I, at thirteen, flirted quietly and relentlessly with my teacher, a man in his mid-thirties, a man with a young family and good standing in the community. She doesn't know how I set my sights on this man, forcing him to stay in the classroom alone with me, on the pretext of needing extra math help. Which is a laugh, since I was shit-hot when it came to math and science, I could have taught the classes myself. She doesn't know how I started to touch him, slowly seducing him, just to prove to myself that I could have anybody I wanted. And then, once I had him, his morals destroyed by his love for me and his belief that I too loved him, I made sure that we were found together, my blouse unbuttoned, my already full breasts on display, and my flimsy panties on the floor. Oh, the disgrace for the poor man. We were found by the religious studies teacher, a hate-filled spinster whose life had passed her by without so much as a how-do. She chewed on the scandal like a yard dog gnawing a piece of gristle until the teacher was sent off to serve his one-year jail sentence. His wife stood by her man for all of four months, following which she fled back to Kamloops, B.C., her hometown, taking their kids with her.

This is why my mother rejected me. When I came home, the day Mr. Carlson and I were discovered together, she sat me down at the kitchen table. She stared at me and I met her gaze with steady calm.

"To look at you," she said, "one would assume all things good and innocent. So pretty." She picked up the salt shaker and pushed it to and fro on the table, like a chess piece. "And," she continued, "I tried to have faith in you. But this? Do you realize what you have done?" She slammed the salt shaker down on the table so hard I jumped. "You have ruined things!" she screamed. "You have ruined my place on the community board, you have ruined my standing in the town. No longer can I show my face. Because what kind of mother brings up a child to do what you did?"

"It was him," I began, "he made me do things—"

"NO!" she screamed. I had never heard my mother raise her voice and something triumphant rose up in my chest and spread its wings. I had provoked this reaction — her anger was my creation. And I felt proud in that moment, proud that I had finally managed to catch her attention. This is what it took, to get a reaction out of her. Sure, she'd help me clean up on that shit-covered day and she'd sent my father to fix things between us but apart from that, it was like I had never existed. She and my father only lived for each other. I was a miscellaneous byproduct, like a side effect indicated in a medication warning list. *Possible side effects of marriage could produce unwanted offspring with lasting negative impact on harmonious marital relations.* That was me. But I'd finally forced my mother to say the things she never wanted to say. The cards were on the table, there was no turning back.

"You!" she shouted. "I know it was you. You, Leonie. I've watched you. Do you think I didn't notice? Your small plays for attention, consequences be damned. Even in gradeschool, you were a troublemaker. I was called in, do you know that? *Leonie is a shit-disturber.*" My mother's soap-washed mouth pursed as if she had trouble even saying the word shit. "That's exactly what one of the teachers said to me. She apologized for her language and she said, "I have to be blunt, Leonie is a shit-disturber. She causes the children to turn on one another." To which I replied, 'I could report you for using inappropriate language like that about my child.' But I knew what she said was true and so I asked her, 'And if she does that, what can be done about it?' And she and I looked one another, knowing full well there was nothing to be done. And for many years I hoped she had been wrong. I hoped your father had been wrong. I watched you and tried to steer you in the right direction. But now this. This terrible thing. And you know the worst of it? We cannot fix it. I can't stand up and tell the world that Don Carlson is a good man, a victim, and that the villain is my thirteen-year-old sociopathic daughter."

She looked at me and I controlled my desire to smile. What would my father think of his "dirty little girl" now? The power was glorious. The damage I had done!

And my mother knew what I was thinking and how I felt. "You are dead to me," she said and she held the salt shaker upside down and we watched the white grains spill onto the table in a small heap. "To all outward appearances, I will do what needs to be done as a mother. But know that I know the truth about you, and I will never forgive you for what you have done. Never mind Don. You have ruined me and everything I have stood for." She stood up and with one swift move, she swept the salt off the table, her gesture of disgust and dismissal a seal upon her vow.

She left the house and I heard her car speeding down the driveway as if she couldn't rush away from me quickly enough. I sat at the table for a while and the glorious feeling inside of me dimmed, the red heart fading inside a dying coal. I tried to breathe on the memory and stir the ember to life, recapture the fiery satisfaction of my victory, but all I could taste were cold, filthy ashes and the silence of being left utterly alone.

And, a couple of days later as I set up my stall at The Rocky Mountain Best Gift Show, I'm as alone as the tree that fell silently in the forest, the tree that no one heard or cared about.

I cannot live with the consequences of destroying my life with my family. They are the only good thing I have. Even although Gerstein doesn't know the full truth of how damaged I am, perhaps her advice will help me stay afloat. I can change. People can change, I have to believe that.

JayRay has yet to arrive and I try not to listen for his voice. I try not to be aware of every single person who enters the conference hall who isn't him.

Sandi waves to me and I grin back. At least I have Sandi.

The day passes uneventfully but I know the moment JayRay arrives. He's still one aisle over but his voice loud and clear and I break out in a sweat. Breathe, breathe. I listen for his deep laugh and his easy banter and the minute the clock signals the day's end, I pack up and shoot out of the conference hall.

I journal furiously throughout the day, using a notebook and pen I stole from a vendor who was leaving the circuit. I justified the theft by telling myself that it wasn't like she needed it any more. I remind myself to tell Gerstein about my stealing; we'll need to deal with it at some point. But, since the urge to steal increases in direct relation to my anxiety and stress levels, I figure we're already treating it. Awareness, awareness, it's all about awareness. I will heal my every ill with awareness.

That night I closet myself up in my hotel room and I carry on writing. When I look up, three hours have passed and I feel worn out but better.

I order room service and Skype with the kids and Dave. I have a bath and fall into bed, worn out with having coped so well.

The next morning, I remind myself that I'm like an alcoholic. I have to see this as the first day of the rest of my life. I can't for a moment think that I'm all good just because I managed one whole day without having to drug myself senseless or get drunk, even though I did steal the pen and notebook — a minor transgression. This brand-new shiny fucking day means only one thing. I have to start all over again.

I walk into the breakfast room and there's JayRay, beaming, holding court, and talking loudly about his honeymoon. Talk about a sucker punch from my sparring partner, life.

"And it's not over yet," he boasts. "That Iris, she's the best. She's got more cruises planned for in between the conferences."

Bully for JayRay. Fucking fantastic. I fetch a plate of eggs and fruit from the buffet table but the food sticks in my throat and I get up abruptly and leave.

I find a Starbucks, pick up a muffin and a latte, and head for my stall. I set up for the day, sit down and take out my notebook.

"Writing your memoirs?" Sandi calls out and I look up and grin.

"A racy novel based on my life."

"Yeah baby, you're going to make millions and leave me alone in this shit hole of a place." Sandi leaves her stall and comes over. "Ah, I guess it's not that bad really. So, how are you, neighbour? We didn't have the chance to catch up yesterday. You look better than you did at the last carnival."

"I am better. Thanks for saving my ass last time." I find an envelope of cash in my petty cash box. "Here, I saved your share of the loot for you."

But Sandi waves me off. "No, man, that's what friends do. My mother was a good old hippie gal and she taught me that we look out for our buddies."

"Much appreciated." I put my hands on my hips and look around. "Here we go again, another two days in paradise. But like you say, it's not so bad."

"It'd be better if Mr. I-Married-Iris-Moneybags would shut up. That guy! For some reason the sound of him seems to carry right into my stall."

"No, we can all hear him," I say.

"Iris is going to land *ka-thunk* on her ass, you mark my words. Everybody knows about that guy, he's a scam artist through and through. He pulled a real shit-bag job on a friend of mine. Her husband think's she cheating, right? Having it on with his best friend in his own house, in his own bed. So, he comes to the show and buys a bunch of cameras and stuff from JayRay. And JayRay's such a regular stand-up guy that he even installs the equipment for the guy, he goes to his house and everything. Next thing, he's set up the remote so that he gets a copy of what the video records and he sees my friend having it on with her husband's best friend. Not that I'm condoning cheating, but my friend's husband was a real piece of work. And what does JayRay do? He blackmails my friend! He shows her the tape and he blackmails her. She doesn't have much money, so he works it out so that she pays him what she can every month. It was supposed to be for a year, but it's already been nearly two. And in return, he wiped the tape clean so the husband didn't know a thing. JayRay ran a shot of the empty bedroom on a loop. How's that for disgusting? JayRay doesn't know that I know her. She came to visit me when we were road-showing in her 'hood and she nearly threw up when she saw JayRay."

"Oh my god. Seriously? That's evil."

"That's JayRay, always in it for the scam. I never liked him. And now Iris is all over him like a rash on a baby's ass. But watch, that kind of love doesn't last long. Either he'll get tired of playing the loving husband toy boy, or she'll figure him out. Iris isn't stupid."

But she's skinny and old and ugly, I want to say, and JayRay makes you feel like the sun's shining on you and only you, and not only that, but that fairy dust and every kind of good voodoo is coming your way.

I hadn't known about this scam. Once again, I am betrayed by the man I thought was my soulmate. I berate myself for being stupid and then I remember Gerstein's words and I tell myself to be more kind and it does help.

"Best I get back to my stand," Sandi says, "You have yourself a scorcher of a day, young lady!"

"You too," I reply and I'm dying to chronicle this development in my journal but a crowd has gathered at my table.

Later in the day, I'm explaining the business of selling cosmetics from home and JayRay walks by. He's wearing a Stetson hat and he winks at me and tips his hat. I stare back at him, incredulous.

"That guy really gets my goat," I say later that evening to Sandi when we're packing up and we can hear JayRay telling tall tales across the aisle. "That thing you told me, I can't stop thinking about it. I wish we could do something to help your friend."

Sandi nods. "But what? Guys like that, you can't touch them."

"Where does your friend live?"

"New York. Why? We hardly ever go there. It was a one-off. She was unlucky JayRay was in town when her husband was looking for gear."

"I'm going to put my thinking cap on. It may take some time but I'm going to come up with something."

I'm proud of how well I'm doing but I wonder if scheming to get back at JayRay is simply another excuse to think about him. But I tell myself it's for Sandi's friend. I have to find a way to help her. And it won't hurt to throw in a good dose of revenge for my own satisfaction too.

27

"**H**E'S A DISGUSTING PIG!" I exclaim. I am back in Gerstein's serene and elegant cottage, telling her about JayRay's antics with the spy cam.

"I understand you want to get justice for this woman and set things right," Gerstein says, "but it's not healthy for you to be engaging with thoughts of him, not at any level."

"I know. You're right. I guess I'm still angry that he scammed me. He's a bad person." Speaking of bad people reminds me how I doctored Iris's creams and I wonder why Iris isn't feeling any ill effects as yet. She sure should be.

"I am a bad person too," I tell Gerstein. "You think I am trying to get better and I am, but I am, or was, whatever, so in love with this guy. I don't want anybody else to have him. I want him to come back to me. He doesn't feel things like he should. He tipped his hat at me, for fuck's sake, and he winked! How could he be so uncaring?"

I start to cry. "All I'm doing, twenty-four seven, is fighting my desire for him. Maybe I should give in and admit that I want him more than anything in the world, and that I miss him more than anything in the world."

"And you will lose everything for a man who has no regard for you. You have to keep fighting this. You are doing well."

"I tell myself that but the truth is, I'm not. I thought he would have come back to me by now. Even you thought he would have come back to me by now."

"Regardless of whether he comes back to you or not, you have to keep fighting. Actually, correction, you don't *have* to do anything. It's your choice and you have to want the alternative more than the fix. How's your relationship with Dave and the girls?"

"Better. But I had a setback with Sandi telling me about her friend. In a weird way, it made me feel close to JayRay again, like we were back together. I withdrew from Dave and the girls, although I didn't want to. They knew, as soon as I came home, that things had changed again for the worse."

"Have you started marriage counseling yet?"

"No. He hasn't mentioned it again and neither have I." I blow my nose and bury my face in my hands. "What a mess. It's a monumental fucking mess."

"If you treat a wound, any wound, with the right medicine, it will heal." Gerstein is implacable. "But you have to be consistent with the treatment, you have to persist."

"Yeah." I look into the distance and gnaw on a nail. "It's not like I've got a choice. He doesn't want me."

"Where is your next conference?"

"St. John's, Newfoundland. Iris will be there. She's the queen bee of the Canadian conferences. I'll have to watch her and JayRay being all lovey-dovey."

"You could leave your job," Gerstein suggests and I glare at her in horror.

"But I love my job! And I could never leave JayRay. The thought of never seeing him again is unthinkable. You see. I'm right. I'm not getting better, am I? If anything, I feel worse."

Gerstein sighs. "Leonie, I'm going to level with you. There's only so much I can do. You think you're the only person who fell in love with the wrong guy and had their heart shattered? This guy did a number on you. You've got a great family, a husband who loves you, and two fantastic kids. And yet, there's a real risk you'll lose it over someone who isn't worth a damn."

"The heart wants what the heart wants," I mutter.

"The addict wants what the addict wants. And screw the rest of the world. Yes, I'm growing impatient with you. Why? Because you came to me with a new story of how this guy screwed some woman over and instead of it making you see what a loser he is, it makes you want him more. I did my best to help you see it for what it is but you're slamming the door on me. You're right, I don't get it. I don't."

Gerstein stands up and I'm immediately confused and afraid. I challenged her and pushed her too far. "I'm not firing you as a client but I am saying this, we're done for the day. Go to your conference, and when you come back, come see me if you really want help. It's up to you. There are people out there that I can help and if you're not one of them, I'm going to have to move on. I do want to help you, but only if you'll meet me halfway."

I get up and grab my purse. "Yeah? Well, fuck you too, doc. Thanks for nothing."

I storm out and slam the door behind me. I march across her perfect garden and sit in my car, wondering how I'll explain this to Dave.

I look back towards Gerstein's cool rooms and something inside me wants to come clean, go back and tell her all my sins, tell her about Don Carlson and how, even as a toddler, I was a shit-disturber. How I stole toys from the school playroom, how day after day, I pocketed tiny bits and pieces, broken or whole, it didn't matter. I shuttled them home to a shoe box under my bed, feeling the shame, the guilt, and the gut-wrenching fear of being caught, but I couldn't stop myself, not even then. I once showed a friend my score, a misshapen ball of orange plasticine studded with floor detritus and stones, and she couldn't understand why I had taken it. Because it was there. Because I had no choice.

But I can't tell Gerstein anything, never mind everything. Everything being my revenge on my father. I can't tell her what I did. Because I poisoned him.

A couple of years after I left home, while I was still at university, I surprised my parents with an unexpected visit, ostensibly to pick up some shit from my room. How I loved watching my mother wince at my crassness. Even after all that time, she had never gotten used to my white trash tongue. I had hooked up with a gothic kid in one of my classes and he was good to his word when he told me he could get me anything I wanted at a price. And I was more than willing to pay whatever it took.

Potassium cyanide. It was the first time I used it. I mixed the powder in with my father's steel-cut oatmeal, hoping that cooking wouldn't lessen the efficacy of the poison but I needn't have worried. I knew my mother was in no danger, she cooked his breakfast but she didn't like oatmeal.

I left that same afternoon to go back to university and the following night, my mother called me. My father had died. He had been fine at breakfast and he had gone to his cabin as usual. But when he didn't return for supper, my mother grew concerned and she went to find him. When she opened the door, he was lying sprawled on the floor. He was dead.

"Heart attacks run in his family," she said and she was crying. "I don't know what I will do with myself now. He was everything I had."

Thanks Mom. Her words made me sorry that she didn't eat oatmeal but, while she had rejected me for what I had done to Don Carlson, she had never hurt me as badly as my father had. Of course I had known about the family tendency on my father's side for heart failure at a young age. In fact, I had been counting on that. While my mother had no regard for what she called "my lack of moral standing," it was clear she hadn't put two and two together. She saw no link between my out-of-the-blue visit and my father's sudden death.

I returned home for the funeral. I put flowers on his grave and I stood by my mother's side while the priest prayed for my father's soul. I wondered if, in his dying moments, my father had realized that he had been murdered by his dirty little girl. I certainly hoped so.

I walked my mother back to the house and I made her take a sleeping pill. "Here," I said, shaking out five pills and putting them in a saucer, "keep these. You can easily get a prescription for this shit if you like. It's Imovane, a harmless sleep aid."

"I'll take one tonight and that will do me," my mother said. "I want to escape my world for at least one night. But I want to say this. I don't want to see you again, Leonie. You may be my daughter but you are not a good person. And if I die alone and am buried alone, that's fine by me. There's enough money left for me to buy a small place in town and I'll get myself a job. I'll get by. And I've made provisions to be buried next to your father when I go. It's all sorted out. I never want to see you again."

I wanted to leave right then but I had unfinished business. "Whatever. I'll go and see if there's crap left in my room that I want."

My mother nodded and I heard her go upstairs and shut her bedroom door.

I went to my old room and lay down on my bed and waited. I eyed Wendy O. Williams wallpapering the walls with her fierce nudity, her duct-taped nipples and her Mohawk hair and wondered if I should rescue Wendy and take her with me. But no, I was over her and besides, why spoil my mother's discomfort at having to face the posters, particularly the one with *Don't be a Wanker!* There was nothing I wanted to take; there were no happy memories in that room for me.

After the scandal with the Don Carlson, people had avoided me like the plague. I retaliated by donning gothic garb and dying my hair black. With my pale skin, crazy light blue eyes and black lipstick, I knew I was striking. I made a point of fucking the most popular boys in school, especially the ones who had girlfriends because it made me feel like I had the upper hand. My sexual prowess was legendary; I was irresistible. The day before graduation, I took my black lipstick and I got to school early. *I fucked you*, I wrote on each of the boys' lockers. Good thing I took two sticks of lipstick, because it turned out I had fucked a lot more dicks than I had realized. It certainly made for a memorable last day, and I made a point of applying my lipstick in front of everyone at assembly. But what could they do? I didn't bother to go to class, I left the girls, crying and furious, and the boys, sheepish and apologetic, and I caught the bus to Toronto. I worked in a coffee shop while I waited for university to start and I dropped the goth look. At university, I stopped working my power plays and I tried to focus on my studies but memories of my father's cruelty plagued me and I knew I had to find closure. Isn't that what they all say? That with closure, you heal. Consider yourself case closed, Daddy Dearest. I had to kill you. I lay on my bed and thought about closure. Revenge, closure, perhaps, at the end of day, they're the same thing.

Late that night, I went to my father's cabin. I was aching to set the place alight and watch it burn but I couldn't do it, it would be too obvious that I was responsible and I wasn't willing to be clapped with a charge of arson.

I unlocked the door, using my mother's key. I stepped inside that hallowed chapel only to find it dark, damp, shabby, and derelict. A mess. Whatever big dreams my father had harboured, they had died a slow and painstaking death because there was nothing inside the shed except for half a dozen ceiling-high stacks of old newspapers and a two-inch layer of dust on everything. The only clean spots were my father's chair and his desk and I sat down in his chair and looked at the world from his view.

I had thought him a giant imaginer of impossible and wondrous things. Instead, he was a nothing more than a depressed hermit, withering away in a cave of his choosing, a failure at life.

I didn't destroy anything in that cabin because there was nothing to destroy. And knowing the truth about my father didn't change what needed to be done. I walked to his grave, pulled down my panties and had a grand old shit.

I wanted to wipe myself with my panties and leave the soiled underwear on the headstone but caution urged me not to.

"So long, Dad," I said and I walked away.

The memory of the funeral is as fresh in my mind as if it had taken place the previous day. I gnaw on my finger and look over at Gerstein's peaceful garden.

No. I can't tell her the truth, what a ridiculous idea. I can't tell her anything and she can't help me. Her and her fucking pathetic little tools. She's laughable. What I can't believe is that I even bought into her bullshit. I really thought for a moment that she was right and that my life was salvageable. Pull the other one, why don't you?

And as for Dave, I decide that I'll lie by omission and not tell him anything. With him, I'll continue to try to play the conservative, cardboard cut-out, perfect wife that he wants. He would never have loved gothic me or the sexual me. I have to get my act together. And it literally is an act. It always has been.

28

I SET UP MY TABLE at the Provincial Craft Wholesale Show in St. John's, Newfoundland. My last evening at home had not gone well. Dave accused me of being distant again, distracted, and I blamed my therapy session. What wasn't great was that we were arguing in front of the kids.

"Frickin' doctor, stirring up all kinds of emotional shit," I said. "Come here, Mack-a-roon, let mommy paint your nails for you."

"Mom!" Kenzie looked up from her homework. "We're not allowed to wear nail polish at school, you know that."

"Right, right." I frowned. "I just wanted to do something nice for you. Do you want me to make my special egg salad sandwiches for your lunch tomorrow?"

"We hate them!" the girls chorused. "Dad makes our lunches, he knows what we like," Maddie added and I sighed.

"I want to do something," I insist.

"You can help me write a poem," Maddie said. "We have to write a poem for school."

I brightened. "About what?"

"Anything. What do you think?"

"*Amore!* The best poems are always about love."

"Eugh," Kenzie said. "Not love. Think of something else."

"Okay," I smile. "What's your most favourite thing in the world?"

"Dad is," Maddie said instantly.

"He is more of a person than a thing," I said. "But he'll do. Start with a line about Dad, anything."

"He's big and strong and manly," Maddie said.

"And his teeth are blocks of candy," Kenzie pitched in and Maddie liked that.

"Good one," she said and she wrote it down. "Um, he's also very handy." She chewed on her pen. "He's patient, he never gets upset, he makes the nicest dinners and he let us get a pet."

"Very good," I said. *Dave the saint.* My mood plummeted, meanwhile Dave grinned from the kitchen sink.

"All the school moms like him," Maddie continued and I shot a look at Dave who shrugged. "And he's never frightened, not even when we watch scary movies."

"That doesn't rhyme properly," Dave said and Kenzie nodded in agreement.

"I know but I'm tired of writing this poem," Maddie said and Dave shook his head.

"Not good enough, young lady. You can't just say you're tired of doing something. You have to wrestle it into submission, make it bend under your will."

"Wrestling!" Maddie giggled. "All right but I only need one more line, the others are fine." She knotted her forehead and concentrated hard. I watched her and thought it was amazing that Maddie was my daughter. I felt no connection to her at all. I needed to mention that to Gerstein, but then I remembered that relationship had gone down the tubes.

"All the school moms like him, at math he likes to win, and he teaches us how to swim." Maddie gave a triumphant glance at Dave who smiled.

"Good enough."

"Then my homework is done. Can me and Kenzie go and play some Xbox before bed?"

"Half an hour," Dave said and he looked pointedly at his watch.

I picked up Muffin and cuddled him but the dog wriggled

out of my grasp, and rushed off to be with the girls. I poured myself another glass of wine, and felt unloved by God, the universe, and my family. Dave sat down next to me.

"I'm sorry therapy is being tough," he said and my eyes filled with tears.

"I'm a bitch. And listen to how they love you. You get love poems while I forget they can't wear nail polish."

"It's nothing," Dave said and he stroked my hair, which only made me cry harder.

"I'm a bad mother," I said. "We both know it. I'm like my father."

"Stop it. You're a fine mother and you are nothing like your father."

Maddie came into the kitchen, took one look at me crying and started wailing herself.

"They're getting a divorce," she shrieked and Kenzie came running in, her eyes wide and her mouth open.

"We are NOT getting a divorce," Dave shouted. "Calm down, everybody. Mom's a bit sad, that's all. We all get sad sometimes, don't we? Yes, we do. Come here, Kenzie, and Maddie, come on, big hug. Everything is fine, isn't it Lee?"

"Yes, fine. Sorry girls. My hormones must be out of whack or something."

"What are hormones?" Maddie asked and Dave handed her a piece of kitchen towel to blow her nose.

"Things that make moms moms," Dave said. "Hormones are chemicals that only moms have and sometimes the mix gets itself wrong and then a mom gets sad."

"Does it get right again?"

"It does," I said and I pulled my girls close to me. "I'm sorry, girls. I'll get my mix right, you'll see. I got sad because I am proud of you and you make me happy."

"That doesn't make any sense," Kenzie was dismissive. "Dad, can we have some hot chocolate? We should, to help Maddie and Mom not be sad."

"Good thinking Kenz, good thinking." Dave reached for the hot chocolate and turned on the kettle. "Marshmallows?"

"Of course," Maddie chimed in, looking shocked. "You can't have hot chocolate without marshmallows!"

I stand at my stall and think about the previous evening's antics and depression, a hundred-pound anchor, fills my chest cavity and drags me down. My mood doesn't improve when I hear JayRay's booming voice.

"Oh god, the king is on his throne," Sandi comments loudly and I laugh.

"I haven't seen Iris. Have you?"

"She's off with morning sickness," Sandi jokes and I stare at her, horrified.

"Seriously?"

"No, duh. Joke. She's much too old to have kids. But apparently, she's got the runs and she's vomiting and shit. She wanted to come but the organizers said not a chance. She could infect us."

She's not infectious, a voice says and I jump. Is that my conscience talking? *She's being poisoned.* I feel sick. Now that it's happening, I'm shocked and terrified. My last increased dose must have done the trick, along with the cumulative onslaught on her system of the previous creams.

"She'll be fine," Sandi says, "don't look so worried. At least we get a show without her fussing about the angle of our displays and how neat we need to keep our stuff."

She won't be fine. She will dehydrate and die. I nod and pretend to focus on my display, but Iris is all I can think about.

I get through the day. I return to my hotel room and I go through my options. Then I reach for my cell phone and text JayRay.

Room 308. Am not hitting on you. Need to see you. Make sure no one sees you.

I don't have to wait long.

Puddytat! I'll be there in ten!

I brace myself for his arrival and when I open the door, he launches into the room, grinning, full wattage. He reaches for me but I put out my hand and stop him. "Like I said, this isn't me welcoming you back into my life."

He sits down on the corner of the bed. "What's up then?"

"Iris is sick?"

"Yeah, she's throwing up and shitting like a pig." He shrugs.

"It's my fault."

"What?"

"It's my fault. I put too much mercury and potassium cyanide in her face cream. You guys got married and she flashed this huge rock at me and she was so fucking happy and she needed more face cream. I swear to god it was an accident, more cyanide fell into the mix than I planned and I should have taken the jar back but she already collected the bag. I didn't know what to do."

"Yeah. Right." JayRay crosses his arms and looks at me, his head to one side. "Cyanide. All this time and you didn't know what to do?"

"What could I do?"

"You could have told me, or you could have told her you were worried you got the mix wrong. There are several thousand things you could have done, and you chose to do none of them."

"I'm sorry. But I'm telling you now."

"Will it kill her?"

"If she's dehydrated enough. They won't be able to rehydrate her and, yes, she'll die."

"If she dies, I get nothing," JayRay says. "You know that, right?"

"No, I didn't know that. I wasn't thinking straight. I was taking tranqs till I was in a coma because I was so fucking upset about you."

JayRay grins. "You were?"

"I was. I wasn't thinking straight."

"Can they trace the shit in her system?"

"Yes. But they'd need a reason to look for those chemicals."

"I don't want her to die." JayRay's angry. "She's good to me. She loves me. She buys the shit I'm selling."

He falls silent. "For starters, give me a new jar of face cream."

"That's what I thought too. I brought you one up for you." I hand him the jar. "Here."

His fingers caress mine and I pull back and drop the jar.

"Stop that, JayRay. You're a fucking monster. You broke my heart. I nearly lost my mind. I tried to kill your wife and now you want to fuck me?"

He winks at me. "Life's such a fascinating thing. You'd better play nice or I'll tell everybody that you did a bad thing. Bad girl did a bad, bad thing."

"Will you? Actually, no, you won't. I've got something on you too."

"Yeah? Really? What?" He looks interested and he sits down, grabbing the jar of cream and juggling it back and forth.

"I know you run a scam with the video cameras. You record people screwing around and you blackmail them."

JayRay goes white. "What the fuck? Who told you that?"

"Doesn't matter. But I've got names. So don't threaten me."

"Hmm. Little girl's all grown up now. She's playing at the big people's table." He gives me a twisted smile. "I miss your juicy pussy. Iris is kind of dried up. She's got this big old wide dry empty cunt, like a doublewide trailer. Not my cup of tea. Now yours, well it's tight and hot and juicy and I miss it."

He rubs his dick through his jeans and the shape of his erection is clearly outlined. My own groin grows hot and tight with need.

"Whatever, JayRay," I keep my voice steady. "You need to go home and take care of Iris. She'll need fluids and hospitalization. No joke. Leave the show. Go home."

"Oh yeah, mama, I'm going home." JayRay stands and he walks over to me. He leans down and his face is only inches away from mine. "You and me, we're not done." He brushes a fingertip down my cheek and I close my eyes.

"See you later. I'm off to save the world. Iris's world at least. And don't worry, we're copacetic, you and me, about who did what to who and where."

He closes the door and I'm left alone.

I unzip my trousers and shove my fingers into my panties and I finger myself hard. I come again and again and I lick my fingers. Then I lie on the bed and start all over again. *You and me, we're not done.*

You're right, daddyo. We're not.

29

IRETURN HOME. I have three whole days before the next
conference. A lifetime in limbo. And yet, I dread the next
conference. I can't forget the feeling of JayRay's finger on my
cheek and, given that I'm full of bad news, I can't return to
Gerstein. I am without allies of any kind. And for the first
time ever, my sales are down. I throw my journal in the trash.
There is no point.

On the first day, I lie to Dave about my appointment with
Gerstein and I pretend to go. Afterwards, when he asks me
about it, I make up something about it being harrowing as per
usual. I'm not lying. My entire life is harrowing.

Time passes with snail pace speed. It's summer and the girls
are at day camp, Maddie for baseball and Kenzie for music.
The house echoes with emptiness. Dave's off until September
and he's decided to try his hand at fixing things up around the
house. I offer to help, because I can't think of anything else to
do with myself. He looks at me with a quizzical expression,
as if there's something else I should be saying, but I just lean
against the door and eye his paint cans. "Nice colour," I say.
He's repainting the dining room a rich dark red.

He fishes around in a bag from the hardware store and takes
out two boxes of Mr. Magic Eraser and he hands them to me.

"I'm hoping to not have to repaint the banisters," he says,
"so if you can give them a good scrubbing with these, you
could save me the task."

I take them from him. He doesn't meet my eyes and goes back to his painting. I wait for a few moments to see if he has anything else to add but he doesn't.

I start working on the banister railings. I never realized we had that many stairs. In a way, the work is soothing and I don't have to think about anything except which spot to clean next.

The girls come back from their camps, dropped off by the ever-helpful Denise, and we watch a movie and Dave makes waffles for supper, the girls' favourite.

The third day, the girls go off again and this time Dave has me sanding the kitchen table. He has hardly said a word to me. I dutifully scrub at the wood for a couple of hours and then I decide what the fuck, I'd rather pay someone to do this tedious shit. I'm going to leave early for my trip. I put down the tools and go and have a shower.

I pack my suitcase and as I zip it shut, I look up. Dave's watching me. He's standing in the doorway with that sad and weary look on his face.

"You never went to your therapy session," he says quietly. He's backed me into a corner. I'm going to deny it but instead, I get angry. I put my hands on my hips and jut my chin out aggressively.

"Are you checking up on me?"

"I saw Andrea Gerstein at the hardware store. She asked me how you were and I said she should know and she said you both agreed a few weeks ago that she wasn't the right therapist for you."

"What the fuck? You never told me you guys knew each other. How did *she* end up being my therapist? How fucking convenient for you."

"Her daughter's in Maddie's class. We live in the same neighbourhood. *You* chose the most convenient therapist. You chose her, not me. And you chose her because she was close and it was the least amount of effort to go and see her. Because you didn't really want to go. I didn't mention that I knew her because I didn't want to give you a reason not to go. But you managed that all by yourself. Of course we never discussed you, not until the day when she told me that you had stopped seeing her. She's worried about you. She cares about you. All she asked me was how you were and we both realized you were lying to me. I'm sure she's thinking that there's no hope for me and my lying wife but of course she was too polite to say so."

"You're excellent buddies with all the mommies, aren't you, Mr. Nice Guy Dave?" I spit the words at him and Dave walks in and faces me across the bed.

"I cannot take your shit any more, Lee. You aren't even trying."

"I am so."

"Then try harder. Or don't. I don't care."

"What are you saying?"

He shrugs and drops his gaze. "Just that we'll resolve this when you get back. I can't go on like this. I won't."

He leaves and I want to throw something after him but I can't find anything except the useless pillows and cushions and I dump them on the floor anyway. I haul my suitcase off the bed and leave. I forget to leave a note for the girls but I figure they wouldn't care anyway. I drive to the airport and book a room at a nearby hotel when I can't change my flight.

I lie awake for hours, furious with Andrea fucking Gerstein. I want to text her and ask her how much she told Dave but I know that she wouldn't have betrayed my confidences. She asked about me because she cared. Although, regardless of her intentions, she shouldn't have asked. That in itself breached doctor patient confidentiality and she should be made to pay.

I finally drink myself to sleep and I'm hungover when I drag myself to the airport. When we land in Houston, I go to the hotel and throw my things into the room. Six months have passed since the Bernice debacle and during that time JayRay dumped me and married Iris. During that time I tried and failed at therapy and at saving my marriage and my family. A year and a half since I started my affair with JayRay. So much dirty water under the bridge of time.

I walk down to the conference centre to set up my display, needing the routine familiarity to settle my nerves. I'm concentrating on getting unpacked when I notice a movement out of the corner of my eye. No! It can't be! And yet, yes, there he is. JayRay, setting up across from me.

I glance at Sandi's stall but Sandi isn't there yet, for which I'm grateful.

I march over to JayRay. "What the fuck are you playing at? Why are you setting up here?"

He folds his arms and looks at me. "Iris had a stroke. By the time I got back, it was too late. She's paralyzed, in a nursing home. She can't talk. She won't ever get better. I changed places with Vic so that I could be here, right in your line of vision. Why? Because *I'm here to remind you of the mess you left when you went away*." He raises his voice as he sings the last line and few people turn and look our way, wondering what's going on. "Just like the song says.*"

"*You* went away," I remind him. "*You* left *me*. You left me to go crazy while you ran off and fucked some skinny old bitch that you married. You never called, you never texted, you left me alone and I nearly lost my mind."

"I was in character," JayRay says, and his face twists with anger. "I had to be. I thought you knew that. I told you what I needed to do. And you said you would support me and then you fucked me over because you thought I betrayed you. You fucking told me how to get Iris to marry me, you practically told me how to fuck her, and then you hated me when I did, and you think I had let you down? You psycho fucking bitch!"

We're arguing loudly and furiously and I'm worried that Sandi will show up. "I have to go," I say. "I cannot be seen with you."

I leave and take my place at my stand just time because Sandi shows up and she raises her eyebrows at JayRay. I meet her glance and shrug.

Iris, paralyzed. It was their fault, not mine. They shouldn't have been together, it was just wrong. JayRay belonged with me. I try to feel bad about poor paralyzed Iris but my heart is singing. Iris is gone! Well, sort of gone.

And I love having JayRay across the aisle. I come to life again, my entire body feels energized and vibrant. I try to contain my joy but Sandi looks at me during a quiet moment and she also knows something's up.

"Your aura's different," she says. "You're like a plant dosed with water and nourishment. But there's darkness too. Are you okay?"

"Just a bit headachy," I lie. "Migraines can make me feel a bit manic before they hit and then they drop me like a stone."

"That's probably it," Sandi agrees but she sounds doubtful.

When the day ends, I rush up to my room. I'm sure I'll hear from him. I shower quickly and I wait.

Midnight comes and goes and there's no word from him. I sit next to my phone. Then I lie down next to my phone and I wait, but there's still no word.

At three in the morning, my phone buzzes. *Room?*

276, I reply and I'm waiting at the door when he arrives.

We fall on each other and devour skin, juice, hair, orgasm.

We finally stop, wrung out and shaking.

"Iris doesn't have any money," JayRay says. He's lying on his back, hands laced behind his head.

"What?"

"She doesn't have any money." He's speaking in a monotone. "Her husband left her the house but she works because she really needs the money not because she enjoys it. I guess she didn't tell me because she thought I was only in it for the money but she wanted me anyway. And now she's in a government-sponsored nursing home. The house goes to the husband's relatives when she dies and I get nothing. She bought her diamond engagement ring on credit. In fact, she's in debt up to her paralyzed fucking eyeballs and here's the clincher. I get to own it all. All her fucking debt. Not only do I end up with nothing, I end up owing. Having nothing would be way fucking better than what I've got now. Fuck. What a joke. What a cosmic joke. And how is your amazing life?'

"Dave wants to end it. My therapist fired me and I lied to Dave and he found out. And, the girls seem happier when I'm not there. What a pair of fuckers we are." I caress his chest and I've never been happier.

He reaches for my hand. "I'm sorry Leo."

"Yeah, me too. It can't get any worse. What are we going to do?"

"I've got one thing left," he says and I sit up. He lights a cigarette and I wave the smoke away.

"Since when do you smoke? JayRay, this is a non-smoking room, I'll get a fine."

"Fuck that. Remember my half-sister, the bitch author? I've got a thing going on with her. It's going down tonight. Remember I told you about Plan B? Well, Plan B is finally happening."

"What is it?"

"I can't say," he says cagily and I'm about to slap him but he grabs my hand.

"I've got nothing left except this," he says. "Okay? We're in this together but for once, fucking trust me. Look what happened when you didn't. Iris would be alive and she'd be responsible for her own fucking debts and Dave wouldn't be ending it with you."

I don't have much to say to that and I nod.

"It's going down tonight at this hotel, nine o' clock. Will you come with me?"

"Of course I will." I kiss his hand. "We have to play it cool at the stalls," I remind him. "No one can know we're together."

"I know," he says and he pulls on his jeans and leaves.

I get ready for the day. When I come out of the shower, I

see a text from Dave. Oh shit, I forgot to Skype with the girls like I said I would. But that's not the clincher. There are more messages from Dave and after I scroll through them, I run to the toilet and throw up, dry heaves. I kneel on the cold floor, heaving nothing but humiliation and shame.

Dave the detective found my marriage certificate to JayRay. It was folded into a tiny square and tucked into a box of sanitary pads.

"The marriage may not be legal," his last message reads, "but at least I know where your heart is. Don't come home. Ever. I'll figure out what to tell the girls. We owe you nothing. I don't want you to damage them any further than you already have. In the meantime, I'll say you're away on business for longer than usual. Don't bother to reply to this. I'm not interested, we're done."

And then my phone rings. I look at the caller ID. It is Ralph.

I make it back to the bedroom and sink down into a chair and take the call, trying to make my voice cheerful, business as usual.

Ralph is calm, which makes what he says even worse. "Seems you're in some hot water, Leonie. The police called me from a hospital. They're claiming that your face creams dehydrated a woman to the extent that she had a stroke and she's paralyzed and there's a good chance she's going to die."

"I don't understand," I stammer. I thought JayRay switched the jars. "That's ridiculous. Of course the creams are fine. But why would they even test them? It doesn't make any sense."

"Because this woman, even when she was taken to hospital, bleeding from every orifice of her body, was adamant that she needed her night creams. She told the nurse she just got married, to some toy boy by the sounds of it, and she was terrified of aging. Even while she was dying, she was slathering herself. And one of the nurses mentioned to the doctor that the face creams may have been the cause of her symptoms. The nurse is one of those biologically aware types who can tell you which

Mac lipstick has more lead in it than Chanel, and she was suspicious of this non-branded, non-government approved line of products. They ran blood tests. And what did they find? Mercury and potassium cyanide. And they tested the cream and what did they find? Mercury and potassium cyanide." Ralph is screaming at me and he isn't so calm any more.

I'm silent. What can I say? Ralph carries on.

"You dosed this woman yourself. God knows why you did it. I don't care, and I don't even want to know. Because of you, a normal healthy woman is now paralyzed, she cannot talk, she cannot see, and she will never recover. Never. June told me you were weird and fucked up but I believed in you. Listen to me. Do not go near the stall. The booth staff will close it up. The credit card has been cancelled. I will be suing you and you will be liable for all legal fees. We have a contract, remember, which clearly states that you're liable for the health effects of the product lines. You signed it. That contract is clear and therefore, the police will be pressing charges of attempted murder and intent to do grievous bodily harm, in addition to which they have a list as long as my arm of other charges. Henceforth, I will correspond with you in writing only via my lawyers."

He hangs up and I clutch the phone, frozen. Then I text JayRay. My fingers are shaking and I can't get the words right. *Dave knows we're married. Ralph knows about Iris & the cream. I thought u switched it? I'm going to be charged, attempted murder.*

He replies. *Couldn't switch it. Happened 2 fast. Leave hotel NOW. Go to diff one, pay $$. Turn your fone off, throw it away. Fone me from new place, tell me where u r, then wait. Can't talk now. C u later as per plan. Don't panic. We'll be ok.*

Okay, I text back. I grab my little suitcase, shove a few random things into it, and I leave the room. I take the stairs and I keep my head down, and I try not to run through the lobby. JayRay's right, they'll be coming for me.

Then

BERNICE UNRAVELS

30

DIRK IS FALLING APART. In the four months since he officially split from Chrizette and his kids and the *Volksraad*, he slowly but surely comes loose at the seams, and there's nothing I can do but watch.

I try to help, of course I do, but the whole thing happens in such slow motion that it's intangible in a way. It's more like a feeling than a set of actual behavioural examples I can call him out on. Although he did leave his job. He said he needed a new direction in life. I couldn't argue with that. He said selling life insurance depended on having good contacts and they're gone. When he first started out, he had his rugby buddies and then he had the *Volksraad* crowd but they're all gone, every last one of them.

"So-called fucking friends," he's bitter. "When the party stops, where are people when you need them, hey?"

Our sex life peters out. The Viagra stops working and he doesn't even care that I know he's been taking it.

I am ashamed to say that I get vicious. "Ag ja, now that's just great," I comment, when his hammerhead cock wilts and dies yet again, "bloody great. The main reason we got together in the first place has now gone back to sleep. The trouble with you, Dirk is that you have a Madonna-whore complex. Chrizette is the Madonna and I am the whore. The fact that your Madonna was actually the real whore in all of this is an ironic joke; she was fucking Gerit while she was *married*. I wasn't even really fucking you, in terms of your pathetic definition, and I wasn't married, and yet, I was, and still am, the whore."

He slaps me hard across the face and my nose starts to bleed.

I should have kicked him out right then. I know I should have, but we have, somehow, developed a passive-aggressive co-dependent relationship and I admit that I feed off the energy of being cruel to him. It's as if I want to see how much I can poke him with needles and pins and barbed wire before he makes me stop.

I look at him; my face is stinging and blood drips onto my silk pajamas. "Nice. Very gentlemanly of you. Something has to change, Dirk." I throw this ultimatum at him with no solution in mind. I just want him to fix this mess, whatever it takes.

He doesn't reply, he pulls on his pajama bottoms and goes out onto the verandah to smoke. To think that he once made me give up smoking. He chain-smokes unfiltered cigarettes and I smoke along with him, but even during my worst days of heavy smoking, I'd never come close to this.

I follow him out, sit next to him and light up. "Aren't you even going to apologize? Hitting your woman is acceptable? That's what *opregte* Afrikaners do?"

"Ag woman, you don't count," he says and he sounds exhausted. "You are not an Afrikaner. You are not pure."

I know he has always thought that. And I should kick him out for saying something that insulting but I'm not ready to let him go, so I change tack. Clearly, it's up to me to find a way out of this black hole we have fallen into.

"Listen, let's stop this war-mongering. What can I do to help you find your way back to yourself? I know you've lost so much. What about racehorses? Can't you get involved in that again? I know you had shares in a few horses. What about getting another one?"

He shrugs. "Chrizette owned them. And they're too expensive. I don't have the money that I used to. I have to watch my spending now."

"I could help you. We could go and look at horses together, pick a winner. It would be fun. Something to do together, get us out of the house. And we could join a gym — get fit, stop smoking. And we could get a dog, go for walks together."

Dirk smokes in silence and I wait for him to say something, anything, but he doesn't. He gazes off into the distance, smoking.

I go back to bed and lie as still as I can, my heart pounding, my eyes wide open. I'm not ready to lose this man yet.

When the weekend comes, he's still in his funk. I watch TV by myself on the Friday night while he drinks himself into a stupor. I make him sleep in the guest room, disgusted by his behaviour. This is becoming intolerable.

The next day I skip breakfast and sit in my study, drinking coffee and looking at the new book on my computer. My story that's going nowhere.

Lunchtime rolls around and I'm famished. I'm about to go and look for Betty when Dirk appears in the doorway. He's clean shaven and his hair is slicked back. He's decked out in one of his good suits and he's even wearing a tie. He resembles the man I fell in love with, only this version is bloated and soft, with fleshy bags under his bloodshot eyes.

"How about you let me take you out to lunch, hey?" he asks and his voice sounds hoarse and strained. "Somewhere special. Go get nicely dressed."

I want to retort with a sarcastic comment but I bite my tongue and nod. He smells fresh and spicy and despite the alkie skin-tone and recently acquired jowls, I feel a pull of the old attraction.

He takes me to Vilamoura, our favourite restaurant, and when the waiter offers us the wine menu, Dirk waves him off and says not today.

"So ja, I thought about what you said," he tells me and he puts his hand on mine. I'm relieved that it still feels good when he does that. "We are going to get happy and healthy and well. I've been struggling with grief but it's time to let it go. We'll join a gym. I love your idea about a racehorse and I've got some ideas about yearlings we can look at. Thank you for that. I'm not sure about a dog, they're a lot of work. But for now, let's start at the beginning. We'll stop smoking and drinking and get our lives on track."

Although I'm relieved to hear him talk this way, concern flutters in my belly. What will we have, if we don't have wine and arguments and cigarettes? I want to ask him about the sex and how he proposes to fix that, but I don't want to ruin his optimistic mood. He reads my mind and squeezes my hand.

"Ja. I know. I'll get some therapy. You're right. I am hung up on some myth of a woman who doesn't exist. She's got my cock in her hand and I need to get it back. We will get that sorted out too."

I smile at him and let myself relax. He's going to take care of everything. Everything is going to be fine.

31

FOR A WHILE THINGS ARE BETTER between us, although we get on each other's nerves a lot. Giving up smoking, going to the gym, and eating healthily isn't nearly as much fun as lying around, smoking, and drinking countless bottles of wine.

But we're committed to the plan and I, for one, start to feel better about myself. But I give up on my writing. It's one too many things on the list and, besides, it's going nowhere.

Dirk and I spend a lot of time looking at horses. He explains the various types of ownership to me: sole ownership versus co-ownership, versus us being part of a syndicate. He says we should form a company, that it's the most financially sound way to run an enterprise. He says that for our purposes, leasing a horse is the best option. We could lease a horse for three years, which would give us a good chance of getting our money back.

There are huge expenses involved and I grow concerned: training fees, farrier fees, vet consultations, race entries, jockey fees, transport and ownership registration fees. I stand next to Dirk, listening to him discuss the pros and cons of a particular horse and my feet grow colder by the minute.

Dirk says it would be a good idea to line up a trainer before we select our horse. This makes sense but I have no interest in that side of the business and Dirk tells me he will take care of it. I'm happy to see him filled with enthusiasm again. It's fantastic to see that great big smile back in play.

"We'll have to register with the National Horseracing Authority," he says. "We must get our own colours, and the jockey will wear them when he races our horse. We'll have to get our silks made up and we'll register the horse."

"There's a lot involved," I comment, and my heart sinks while my feet grow even more cold.

"Ja, I know it seems complicated. Don't worry. I'll take care of everything. All you have to do is help me choose our horse. I'll do the rest."

"Dirk, I'm a bit worried about costs. A good horse can cost half a million rand, never mind the other things you mentioned. How much is this going to put me out of pocket? I need a number."

"*Liefie*," he says and my heart skips a few beats. That was his term of endearment for Chrizette. I heard him use this when he was phoning to tell her he was working late when he was with me. He finally uses the expression for me and I melt. "I know it seems overwhelming right now. I'll work it out and let you know. I'm confident I can bring it in under a million."

"A million rand! That's a lot! Well, see what you can do."

As much as I love this energized, revitalized Dirk, a million rand is a lot of money to spend on a horse. But I said I would help, so I am committed. I guess I should have asked him upfront for a ballpark figure but it's too late now.

I just wish his happy vibrancy would extend to the full length of his dick, but unfortunately that particular area remains quiet and subdued.

A few days later, he comes to me with his laptop. "I have done the math. Come sit with me, *liefie,* I will show you."

I have to admit, spreadsheets and the like hurt my brain like nothing else. But I nod and we sit together and I try to make sense of the columns and rows and how it adds up.

"A million rand? No way you can do it for less?"

"Ja, well, hopefully I can bring some change home for you," Dirk sounds confident. "If we set this up as a company, we'll save on taxes and it'll be better in the long run. I've set up a company, VilliersVanColler Pty (Ltd)." He pulls his briefcase onto the sofa, opens it and takes out an official looking form with a South African Registrations logo at top. "Here. Sign and date it here, give me a cheque, and we'll be off to the races!"

It looks fine. What can I do? He's sitting there, the document is ready, he's holding out a pen. What can I do?

"Coffee, Madam?" Betty asks at that moment and Dirk glares at her.

"Ja, Betty, that would be lovely. Dirk, let me look at this for a moment, it looks very official. I'm sure it's fine but give me a moment."

A look of terrible hurt crosses Dirk's face and I grab the pen. "Betty, why don't you bring out that lovely cake you made yesterday? Dirk and I need to celebrate this new journey together. We're going to have a lovely horse racing adventure!"

I sign and date the form and give it back to Dirk who beams. Betty vanishes into the kitchen.

"*Liefie*," Dirk says as he rests his hand on my knee, "I wish I could make love to you right here and now. I'm sorry the boy has not been co-operative. You do know you're the love of my life? I'm sorry my brain and my cock are so fucked up. They'll come right. Thank you for believing in me."

He gives me a deep kiss and I too wish his cock and his brain worked better. I have slight misgiving at how fast the whole horse thing has happened and how much I have invested, but it's too late now.

"I'm going to the bank," Dirk says and he closes his briefcase with a satisfied little click and rushes out the door, pausing to wave on his way out. "I'm getting us a bottle of wine. We're falling off the wagon tonight, we earned it!"

I listen to his car leave and I wonder what I've done.

DIRK IS HAPPIER than I have ever seen him. The night after he deposited the cheque, we drank wine and we even had some sex. I wasn't even keen on trying, that's how bad it had become, but he persisted and in the end we managed.

I couldn't help hearing a little voice in my head tell me I just paid a million rand for a fuck. I told myself I should be happy, but I could feel that awful depression slinking back into my life.

In the past, baking with Betty and writing my books were a sure-fire way to keep anxiety and depression at bay, but Betty and the books have both deserted me. All I have left is this sick feeling like everything's going horribly wrong and I won't be able to put the pieces back together when it falls apart. I'm waiting for the worst to happen and there's nothing I can do to speed up the inevitable or make it go away.

I need something to do with my time. But what? Maybe I need to take up volunteering, give back to the community. But that's a cliché for post-menopausal matrons whose kids have fled the nest. And I don't care about the world except for my tiny patch of lawn. I don't follow the news, local or international; my focus has always been me.

In the week following the cheque exchange, I spend more time in the gym we joined, swimming lengths in the pool, hoping to exhaust the anxiety in me, drive it away by doing laps up and down, up and down. When that fails, I go to the

Rosebank mall and wander around the various stores. I pick up this and that, but I don't see anything that interests me.

I sit in my car in the parking lot, listening to Fleetwood Mac from yesteryear and staring at nothing, unwilling to go home.

I'm stuck. And I don't know what would have become of me if Dirk hadn't left me. But he did leave. He took my money and he left.

33.

"I COULDN'T HAVE BEEN MORE STUPID, could I?" I ask Betty and Theresa.

"Ag no, shame man, how on earth could you have known?" Theresa is supportive whereas Betty is silent, for which I cannot blame her.

"A million rand," I say. "To an impotent fool. This is my most stupid love *faux pas* ever."

"I want to *bliksem* the fool," Theresa says. "But don't you be so hard on yourself. We've all make mistakes in the name of love. You've called his cell again?"

"A thousand times. It goes straight to voicemail."

"Let me phone Chrizette for you," Theresa says and she takes it out of her new Kate Spade purse.

"Nice handbag. You've got her number?" I think back to the first time Dirk vanished and how I wanted to call Chrizette to see if he was with her, but Theresa said she didn't know her number. Why would she have lied?

"Ja, for sure. We did a charity event together, recently. I didn't tell you because I know you're not exactly fond of her." She searches through the contacts on her phone. "Here we go. Don't say anything."

I nod and Theresa switches the phone to speaker and we listen to the phone ringing.

"Hello?"

"Chrizette?"

"Yes? Who is this?"

"Theresa, from the fundraiser at the Kruger Park. I'm sorry to trouble you. I'm trying to find your husband, Dirk."

Chrizette gives a snort. "Shows how much you know. We split up ages ago."

"Do you know where can I can reach him? He isn't answering his cell."

"You might want to try Bernice Van Coller. I heard he was sponging off her these days. If you speak to her, tell her she's got my sympathies."

"She hasn't heard from him either."

"Then sorry to say but you're out of luck. Does he owe you money? If he does, you can forget about getting it back. I have to go." And she hangs up.

"You want to call the cops?" Theresa suggests, after we sit in silence for a while.

"I gave him the money. No gun was held to my head. It was all me, my stupidity."

"Was he really impotent?" Theresa wants to know and I nod.

"He did kind of okay the night I gave him the money but a million rand is a lot to pay for a fuck, wouldn't you say?"

"Ja, I would." Theresa agrees. "Listen my friend, I have to go. I'm sorry about this. I hope he turns up soon. Maybe he just went on a bender."

Something clenches in my belly. *My friend.* She's never called me that before. Usually when people call me *my friend*, they are trying to con me into something and it reminds me of something Dirk said.

"*Liefie*. He called me *Liefie*. He only called Chrizette that when he was lying to her. And, when he was lying to me. I should have known then that something was wrong."

"You couldn't have known anything. Stop blaming yourself. Blame him. He's the one to blame, not you. Do you want me to come by later?"

"No, thank you. I'll be okay. I need to think."

Betty lets Theresa out the front and I go into the kitchen and turn the kettle on just for something to do. What a mess.

"Rosie wants to talk to you," Betty announces and I jump. I hadn't heard her come into the kitchen.

"Me? About what? Does she know where Dirk is?"

"She doesn't know anything about Dirk," Betty replies and I'm confused.

"Then why does she want to talk to me?"

"She will tell you." Betty is implacable.

"When does she want to have this talk?"

Betty looks up at the apple-shaped wall clock. "In half an hour."

I shrug. I soon forget about Rosie and go back thinking about Dirk and my money.

He took all his clothes too. He planned the whole thing in careful detail, packing when Betty was in her room and I was at the gym, leaving before I got home.

I waited for him when I came back from the gym, and when he didn't come home, I thought he was meeting with a trainer or some such, and there wasn't anything more to it. Although it was odd of him not to have called.

I went to bed at my usual time, not even considering the possibility that I would wake up without him. But when I woke, startled out of a nightmare, it was with a sick feeling and no Dirk, and I knew then that something was horribly wrong.

He kept his toiletries in the guest bathroom and his clothes in the adjoining spare room, and I rushed into his bathroom, expecting to see his toothbrush and shaving kit in their usual place, but the counter was bare.

That's when it hit me. He was gone. I ran into the spare bedroom and yanked the closet open. It was empty, apart from a few misshapen metal hangers, an old pair of tracksuit pants on one shelf, and a broken pair of old running shoes.

I shouted for Betty and she came running. "Gone," I said. "He took my money and he left me."

I sank down onto the carpet. Betty didn't say anything.

I managed to get up and I tried to phone him and that's when it went from bad to worse. I called Theresa who drove over as fast as she could.

"Rosie is here," Betty announces and I look up. I'm in my study, scrolling through my emails trying to find someone else who knows Dirk but I'm not coming up with anything.

"Hi Rosie," I say distantly to the figure in front of me, my eyes on the screen. "What can I do for you?"

"You can pay my mother back the money you owe her," Rosie says curtly and that snaps me to attention and I spin around to face her.

"I beg your pardon? What are you talking about?"

Rosie sits down across from me. She sits down uninvited. I want to point that out to her but I'm too shocked by what she has said to correct her manners. I look up, expecting to see Betty hovering in the doorway like she usually does, about to offer tea or coffee, but she's nowhere to be seen.

And then, out of the blue, I'm hit by a blinding headache that knocks me sideways. I've never had a headache before, although my mother suffered constantly and most terribly. I always dismissed her as being a hypochondriac, a weak and lazy person who used headaches to cover up her depression and her unwillingness to do anything that required effort. But right now, she had my heartfelt sympathy and I squint, trying to see Rosie through the blackness of my pain.

"Ag come now, Rosie, I don't know what you are talking about," I say, and I lean my forehead on the palms of my hands and close my eyes.

To my shock, Rosie slams her hand down on the desk and I jump. The pain is nearly intolerable. I want to throw up, gouge my eyes out, howl with agony.

"Rosie, please, don't make so much noise. My head is killing me. What's going on? I don't understand. Please, close the blinds, the light is hurting me."

"I am not your servant. Close your own blinds. And don't act confused. Your books. You used my mother's recipes for every single one of them. And you never gave her credit. And you never paid her either. I am suing you, on behalf of my mother, for half of every cent you have ever earned."

"Have you lost your mind?" I ask. "Tell me this, could your mother ever have done a book without me? All she did was show me how to cook and bake. I did everything else."

"Yes. She showed you how to cook and bake. She contributed half of the content of each and every one of your books. I am glad you see it that way too. I am, by the way, recording this conversation, so thank you for being obliging in admitting that my mother is responsible for half of the proceeds of what your books have earned."

She pushes a phone across the desk and I see the red recording light.

She reaches into her leather briefcase and pulls out a thin binder. "In this binder you will find the legal notices that require you to pay my mother. Should you fail to pay her, legal proceedings will be put in place."

"What about your school fees? My father paid for that. And your university. And I paid your mother a monthly wage and gave her a room to live in."

"Yes. A room. With a toilet in another room outside and a basin to wash in. Not even a bath. Not even a shower."

"The room has always been like that," I object. "If Betty was unhappy, why didn't she tell me, hey?"

"And you would have done what? Told her oh, you're sorry, or offered her another fifty rand a month? You wouldn't have done anything. And to your point about my school fees and varsity fees, I anticipated that and I deducted them, although in reality it was your father who paid for that. You had nothing to do with it. Tell me, would you, out of the kindness of your heart, have sent me to such a good school, to your school, if it had been up to you? Somehow, I don't think so. And in case you are wondering how I arrived at the sum I did, with regard to my mother's share of the royalties, a friend of mine is a publishing agent and she got a copy of the sales figures. I am very glad to see that my mother is entitled to so many American dollars.

She stands up. "I am taking my mother home with me now. I wonder how you will manage all by your fragile little self."

I squint at Rosie. She has straightened her hair and she looks different from the last time I saw her. Something about her reminds me of someone, in a good way, but I can't think of who. And I am too distracted by what she's said to think about it.

"Now? Betty is leaving now? But she can't go. I need her. Dirk left me, everything is going wrong. This explains why she wouldn't give me any new recipes. It's because of you. Fine, I will pay her but I want her to stay. I am certain she wants to stay, why don't we ask her?"

"I want to leave," Betty says quietly from the doorway. I hadn't seen her arrive. "I am sorry Madam, but I want to go home to my family in KwaZulu Natal and I want to rest. I am very tired."

"Tired from what?" I ask, incredulous. "You can't leave me, Betty. Not now. I need you. What's in KwaZulu Natal anyway?"

Rosie laughs. "You see. You know nothing about my mother. Nothing." She pushes the binder towards me. "You'll see on the papers who you have to send the money to and you've got my email address to let me know when it's done. Now I'm taking my mother and we're leaving."

There's nothing I can do. And then Betty is gone.

And the pain in my head is unbearable.

I manage to reach for the phone and I call my family doctor. "I'm dying. I need you to send an ambulance."

A voice tells me help is on its way and I pass out cold.

WHEN I WAKE UP, I have no idea what happened. I'm in a hospital bed, in a hospital gown, with a needle in my arm and tubes up my nose. I am trussed up and confused and I start tugging the wires from my face. I'm about to yank the IV from my arm when the nurse comes in and stops me.

"How's your head?" she asks which is a strange question.

"Fine. Why?"

"You lost consciousness due to a migraine," the nurse says and I shake my head.

"I don't get headaches." I'm annoyed by her mistake, but I start to remember what happened and even the vaguest memory of that pain hurts like blazes. I lie back on the pillow.

"Your family doctor will be here in a few hours, as soon as he is done with the patients in his clinic. He works in the hospital too."

"I didn't know that." I speak automatically. Betty is suing me for half of my book money and she's gone. I'm sure that Rosie has been after Betty for years to get repayment for her contribution to the books, but I'm equally sure that Betty resisted. It's clear to me now that she hasn't been happy for a while, and it culminated in her quiet refusal to talk about new recipes. But would she have agreed to this enormous betrayal had I not foolishly handed over an obscene amount of money to a useless fool? But the only fool in all of this mess is me.

IHAVE A CAT SCAN AND AN MRI and I'm released from hospital the following day. My doctor concludes that the headache was a medical anomaly triggered by extreme stress. He doubts it will reoccur, unless the stakes once again rise to that level. I don't tell him all the details, except to say I have been conned out of millions of rands with only myself to blame. He agrees that would indeed cause a crippling headache in the most hardy of fellows. That's how he put it.

I take a taxi home and let myself inside. The house has been unlocked for two days and it's a miracle that I haven't been burgled to hell and back. I pause in the hallway. The sun is shining through the tall stained-glass windows and I watch dust motes float down on a diagonal beam. I remember reading that the dust motes are skin flakes that we've shed and I shudder. There's a lot of skin floating around my house.

It's so quiet. And perhaps it's my imagination but the rooms already have a dusty, unloved, unlived-in look.

I wonder if I should lock the door behind me but I have the sudden thought that perhaps an intruder has found his way into the house in my absence and, if so, I want to be able to make a run for it.

I tiptoe quietly into my study and pad around to my desk. I open a drawer and take out a key. I remove the entire drawer and unlock a secret drawer behind that. I reach for the tiny revolver that my father gave me. It is loaded.

I check the house, room by room, as silently as I can, with my senses on high alert for the smallest sound. I'm terrified the stress of being there alone and being so frightened will spark off another headache and I'm relieved when I finally make it through the house and everything is fine. I lock the front door and set the alarm.

I pick up my phone. Theresa called a bunch of times. And there is a text message from an unknown number, caller ID blocked.

> Bernice. Sorry. I never meant to steal from you. But I ran out of money. I ran out of faith. Everything and everyone has betrayed me and they must pay. I will make them pay and you will see my retribution.

There are more texts:

> I will have my justice. Like my fathers before me, I will do the Afrikaner nation proud. I will make them stand up and be counted. They have lost their way. But I will show them.

And then:

> When I am finished, they will rise up again, as a nation.

And:

> I am sorry I could not love you. I was a married man. I was a father. That should not have been taken from me.

Dickhead. I hate him. I hate being in this house. I miss Betty. The weight of her loss fills my heart. Tears run down my face and I half-heartedly wipe them away on my sleeve.

I go to my desk and remove Rosie's paperwork from the binder and I read it. I sign where she wants to me to and I make out a cheque. I seal the papers and the cheque in an envelope and I address it. I put a stamp on it and put it in my purse.

I get my computer going and I send Rosie a message: *I have done what you asked. The letter and cheque will be posted tomorrow. Please tell your mother that I miss her very much and that I hope she is well.*

I can't apologize for my actions, as much as I want to. I can't say I'm sorry for never having acknowledged Betty's role in the cookbooks. I can't even thank Betty for everything she did for me. I want to, but I can't.

I send Theresa a message to say I'm fine, that I collapsed and was taken to hospital but I am better now. I tell her that I'm going to take a vacation and that I'll phone her as soon as I get back.

I hurry to my bedroom. I pack a suitcase and I call a taxi to take me to the airport. When I get there, I'm told I'll have to wait for a few hours for the next flight to Pilanesburg but I don't mind. I sit neatly and primly in my chair, with my large purse balanced on my knees, and my suitcase at my side. I sit and wait. And every now and then a tear escapes from my eye and I don't care who sees.

36

THE WOMAN AT THE AIRLINE COUNTER misled me. The flight to Pilanesburg is only the following day. I wasted hours waiting.

I'm tempted to rent a car and head straight to the farm as it's only a three and a half hour drive, but it's already evening and I would be stupid to drive at night.

I check myself into an airport hotel and dump my luggage in the room. I don't know what to do with myself. I'm wound up, stretched like a bowstring. I check my phone. I'm hoping to hear from Betty. I'm hoping she will say she's sorry she left me and that she wants to come back. Instead, Dirk has fired off another volley of texts:

Where are you? Why were you in hospital? Email me.

Then:

Watch the news.

Then:

They made me do this. They brought me to this.

"Betty," I say out loud. "Ag man, you were like a mother to me. Why didn't you say something to me, about the cookbooks, hey?" But I know the answer to that one. Because I wouldn't have listened.

And Dirk. Wait a minute, how does he know I've been in hospital? The only person I told was Theresa. Oh. My. God. Theresa is fucking Dirk.

I immediately call her.

"Where are you?" she asks. "What do you mean, you are going on vacation? Where to?"

"Cut the crap. How long have you been fucking Dirk?"

A resounding silence follows. "Since he moved in with you," she finally admits in a small voice. "He came to see me when he couldn't get it up. Turns out he managed fine with me. He said it's because my parents were Afrikaans. He said I'm a lapsed Afrikaner and there's still hope for me. And I fell in love with him. He doesn't love me, he never did. I am sorry, Bee."

I want to hang up on her but I need to hear more.

"Where is he now?"

"I don't know. He texts me from a phone with no ID. I can't even text him back."

"And did you know he was going to steal from me?"

"Of course not! What kind of friend do you think I am?"

"A friend who fucks her best friend's lover. That the kind of friend I know you are. That fancy new Kate Spade handbag you got. Dirk paid for that with my money, isn't that so?"

Theresa starts crying but she manages to tell me that I'm right. It was a gift from Dirk.

"Ag stop crying for god's sake," I tell her. "What is he planning to do?"

"I don't know. I swear. He hates the fact that he was betrayed by the *Volksraad*. He says the Afrikaners need a wake-up call and that he's going to give it to them. I told him not to be stupid but he won't listen to me."

"Dirk stole from me and cheated on me. You lied and cheated on me. Betty left me. Rosie sued me. You all deserve to die."

"What? What do you mean? About Betty and Rosie?"

"You are dead to me. Don't ever contact me again." I want to add a childish, vicious remark like I hope she'll get syphilis and go mad but I'm not sure if women get syphilis and I can also, on some level, understand her having fallen for Dirk. Hadn't I? He cheated on me but then I was his cheat when he was with Chrizette. And so it went around. What had I expected?

I end the call abruptly. I need to get drunk. All I can see is Betty's sweet face, with her dark eyes, and her concerned look as she cocks her head to one side when she looks at me. Was her concern fake? We have been through so much together. I can't believe I'll never hug her again. But, come to think of it, she never hugged me. I always hugged her. I thought she liked it when I hugged her. Now I wonder if I have unwittingly forced myself on her my entire life. Had she, like Rosie, hated me all along? I can't bear the thought.

I go down to the bar and order a bottle of wine. I down the first glass and try to sip the second one more slowly. I need faster action to numb my pain and I order a shot of scotch on the side and I throw it back.

"A beautiful woman such as yourself should never drink alone," a British accent pronounces and I look up.

"I drink alone by choice," I retort. "And if you want to join me, best you don't make stupid remarks like that."

The man laughs and sits down. He's good-looking and well dressed, the kind of man who could be a lawyer or a serial killer. I look at him sharply. "What made you think that was an invitation? The next thing you say will determine whether you stay or go."

"My sister loved your last book," the man says.

"Only the last one? But not the previous ones hey?"

"Whoa. You're not exactly friendly, are you?" The man leaves and I make no move to stop him.

The bartender grins at me and puts another shot of scotch in front of me.

"On me," he says and he goes back to texting on his phone while I admire his muscled forearms.

I would have preferred to be hit on by him, a muscular young stud, but I'm too old for him. I sigh. No wonder Dirk couldn't get it up with me, but he could with Theresa. Theresa is a simple person really. Saying that makes me sound like a bitch but it's true. She would no doubt have tried to make him feel better, whereas I only ever worried about what I was feeling. I have always been too intense, too deeply mired in the darkness of my own thoughts. Selfish, that's me.

It's all my fault. Even Betty said that. After I split with one of my many lovers, I told Betty that he had turned out to be boring. I said it wasn't my fault, that I had to end it, that no one could be expected to stay with boring.

Betty sniffed. "You. Even when you were a little girl, one day you wanted your friends to visit and the next day, no, you didn't want them. Then boyfriends. One day you liked a boy, then no, he was boring. It is not the man, it is you."

I had no reply for Betty at first. I knew what she said was true.

"I am who I am," I finally said. "And if that makes me a bad person, so be it."

"*Eish*! I never said you were bad," Betty scolded me. "But I am saying don't blame the men."

I don't want to think about Betty. I look at myself in the bar mirror and I see that the bartender is watching me.

He leans on the bar. "You have a fascinating face. I just watched a thousand expressions move across it, none of them happy. What were you thinking about?"

"Lost opportunities. But how can you regret losing something you never had?"

"There's always time to want something new," he says and I notice that he has fantastic upper arms, strong and shapely, while his hands are elegant and his fingers are long and somewhat bony.

"But is there?" I ask absently. "That's the trouble with me.

I constantly want something new. How long can that go on? I've never been happy."

"I'm always up for a new adventure," the bartender says, missing my point. "I'm Keith. Would you like to go on an adventure with me, go on a *jol*?"

"Where?"

"A party. I know a guy." He looks at his watch. "I'm knocking off in fifteen minutes. Come with me, you'll have fun."

I nod. Ja well no fine, I will go with him. Maybe it isn't too late to try something new.

Half an hour later, I follow him to his car. It's a *skedonk* of a thing, and the door makes a groaning noise when he opens it for me. The chassis is nearly on the ground and I want to run away, but I remind myself that this is an adventure. I'm thirty-six years old and I need to have some fun. This is fun, right?

We drive away from the airport and I'm suddenly tired. Such a party animal, not. I would prefer to be in my hotel bed, with a glass of wine in one hand and the TV remote in the other.

Keith glances at me as if he senses my discontent and he opens up the glove box and fumbles inside.

We're speeding down the highway and I want him to focus on the road, not on whatever's inside the glove box. I distract myself by watching the city lights flash by. Johannesburg has a few tall buildings but they're nothing like the skyscrapers of America where I do my book tours. Johannesburg is a small city, a broken city filled with desperate people scavenging like rats to survive.

The smell of marijuana fills the air and I turn to Keith who holds the joint in my direction. I take it, inhale deeply and hold the smoke in my lungs.

I'm immediately stoned. "Good dagga, hey?" Keith grins. "Durban Poison."

I nod as he veers off and takes the Parktown off-ramp.

"Where are we going?" I ask and my voice comes from faraway and it sounds growly, belly-based.

"Hyde Park."

Hyde Park is a good area. I'm relieved. For some reason I assumed we'd be going to some shady *shebeen*. But my peace of mind, such as it was, evaporates as soon as we pull up at the party and I feel lost and alone. Keith parks outside and presses a buzzer. An ornate steel gate swings open and the parklike grounds are filled with shadowy people. The place is spotlit like a stage set and I'm confused.

"What's going on?"

"Film crew. Wrap party. I had a part in the movie. I played a security guard." Keith laughs. "I got to say, 'hey mister, let me see some ID.' That was the extent of my role. I'm a model too. *Men's Health* loves me." He sounds proud and I nod.

"How old are you?" I ask.

"Thirty-two. Time I got my shit together, wouldn't you say. But not tonight. Tonight we *jol*, do whatever we want, right hey?" We're standing in the shadow of the high wall that runs the perimeter of the grounds and I nod and run my tongue over my lips. The gesture isn't intended to be sexual, my lips are dry and chapped from the dagga, and I can't be bothered to find my lipstick in my purse. But Keith misunderstands and he leans in and kisses me, tonguing me deeply and I'm instantly on fire. At last! A real fuck! I grab his neck and pull him close.

"We do anything we want," I agree breathlessly and I kneel down and I unzip his fly. I go down on him, nearly impaling myself on his cock and he groans. I'm so into it that he comes almost immediately and he apologizes, wiping himself off with his T-shirt.

"I'll satisfy you later," he says. "I'm sorry, I didn't mean to come so fast but man, you had me so good. Come on, let's go find some people that I know."

We cross the garden, and walk between oil drums with fires burning high and Keith stops to talk to some people passing a bong around. I take a deep hit, thinking for a moment that

I've got no idea what I'm smoking but I don't care. I want to punish myself and punish the world.

"You look like Lauren Hutton," a young girl says to me. "Not like she is now, of course. Like when she was young and beautiful and famous."

"Thank you," I say and I would like to kiss the girl but I have no idea if the she will be agreeable and I decide that it's best not to find out. I've never kissed a girl but my anger and hurt is making me want to act out, do crazy things.

The girl hands me a joint. "Hash," she says and I take it.

I sit down on the grass, holding the joint and she joins me and we pass it back and forth.

"I would love to kiss you," I say. "But I'm too old, aren't I?"

The girl takes my face in her hands and she kisses me and it feels so different, her tongue is too soft and gentle and her face is delicate and smooth. I pull back and she smiles.

"It's okay," she says. She passes me a bottle and I take a long drink. Tequila. I hate tequila.

The pool is lit up like an aqua jewel and a woman jumps in. She's naked. Around us, people follow her lead, stripping off their clothes and diving in. The spotlights make the blackness of the night more intense, and the Spanish-styled house glows white in the background, while palm trees blow back and forth, making rustling noises. A strong wind whips across the lawn as if a storm is on its way.

"I'm going for a swim," the girl says and she strips bare. "Are you coming with?" She smiles at me and walks towards the pool.

"Ja, sure, just now," I say and I reach to pull my top off but I suddenly feel stupid and vulnerable. I don't want people to see me naked. And what if someone steals my purse while I'm in the water? I hate myself for being mundane and practical while others are happily losing their minds and their inhibitions, but I can't help myself. Oh god. I'm such a loser. No wonder everyone leaves me.

I turn and walk away from the pool. I've lost Keith and I've got no idea how I'm going to get back to my hotel. I sit down on a lawn chair and start to cry.

"Too many drugs?" a sympathetic voice asks me, and a boy with blond dreadlocks offers me a cigarette.

I take it and light it from the match he offers. "Don't you love matches?" he asks conversationally. "I love the way they smell."

"Ja, for sure. They smell decadent, poisonous."

The boy agrees and he lights another match and we watch it burn close to his fingers. "If you don't mind my saying so," the boy comments, "you look a bit out of place here."

"I am out of place. I fell down the rabbit hole, looking for adventure, and now I wish I hadn't." I blow smoke out of my nostrils. "And I don't know how I'll get home."

"Where is home?"

"The hotel next to the airport."

"I'll take you back. Come on. I don't care. This party's boring."

I follow him inside the house to the kitchen where he grabs a bunch of car keys off a hook.

"Only the best for you," he said and he led me to a low-slung black Porsche.

"You weren't joking," I tell him and he grins.

"My daddy's the director of the movie. Married to mommy, the money. I couldn't give a fuck about any of it, fame or money."

"Because you already have both," I say and he laughs.

"Maybe so." He starts the car and I close my eyes.

"The most perfect sound in the whole world," I said, "Hey, I don't even know your name."

"Kai. My mother's Finnish."

"I'm Bernice."

"Cool. You want to fly, Bernice?"

"Yes, please."

The boy obliges and we fly down the highway, with the city now on my left, and I lean back against the smooth leather stroke my thighs, and when Kai lifts my skirt and thrusts his fingers inside me, I moan and come, not once but again and again, and I lift myself hard against his fingers.

When I'm finished, he holds his fingers under my nose and presses them inside my mouth and I suck, thinking his fingers are rather thick for a slender young man.

He pulls up outside my hotel lobby and I smooth down my skirt.

"Well," I say, "thank you. Stay interesting, young man."

He chuckles. "I'll do my best."

I ease out of the car and walk into the reception area, and I don't look back. The engine roars off into the night and I'm filled with equal parts exhilaration and loss.

I take the elevator up to my hotel room and look at my phone. There are several texts and emails from Theresa. She is so very sorry. *Blah blah blah.*

And another text from Dirk.

Tomorrow is the day of reckoning.

Whatever. The man isn't capable of doing anything.

I run a hot bath and luxuriate in it, reliving my time with Keith and Kai. Two K's in one night. No actual sex. I want to laugh. What, am I like Dirk now? *I was never inside you, you were never inside me...*

No, I wouldn't lie to myself like Dirk did.

I wonder again, if Betty's right? Is there something wrong with me? What is it that makes me the eternally restless child that I am?

Do I have abandonment issues stemming from the early departure of my biological father? But that doesn't resonate. I have more anger at my mother, anger at her for being nothing more than a social butterfly, a butterfly resigned to being pinned down by life and headaches, and possessed by the need to flit from party to party, finding the meaning of life in the pages of a fashion magazine and a bolt of cloth and ignoring her daughter's very existence. And not sharing any of her beauty. Now that was selfish. A mother should share.

"Ja, Ma, I think the blame is more with you than the sperm donor," I say out loud. "But how pathetic, I'm nearly middle-aged and I still have mommy-issues. I'm quite sure you never wanted me."

I had leveled that accusation at my mother once.

"You never wanted me," I screamed and my mother looked at me, open-mouthed and wide-eyed, and she was about to answer but I ran out because I feared the answer. I feared that she would say, *You're right! I don't like you! You're unlikeable and plain and unlovable which is no fault of mine! So there, take that!*

I couldn't bear to hear those words said out loud, so I left the room and went to fire my rifle with my father instead.

I'm tired of thinking about the past and I'm getting sleepy. I climb out of the bath and pour another glass of wine. I get into bed and flick on the TV. I have a sudden vision of myself at that wild party, wishing I was in bed and I grin.

"Ja, me. Not the world's greatest adventurer, despite my best efforts. I like my creature comforts."

But I remember the feeling of Keith's thick hot cock in my mouth, and Kai's fingers deep inside me, and, at the end of the day, the evening hasn't been a total loss, not by a long shot.

37.

I WAKE AT MIDDAY. It's nearly checkout time. My head is aching and I down two painkillers with half a bottle of water. I turn on my phone and there are more text messages from Dirk. I can't be bothered to read them and I throw the phone back into my purse.

I missed the plane. Goddammit, I'm going to drive. I check out of the hotel and walk to the car rental booth and I sign out a BMW SUV.

And if any of those mothers try to highjack me, I'll show them what-for. I brought my little revolver with me and I lay it on the seat next to me, under a sweater, easy access. I'm in control at the wheel of this powerful car. I turn onto the highway off-ramp and I think of Kai, *do you want to fly? Yes!*

I step on the gas and pull into the fast lane. I glide across the highway like a snake sloughing off an old skin. I leave my lying existence with Dirk on the tar road behind me. I am wild and free. I am my true self.

Soon, the city is no more than a speck in my rearview mirror and I fly through the African veldt under a blue sky. I fly on a black tarmac strip of road that is lined with rubbish and de-tritus. How did this much garbage get here? Is there nowhere else for these people to take it? Apparently not, or maybe they don't care.

I keep my phone and my gun on the passenger seat next to me and I check my rearview mirror regularly. Pa trained me well.

"You cannot live in Africa without being vigilant," he said. "Always be prepared for the worst. It's the only way to survive."

When I tire of the silence, I switch on the radio and flick through the channels, trying to find a music station, but all I get is frenzied reporting and babbling voices. Eventually I leave the channel where it is, to hear what's going on. And I nearly swerve off the road when I hear the news.

Dirk has blown up the Voortrekker Monument.

What the fuck? And, *how* the fuck had he pulled it off?

I turn up the news and try to make sense of what's going on. Of course, no one knows Dirk is responsible but I know.

I pull over for a moment and check the messages I had thus far ignored.

Listen to the news!
Watch TV!
Now they will rally, as they should.

What exactly had he hoped to achieve? By all accounts, the forty-metre-square granite monument had been laid flat. Experts estimated it would have taken nearly forty pounds of explosive and nearly as many detonators. It seems ironic to me that it had taken forty pounds of explosive to level the forty-metre-square structure. I wonder about the symbolism of the number forty. But forget about that, I must to concentrate on what matters. How had Dirk got his hands on the explosives?

Oh my god. He used my money to fund it. I'm ice cold and I flick the seat warmer on even although it's a hot day. Freezing sweat runs down my armpits.

Should I call the police and tell them what I know? But would they consider me an accomplice? I wish I had looked more carefully at the papers Dirk asked me to sign. For that and nothing else, I deserve this. My stupidity has brought me to this. That, and my lust. There's no other reason for it. I fooled myself into thinking that I loved Dirk when in reality, my ego couldn't bear the thought of losing him and I would have done anything, even pay him a million rand, to keep him by my side.

I listen to the newscaster who is reading a press release issued by the police.

An Afrikaans man has claimed responsibility for the attack on the Voortrekker Monument. Here is an excerpt from a five-page letter that the man wrote, explaining his actions: "Afrikaaners no longer deserve the monument and what it stands for. We have lost our way. We have lost our morality. If they want to have monuments, we have to earn them. Have we forgotten Bibault's cry from the heart; *'Ik been een Africaander'*? It seems we have.

"Stephanus Johannes Paulus Kruger stated that 'in the voice of my people, I have heard the voice of God' but no longer do we speak with the voice of God. We have become godless, rudderless, empty. Our Bible came from our Afrikaner tongue, forging our Christian morality but where is that now?

We are a nation of fornicators, liars, and thieves. The *Regte* Afrikaners, the true Afrikaners, are dead. We had a divine sanction and we ignored it.

The Dear Lord placed us in Africa and provided us with the Afrikaans language and what have we done with it?

Have we forgotten everything the Great Trek stood for? We fought for our freedom as a people, as a nation and now look at us, content to be ruled by the savages from whom we took the land.

Die Ossewabrandwag (the Ox Wagon Sentinel) told us *Gesonde Huisgesinne Bou 'n Lewenskragtige Volk*. Yes, Healthy Families Build a Vibrant Nation! Where are our families now? We are divorced and divided.

Where is our blood *suiwerheid*, our blood purity?

We have lost *gesin* (family), *bloed suiwerheid* (blood purity), *godsdiens* (religion), *vaderlandse bodem* (fatherland), *vryheidsliefde* (a love of freedom) and we have lost our greatest cultural and national inheritances of our *volkerfenis*, of our nation.

The monument is gone because we did not deserve it any longer. Perhaps one day we will earn it again. And if and when that day comes, we will build it again.

I turn the radio off. I don't want to hear any more. A part of me isn't surprised this has happened. What an idiot the man is.

And so what if I gave him the money? I thought it was for a racehorse. I wasn't responsible for what he did with it. He stole from me. I'm as much a victim in this as anybody.

Luckily, no one was killed when the monument went down. At least he got that right. But the logistics of it…. I still wonder how he orchestrated it. The thing was huge, a granite man-made monolith and ugly as shit. I'm not sorry it's gone.

I concentrate on driving and I pick up speed. I'm going way over the speed limit but I don't care. I need to get to the farm as soon as possible.

I haven't visited my childhood home in the eight years since my father's death and, truth be told, I have hardly thought about it. I realize that I should have called Isaac, the groundsman, to tell him I'm coming. I also know I should stop in at the police station in the town to tell them I'll be at the farm, and get hooked up to the farmer's radio for the security network but first, I just want to get there. I'll sort out everything later. Let me be inside that cool house, that quiet, peaceful house where light falls through the windows like liquid gold and where everything is serene and lovely. I'll find peace there. I drive even faster, my need increasing as I grow closer.

When I arrive, I get out of the car and stretch, my hands firm against the the small of my back. Yes, there's the smell that brings my soul back to life. The hot dry dust of the baking earth. I dig out my keys and unlock the front gates. The padlock is rusty and stiff and the steel chain grumbles as I unwind it. The gate creaks with protest as I push it open. Yes, it has been a long time since I have been home. I get back into the car and turn into the long driveway. My shoulders relax and I slow down. The grounds look good. I drive past the cottage where Pa's mother stayed until she died and I drive past the stables that haven't been used in years. The sheep sheds are quiet and empty.

A rusty old windmill turns idly in the breeze and there is a quietness to the place as if the heat and dust have silenced even the birds and crickets.

I drive past the empty swimming pool. The grass around it looks dried out and burnt. I'll need to get the pool filled.

I pull up outside the house and switch the engine off. The car makes ticking noises, and it seems to shake slightly from exertion of the drive, like a panting dog.

I tuck my gun and phone into my purse and get out of the car. I slam the door behind me and the sound echoes in afternoon silence.

The house looks exactly the same as when I left it. Colonial and yet African at the same time. Built in the late 1800s in the traditional Cape Dutch style, the high rounded gables and white-washed walls with their green wooden window shutters gladden my heart as I approach. The wide, wrap-around verandah welcomes me, the floor polished and shiny, and even from a distance, I can imagine the smell of Cobra wax polish.

The steps leading up to the main door are lined with pink and scarlet bougainvillea and wild roses, yellow, white and red, while thick cactuses grow against the low verandah wall. The flowerbeds are filled with crimson geraniums and orange nasturtiums and vibrant marigolds, hardy plants that thrive in the heat and don't need much water.

The burglar bars are a cruel reminder of a harsher reality,

marring the loveliness of the idyllic house with their prisonlike appearance.

I walk up the verandah steps and yes, there's that smell of floor polish. The chairs on the verandah are as I remember; a white wicker set with a low coffee table in between them. Everything gleams and shines.

Being home is a like a hug and I inhale deeply. Yes, coming here was the right thing to do.

I unlock the door and walk through the house, from room to room. The curtains are drawn and the drop cloths are in place. There's a stillness to the house, and the air is stale, like the breath of an old person with unwashed teeth. The first thing I will do is air it all out.

I'm sitting on my old bed, running my hands over the duvet cover. It's dark blue with tiny daisies in a paisley pattern, and I feel a surge of affection for my younger self. And that's when I hear the sound of footsteps, and I pull my handbag towards me.

The footsteps stop and my heart is a hammer drill in my ears, so loud I am sure that whoever is in the house can hear me.

I cock the gun. I sit dead-still, the gun pointed at the door. The footsteps get louder and I can't blink, I mustn't blink, if I blink they will kill me, me sitting there with my eyes closed like an idiot.

When a face cautiously eases around the door, I scream like a banshee. My voice is stuck at first, a squeak, but it loads up well and the person drops to floor and starts screaming.

Dear god, it's Isaac. I lower the gun.

"Don't shoot, Madam, don't shoot," Isaac sounds terrified and I kneel down on the floor next to him, leaving the gun on the bed.

"Isaac. I am so sorry. Ag shame man, I should have come and found you first. Come on, get up. I am very sorry. I came home without telling you or anybody. I should have told you."

His dear face has aged and is a study in wrinkles. It's been that long since I saw him.

"You nearly gave me a heart attack, Madam," he tells me with a toothless grin and I laugh and hug him. "How are you?" I ask. "How are Elsie and your children?"

"They are fine Madam, thank you. The children are all big now. At school. Elsie has got work, that is good." He looks around, uncomfortable at being in my room.

"Let's go to the kitchen," I say and he turns and limps off speedily. I wonder why he is limping. I follow him. "Isaac, why are you limping?" I ask him.

"I was moving some machinery the other day," he says, "and it fell and hit me. My leg was broken. It only got better the other day."

He looks like the last place he wants to be in the kitchen with me and he shifts uneasily. I'm a bit hurt by his reticence.

"So the place looks in good shape," I say. "You took good care of it. Thank you. You got the bonuses I sent you?"

"Yes Madam, thank you." He studies his hands.

"Is there anything I should know, Isaac?"

"No Madam. The borehole is working well. Lots of water, we are lucky. Lots of farmers around ask me if they can take our water but I say no, they must ask you."

"They never did ask me. Well, a lot of water is good. The land in good shape?"

"Yes, everything is good. We had rain too. This is a good farm. Madam, how long will you be here?"

"I don't know Isaac. Listen, do you want to take off and go and see Elsie for a couple of days? Be with your kids. I'll be fine here by myself. I'm sure you must miss your family, living here all by yourself, so much of the time."

An expression crosses Isaac's face that is hard to read. Where has he gone, my old friend who used to lead me around on my pony, the man I've known since he was a boy and I was a baby? He's treating me like a stranger.

"I would like that very much, Madam," he says and without further ado, he bolts out the door.

I watch him hurry across the back yard to the servant's quarters, as fast as his limp will allow him to.

I go out the back and watch him as he hobbles down the driveway. Very strange, his sudden departure. His whole manner is odd. My curiosity is aroused and I decide to take a peek around the servants' quarters.

The servants' quarters. I haven't been back there since I was a child. Not since I was seven years old and hungry, annoyed that Betty wasn't in the kitchen.

I knew that she lived in the mysterious rooms that lay in the shadow of the house, across the broom-swept red dirt back-yard, hidden from view by the washing lines. There was no washing on the lines that day long ago and I, full of fury and self-righteous authority, crossed the expansive space, ready to find Betty and scold her for neglecting me.

The first room was a washroom, narrow and dark, a tiny cave. The toilet didn't have a lid or a seat, and the small, oval, rust-stained basin had one tap. I didn't find Betty there.

The next room was Isaac's. His room was spotless, with a thin mattress on the floor and a pair of overalls hanging from a nail on the wall. A small, battery-operated silver radio was next to the bed, as well as a dented candlestick holder with a stub of a white wax candle and a box of Lion matches. I had seen Isaac carrying the radio on his shoulder, holding it close to his ear as he walked down the driveway and into town.

Betty was in the next room, with Rosie. I was about to shout at Betty when Rosie's look stopped me. Rosie was cross-legged on the floor, the broken piece of a wax crayon in her hand. She was leaning over her colouring book, and Betty was asleep on the single bed, her mouth open and her hands folded across her chest.

The bed was high off the ground and I wondered about that. Why was Betty's bed so high and Isaac's just a mattress on the floor? Later I learned about the *tokoloshe*, which Betty feared and Isaac scorned.

A faded orange rope of twisted hay-baling twine was stretched across the room, nail to nail, hanging below the flat corrugated ceiling that clicked and creaked in the heat.

Betty and Rosie's clothes hung on bent wire hangers, the kind I had seen my father twist and throw out after he got his special church shirts back from the dry cleaners. The shirts he didn't even trust Betty with. When the shirts were returned home, they were protected by a filmy, thin sheet of delicate plastic and collared with a mysterious white paper wimple, similar to those worn by the Catholic Sisters of Mercy. I always tried to grab the white paper to play with it, before my father crushed it into a ball in his hand.

Betty's white-and-blue Church of Zion uniform had pride of place at front of the clothes line, and it was so starched and immaculately ironed that I could smell its cleanliness from where I stood. I wondered, in one of those thoughts that flashes through your mind and vanishes before you know it, where Betty ironed her clothes. The room was surely too small for an ironing board.

A battered kerosene stove was pushed underneath a rough pine plank that was held up on either side by four red bricks. Chipped yellow and green enamel tin mugs and plates were stacked next to a pile of bent tin knives and forks, alongside, a half-full bag of Mielie-pap, with a frying pan and two tin cooking pots with flat, thin lids.

I was but a child and yet, in the time it took for a fat housefly to buzz into the room and settle on the windowsill, I saw it all.

And Rosie's eyes, filled with hatred, made me scramble away, my heart pounding.

I scurried back to the big house, my hunger forgotten. What other land had I just visited?

And I never returned. I took care to avoid the servants' quarters. I didn't want to know, it was all too complicated.

When Betty came to stay with me in Westcliffe, I made sure that her room had a brand new bed and I got it made as high as she wanted it and I made sure it was sturdy. I bought her a brand new pillow and a duvet and a pine chest of drawers. I bought her a kettle and I even got her a microwave. I made sure her toilet had a seat and a lid, and that her basin had two taps, with hot and cold water. And then I left her to it and never thought about it again.

And I am not thinking about Betty's room now. I am thinking about Isaac's. Because as soon as I push open the door to his room, I know the answer to his hasty retreat. He hasn't been staying here alone. It's clear that Elsie is living there with the kids. There are thin foam mattresses in each of the rooms and the place looks lived in and organized.

I close the doors to each of the rooms and lean against the brick wall, thinking. Why didn't he tell me? I wouldn't have cared. Or would I?

I feel very tired all of a sudden. Between Betty and Isaac, it's clear to me that I haven't behaved very well towards my employees. In fact, I'd never even seen them as employees to be respected and looked after, rather they were simply incidental people who had been a part of my life forever, there to do whatever it was that I wanted. Such was my upbringing. What would I have said if Isaac had asked me if Elsie and the kids could move in? Would I have said no? I don't know the answer. I'd like to tell myself that I would have said yes, but I never liked Elsie and maybe it would have made me nervous, the thought of all those people living here. All those people? Most of them were children. And had I expected Isaac to live alone all that time? The truth was that I'd never given it any thought at all. And I am too tired to think about it now.

I sink down to my haunches and look around. The farm is very quiet. The old windmill creaks and turns against a clear blue sky and the veldt grasses rustle with the heat. I smell the beautiful dusty red sand and the air is perfect. A few crickets chirp and a bird calls *Piet, my vrou,* over and over again and I smile. A red-chested cuckoo.

And that's when I realize how very alone I am. And that no one knows I am here, none of the farmers or the people in the town. I stand up, dizzy from the sudden movement, there is a blackness to my vision and my heart flutters in my chest like a tiny trapped bird. I gather myself and run across the yard, into the kitchen, and through the house. The panic room. I will be safe in the panic room.

I run down the hall, my footsteps echoing through the house. I reach my father's bedroom. It is like a beautifully decorated prison cell, a barred-in box with a sliding security barrier. I draw the steel-barred door closed and insert the key into the lock. But the lock has been tampered with. It is broken. I jiggle it back and forth, as if I can fix it by desperate action. But it is broken and the sliding bolt has been sawn off.

Despite the heat of the day, my armpits are filled with ice cold sweat and goosebumps prickle my skin. A metallic click echoes through the house and I press myself back against the wall, my hand to my mouth to stifle my scream. *Don't let them know where you are.* But it's just the grandfather clock in the living room, stretching out in the heat of the day. It used to be a family joke, how, when you least expected it, the clock would make a chirp as if to say "I am here!" and then go back to sleep.

And still, I remain pressed against the wall, my thoughts spinning. The panic room is broken. What have I done by coming here?

And I can hear my father's voice in my head.

My girlie, what were you thinking? All alone? On the farm? Have you lost your mind?

And he's right. I press my palms against the cool wall. I am here because I lost my temper. I didn't think things through. I let my anger and my hurt get the better of me. I ran home without thinking clearly. Should I go to a hotel? But where? I don't even know if there is one in town and I suddenly feel too tired to talk to anybody. It took all of my energy to get myself here, and now that I am here, I can't bear to leave. But slowly, like a red tide rising, the rage builds inside me again and I feel my energy returning. I straighten up and stand tall, my hands balled into fists at my side. I have been fucked over by just about everybody I know. I don't know if my fears are founded but one thing is for sure. I will be ready for these fuckers if they come. They sawed off the bolt. The broke the lock. They have been preparing for this moment. I cannot afford to assume anything otherwise.

My rage is like an amphetamine. Time to get started. I walk around the outside of the house. The security lights are still in place, but there's no way of telling if they will work until darkness falls.

"What should I do, Pa?" I ask my father. "Tell me."

And he does. He asks me, one final time, if I really do want to stay, and I tell him I have no choice. This is my home. MY home.

Then fine, we deal with it. Worst case scenario, they will come and kill you in your sleep. They will rape you first. And maybe after. But by then you will be past caring. You don't want to be killed in your sleep, do you?

"No, Pa, I don't."

Then think. Where will they come in? Let's start there. Remember cookie, what they say, a boer maak a plan. So, make a plan.

"Okay, Pa."

I go to my father's study. The safe is hidden behind a large bookcase and Isaac had no way of knowing it was there. I take the books off the shelves and move the bookcase. I open the safe and remove one of the rifles and I load it, taking the spare ammunition with me. I pull on a pair of tactical hunting gloves that Pa kept for me in the safe, and I reach for what he called my last resort, the Glock 21. It is already fitted with a silencer. With a thirteen-round magazine capacity, and hollow-point bullets, I have no doubt that this ugly brute will save my life.

The gun is a stolen one, with the serial number removed and Pa said that even the ammunition had fallen off a truck and could not be traced. I load the gun and put it on the table.

I lock the safe and move the bookcase back into place and replace the books on the shelves.

Maybe it is stupid of me to stay. But I have had enough of being the victim. I let Dirk fuck me over and steal from me. I let Theresa pretend to be my friend and she fucked me over. Rosie and Betty took what half of what was left of my money and Betty abandoned me. Everyone has left me. I have nowhere left to go. This is my home. And if they are coming for me, then so be it but I will be ready. I have five hours before nightfall. Best I get busy.

38

I SIT IN THE DARK, WAITING. The whole world is utterly silent. It's the middle of the night and there isn't a sound to be
heard. If they come, they will enter via the kitchen because it
is the easiest access point and then they will hunt me down in
the house, me, a trapped rabbit quivering with fear, knowing
I am about to die.

I am inside the servants' quarters. I am not in Isaac's room
but one belonging to the children. The toys and clothes are
old and broken and in bad shape and I wonder what it must
be have been like to live in those rooms, to look over at the
main house and know there was all that luxury inside, all that
unfairly distributed luxury that could so easily be taken. And
wouldn't anyone deserve to take it, after years of servitude,
injustice, and inequality? But the farm belongs to me, and
before me, it belonged to my father, and his father before him.
This is our land too.

I sit there, pondering the ethics of the thing and I hope that
nothing will happen. I hope that the night will pass peacefully
and I will get the locksmith over in the morning and all of this
will have been for nothing.

*But you know that's not the case, cookie. You know how
it goes. You haven't had your head in the sand all this time.
The black government is urging the people to take back the
land, the land that was theirs to begin with. It's not stealing
if it was yours to begin with. And Isaac will have told them*

about Madam, at the farm, all alone. Even if he didn't mean to, he will have told. He will have told Elsie and she would have told everyone. You're a sitting duck.

"It's our house too," I say, and my voice is fierce in my head. "You've had this land forever. It's our home."

Then you must defend it and live with the consequences.

There are always consequences. This I know. I rub my hand over my face. I am tired. The rage is still there but my body is worn out by my preparations. I shake out two Bennies from an old exam stash I found in my room and I swallow them with some bottled water. I cannot let myself drift off, not for second.

They finally come. It's just after one a.m. Their shadows ease around the corner of the house and in spite of my preparations, my throat closes and I push back against the wall, hard. *Breathe. You think your heart will burst with fear but it won't. Just breathe. There you go, breathe, in, out, in.* This is real. This is happening. There are three men. They open the kitchen door and slip inside exactly as I predicted they would. But before they vanish into the darkness of the house, the security lights throw a spotlight on their faces. To my horror, Isaac is one of the men. Isaac. Yet another vicious betrayal in my life. Isaac is the smallest of the men, and he is the oldest. I don't recognize the other two. They are in their mid-thirties, strangers to me. Their faces are bare, they hadn't even worn balaclavas; they planned to kill me. My mind is scrambling. I was so stupid to stay here. What was I thinking? That I was Rambo or Schwarzenegger? Maybe I should abandon my foolish, foolhardy plan and hide? Perhaps they will believe I have left. I had hidden the car, so they could easily believe that I had gone. But just then my Bennies kick in and my red rage returns and I stand up. Fuck this. I won't take this lying down. I won't be a sitting duck or a quivering rabbit, accepting my fate.

A sense of righteous justice washes over me and I feel powerful, purposeful. I have come this far and I will see my plan through. I listened to Pa and I thought it all out. If I don't stick to my plan, then I will be killed and if not killed, then caught and raped until there is nothing left of me.

I wonder how many of them have guns. I know the law. If I shoot them inside the house, it's a manslaughter charge for me, regardless of the fact that they are in my house with the premeditated intent to rape and kill me.

I creep silently across the sandy backyard, duck underneath the empty washing lines and slip inside the kitchen door. I tiptoe down the hallway and strain to hear where the men are. I'm satisfied to note that they're exactly where I thought they would be. They're in Pa's bedroom, and their torches are sweeping back and forth. They are searching for me.

I swing into the bedroom, flip the light switch and aim my gun. The men turn towards me, shocked, off guard, blinking in the unexpected light. I shoot two of them in quick succession, one after the other, in the chest and head, with perfect aim and precision. They are both too surprised to do anything and they drop to the floor.

I turn to Isaac. He is pleading for his life. He's on his knees now, holding his hands high and he's crying.

"Easy for you to beg me now, Isaac," I tell him. 'You planned to kill me."

"Please, please Madam, don't—"

And I hesitate for a moment. This is Isaac, after all. I've known him my whole life. He was a young man when I was a child. He used to put the wheelbarrow in the shade of a tree on a hot day, and he'd fill it with water, for me to sit in. He helped me with my pony when I was learning to ride, and he led me around, while I clung to the saddle. He watched me grow from a toddler into a young woman, and then he helped me dig the graves for my mother and my father. I had always liked and trusted Isaac. I lower my gun slightly and he sees my doubt. He immediately takes advantage. He grabs the hammer that he had dropped and he swings it at me wildly. He catches me hard on the thigh and I wince at the white-hot pain.

I'm bent over, trying to breathe through the burn, and Isaac raises the hammer above his head, using both hands this time. I jump back, out of reach, and he swings at the air.

"You were going to kill me," I say. "Me, Isaac, after all these years." And he looks at me with hatred and lunges for me, and I shoot him in the heart. He drops to the floor.

"For *fok's* sake, Isaac," I say. "You gave me no choice. "

During my preparations, I had moved Pa's bed against the furthermost wall and I had stripped it down. I had lined the carpet with half a dozen plastic tarps and I had been worried that the plastic underfoot would alert the men that something was up, but they never noticed. My thigh burns where Isaac hit me and I touch it gingerly. But I can't think about it now, I have to get busy.

I step over the men, favouring my good leg and I open a door that leads out to a side patio. This was my father's favourite place to take breakfast, with a view of the mountains to the west and a cool breeze coming off the veldt grasses.

I had driven the small farm truck, the bakkie, right up to the patio door and left the tailgate open. I had put a small trestle table top into the back and I drag that to the edge of the tailgate to serve as a ramp. I limp back into the room, roll the first man up in his own tarp and drag him onto the back of the bakkie. I pull him onto the ramp so he's half way into the bed of the truck. The bakkie is a simple, old model, not like the modern-day SUVs that stand five feet off the ground, which makes my job easier. I climb into the back and pull the man the whole way inside. I do the same with the second man and the same with Isaac.

The men are heavy, except for Isaac who is skin and bone, but I'm fired up with adrenalin and the plastic slides fairly easily across the carpet and up into the back of the bakkie.

I forget about my bruised leg as I grunt and swear and tug and pull.

I gather up the men's knives, their bag with duct tape and rope, Isaac's hammer, a steel pipe, and a crowbar. I gather everything, put it into the bag and throw it in the back of the bakkie.

I turn the light off in the bedroom, close the patio door and drive off, relieved it's still dark. I look at my watch. It's 1:45 a.m. The sun will rise at 5:41 a.m. I will make it back in good time. The bakkie has half a tank of gas and I hope it will be enough to get me where I want to go and back home again, without having to stop and fill up. It's the one thing I forgot to do, fill the van up with petrol.

I drive west for over an hour. I change gears and grind up a steep mountainside and the engine strains. I pull over at a lookout where tour busses bring camera-happy tourists to admire the view. I reverse and back the bakkie up to edge of the lookout. The rocky crevice at the bottom of the mountain is home to nothing but scrub, rocks, and stunted trees.

I open the back and, one by one, I empty the bodies out of their tarps and roll them off the mountainside. They tumble out of view in the blink of an eye and fall to a place where no one will ever find them again. I hear a terrible thumping sound as the bodies bounce off the mountain, a gruesome, heavy sound I will never forget.

"If you ever need to," my father had told me, "this is a good place to get rid of evidence of any kind. Never admit to a crime. I'm telling you my girl, if they come after me in my own home, I will take them out. What, me, stand trial for defending myself and my family in my own home? I don't think so. This is where I would throw away the rubbish that would kill me and take the things I have worked for my whole life. And if you ever need to, you do the same. And how come they wouldn't go to prison, hey? They would get off with a warning, wander the streets and kill again, while my life and my family's life would be ruined. No way. You remember this, if you ever need to, okay?"

I remember, oh yes, I remember. I take the bag with the knife, the crowbar, the hammer, and their other tools, and put it in the middle of the tarps that I have stacked. I roll the tarps tightly and secure them with the duct tape they brought to cover my screams while they killed me. I use half a roll on the tarps, and I kneel on the bundle while I do it, squashing it until it's no bigger than the size of a large rock. I throw that off the mountain too. I remove the silencer from the Glock and throw it, and the gun, as far as I can.

All the adrenalin is gone. The Bennies are long gone. I'm shaking with exhaustion and fear and a cold sweat runs down my body, making me shiver. My clothes stick to my body as if I got caught in a winter storm. My leg burns and to make matters worse, a screaming headache has taken up residence in my skull. Nothing like the one that knocked me out cold but, nevertheless, the pain is brutal.

The doctor gave me a bottle of pills when I was in hospital but they are back at the farm. There's nothing I can do except put one foot in front of the other and try to get back home in one piece. But there's still evidence I have to get rid of, my clothes and my gloves, all of which are covered in gunshot residue and the bloody back spatter from Isaac.

I peel those wet clothes off me, tugging and yanking as they catch around my head and ankles, and change into a clean tracksuit. I bundle up the soiled clothes and put them into the back of the bakkie. And now it's time to start heading home.

I ease in behind the wheel and hold my head in my hands. I just need a moment. I press my palms against my temples, praying the pain will ease. I dig my thumbs into my forehead. I can't afford to pass out now. I hold my breath, which seems to ease the pain slightly. I check the time. It's four-fifteen a.m. The drive and clean up has taken me longer than I figured it would. I turn the key in the ignition and adjust the heat to high.

I drive slowly, hunched over the steering wheel like an old woman hanging on for dear life. I stop at an abandoned petrol station and I get lucky, there's a rusty oil drum half-full of rubbish around the back. I dump the bundle of clothing into it and throw in a few lit matches, making sure the clothes catch fire. If anyone sees the smoke, they'll assume the fire was lit by some vagrant for warmth.

I get back into the bakkie and focus on the gas tank and the road ahead of me. The gas tank level looks horribly low. I try not to watch the needle as it dips and bobs. I follow the white line in the middle of the road as if it's a lifesaving trail. I moan softly and tears spill down my face. It hurts to cry, the pain cranks up several notches but I have to let the tears come. My bruised leg throbs where Isaac took the hammer to it, adding to the agony.

It takes me an hour and a half to get home and when I finally turn into my driveway, I can see the start of dawn's fiery crimson ascent edging over the horizon. And I am lucky. The red light of the reserve tank comes on just as I turn into the farm road. That was too close for comfort.

I drive the bakkie behind the garage and park it. It's an old white Nissan model, not worth much at all, but it helped save my life tonight. I pat it in thanks. Then, I go and check the room where I killed the men. I crawl around on the carpet and find the cartridge cases, accounting for all six rounds.

I check outside the patio side door where I parked the bakkie to load the men and I can't see anything out of place there.

I go back to the bakkie, and hose off the truckbed, with my thumb pressed against the open valve to create as strong a spray as I can. There are a few small leaks in the hose and I'm soon soaked and shivering again. The African veldt doesn't retain its heat at night and I can't imagine ever feeling warm again. My head is blisteringly painful, my eyes are mere slits and I can hardly see. My breath makes a strange sound, like the rhythmic pant of a dying dog we had before the vet had to put him down. I'm driven by sheer force of will and the sound of my father's voice, he is urging me to see this thing through, he tells me what to do. I retrieve the unused rifle from the servants' quarters and lock it in the glass cabinet of my father's study.

I lock the kitchen door and I crawl back to my room. I shed my wet clothes and rub my body dry with a towel. I'd love to take a shower but the pain is overwhelming. I pull on a pair of pajamas. My movements are slowing down, like a wound-up toy that is coming to a stuttering halt. I don't have much left. I scrabble through my handbag to find my headache meds, emptying the contents onto the floor in desperation. I find the vial and struggle to get it open, damn childproof lids. I chew on two tablets and haul myself onto my bed. A dirty bomb is exploding in my skull. Is it possible to die from such agony? I pass out without even pulling a blanket over me or closing the curtains.

I wake in a hot sweat with my heart banging like an African drum in my chest. I spring upright. What happened? I can't remember anything, but I know that something happened, something terrible. What was it? I am in my old room at the farm. Why am I there? And then it comes back to me. I see myself sitting on the bed, looking at my duvet cover, and then Isaac appears and I nearly mistake him for an intruder. And then I do shoot Isaac, along with two other men. My thoughts fly around like frantic birds, whirling and seizing fragments as the events of the whole night come back to me. I touch my thigh and wince. I pull my pajama bottoms down and the bruise is godawful, the skin is red and tender, and the bone feels bruised. But the skin is not broken, for which I am grateful. What is the time? I have to get the locksmith in to fix the safe room.

I scrabble around on the floor and find my phone. It's after lunch time. I need to get moving. My pajama top is stuck to me like glue. I'm drenched in sweat from a bad dream that I can't remember and from sleeping with the hot sun shining down on me.

I have a quick shower and get into a pair of shorts and a T-shirt. *Calm down Bernice, calm down.* You arrived yesterday, last night passed without incident but you need that safety door fixed. That's your story, there's nothing more to it.

I drive into town and find the locksmith. I tell him I'll pay him double if he can fix the door today and he says he'll come by in a couple of hours.

I find a coffee shop in town. I order a Farmer's Breakfast with eggs, bacon, toast, grilled tomatoes, grilled mushrooms, sausages and hash browns, with lots of coffee to wash it down. But the minute I finish eating, I rush to the toilet and throw it all back up, my stomach rejecting the rich food and the grease.

I can still smell the spilled blood and the acrid sweat that rose from the men's skin as they died. I lean over the cool toilet, hugging the bowl. *You'll have to live with the consequences,* Pa had said. He's right. I have to get my act together. I wash my face and hands and go out and pay, buying a bottle of cold water that helps settle my stomach.

I wonder when Elsie will start to worry about Isaac and when she'll alert the cops. I stop by the police station to tell them I am home at the farm.

"Just you *Mevrou*?" the sergeant asks and I nod.

"You're hooked up to the farmers' radio?" he asks and I shake my head.

"Not yet. I'll need to let them know I'm back."

"When did you get back?"

"Late yesterday evening."

"And it's just you there?"

"Ja. Like I said, just me." I don't tell him that Isaac was there when I arrived. It's better if I say Isaac wasn't there, that I never saw him. "I know how to look after myself."

"You're taking a big chance. A bit stupid if you ask me. *Stoksiel alleen,* all by yourself. But it's up to you."

I am careful not to limp when I leave the police station. I walk out with a careful, even stride although the pain is fierce.

I stop to buy a few supplies for the night ahead and when I get home, the locksmith is waiting for me, smoking a cigarette. He installs a shiny new lock and bolt on the safe room door and I get him to do the front door, the kitchen door and the patio door too. He grumbles at the extra work but I tell him I'll pay him double which cheers him up.

With nightfall only an hour away, I close up the house and I lock myself in Pa's room. I have my supplies and my gun and I lie down on Pa's bed. I had moved the bed back into the centre of the room and I made it up with fresh linens and a pretty yellow duvet from one of the spare rooms. I bought a big bunch of yellow, orange, and pink daisies and arranged them in a crystal vase in an effort to brighten up the brown masculinity of the room. I even bought half a dozen votive candles which I remind myself are a safety hazard, best I don't burn the place down, with me locked inside it.

My headache has backed off but my leg is burning. I crack open a bottle of painkillers that I picked up at the chemist and I wash down a couple of pills with the red wine I bought at the bottle store. I still don't feel like eating anything but I half-heartedly chew on some soda crackers.

My phone lights up with more texts from Dirk but I can't be bothered to read them.

I look around. I've transformed the room; it's brightly-coloured, pretty and girly. But I killed three men in this room. I can still see their faces, Isaac's in particular. Such hatred he had for me. I remind myself that the barred room will keep me safe. But still, despite the wine and the painkillers and the fresh new locks, I cannot sleep. I doze fitfully, wondering what I am going to do with myself. Perhaps this was a thoroughly stupid idea and I'll have to go back to Joburg with my tail between my legs.

39

THE NEXT MORNING I WAKE EARLY and I decide to explore the house before I just turn tail and run.

I open the door to my mother's bedroom. I take a cautious seat at her dressing table, and stare at myself in the mirror. I pick up her lovely silver-backed brush and run it through my hair, which immediately looks as if I've driven through a static wind-tunnel. I sigh and put the brush down.

My mother's bedroom is a world away from real life. I now understand why she spent so much time closeted away. The room is serene and sunny. Her sewing machine stands quietly in the corner of the room but I can still hear the whirring sound of her hard at work.

I wish I could understand my mother's constant desire for parties; why emerge from this sunlit glade into busy rooms filled with silly chatter and foolish laughter? Because clearly the socializing had not agreed with her, no sooner had she emerged, than she had to scuttle back, felled by a headache.

I open and close the drawers of the dressing table, half-expecting my mother to march in and slap my hand and shoo me out of the room for touching things I had no right to. I notice that the bottom drawer is not properly closed and I give it a gentle nudge but something is blocking it at the back. I pull the drawer out and get down on my hands and knees. I reach my hand inside. Yes, something's definitely in there, papers, tied with a ribbon. I don't want to rip or tear anything and it takes some time to negotiate the package out of its narrow confinement. It's a bundle of notes and letters, tied neatly with a faded pink satin ribbon.

I look at the package for a while, thinking that perhaps the letters are from a member of my mother's family. But no, my mother has no other family. She grew up an orphan in a foster home, she has no relatives to speak of and these letters look too adult. I harbour the fleeting thought that perhaps the letters are from my biological father, addressed to me, and my mother hoarded them, not wanting me to see them.

I take the package to the kitchen, untie the ribbon and pick up the first letter. The writing is a feminine script, laced with decorative curves and swirls and long descenders. The envelopes are formally addressed, with the return address from a farm just down the way. Which doesn't make any sense. Why would a farmer's wife write to my mother when she lived a mere half an hour's drive away?

Marika Lamerdin. Who was she? I put the letter back on the table with the others and turn on the kettle. I need to prepare myself for whatever the letters hold. They must have been important for my mother to take such care to keep and hide them, and I'm a little fearful of what I'll discover.

The kettle boils noisily and I only realize that a car has pulled up in my driveway when I hear the slamming doors. I rush to the front window. It is the police.

I grab my little revolver off the sideboard in the hallway and shove it into a drawer. Then I go outside.

Two men walk towards me. One man is the same sergeant I spoke to the previous day, Lester du Toit, and he is with a partner, a man he introduces as Don Bethell.

"*Goeie moere Mevrou*, good morning madam," du Toit says. "*Asseblief*, please can we come in?"

"Of course yes, I just put the kettle on, would you like some coffee?"

I lead them through to the kitchen, taking care not to limp, and I make the coffee, and arrange Marie biscuits on a plate.

"I've only got Ricoffy," I say. "I hope that's okay. Now, what can I do for you?"

"You arrived the night before last," he says and he looks at his notepad.

"I did, ja."

"What time was that? And did you see Isaac when you arrived?"

"Um, I came around four o clock and no, he wasn't here. No one was here."

"You stayed the night all by yourself?" Bethell interjects. "Pretty stupid, né?"

"I can look after myself. I was a bit worried when I saw that the door to the safe room was broken, but nothing happened and yesterday I got the locksmith in and he fixed it."

"Did you know that Isaac was implicated in a farm attack a couple of weeks ago?" du Toit asks the question and I am shocked.

"No! What do you mean? Isaac would never do anything like that."

"He did. At least he allegedly did. The farmer's wife swears she recognized him plus the farmer shot one of the men in the shin and Isaac was seen limping afterwards."

"Hardly hard evidence," I say. "Isaac wouldn't do a thing like that."

"And yet now, one night after you arrive, Isaac is missing. And not only him but Elsie's brother and her nephew." This from Bethell who manages to sound accusing.

"Oh?" I reply. I shrug. "Maybe they went to look for work?" I suggest. "In Magaliesberg?"

"All three of them? At night? I don't think so, no." Bethell takes another Marie biscuit and dunks it in his coffee. "And why would Isaac look for work if he already had a job with you?"

"Maybe he wanted more from life, how should I know? I

never saw him when I got here. Maybe he's been gone from here for a while. I've got no idea."

"Elsie says he was here when you got home. She says he left after you arrived."

"And did she say he told her he was coming back here?"

"No." Du Toit shifts in his seat. "She just said he went out with the other two."

"He didn't come back here. What do you think happened?" I ask, my heart beating fast.

"That he met with foul play. That they all did."

I laugh. "Foul play! What an old-fashioned thing to say!"

The men exchange a glance. "Can we see your guns?" Du Toit asks apologetically. "We have to ask."

"Of course." I lead them to my father's study, unlock the glass cabinet, and I take out the rifle. "It hasn't been fired. Check it."

I hand the rifle to du Toit who examines it. "Nice piece." he says.

"It was my father's. He taught me how to shoot. I also have a revolver. I'll go and get it."

I retrieve the revolver from the drawer and hand it to the constable.

"You've got a lot of guns for a woman," Bethell observes and I don't bother to reply. I show them my gun permits then I lock them back in my father's desk drawer.

"If that's all in order, is there anything else I can help you with?" I ask and I make a show of locking the rifle back into the cabinet.

"Can we look around the house?" Bethell asks and I stiffen. "Why?"

"Just to check the lay of the land, so to speak." He takes a toothpick out of his pocket and starts to dig deep.

"Follow me," I say with ice in my voice and I lead them from room to room.

"A *groot* big place for a single little *vrou* like you," Bethell says and I turn to him.

"I've had just about enough from you. We're done here."

"Ja, we won't trouble you any further." Du Toit is uncomfortable. "But Bethell is right, maybe it's not safe here for you, maybe you should to go back to Joeys."

"At least get a dog," Bethell chimes in. "Get a boerboel. Tear those *kaffirs* apart, ja."

"How can you even speak like that? You disgust me. I respect all humankind. Get out of my house." I herd them down the hallway, the irony of my words causing my ears to ring with the gruesome heavy sounds the bodies made as they tumbled down the mountainside, a sound I will never forget.

"Ja *jong*, you must not have seen the things I have," Bethell retorts but I ignore him and march them out the front door.

"Wait one moment," I call out as the men turn to leave. "Do you know Marika Lamerdin? She lives in the farm across the way, I believe?"

"She's been dead for years," du Toit replies. "Why do you ask about her?"

"I found a letter she wrote to my mother. I'd like to have talked to her. I have so few links to my childhood, it seems like everything has changed or gone."

"She killed herself," Bethell says bluntly. "Hung herself."

"Hanged," du Toit corrects him.

"Ja. With her husband's ties. Franz Lamerdin. The police thought maybe it was him who killed her and made it look like suicide but no, she offed herself. The evidence proved it. Plus Franz said if he was going to kill her, he wouldn't have used his favourite church ties to do it."

"When did she die?"

Du Toit scratches his head. "About sixteen, seventeen years ago, give or take?"

Shortly after my mother passed away.

"We'll be on our way then," he says and I can see he wants say something else but he turns away.

"Maybe you need some friends," Bethell offers. "You must

get lonely here, hey? Maybe I'll come back later and see if you are okay."

"No. Don't come back." I am sharp. "I don't want you here, do you hear me? I want nothing to do with you."

"I'll remember that when some *kaffir* comes to rape and kill you and you need my help. Oh wait, maybe that already happened, né, and you took care of everything." He walks back up to me and I can smell his breath, a hot foul wind on my face and I try not to breathe. "Little girl thinks she can take the law into her own hands? I think Isaac came back here, with Elsie's brother and her nephew. I'm not saying they were up to any good, but still. Elsie said everybody knows you've got a bad temper. And Elsie also said your father taught you all about guns and how to hunt. And then suddenly, the men disappear off the face of the earth. Strange coincidence, né? Something smells very fishy here."

"How come you believe Elsie over me? Given your racial tendencies, I would have thought you would give me credence over her." My thigh throbs as if objecting to the whole situation and I want to touch the wound, comfort it, but I fold my arms across my chest and glare at Bethell.

"I don't like it when farmers take matters into their own hands. I'm the law here, not you. I'm not finished with you, missy."

"But I'm finished with you," I say. My whole body is shaking and my coffee rises in my throat but I choke it down. I turn to du Toit. "Give me the name of your superior officer. I'm going to phone him and complain about abuse and harassment."

"Ag now, that's not necessary," du Toit says placatingly. "Come now Bethell, let's leave, man. No need for rudeness from anyone. These are not easy times, for any of us. We are here if you need us," he says to me.

"I want your private number," I tell du Toit. "Your cell. In case your friend here comes back, in which case I will call you. But you should strongly encourage him not to return."

Du Toit hesitates for a moment but then he pulls out a pen and writes his number on the back of a police business card. I nod my thanks and take the card.

I stand on the verandah and watch them drive off in a cloud of dust. My heart is a beating fist against the wall of my ribcage. I sink down on the polished red steps and hug my arms around my chest. My clothes are damp with sweat and there's a ringing in my ears.

I try to focus on the dust devils dancing across the dry land and I tell myself I'm fine. They'll never find the bodies. Pa had said so and Pa was never wrong.

It's only midday but I mix a stiff gin and tonic and return to my easy chair on the verandah, sipping and thinking. My phone buzzes while I'm in the kitchen mixing the drink. It's Dirk, and once again, I ignore him.

I sit with my feet propped up on the railing. Secret lives. Lives with secrets. Fewer are those who travel through life without secrets than those who do not.

I'm afraid to read what Marika wrote. I'm afraid to find out who my mother was. The answers to my questions lie in those letters but I can't bring myself to read them. Not here, anyway.

I finish my gin and tonic and go inside. I need some peace and quiet and I know just where to find it.

40

I PACK AN OVERNIGHT BAG. I lock the house and put a new padlock on the gate. I drive to Sun City, a luxurious resort like a mini Las Vegas in the middle of the scrub and veldt. Within an hour and a half, I'm in a room overlooking the golf course, with the enormous swimming pool off to the side.

I've come to this hotel because I could not read the letters in my father's house. Now I'm sitting on the edge of the bed, trying to pluck up my courage. But still, I cannot not read them.

I have a long bath, then I order a steak sandwich with monkey gland sauce and a bottle of wine from room service. Then I force myself to begin.

The letters are not in any particular order and I organize them by date. This takes me much longer than I planned and it's close to midnight by the time I'm done. I tell myself that I'm not procrastinating, I'm justifiably tired, and I decide I'll read them in the morning.

But when I wake in the blue-black hour of predawn, I can put it off no longer.

Hands shaking, I begin to read. I'm grateful for Marika's precise penmanship, although the ink has faded and it is hard to make out a few of the words.

The first letter is brief. It is an apology.

Dear Ariana, I am so sorry, please, forgive me. I never meant to be so forward. I meant what I said, I do love you. I am in love with you. But please forgive me for approaching you with too much honesty. It will never happen again.

The letter is dated: 1st February, 1985. I was three years old at the time. My mother was twenty-two and she would have been married to my father for little more than two years.

The next letter is happier.

Ariana, Liefling, you gladden my heart! Thank you for not being angry with me, I can't tell you. You mean the world to me! See you at the next party, I cannot wait.

I read the letters slowly. Some are no more than party thank you notes bearing loving words filled with longing for the next meeting. I wonder how the women managed to slip away and be together and how no one else noticed what was going on. Or perhaps they did, but they didn't comment or care. At least those ridiculous parties made sense now. This also explained my mother's headaches. She must have been anxious about being discovered, while excited at the same time. Because she clearly reciprocated Marika's feelings.

The next letter tells me all I need to know.

My Liefie Ariana, how I long to see you again. Your loveliness is the medicine my life craves. You are the only one who gives my life meaning with your grace and your beauty. I watch with wonder as you fill the room with your laughter and I live for the moments when I see you. Even when we are with others, just to be in the same room as you fills me with joy.

Franz is such a boor, not that that surprises me, or you! I told him I have terrible women's problems down there and cannot have him in my bed any longer, because no one belongs in my bed but you. He told me I am doing him a favour.

I wish I could tell him, like you told Ruan. That was very brave of you. Ruan is a good man. I wish Franz was a good man like him. But I am only a plain farmer's wife who must earn her keep, while you are so beautiful and Ruan loves you as much I do. He would do anything for you. You do know that, don't you? That I would do anything for you.

I wish we could run away but I know we would not survive.

Running away together is a pipe dream. Sometimes, when I am milking the cows, or feeding the pigs, I let myself dream. I dream we are far away and have a place of our own and I have you all to myself, all day and all night.

Please, let us make a plan to meet soon. You and me, alone. Perhaps I can pick you up and take you into town to get more fabric. I miss you so much.

My father had known all along.

Ag Pa. Not only was I not yours by birth, but then Ma betrayed you and yet you still looked after us. You gave me such a good life. Imagine me and Ma and Marika living together. Although that said, Marika never mentioned me in her daydreams, it was only her and my mother. I guess I would have been left behind.

I force myself to carry on reading. It is harder near the end when I read about my mother's illness and how frightened she was. I feel bad. I should have been home. I should have been with my mother at the end. But she had Marika and my father, and she didn't die alone. And besides, she never mentioned me anyway. That stings but it shouldn't be news to me.

The penultimate letter sucker-punches me. Literally knocks the wind out of me. I can't believe what I'm reading. I put the letter down, hardly able to breathe.

No,way. It can't be true. Well, I won't think about it, I simply will not.

I go to the window and look down at the luxury golf course, at the lagoon and the enormous palm trees, and I'm as winded as if I've been thrown from a horse.

I rush to the mini bar and crack open a tiny bottle of scotch and swallow it in one gulp. I open the vodka and do the same.

No, this will never be thought of again. I will banish what I have just read, it has no place in my life. It will not change who I am.

I sit down and read the final letter. It is the longest one and it was written after my mother had died although it was still

addressed to her and it had been opened. In it, Marika jour-
naled her relationship with my mother, as if revisiting their
love in her mind for the last time. I learned more about how
they met, when they met. Marika recounted conversations
and I learned more about my life and my birth father and the
despicable man my mother first married.

Marika and my mother had celebrated their sixteenth
anniversary shortly before my mother's death and Marika
wrote about her love for Ariana and how life was worthless
without her. How she had to join her by taking her own life,
rather than remaining in this world, so alone. She asked to be
cremated and have her ashes scattered on my mother's grave
and I wondered if that had happened.

Which is when I realize my father must have read the letters
too. Who else would have opened the last one? And he hid
them in a way that I would find them. Had he wanted me to
know the truth about my mother? About me? I have no idea
what to think.

I need to get out of the room. I can't bear to be alone with
the letters for one more minute. It's nearly suppertime. The
entire day has passed and I'm starving, and my head is spinning
a bit from the alcohol, of which I need a lot more. I pull on a
tight black mini dress and high heels and go down to the bar.

I order a large glass of wine and look around. Slim pickings.
Married couples, gay couples, hen parties, and rowdy golf men.
Hmm, maybe a golfing boy will help me forget my problems. I
look at the group who have clearly been drinking for a while
and I suddenly miss Dirk. I miss his sense of humour, his sarcasm, his uncompromising perspective.

Oh god, what if Dirk ever finds out? What if anybody ever
finds out? My face flushes that meaty colour at the thought.
But what am I thinking? Dirk and I are history. What stupid
thoughts are these? Do I imagine that he'll reappear, money in
hand, an apology as long as his arm, and a wedding proposal
for a happy-ever-after? I'm beyond stupid. He's a home-grown

terrorist, and never mind that, he's also fucking my best friend. And, by all accounts, managing to fuck her much better than he had ever fucked me. So really, missing Dirk is the biggest waste of time. Missing him is a reflex, a bad habit. I'm just so painfully lonely. It feels like I've swallowed a boa constrictor of loneliness. If only I had a book to work on. I wouldn't feel so all alone.

I'm deep in thought and I barely notice when a good-looking man in his early thirties leans suggestively on the table next to me.

Ja, that's it! I know what the book will be about! I've got it! The memoir wasn't going to work but this affair of my mother's would make for a great book. I can change it into a work of fiction, using the secrets and lies, and who knows, maybe I can work the killings in too, not, of course, in any self-incriminating way, of course not, but maybe Marika killed to protect Ariana? How far would a person go for their lover? I'll turn the whole thing into a crime novel!

I'm fired up. I have a sense of purpose. I'll be a real writer. For the first time in months, I feel like myself again and I grin.

"Hey good-lookin'," the man says to me as I hop off my chair, "Whatcha got cookin'?"

"Nothing for you," I say, "not now, and not ever." I slug back the rest of my wine. I need to get back upstairs and make notes. And that other thing, can I put that in the book? I shake my head. No way. I can't even think about it. Besides, I have enough material to work with. I don't need that too.

I get back to my room and haul out my laptop. Ja for sure, this is going to be a great success.

41.

THE NEXT DAY, I DRIVE BACK to the farm and set up a study in my mother's bedroom. I arrange some of her dresses on the bed along with her jewelry. I sit down to write and I'm instantly stymied. I have nothing. I expected a waterfall of copy and there isn't even a tap drip. I am stuck staring at a blank page that stares back at me. I stare with desperation, the page, with accusation. Standoff.

I need a picture of Marika. I have no clue what she looked like.

I decide to try my luck at the public library and I drive into town. I ask the librarian if she has anything on file about my parents or perhaps my mother's good friend, Marika Lamerdin. She says that a rich farmer in the area funded the archiving of the local newspapers into digital format and that it will be easy enough to check. We find a few pictures of my father winning hunting contests and there's even a full-page article about me, how I won the gold medal in the South African Practical Shooting Association's Junior Division, but the search seems to end there. I look at the grainy photograph of my earnest young self and think I still wear the same expression to this day. Like I know I don't fit in and I'm embarrassed for even trying.

I have another idea and I ask the librarian to search ladies golfing tournaments, recalling from one of the letters that Marika had won a golf tournament. And yes, there she is. But it's disappointingly hard to see any kind of detail in the woman's face. All I could discern is that Marika was tall and stout, strong.

"How exactly do I would get to the Lamerdin farm?" I ask and the librarian draws me a map.

I speed off to the farm. I know when I reach the perimeter because it is fenced off and sign-posted. These guys are big into security, the tall fences are topped with barbed wire and I pull up at a double-wide, double-high steel security gate. This working farm is a whole different operation to my father's gentlemanly patch.

It's so intimidating that I nearly change my mind and turn back for home, but I press my finger to the intercom and speak into the buzzer. "Hello, yes, I am a neighbour, calling for a visit, Bernice Van Coller."

The gates swing open slowly. As I drive in, I marvel at the farm. No wonder they need this much barbed wire and enormous electronic gates. This farm is worth a fortune.

I'm reluctant to get out of the car, what with the massive boerboel dogs circling the car and I stay where I am, lowering the window slightly when a woman comes out to greet me.

"Can I help you?" she says, drying her hands on an apron and I apologize for inconveniencing her. I explain I'm back at my family home for a while and I have been going through my mother's things and I realized that Marika and my mother had been friends and—

"Friends?" the woman gives a bark of laughter. "Ja nee *jong*, they were more than that. Not that anybody spoke about it, mind you. Come on in, the dogs won't bite. Come, have some cake and tea with me. The men are with the sheep. I get lonely. I'm Deanna."

I climb cautiously out of the car, not sure if the dogs are to be trusted but they quiet down when Deanna tells them to. I follow her into the cool house that is a close match to my own and I sit down at the kitchen table while Deanna puts the kettle on and fetches a cake out of the pantry.

"Bundt. Double chocolate, I hope you like it. So yes, I know about our mothers."

"Why did you and I never meet?" I wonder out loud and the woman gives her strange barking laugh again.

"We did, you just don't remember. We saw a lot of each other when we were little kids. But I was older than you maybe that's why I remember and you don't. Then they sent us both away to boarding schools, me to the Afrikaans one and you to the fancy English convent.

"Did they send us away because of our mothers?" I ask and the woman shakes her head.

"No. Kids went away to school, that's all. My brothers did too, all the kids did. It's the way it was. We were at primary school together here, but then we were sent to different high schools."

"And you knew about our mothers? What's the story?"

"I knew my mother loved your mother. Takes one to know one? I'm a lezzie too, never married. I live here with my three brothers, two of them are married and have kids. We're like *Dallas* or *Dynasty*. All of us living on a farm together, sounds hunky dory but in reality ... oh, in reality, it's fine too. Family, you know how it goes."

"I don't. My family are all gone." I drink half my tea, surprised how hungry and thirsty I am.

"But you've still got your half-brother," Deanna comments and she looks sly and I sit up startled, my mouth full of cake.

"I saw you on TV. You're famous around these parts, at least among those of us who read books. I read a lot of cookbooks. I can't be bothered with self-help shit, but I liked the baking side of it. This might even be one of your recipes." She grins. "It was quite a shock to us that you have a brother."

"Half-brother," I correct her and Deanna shrugs.

"Whatever. Why didn't you talk to him on the show? Did you speak to him afterwards? Was that just for the cameras that you were all fired up?"

I regret having come and I once again realize the merits of a hermetic existence. I push my cake away.

"Ag, now don't be like that." Deanna refills my tea. "Eat your cake. I'll shut up about issues that aren't my beeswax. And yet, you want to know about our mothers."

"I only found out now. I came across a bunch of letters."

"Ag, ja. The letters. There were many, over the years. My father burnt the ones from your mother. My mother tried to hide them, but he always found them and he burned them. He loved burning them. He was horrible in that, and many ways."

"Do you have a picture of your mother?"

"Of course I do!"

Deanna gets up and returns with a large old-fashioned photo album, which crackles and snaps when she opens it. Clear plastic sheets peel off the old, discoloured photographs. No doubt it was the film used but the whole world looked orange and brown.

"What a time it was," she says absently. "And then she killed herself, after your mother died. She had nothing to live for. I knew it was going to happen. I didn't blame her. My father and my brothers hated your mother. They were ashamed. But I understood."

"Is she buried on your farm?" I ask, curious about Marika's request to be cremated and scattered on my mother's grave.

"She is not. Your father had a talk with my father. Funny. Your father was a small little fellow and my father was a big ugly hulk, but he did what your father asked him. My mother's got a fancy big gravestone here on the farm and we buried a coffin but my mother was not in it. Only I knew. I hid and listened when your father came. My mother was cremated and your father and I scattered her ashes on your mother's grave."

More secrets my father kept from me. Had I even known him the way I thought?

Deanna turns to a page. "My mother was more handsome than pretty." I study the photograph and silently agree. Marika was mannish, with a clean, strong jaw, a straight nose and clear penetrating eyes.

"She's lovely," I say.

"Ja. I thought so too. She was a good woman; my father was a bastard. Your father, step-father, whatever, he was a gentleman. He was always kind to me."

"He was kind to everyone. That's who he was. But he taught me how to fight in this life, he taught me that few things are free."

"But still, you never had to work like I did," Deanna is bitter. "You were born into money and you could sit your expensive bottom down on a nice fat cushion and make more money. Isn't that always the way? I knew you would be successful, everybody who met you knew. You lived in your own head, in that place of the future where you would be the queen of the castle and the rest of the world would serve you."

"That's how you remember me?"

"It's how you were, *jong*. When you were a teenager and home from school, you were a heart-breaker. You broke two of my brother's hearts."

"I don't even remember dating them."

"You see. That's who you are. I wouldn't call you a user but you were always number one in your mind, the rest of the world never mattered."

"You are very blunt. Gets you many friends, does it?"

Deanna barks again. "Haha. I can say what I like. It's all I've got in life."

"Why don't you move to the city, find work? Find a partner?"

"It's safer here. Life is easier here. Besides, it's not like I'm that lonely. You'd be surprised at how many people play under the table in this town. I get my share of good times."

I don't know what to say to that. I page through the album and stop when I come to pictures of Betty.

My eyes fill with tears. "She left me," I say and point to a picture, "Betty left me. Recently. I miss her terribly. She went to live with her family in KwaZulu Natal. I didn't even know she had family there. The only contact I have for her is Rosie's email and Rosie hates me."

"Ag man, Rosie hates everyone. Wait a moment, I've got Betty's telephone number if you want." She gets up, leaves the room, and then comes back with a piece of paper with a phone number on it.

"How come you have this?" I ask.

"Betty's sister worked for us for years. I still speak to her regularly."

I take the piece of paper and put it in my pocket. I can't imagine myself phoning Betty. The idea of contacting her is as alien as me calling a psychic to talk to my mother. But it's nice of Deanna to try to help.

I don't know what to say after that. "I should go. Thank you. You've been very kind."

"Not at all. And I wasn't. That's your lying English manners. Here, take some cake with you."

She cuts a few slices, wraps them in some cling wrap, and holds them out. I thank her and say, "I don't judge her. It was a shock to find out, that's true. But I never understood why she stayed all these years when she seemed so out of place. I thought she stayed because she lacked the courage to leave my father and support herself and maybe that was true too, but she stayed because she loved your mother."

"My mother would have left here in heartbeat. She would have taken me and you and the four of us would have gone. Wouldn't that have been something? But your mother said she loved your father, that he had rescued her when she needed it most, and that he loved you too much. She couldn't do that to him. She couldn't repay the kindness he had shown her by taking you from him and leaving him. Who ever gets through this world happy? No one I know."

"Happiness is a myth. Like closure. They are just theories. All we have is the day ahead of us and the one we left behind.

Labels don't change what it was or what it will be. We walk the tightrope of time throughout our lives, balancing over the present, tiptoeing away from the past, and inching forwards to the future. That's all we can do."

Deanna laughed. "Very deep, *jong*. Listen, it was nice to see you. You can come again, though, if you like."

"Maybe," I say, although we both know I probably won't.

"Hey, *jong*," Deanna says, suddenly, "you want a puppy?"

"A puppy? No! What, a boerboel? They're vicious."

"Listen *juffrou*, let me tell you something for nothing. You are being stupid as pigshit to be out there on the farm alone. And I hear Elsie thinks you got rid of Isaac and half of her family. If I were you, I'd get back to city before they *donder* the shit out of you and worse. A puppy won't protect you, but he will alert you if you hear a noise. I breed boerboels. That's my thing. They cost a pretty penny, a hundred thousand rand a puppy, and I've got a long waiting list."

"A hundred thousand for a dog? I'm in the wrong business."

"Not just any dog. Come and see."

"I thought you said your brothers would be home soon?"

"Ja, but if they think you are here for the dogs, they won't mind. It's the stuff with Ma they hate to hear about."

I follow Deanna out to a large barn behind the house and I lean over a stable door to look at the puppies.

"Ag shame, look at them," I say smiling like a fool. "I've fallen in love."

"From what I remember, that doesn't mean much," Deanna comments, and she opens the door, and I can hear she's teasing me. "You can go in, pick them up if you like."

"These are the cutest things I've ever seen in my entire life." I kneel down in the straw. "Are they old enough to leave their mother?"

"Ja, the other owners are coming to pick them up in a few days. They're house-trained and everything."

"Which of them are taken?"

"All of them actually, except for this one. I was going to keep him for myself but something about you says you need a dog."

"I do, do I?" But I laugh again and I take the puppy that Deanna is holding out to me. "I haven't had a dog since I was a kid. I won't remember what to do." I take the puppy. He's the colour of Lyles Golden Syrup and he's a solid weight in my arms, warm and reassuring. "Look at his wrinkled forehead. He's got a head like a Shar Pei!"

"You don't *do* anything. You just love him. But when you go back to Johannesburg, you must take him for walks."

"I can manage that. I want to pay you, it's not fair you should be out of pocket for this."

"He's a present, stupid. I told you. I was going to keep him, but now he's yours. You weren't my favourite person growing up but that doesn't mean I want to see you killed. What are you going to call him?"

"I don't know yet. I'll have to see. Can I take him now?"

"Sure. I'll get a box for you to put him in. And I'll get his food."

She leaves me with the dog and when she comes back, I look up at her. "I was wrong," I say, smiling, "I do know what happiness feels like. It feels like this."

"Good to hear," Deanna says and she looks around and I see someone standing behind her. "This is my brother, Johan."

"Hello," I stand up and shake the man's hand. He was a carbon copy of his mother, with the same square-jaw, cleft chin, high cheek bones, and wide set dark eyes. I know what my mother saw in Marika and I hold his hand for a moment too long.

"You don't remember me? You got off with me all night at a drive-in one time, and then you wouldn't return my calls," Johan says good-naturedly.

"I'm sorry," I reply and I wonder about my teenage self about whom I have no recollection. Johan shakes his head.

"No way, it was a fantastic night. You came to buy a puppy?"

"I did," I lie. "I'm alone in the farmhouse across the way. I wonder what I should call him."

"It'll come to you," Johan says. "You've got a half-brother, hey? That was quite the TV show."

"Don't you guys ever do anything except watch TV?" I ask, and they both laugh.

We are lining the puppy's box with newspaper when I spot the headline: *Monument Slayer Suspect Identified.*

"Wait," I stop them. "I need to read this." And I understand when cheap crime novels say a person's blood ran cold because that is what mine does when I see the picture of Dirk, right underneath that headline. I start to scan the paper.

"I wouldn't have thought you would be interested in the Voortrekker Monument," Deanna says and I shake my head, distracted. "I'm not. I dated him."

"What a moron," Johan says. "He tried to re-ignite old-school Afrikaner tribal values by blowing up the monument. The only problem is that no one believes in those antiquated values except for him."

"How did they find out it was him?"

"You haven't been watching the news, have you? It's been a huge deal. The ANC have been panic-stricken that this would start a war so they've had the whole police force on it. The funny thing, they were more worried about it than the Afrikaners were. I mean the Afrikaners were upset, but it wasn't going to start a war."

"Aren't you Afrikaans?" I ask and both Johan and Deanna shrug.

"Sort of," Johan says. "Ja nee, yes and no. I mean yes, but it doesn't define me. Life goes on."

"How did they catch this guy?"

Johan laughs. "This *oke* wasn't exactly a brain surgeon. He kept sending them emails, ranting about how the new-wave Afrikaner had betrayed his *volk*. They found him through the IP addresses. The guy just couldn't shut up."

"Is he in prison?"

Johan shook his head. "That's just how they identified him. They didn't catch him. He skipped the country. They think he is somewhere in the U.S."

"IP addresses? He's been texting me but I haven't read them. I don't even know what he's been saying. But what if they ask me about him?"

"What if they do? It's not like you had anything to do with blowing up the monument. Just show them the texts on your phone."

"In which he told me he had something planned. I should have said something to the police and I didn't. Can they charge me for that?"

"No one would have believed you. Were you still seeing each other?"

"No, we had broken up."

"There you go then. The police would just have said it was a private relationship issue and left you to it. I wouldn't worry."

But I am worried. I gave Dirk a million rand and he used it to blow up the monument. But I can't tell Deanna or Johan that.

"Maybe I should call the police myself," I said. "Tell them what I know."

"No." Johan is adamant and Deanna agrees.

"Don't say anything. That article isn't exactly new, and that's when they figured out who it was. They would have contacted you by now."

"When did he leave the country?"

"They discovered he was gone right after that was published. They should have waited till they caught him but you know the media. All eager beaver to break a story, no matter what the consequences."

I check the newspaper date. It was the day I had the locksmith come to the house. People had seen me at home and in the town having breakfast. At least there's no way they can tie me to his leaving. But the money. It will find its way back to me eventually, I'm sure of it.

Johan hefts the box with my dog in it and I force myself back into the moment. "Ja, you're right," I say, although he hasn't said anything further. "There's no use thinking about it now. Let's get this baby home."

We walk to my car.

"Nice ride," Johan comments.

"Rental. But yes, I do enjoy driving it."

"It's not safe, you being there at the farm all alone. I am going to follow you. Don't worry, I'm not looking for Drive-In Make Out Session Number Two. I just want to see you safely inside your house."

"I am not going to argue." It's getting dark and I'm not looking forward to going back my house by myself. I wonder again if Elsie is finished with me or if she has anything else in store.

"Deanna, can you give me your phone number? I mean what if SunnyBoy gets sick or something?"

"SunnyBoy?"

"The dog! *Miami Vice*, don't you know?"

"Not bad. Johan, give her our number. Listen, you crazy woman, I'm glad we met all these years later even if you're still exactly the same as you ever were and you still don't remember anything or anyone unless it pertains to your needs. That said, I really hope you will come visit again, okay? I wasn't just saying that, before. Goodbye SunnyBoy. I hope I haven't sent you to the dark side of the moon, with this new home of yours."

"She likes you," Johan says after Deanna marches off into the house.

"I like her too." I get into the car. "Race you there," I say and I speed down the driveway, forgetting about the electronic gates and having to come to a grinding halt which is a tiny bit embarrassing.

42

JOHAN MAKES ME WAIT AT THE GATE until he pulls up right behind me. And he sits there, grinning at me while I watch him in the rearview mirror. He finally opens the gate and lets me out.

I'm relieved he's with me when we arrive at the farm because the place is in darkness. I let us into the house with Johan carrying SunnyBoy. We go into the kitchen and settle the puppy.

"You want some coffee?" I'm reluctant to see Johan go.

"Dinner maybe?" Johan suggests and I pull open the freezer door.

"The world's cuisine is at your door," I wave a hand in front of the stocked freezer. "I went shopping. Pizza, Indian, Chinese, Thai, veg, burgers, you name it."

Johan is horrified. "It's all frozen! Where's the real food?"

"What do you mean? That is real. Oh, you mean ingredients, like making a thing from scratch. I can't do that."

"Why not? Your books are cookbooks."

"Don't believe everything you read! I have zero interest in cooking. It's a waste of time. Anyway, Betty cooks for me. Correction, she used to cook for me. I am going to have to learn to cook or learn to eat like this."

"This is a wasteland! You've got Siberia in your freezer!"

"It's not so bad! I suggest we have pizza. I will add extra cheese: parmesan, mozzarella and blue cheese. It will be fantastic. You'll be amazed."

"Fine, amaze me," Johan said and he sits down at the table. "So you were seeing Mr. *Opregte* Afrikaner. When did that end?"

"Why did you call him that?"

"He called himself that, not me. It was his signoff."

I read the instructions on the back of the pizza box and turn on the oven.

"It ended a couple of weeks before he blew up the monument. Are you married?" I want to deflect the conversation away from Dirk and me. Besides, I'm curious.

"My wife died of breast cancer two years ago. She was only thirty-seven. Broke my heart."

"Ag shame, I'm very sorry. Do you have kids?"

"Nope. We thought we had lots of time. But now I'm glad we didn't have any. I don't think I would have made a good dad. I'm too into my own things. I neglected my wife, I know I did, and I feel bad about that."

"What kind of things are you into? Red or white wine?"

"Red, and I am assuming your question isn't limited to my wine selection. I fly planes, I like to travel, I have won a handful of photography awards, and I'm a local member of parliament."

"Whoa. Now me, I have my books and my writing and that's about it." I hand him his wine and start grating the cheese.

Johan looks around. "Don't you get lonely here at night, all by yourself? And no, that wasn't a come-on."

"I haven't been back here that long. It is scary, actually. I'm going to get some proper security fences installed around the perimeter of the property. All I've got is some old barbwire. Hardly a deterrent. But now I have SunnyBoy."

"He's a puppy, not a guard dog," Johan points out.

"True but he can sound an alarm by barking. At least I hope so."

We both hear a car pull up and Johan looks at me. "You expecting visitors?"

I shake my head.

"Come on, let's go and see who it is. Maybe Deanna got psychic about the incredible pizza you are going to serve and she wants in."

I follow Johan down the hallway and I peer through the peephole.

"It's that policeman, Bethell," I whisper to Johan. "He thinks I am responsible for Isaac's disappearance as well as two other men. He was here earlier and he is a nasty piece of work."

Johan pulls the door open. "*Goie nag*, Donnie," he says cordially. "*Wat doen jy here?*"

My Afrikaans is fairly bad but I understand he's asking him what he's doing here.

"I came by to see if this lovely lady is okay. Is that a crime, Johan?" Bethell says in English and he sways back and forth, his eyes bloodshot.

"As a matter of fact, I don't think it is all right for you to be here." Johan pulls out his phone and holds it up to Bethell. "You want me to phone the Colonel and tell him you need to be transferred for yet another indiscretion? You got away with it last time because the girl wouldn't press charges, but you've got no right to be here now. Get lost and don't come back. In fact, I'm going to call the Colonel anyway, because you're as trustworthy as a puff adder snake."

"*Fok's* sakes, I'm going, I'm going," Bethell says but Johan is already talking into the phone and Bethell turns and runs. He jumps into his car and races off.

"Thank you," I say after he hangs up. "I hate to think of what would have happened if you hadn't been here."

"I am glad I could help. No way am I leaving you alone though. I'm going to phone Deanna and tell her I'm staying here tonight. I don't trust Bethell. He might come back."

"Why don't you invite Deanna over for supper?" I ask. "I don't want her to think I am up to my old tricks with you. I like her and if you tell her you're staying with me, she'll lose what little respect I may have earned back."

Johan dials his sister's number. "Yes, she really does want you to come," he says when Deanna questions the invitation and I shout affirmation.

"Tell her to hurry up, the pizza is nearly ready."

"She said move your arse," Johan speaks into the phone, grins and hangs up.

"Who's the Colonel when he's at home? I meant to ask."

"Chief of police. He's a good friend. I don't know why he doesn't fire that creep Bethell. Do you have any frozen dessert for after our unfrozen pizza?"

I point at the freezer. "A veritable plethora of ice cream," I say to his delight.

Deanna arrives just as the pizza is ready and we carry the food into the living room.

"Since I am the hostess," I say, "I get to choose what we will watch with our fine dining."

Deanna groans. "Is it? Okay well as long as it's not *The Notebook,* or anything with Julia Roberts."

"Give me credit for having some taste." I say and I click the remote at the TV.

When the theme song for *Miami Vice* sounds, they both look at me, open-mouthed.

"Given what you named your dog, I should have expected that," Johan grins at me.

"I have seasons one to five. Both here and at my house in Johannesburg. We have ourselves some watching to do."

"Bernice," Deanna says as a long cheese pull attaches itself to her chin, "you are one sick puppy. SunnyBoy, I apologize. I shouldn't insult puppies."

We watch five episodes in a row. And I can't remember the last time I had such fun.

We eat the pizza, finish off two bottles of wine and a bottle of schnapps. We also eat an entire tub of chocolate and fudge ice cream.

"I am drunk," Deanna says, weaving to the bathroom. "I

admit it without shame. I am drunk."

"You're staying here too for sure," I say and I yawn. "I'll sleep in my mom's room, Johan, you take my dad's, and Deanna, you take mine."

I get them settled and I coax SunnyBoy to jump onto my bed.

"Teaching him bad habits," Johan says, from the doorway and I jump.

"Sorry, I didn't mean to startle you." He comes over to the bed and lies down next to me. He's wearing boxer shorts and a T-shirt and he smells so good, spicy and warm. I quite forget about SunnyBoy and I turn to him.

"I thought you weren't interested?" I tease him.

"I lied. Come here, you."

When I wake the next morning, SunnyBoy is whining to go outside and both Johan and Deanna are gone.

They scribbled me a note saying they were off to do some real work, not like writing books which meant you could stay up as late as you like and get up as late as you like too, and I smile. It's weird and wonderful how life can change, from one moment to the next. I text Johan, and ask him if he's be interested in a third make-out date and I'm happy when my phone resounds almost immediately with a YES! and a happy face.

I grab SunnyBoy and take him outside. I know I should be writing but all I want to do is think about how happy I am. But I decide to check the messages from Dirk and when I do, I realize that my happiness has been extinguished.

I will be leaving the farm again and much sooner than I had planned.

But before I go anywhere, I need to phone Betty.

I find the piece of paper with her number on it and I dial, my hands shaking. I know she doesn't want to speak to me but I don't care. I'm going to thank her for taking care of me and I'm going to tell her that I love her and that I miss her. The phone rings forever and I'm about to hang up when a child's voice speaks.

"Hello?" a boy says.

"Is Betty there?"

"Betty?" he repeats and my voice gets stuck in my throat. Betty must be there.

"Hello?" Another voice comes to the phone. "Who are you looking for?"

"Betty." For god's sake, I don't even know her surname. How ignorant am I? I saw Rosie's surname on the email but I can't remember it. I hate myself so much in that moment. I treated Betty like a robot or, much worse, a slave. Nothing more than my caretaker, my nanny, my maid.

"I'm Bernice von Coller. Betty looked after me for years. Her daughter is Rosie. I got this number from Deanna Lamerdin. Please tell me that Betty's there. I need to speak to her urgently."

"*Yebo,* Betty is here. Wait."

I wait. And I wait and wait.

Eventually I hear footsteps approaching and I stand up straight.

"Hello?" It is Betty.

"Betty?" My own voice breaks. "It's me, Bernice. How are you?"

"Fine, thank you." Betty is reticent and polite.

"I'm at the farm. Betty, Dirk used my money to blow up the Voortrekker Monument."

"I saw that."

"I was so stupid. More stupid than usual. I'm very sorry. You must think I am such an idiot."

"You thought it was for a horse. But he was a rubbish, that man."

"Yes, he was. He is. But I shouldn't have given him money for a horse. I shouldn't have given him money for anything. What was I thinking? I completely lost my way. And Theresa's having an affair with him. She has been with him the whole time since he left Chrizette. So anyway, I came back to the farm. And now Isaac and two of his friends have disappeared and the police think maybe I had something to do with it. They asked me all kinds of questions."

I am silent after that and Betty doesn't say anything either.

"I got your number from Deanna Lamerdin," I say, desperate to keep her on the line. "I got a puppy from her too. And I met her brother again, Johan. Apparently I went on a date with him when I was a teenager."

"Yes, you did. Did you finish your new book?"

I sigh. "Ag Betty, I have no new book. I thought I was going to write a memoir. That didn't work out. Then I thought I could write a crime novel. But the truth is I'm not a fiction writer. I'm a psychologist not a writer. And let's face it, I'm not a cook in any way, shape or form. You are. I'm sorry I took you for granted, Betty. I'm sorry I never gave you credit for everything you did. The recipes were all yours. Rosie was right to do what she did. I should have done it long ago. I wish you had said something to me."

"If I said anything to you, you wouldn't have listened."

"You are right. I never realized how pig-headed I am. I didn't treat you well at all and I wanted to tell you how sorry I am. I should have got a proper bathroom for you in the back and done your rooms up properly. I should have made sure you got enough rest. I behaved like a spoiled child. Please know how sorry I am. I would do anything to make things right. But tell me about you, how are you? Are you enjoying your retirement?"

Betty laughs, a beautiful sound I never thought I'd hear again and the iceberg of tension melts from my shoulders. "No, I am not. There are too many children running around making so much noise and needing attention and I don't have any peace. Nobody is interested in my recipes; they want the same things every day or they want MacDonald's. And I don't like the weather here. The humidity is very unpleasant. Everything is sticky."

"So, come to the farm. Come and live in the house with me.

You can have the main bedroom with the en suite bathroom or any room you like. Please come back, Betty. I miss you so much."

"Even after what Rosie did to you?"

"Rosie was right to do what she did. What do you say? Will you come back? But first I have to go to Houston and fix something. I'll be back in a week. Will you come in a week?"

Betty hesitates. "Well, I have got some new recipe ideas. Can we do another book?"

"Of course we can do another book!" I'm so excited I turn that awful purple colour but I don't care. I want to jump up and down for joy. "And this time you will be called co-author. And we'll republish the other books to say that too. Betty, what is your surname?"

"Khumalo."

"Betty Khumalo. I never even knew that. Betty, can I ask you something?"

There is a long pause. "Yes, what is it?"

I clear my throat. It is hard for me to say the words, despite my conviction that I know the truth. "Who is Rosie's father?"

There is silence. Betty holds firm in not saying a word.

"My father is Rosie's father," I say. "I noticed the other day, when she came with the papers, that something about her was familiar. She reminded me of someone and later I realized it was my father. I hadn't noticed it before but she straightened her hair. And I looked through photographs at Deanna's and that's when I saw it for sure. Please tell me the truth, Betty."

Betty gives a great big sigh. "I promised I would never say."

"He's dead, Betty. And if Rosie is his daughter, she's entitled to half of the estate."

"You would give Rosie half of everything?"

"I would keep the farm, she can have the Westcliffe house. And I don't have much of Pa's money left since I gave Dirk such a lot, but there's still over a million left."

"Rosie hates you."

"With good reason, wouldn't you say? Does she know who her father is?"

"She always suspected but I never told her she was right. It used to make her very angry. She said why else would he pay for her schools? There were other children on the farm and he never paid for them. She hated him because he paid for her silence. That's what she said. He never acknowledged her. But how could he? Nobody in his position would have said the truth. I told her that."

"I would have been angry too." I pause. "So, um, did you and my father, um, see each other for a long time?"

"We did. Until I went to Johannesburg with you."

"But I never saw you with him, like that. You were so formal with him. Why didn't you get together after my mother died?"

"Because I was the housekeeper. And things were very different then, between black and white people. It had to be a secret. Today nobody would care. But then they would have cared a lot. The whole town would have hated him. His friends would have spit on him. And you would have cared too. You maybe say you wouldn't but you would have."

I am silent, trying to imagine it. "I don't know what I would have said or done. But you're right Betty, I can't imagine I would have behaved well. This explains why Rosie hates me so much."

"*Eish,* yes, but Rosie hates everybody. I don't know what her problem is."

"She was rejected by her father, that's what her problem is. She was abandoned by him and, unlike me, she didn't get an A-grade replacement. She had to watch me getting all his love and affection while really, he was her father. That's a lot to deal with. And the racial injustices on top of that. Betty, we need to focus on parental rejection in the new book. I don't mean we'll make it about Rosie because she would kill us, but I bet there are a lot of adults out there who had a parent, or maybe both parents, who abandoned them emotionally or were cruel to them when they were growing up."

"That is your side of things! But it is a good idea."

"I'm glad you like it. I'll have to think of a good title. Maybe *Bake Your Way to Healing Your Inner Child*. No, that's too long. We'll see. So, I have to go to Houston. Don't say anything to Rosie about any of this until I get back and we'll do it together."

"I won't say anything. I will be at the Pilanesburg train station in one week. I will see you next Friday. I will send a text to let you know the time."

I want to ask Betty if she loved my father and if he had loved her. I want to ask her how often they met. I want to say how sad it was that she had to watch him being buried and she couldn't say a word. But I have to respect her privacy. Perhaps, one day, she will tell me of her own accord.

"Wonderful. I love you, Betty."

"I love you too, Bernice."

And then Betty is gone and I stand there, crying because I am so blessed. And then I gather my resolve. It is time to fix this thing, once and for all.

Now
THE END OF THE WORLD

43. LEONIE

I AM NOT A KILLER. I just fell in love with the wrong man. And I went too far this time, there's no going back. There's no going anywhere, period.

I was close to staying afloat but my luck ran out. Luck, that mystical mythical glue that holds the shards of despair together and makes life navigable. But fragmented despair, that's what sinks you.

I did what JayRay said. I left my room after the call from Ralph and maybe it was just a coincidence but as I walked away, a police car pulled up and the officers ran into the hotel.

I darted around the corner, my heart hammering and my mouth dry. I found a cash machine and withdrew as much money as I could. I spotted a dollar store and I bought a floppy fishing hat with a wide brim. I bought cheap dark brown lipstick and a pair of reading glasses with the lowest prescription. I tied my hair in a bun and tucked it under the hat.

I thought about what JayRay had said, that I should go to a hotel and I thought he was wrong. I needed to save the cash. But I was beyond tired. Besides, I couldn't sit out in the open all day either. I needed to be hidden.

I checked into the Magnolia Hotel, thinking what the fuck, at least I could spend the day in the lap of luxury. I paid cash and I gave my name as Marian Applewhite, using a driver's license that I stole as a lark because I thought the girl looked like me only younger, and I got a kick out of that.

I went up to my room and wondered what to do with myself. I didn't feel anything except a gnawingly horrible awakeness. The world was too bright and everything hurt. I threw the reading glasses on the floor and I wiped off the lipstick and untied my hair. I fumbled for my meds and I put two tranqs under my tongue.

I phoned JayRay before I forgot and his phone went straight to voicemail. I left him a message with my whereabouts and the room number and the name I had checked in with.

I shed my clothes and left them in an untidy puddle at my feet.

I pulled the bedding out from its military-style tuck and climbed under the covers. I added a sleeping pill to the pharmaceuticals in my bloodstream and I sank down into the sheets and pillows. My meds soon kicked in but I was too fired up to sleep. All I could do was doze fitfully and be woken by nightmares of shame and terror. I dozed on and off and the sun was blinding and the ghost of a cat walked on my back. I forced myself up to take another tranq and my body felt like it had forgotten how to move and I couldn't keep my eyes open although it was impossible to sleep.

The day turned to night and the cat left me. It went to join God and luck and all the missing socks of my life and it joined the childhood assumption that life got easier when you get older, not harder, and that courage was rewarded and that fortune-cookie, guru-zen crapfests still made a modicum of sense.

And finally, it is time, it is time. Game on.

There's a knock at the door and I want to answer it, I need to answer it but I can't move, my body won't move. I hear the door being opened and I am relieved. He's come to get me.

"Leo, baby," a voice says and I blink.

I want to move but I can't. I can't even tell him that I can't move.

He tells the manager that he's got this, and the manager makes a few cursory protesting noises but he sounds happy to leave this mess for someone else to clean up.

"Baby, we've got to be somewhere," he says and his voice makes my groin hot and tight and I hate myself for my reaction, hate myself like I always do when I am around him.

He helps me sit up and he props a pillow behind my back.

He puts the coffee machine to work and he feeds me some water, a little at a time and the fog starts to clear.

"What the fuck, JayRay?" I manage to ask. "What the fuck?"

He looks at me.

"It's time to get our shit together," he tells me. "It's time, Leo, it's time."

"Only if you tell me what's going on, JayRay."

"Fine. But this plan's going ahead, no matter what you say. Remember my half-sister, the bitch author? Well, I got an email from her so-called lover who she ditched."

"Yeah, so?"

"He doesn't want to leave empty-handed either. After the TV show, Bernice told him that I told her I knew a big secret about her that would ruin her. She thought he wasn't listening when she said it but he was, and later he checked out the email on her computer and wrote down my address. It must have been true love from the start, for him to be doing shit like that. Anyway, he said he's got something big on her too. He said he can get her to come to here and then I lay my shit on her, he lays his, and we all split the money. Well, him and me, not you. I said yeah sure, but good luck with that getting her here, especially if she's not into him anymore and he said he's got a way, that he'll meet me here tonight and she'll be there too."

I sit up slowly. For some reason, every bone in my body feels beaten and bruised. "I don't get why he needs you there. If he's got something on her, why does he need you?"

"I asked him that. He said it's because he wants to bring her to her knees. He said he's not only after the money, he wants her to be in the same position he is now, having lost every-thing. He said Bernice cost him his marriage and his kids and he wants payback for that. He started rambling about losing his folk and his language and his culture and he lost me there. He's got a lot of anger, that boy."

"He told you all this in an email?"

"No, he phoned me. Rambled on for hours. Wouldn't give me details of what he's got on her, but it must be big."

"And what do you have on her?"

"I can't say," he says cagily and I'm about to slap him but he grabs my hand.

"You fucked things up before by not trusting me. I'm not telling you, Leo. I am not going to make the same mistake again."

What choice do I have? I have nothing left. I nod.

"I'm going to get you some strong coffee. We'll come out winners, Leo. Trust me."

44. BERNICE

I HAD NO CHOICE. I had to go. Dirk's message was clear:

> You blew up the monument. Your money. It all traces back to you
> and the contract you signed. Come to Houston and I will give you
> the evidence and a way out.

I had to go and fix this thing, once and for all. I needed to
stand up for myself. He stole from me, this pathetic excuse
for a man. I had to put an end to his nonsense and I wanted
to be able to look him in the eye one more time and tell him
what a loser he is.

I phoned Deanna. "It's me, Bernice," I said when she answered
the phone and she gave a deep groan.

"*Fok!* My head is killing me! What a *babbelas*! Still, it was
fun. What can I do you for?"

"I have to go and deal with a situation. With Dirk. Can you
look after SunnyBoy for me? I won't be gone long. I'm sorry
to have to ask."

"Ag for sure, bring him over."

I thanked her and loaded SunnyBoy into the car. Deanna
was waiting for me in the front yard. She looked worse for
wear and was guzzling water. "What are you going to do?"
she asked me. "Set the cops on him?"

"Worse than that. I'll let you know as soon as I'm back." I
grinned at her. "Johan around?"

"No, he's up in the top field, fixing a tractor that broke down. Why, you want to see him? You can text him to come down." She looks at me keenly and I blush.

"Thought I'd say goodbye but I'll see him when I get back," I said. "Take care of my baby." I gave SunnyBoy a last kiss on his nose. "See you soon."

I texted Johan to say I was going to deal with Dirk and that I'd be home soon.

Be careful, he wrote back. *Don't forget about me.*

* * *

I check into La Quinta Inn & Suites, $69 a night. Dirk certainly wasn't living large. A hotel whose big draw was free coffee and free wireless Internet. Still, the place is close to all the tourist attractions, should I desire. I do not desire.

And now here I am, sitting across from Dirk at a table set for four in the Steak 48 restaurant in Houston. The place is fancy, with a polished interlocking marble floor patterned in black, chocolate brown, and cream, with rows of low-hanging ornate cacti chandeliers, and yellow and dark wood glass partitions that give the diners their privacy — the kind where it looks like the glass is melting or there's a downpour outside. The bench seats are burnt caramel Nappa leather and the linen tablecloth is snow white with sharp, freshly-ironed creases.

Dirk looks tired and unhealthy. His face is a red balloon that is starting to pinch and sag. His blood pressure is about to blow, he's added a few jowls, and he's lost a bunch of hair.

"So," I say as my opening greeting. "You and Theresa. And apparently your dick worked much better with her."

"You were a controlling bitch," he shoots back. "Fucking your cunt was like fucking a barbed wire fence."

The waiter comes over and I order a lime and soda while Dirk orders a bottle of red wine. Macauley Reserve Cabernet. A hundred and fifty dollars a bottle. I guess he thinks I'm paying for this joyful reunion and plans to make the most of it.

I have taken care with my appearance. My hair is in a chignon and I'm wearing a black cocktail dress, pearls, and high heels.

"Get on with it, Dirk," I tell him. "I'm here now, let's get this party started."

"We're waiting for company. And there they are." He waves and I turn around to see Leonie and JayRay walking towards us.

I don't move. Not a twitch of a muscle, not even when they both sit down and JayRay pours himself and Leonie a glass of wine from Dirk's bottle.

I cross my arms and wait.

Dirk begins. "We, each of us, me and your brother, both have evidence of your wrongdoing, evidence of the lies you have lived. We are going to show you this evidence and once we are done, you are going to give us each a million dollars. Not rand but dollars. And then we, and you, can go our separate ways and pretend like we never knew each other.

"I will go first," he says and he pushes a stapled pile of pages at me. I make no move to look at them. I keep my arms folded and Dirk sighs.

"Be like that. I will tell you then. The money you signed over to me, the money you thought was for a horse? You should have read the fine print better. The company was called VilliersVanColler PTY, but it was also called *Die Vryheidsoorloë*, The Wars of Liberation. And you will see that the contract says that this money will be used to further the cause of the currently oppressed Afrikaaner nation. By signing, you affirmed that you support this war in every guise that it might take."

He takes a large swallow of his wine. "I will send this to the police. They will know it was you and not me, who funded the blowing up of the monument and you will be arrested and put away for the rest of your life."

I laugh. "Right. You may have conned me into funding it by stealing my money, but there's nothing to tie me to the bombing. You took credit for it with all that ridiculous rhetoric about *volk* and *taal* and the other rubbish. Plus, they have a man's voice on the messages you left the newspapers, and they pinned the IP address to you for the emails you sent, and they traced the calls to where you were staying."

"Facts are facts," he says and his face is ugly as he stabs his forefinger hard on the paper. "It's all here. You did it. It was you. You signed along the dotted line. It all comes down to you."

"Hmmm. We will see." I turn to JayRay. His partner-in-crime, Leonie, looks pale and distracted as if she isn't really a part of what's going on, but I don't have time to think about her and I address JayRay.

"And what do you have, cookie? What do you have in your little bundle of gifts for me? I must admit, I am not sure why you and Dirk thought you had to meet me together like this? Safety in numbers? Who called who? Before we go any further, I'd like to know how this meeting came to be. I deserve at least that much."

"Remember one of the many times when you wanted me to fuck you?" Dirk asks. "You were like a bloody machine, woman, always wanting more sex. You got back from your TV stint and you were all *me, me, me,* and look how hard my life is and why can't we have real sex and *whine, whine, whine.* And you told me that JayRay said, as a parting shot, that he had some big evidence on you that would change your life, but that you were going to ignore it. I got on your computer and found his email address. I knew you wouldn't be in my life forever, because you are a bitch and a user. You use people and you spit them out. I swore to myself that I would be ready for you. You treat everybody like shit but I wasn't going to sit back and let it happen to me. Even Betty couldn't put up with you in the end. No one can."

It's tough listening to him and not being able to say anything, not being able to get up and leave. How dare he? The tears come and I swallow them down, hoping he won't see how much he's affecting me. He thought all those things about *me,* back when I thought we were in love. He never loved me. He was the one who used me and I want to shout that at him, bang my fist on the table and leave. But I can't do that. I have to sit quietly and let his sewer filth wash over me.

"And what's more," he continues, "you cost me everything. You cost me my family, my nationality, my pride, my place in the *Volksraad*. You took all that away from me. I don't just want your money, although that will certainly help. I want to watch JayRay bring you to your knees too, double whammy, so you've got nothing left, just like me."

"And you emailed JayRay and you both set this up?" I looked at my half-brother. "Tell me, what have you got? Bring it on."

"I have evidence," JayRay says, and he sounds pompous and ridiculous, "evidence that we will release to the press, unless you agree to pay us the sum of one million dollars each, that your father was not my father. Your father, your true biological father was a black man. You, therefore, are a black person."

Leonie, sitting next to JayRay, gives a snort of laughter. "JayRay," she says, "look at her. She's pure white, a white princess. That's not true."

Clearly JayRay hadn't looped his partner in on the goods. Another trusting, loving relationship.

JayRay takes a birth certificate out of his pocket, as well as a photograph.

I take them from him, my hands shaking, and I study the photograph.

"These are only copies, of course, and you can keep them," JayRay says. "Look at them. That's a picture of your real father and there's his name on the original birth certificate. Your mother lied and had an affair with a black man and you are the resulting child. Why your mother put your real father's name on the certificate when she was married to my dad is beyond me, but she did. And a year later, your new rich father paid to have it changed to his name. Apparently you can do shit like that in South Africa if you pay the right people. But my father got to it first."

"I was fucking a *kaffir*?" Dirk turns green and he wheezes like he can't breathe. His face is the colour of a lizard's underbelly and his throat jerks like a cat about to toss a fur ball.

"It would be more accurate to say you were *trying* to fuck one," I suggest and I turn back to the picture. "You didn't actually succeed."

"No wonder I couldn't get it up. I knew it! I knew there was something wrong with you. No wonder! My dick knew better than me, my dick knew you were not pure."

"David Okoro," I say, studying the picture. My birth father had a sensitive, fine-boned face with high cheekbones and a sensual mouth and I can see myself in his shape of his wideset eyes. I put the photograph and the birth certificate into my purse.

"You say you want a million dollars for this?" I asked JayRay. "A million dollars to keep this a secret?"

He nodded.

"And Dirk, you want a million dollars or you will tell everybody I funded the bombing of the Voortrekker Monument?"

He nods and I chuckle.

"You guys are hilarious," I say. "You crack me up."

"I'm not sure I follow the joke," JayRay says, and his face is pinched and hard.

"I will explain it to you. Firstly, how happy am I that we do not share a father. I could not be more delighted that we do not have one drop of mutual blood between us. I know all about my biological father. He was a musician, and my mother had a fling with him while she was married to your father. She married your father because she had nothing and she was poor and that was what she did, she lived off her looks. She married my father for that reason too. And he, by the grace of his good and kind heart, loved me like a real father would. My mother met my biological father on a shoot. He was a model and a jazz musician and they had a brief affair. But he didn't have any money and my mother would never have left your father for him because she needed someone who would take care of her.

"My biological father died years later, working in the mines. You want me to be ashamed of him? Ashamed of who I am? I am not ashamed. Tell the world. Tell whomever you like. And if you don't, I will, in my next book. There are many other things that you don't know about me and my family, but you can read about them when the book comes out."

I discovered the truth about my birth father from the second to last letter Marika had written to my mother. At first, I didn't want anyone to know. My old-school White South African values made me feel ashamed, as if it was something that needed to be hidden. But the world is a different place today and it was interesting how quickly I adapted to this new truth. I felt, for the first time in my life, as if I was properly explained. The strange colour of my skin tone when I blushed. The texture of my hair. It was a relief to finally know the full truth about myself. According to Marika's letter, my father, Ruan, had never known. It was the one secret my mother withheld from him. But he would have known before he died because he had read Marika's letters. I wondered what his reaction would have been.

My first conditioned response had been to hide it, run from it, pretend it never existed. Was that how my father had reacted? In all probability, yes. But to his credit, my father never changed his manner or affection for me, not one iota. I just wish it had encouraged him to embrace Rosie and admit to the world that he was her father.

I look at JayRay. "I am not buying what you are selling. But thank you for the picture and my birth certificate."

"I want them back then," JayRay stands up, threatening me, and I gesture to my phone on the table. "This has been recording everything. And you clearly said I could have them. You said these are for you and I thank you for that. As it stands, none of you have anything on me and I should have known it. In a way, I did know it, but I wanted one last opportunity to look Dirk in the eye. And, bonus, I got to see you JayRay and I got the chance to tell you that your smoke and mirrors and con man plans are no more than a bad magician's trick that everyone can see through. And Dirk, as far as your demands go, I will take this copy of the document that you so kindly brought along for me. And I will give them to the police who along with a recording of this conversation. You know, I thought about alerting the police to this meeting and have them arrest you and take you home to stand trial for terrorism on home soil."

Dirk grips the table and starts searching the room, as if expecting to see the police streaming out from behind the pillars and kitchen.

"But," I continue, "I realized that taking you home was much too good for you."

Dirk visibly relaxes and he folds his arms and leans back in his chair.

"Because here, in America, you have nothing." I continue. "No friends, no family, no livelihood. No past and certainly no future. Remember how you loved watching that movie *Stander*? How he was such a hero to you, a high-profile white cop, robbing banks in Joburg and getting away with it? And he ended up dying alone in Fort Lauderdale, all by himself. Shot like a dog by the police. He died in the street with no one. And you will die in the street, all alone."

"And you will die on your farm," Dirk says, full of spite and he smiles. "Yes, I heard you moved back there. How long do you think you will last? They'll come for you. You think you've got a future? You're more stupid than me."

"But at least I will die on my home soil. I will die in my bed, on my farm. Of course I will take every measure to stop that from happening but if it does, then so be it. But you are here, a drunk, alone in a place of exile."

I gather up my papers and my phone.

"And that," I say to JayRay and Leonie, "as they say, is that."

I walk away and I don't give the losers left at the table a second glance.

I'm going home to Betty and SunnyBoy and the farm and I'm going to give myself the chance to be happy. And if not happy, then at least at peace with the choices I have made. *Yes, Pa,* I say silently. *I will live with the consequences of my actions.*

45. LEONIE

DIRK POURS THE REST OF THE WINE into his glass, downs it and leaves. JayRay and I watch him waddle out into the night, his hands paddling through the air as if he is wading through water.

"What the fuck did she see in him?" JayRay says. He gets up. "That fucking bitch. Come on Leo, let's blow this pop stand before I lose my shit in here."

He's right. We can't afford to draw any attention to ourselves, I'm already wanted by the police and dollars to doughnuts, Dave contacted Ralphie and told him how I was connected to JayRay. Which would implicate JayRay in what happened to Iris.

The waiter brings the bill. "That fucker," JayRay says, "he stiffed us." He passes me the bill. "Fuck," I say. "Will any of your cards work?"

"Yeah. Maybe. But that's big bucks for us to lose right now. Maybe we can duck out. You get up and make like you're going to the washroom. Then dig in your purse like you can't find something, and walk out like you're going to get something from the car. I'll go and order a drink at the bar and I'll be right behind you."

I do as he says. I slip out and no one notices me leave. I go the car and wait. And I wait and wait. What the fuck? Where is he? I sit down on the kerb and text him. *Where are u?*

Nothing. I don't have the keys for the car, he does. What's

going on? Has he dumped me? Why wouldn't he? What will I do? *Are u ok?* I text again. Then I see him, he's walking fast, keys in hand.

"What the fuck Leo, you're like my fucking nanny," he says. "I lifted a fat juicy wallet. Now we'd better get the fuck out of here."

I get in the car and he does a quick three-point turn and heads southwest. "What about our stuff at the hotel?" I ask.

"Fuck it." He's gnawing on a finger. "Shut up Leo, I'm thinking."

I glare at him and turn away. We drive for an hour and a half and he pulls up at a strip mall in El Campo. It's ten p.m. and a bunch of teenagers are drinking and partying outside a 7-Eleven. I go in and use the washroom and buy a Coke and a Hershey bar. While I'm paying, I see a job posting for a night shift Sales Associate.

> Cultivate a G•U•E•S•T in Mind Culture.
> Focus on the wildly important.
> Be a leader.
> Be committed to the guest.

I'm studying the poster when JayRay walks in. "Maybe I should apply," I say and I point.

He ignores me and goes to the washroom. When he comes out, his hair is wet and he looks like he had a whore's bath. He grabs a bunch of Cokes, chips, chocolate bars, and cookies. He pays and I follow him out.

"So you're not talking to me?" I ask. "A bit childish, wouldn't you say? I realize another one of your big Bernice dreams just went bust but that's not my fault. I knew that bitch would never deliver."

JayRay stops. He digs in the bag and pulls out a Coke and he fires it at the wall of the 7-Eleven. "You drive me fucking crazy!" he yells. "My whole life is fucked up because of you!"

The partying kids fall silent and watch us, bemused, slightly bored. I notice that one girl, with purple hair and a face full of piercings, is watching me intently.

"You are the reason everything has gone wrong!" JayRay fires another Coke at the wall and the Sales Associate comes out from behind his desk and watches us through the glass.

"Stop it JayRay," I say, "everybody is watching us. They'll call the cops soon."

"I. Don't. Give. A. Fuck. Let them arrest me. Let them free me from you, you poisonous fucking bitch. What did I ever do to you? I hope they take you away." He reaches into the bag and pulls out a bag of Chips Ahoy Oreo Créme Filled cookies. He tears the bag open and throws the cookies at me, one at a time. The kids and the 7-Eleven Sales Associate are mesmerized. I dodge as a cookie hits me on the cheek and I wonder if JayRay's lost his mind.

He runs out of cookies and he empties the rest of his purchases on the ground. He jumps on the bags of chips and they make a loud popping sound.

"Sir?" The Sales Associate has finally emerged from behind the glass door. "Sir, you are creating a disturbance and creating a mess on the forecourt. I'll have to ask you to leave."

JayRay replies by sitting down on the pile of chip bags. He puts his head in his hands and screams. I fold my arms and wait for his histrionics to subside.

"He lost a winning lottery ticket," I explain to the Sales Associate and the kids.

"That blows," one of the kids says and JayRay starts crying. "We're so fucked," he sobs. The girl with the purple hair goes over to him and hunkers down next to him and puts her arm around him. She hands him a bottle of Wild Turkey and JayRay takes a big slug. The girl helps him to his feet and she leads him out of the gas island to sit on the kerb. JayRay is still crying. The Sales Associate vanishes inside and comes out with a long-handled dustpan and broom.

"We have to go," I tell JayRay and I shout so he can hear me over his muffled sobs. I go over to him and dig the car keys out of his pocket.

"We're late for a family wedding," I tell the girl. "Can you help me get him into the car?" I dig through the wallet JayRay scored in the Steak 48 and I pull out a twenty. "Can we keep the booze?" She nods and a boy comes over and they haul the sniffing JayRay to the car and load him into the passenger seat.

"Man, you've got a shit-load of stuff," the boy says and I want to belt him for being so nosy. "Moving back home," I say vaguely. "Thanks for all your help."

The girl kisses JayRay for longer than she had any right and I look away. She wipes his face with her T-shirt. I fire up the car and start reversing before she's fully closed the door and as I spin out, I give her the finger.

JayRay drinks out of the bottle, moaning to himself and muttering less than kind things about me. But we're in this together. We have been, from the start. I was wrong to think he'd leave me. He needs me as much as I need him. He finally passes out and I drive through the night.

I drive us all the way to Mexico. It takes one night and one day and the whole way, I try to tell myself I'm living the dream while next to me, JayRay is silent, swollen-eyed and sullen.

* * *

Two years later, my life finds me working the night shift in a pharmacy in Mexico City. JayRay's buddy got me the job soon after we arrived. JayRay has yet to get a job. He says he's keeping his options open, looking for the right thing.

We change our names and dye our hair and it's a whole different ball game only it's the same old shit.

JayRay's buddy, Brett, isn't what I imagined. He's an aging catalogue fashion model and when he's not on set, he's pumping iron or working on his tan. He encourages JayRay to go to the gym with him and JayRay does, to shoot the breeze and hang out.

"I'll put in the work when I have to," he's fond of saying, while he pats his smooth belly. He's happy to lie on the beach with Brett and he soon turns butterscotch.

"You'll get wrinkles later," I say but he just laughs at me. Life's a beach for JayRay and he's perfectly happy to roll from one day to the next, living off me and Brett. I figure Brett has a crush on JayRay. Why else would he be so supportive of him?

I tell JayRay and he shrugs his tanned shoulders. "What's not to love?" he grins, his teeth white and even, his eyes beautiful and clear.

While I, tired, out of sync with life, and pale as a ghost, live among the moths of the darkness, dispensing drugs under the watchful eyes of my own personal security detail who is armed to the teeth in case the addicts try to make any fast moves.

The pharmacy is a tiny fluorescent-lit cave, situated on a busy main street and I grow accustomed to the sounds of sirens, shots, car tires, and shouts. My security guard acts as an interpreter and I have no idea how I would manage without him. I rely on my computer to translate prescriptions and I'm learning Spanish and I'm doing pretty well. I get a lot of practice time, there are long hours when no one comes in at all, and I sit with my book and my earbuds, repeating words and phrases.

I often think about Dave and the girls and how much better off they are without me. About a year after JayRay and I started our new lives, I couldn't help myself and I used the pharmacy computer to go on Facebook. Dave has remarried. He married Denise, Sam's mother, no surprises there. They even have a new little kiddie of their own, so sweet, and there are great big smiles everywhere.

I never belonged with them. Strangely, I do belong here, in this no-man's land, but it is more about my aloneness, than being in Mexico. And most of the time, JayRay's like an annoying roommate who makes a mess and sleeps a lot and is noisy when I'm trying to sleep.

Although, he still only has to touch me and I melt like candlewax under a flame. It's annoying how my body responds to him and I wish it didn't.

I googled *SuperBeauty* and saw that it had gone belly up. Even though Ralph went to great pains to explain that I'd gone rogue and I was solely and personally responsible for Iris's murder, faith in the product line plummeted and, thanks to me, everyone lost their jobs. I felt bad about that for a couple of nanoseconds and then I remembered what annoying assholes they all were, and how quick Ralph was to throw me under the bus, to used one of his well-worn phrases, and I didn't feel so bad at all.

I googled myself and it was fascinating. Newspapers dubbed me the Killer Cosmetics Queen, which no doubt helped hammer the nails into the coffin of the beauty line. And, what a laugh, Don Carlson crawled out of the woodwork and wrote a bestselling novel, *BORN BAD: How the Killer Cosmetics Queen Ruined My Life*. Looks like I did you a favour, bud, look, you're rich and famous now. Of my mother, Dave and the kids, there was no word. Nancy was spitting mad which made me laugh. I bet she wasn't quite so happy anymore about the extra zing I added to her jars. But her friends rallied around her and she ended up marrying Oscar Dallaire, a billionaire, so she got what she wanted even if her system was loaded with slow-acting, irreversible poisons. Dosing her added an extra attempted murder charge to my rap sheet. My ex-school buddies had a field day, trashing me liberally and Marcia Gray ran a two-hour feature on *Who Was Leonie Logan?* All the pictures of me were flattering, of JayRay, not so much. I told him what I had found and he looked at me, startled.

"They can trace that shit you know. Who's googling what, and from where. Don't be stupid Leo, think for once. We're on the run. We're never safe, not from anyone, ever."

"I won't do it again. I needed to know, and now I know. There's something else I need to know." I studied my nails and JayRay chugged orange juice from the cartoon.

"The fridge is dying," he pulled a face. "Nothing's cold anymore. What else do you want to know, cupcakes?"

I felt like he knew what was coming. "I want to know why you didn't switch up that jar in the hospital? I know you lied. You could have done it, but you didn't."

He wiped his mouth and considered the question. "Yeah, I wondered when you'd get to that. Well, puddytat, I didn't want them to pin it on me. Look at it this way. I marry Iris and next thing, she dies. Who do they look at? They look at the spouse. First and foremost. And for sure she was poisoned. So I had to." He grins. "But you'd been kicked out by Dave and it all worked out just like it was supposed to. And here we are, in sunny Mexico, living the dream."

"You pointed the nurse to the cream, didn't you? Like, oh, maybe it was that...?"

He shrugged. "I did what I had to do. You would have done the same. Hell, you did worse."

I think about his words early one morning when I arrive home from my shift. I sit at the kitchen table in our basement apartment. Calling it an apartment is a wild exaggeration. We rent three rooms in the basement of a rundown house; we have a tiny bedroom with a mattress on the floor and a doorless, leaning closet, a walk-in shower with a toilet that's inches away from the cracked shower door, and a kitchen that used to be a bedroom. It has a broken cupboard, a filthy old stove, a microwave, and a wobbly table. I keep meaning to get us a table that doesn't wobble but it seems I like I never remember until I'm actually sitting at the thing.

I'm waiting for JayRay to wake up. When it looks like he's going to sleep till noon, I wake him up.

"I'm making eggs," I tell him, just like I do every morning when I come back. "You want some?"

He mumbles agreement and I push the dark black hair back from his face. He looks beautiful, with his tan and his white teeth and startling green eyes.

I whip up two bowls of his and hers scrambled eggs, whites only for me, extra pepper for him, and when they're ready, I dish them onto plastic plates with yellow daisies.

"They're getting cold," I call out, forking in a mouthful. "Come on already."

I stop eating to wedge a folded-up piece of newspaper under the gimpy table leg and I test the table. "Piece of shit," I say, like I always do. "Come on, you're wasting good food."

"Yeah, yeah," JayRay says and he stumbles into the room. "I don't think I can eat. I don't feel good."

"You need some protein. That's what you need. Breakfast will make you feel better. You're just hungry."

"Yeah, maybe. I've got like no energy. I don't know what's wrong with me." He shovels some eggs into his mouth. "These are good. You added lots of hot sauce, just like I like it. Thank you, baby."

He cleans his plate and sit back, rubbing his belly. He shakes his head. "Man, I still feel bad. I'm going to lie down for a bit."

"I'll come with you. I'm beat. Busy night."

I draw the curtains, which are weak protection against the tough sun, and the basement room is hot as Hades as the heat pours through the tiny street level window. I lie down in my panties and singlet and feel the sweat running down my ribs.

We lie there, and I wait. JayRay's breathing grows laboured and he starts grunting.

"JayRay? Are you okay?" But he can't answer me; he's lost consciousness.

I help him onto his back and I stroke his chest and hands and say soothing things to him. He throws up and chokes on the vomit and the whole thing doesn't last long.

I smooth the hair off his forehead and close his eyes. "My poor baby," I say. "My beautiful boy."

I have been siphoning off tiny amounts of sleeping pills and tranquillizers for months, waiting patiently until I had a lethal dose. I had to make sure I did it right, and I was careful to mix up a concoction with no scent or taste. I was panic stricken when it looked like JayRay wasn't going to eat the breakfast I made. It would have ruined everything. What were the odds that he'd some kind of stomach bug on the very day I needed to kill him? But it all worked out in the end.

"I am sorry, baby, but you deserved it," I tell his dead body. "You ruined my life. I loved you more than anything, but you ruined my life."

I pack my meagre belongings along with my stash of accumulated money and leave the apartment. The sun is shining and the street is full of little kids playing. And in that moment, I feel the tiniest glimmer of happiness and hope.

ACKNOWLEDGEMENTS

Many thanks to my beloved Inanna Publications for this book (and all my books), with huge thanks to our beyond-amazing Editor-in-Chief, Luciana Ricciutelli, for her skillful and detailed sculpting of this work. And huge thanks as always to our fantastic publicist, Renée Knapp.

Thanks to my lovely Bradford for his tireless support of my writing endeavours and to my family for always believing in me and for supporting me every step of the way.

Special thanks to Jennifer Shelswell for the beautiful portraiture for the cover.

Many grateful thanks to Terri Favro for reading various incarnations of the manuscript along the way and for offering invaluable insights with regard to character, plot and motivation and also, a huge shout out to Toronto Police Services Forensic Specialist, Detective Ed Adach, for his detailed and critical help with the crime scene and crime insights. You both strenghtened the book immeasurably!

Grateful thanks to all the early readers of the novel and to all who endorsed the book: Stacy Lee Kong, Carol Bruneau, Karen Dionne, Terri Favro, Shirley McDaniel, Robin Richardson, Marilyn Riesz, Jennifer Soosar, Karen Smythe.

Thanks to my dear friend and colleague, Beth Fraser, who let me channel the beauty of her adorable twins, Maddie and Kenzie, by letting me borrow their names for the two girls in this book.

Thanks to my friends who have patience with my lengthy absences and vocal preoccupations with my craft, who listen to my ideas, and indulge my flights of fantasy! There are too many to be named; I am very blessed and grateful to all.

Thanks to the Mesdames of Mayhem, the Sisters in Crime, the Crime Writers of Canada and the Toronto Public Libraries. We are a community above all else, fostering friendship, creativity and a commitment to the written word.

And I would be very remiss if I didn't thank my fellow collaborators for making *Bake Your Way to Happiness* come to life! Thanks to registered psychotherapist Marilyn Riesz (Evii), MA, RP, and to talented food editor Gilean Watts for turning an idea in *Rotten Peaches* into a beautiful, well-received self-help book that would have made both Betty and Bernice proud!

I acknowledge the following sources from which I have borrowed fragements:

"Daddy, I have had to kill you." From "Daddy" from Sylvia Plath's *Collected Poems,* Copyright 1960, 1965, 1971, 1981 Estate of Sylvia Plath (HarperCollins Publishers Inc, 1992).

"I was much too far out all my life / And not waving but drowning." From "Not Waving but Drowning" by Stevie Smith, *New Selected Poems,* Copyright 1972 Stevie Smith (New Directions Publishing Corporation, 1988).

And from songs:

"Rotten Peaches," written by Elton John, Madman Across The Water, 1971.

"You Oughta Know," written by Alanis Morrisette, *Jagged Little Pill*, 1995.

"Echo Beach," Martha and The Muffins, Copyright: Sony/ATV Music Publishing.

I am also grateful for the information provided by *The Afrikaaners of South Africa* by Vernon February (London: Kegan Paul International Limited, 1991).

Note to the readers:

With regard to the South African aspects of this book, I wanted to present the psyche of apartheid, including the abhorrent language and the prevalent attitudes of the time.

We write in order to make amends — if we pretend that things never happened, we are complicit. I ask readers not to confuse the attitude and opinions of any of the characters with those of the author.

Photo: Bradford Dunlop

Lisa de Nikolits is the award-winning author of eight novels: *The Hungry Mirror, West of Wawa, A Glittering Chaos, The Witchdoctor's Bones, Between The Cracks She Fell, The Nearly Girl, No Fury Like That,* and *Rotten Peache*s. *No Fury Like That* will be published in Italian in 2019 by Edizione Le Assassine under the title *Una furia dell'altro mondo.* Her ninth novel, *The Occult Persuasion and the Anarchist's Solution,* is scheduled to be published in 2019 by Inanna Publications. Her short fiction and poetry have also been published in various anthologies and journals across the country. She is a member of the Mesdames of Mayhem, the Crime Writers of Canada, Sisters in Crime, and the International Thriller Writers. Originally from South Africa, Lisa de Nikolits came to Canada in 2000. She lives and writes in Toronto.